Born in the Irish Republic and brought up in Northern Ireland, Malcolm Haslett has been involved in conflict situations from an early age. After spending two years as a volunteer in Rwanda, he completed a postgraduate degree in Russian and worked for most of his career at the BBC World Service, trying to explain Russia to the world and – rather more difficult – the world to Russia. He is very happily married, with three adult children, and lives near London.

Other Books by the Author:

The Mountain on the Other Side of Light

PART ONE

A Cry for Help

PART TWO

The Search for the Opening

PART THREE

Fles

To Dottie, Ali, Ruth and Trish – who sustain my belief in the Other Side of Light.

Malcolm Haslett

THE MOUNTAIN ON THE OTHER SIDE OF LIGHT

THE SEARCH FOR THE OPENING

AUSTIN MACAULEY PUBLISHERS™

LONDON • CAMBRIDGE • NEW YORK • SHARJAH

A CIP catalogue record for this title is available from the British Library.

ISBN 9781528917858 (Paperback)
ISBN 9781528962087 (ePub e-book)

www.austinmacauley.com

First Published (2019)
Austin Macauley Publishers Ltd
25 Canada Square
Canary Wharf
London
E14 5LQ

I am deeply grateful to all those friends who have encouraged me in writing these books, particularly my sister, Margaret (Maggie); and my good friend Pete Keogh.

The Mountain on the Other Side of Light

Part Two

The Search for the Opening

The story so far…

Bridget and her friend Tom have entered the beautiful but tortured Realm of the Elonym in the airship Goodcheer, piloted by Tom's aunt Madge. They are following a trail of coded messages left by the shadowy mystic Kalmom, who has appealed for help to combat the cloud-born Grey Pestilence devastating the Realm, which he believes emanates from the giant volcano of Fles. On their way they have encountered trouble in the form of the Skomiar, a wild tribe of horsemen who say it is their aim to free the Realm from the dominance of their traditional rivals, the proud and arrogant Yenomi. The companions escape from the Skomiar capital Teivos, but their friend Pageya, a beautiful Elonym girl with remarkably keen senses, is subsequently abducted by the sinister sorceress Vencengea, who shows an unhealthy interest in the curiously shaped pendant she wears round her neck. Bridget is particularly alarmed because Pageya's pendant is remarkably similar to one she herself has worn since early childhood… Now the search is not just for the elusive Kalmom but also for Bridget's lost friend Pageya. Tom and Bridget have been parted, but each is determined to continue their quest with the help of the eccentric seer Quenrie and the giant river captain Stigrath…

THE COUNTRY OF THE ELONYM, BEING ALSO THE LAND OF THE GREEN VALE, AND SURROUNDING AREAS, UP TO AND INCLUDING THE VOLCANO OF FLES.

Part Two
The Search for the Opening

Chapter One
A Crucial Decision

Tom had been aware of the lights for some time. They flickered, bluish, through the door of his cell. And if he went out into the main room, with its windows looking out over the Lake of Nirei, they were brighter, flickering from behind the heavy curtains that the servants drew across the windows after they cleared the supper away.

More sinister still, when on their third night back at Nirei he had gone out into the corridor that led from the main part of the castle, thinking to find out whether their quarters were still being guarded after nightfall, he saw the same eerie blue glow filtering up a dark stone staircase to one side of the passage, not far from their rooms.

Immediately, he scampered back to the door of their apartment and shut it fast, hastily drawing across the heavy iron bolt.

They had been back now for almost four days, and Tom was growing impatient. The airship was moored alongside one of the castle's towers, and he had been pleading with Madge almost since they got back to agree to a return to Teivos to find Bridget, Pageya and Orin.

"We can't just leave them there, even if our friends in the underground are looking after them! If they're still in the vicinity of Teivos, they run the risk of being captured by the Skomiars any time. The Skomiar are bound to have stepped up their search for Asnelav and Levah and their followers after our escape." (Asnelav and Levah were the leaders of the dissidents from the huge slave city of Teivos, the Igremes, who had helped Tom and his friends infiltrate the city in search of their lost friends Pageya and Orin.)

But Madge seemed to be taking everything even more calmly than she usually did. "Don't get so worked up about it, Tom. There's not a great deal we can do to help them since we don't even know where they are. What do you suggest? That we just park outside that great pyramid thing and go in to ask those Skomiar guys: We've come to take our friends back. Do you mind?"

"No, we go back to the Igreme community in the forest above Teivos. That's where Levah and Asnelav will have taken them…"

"But we would still have to fly back in the airship. Our friend Stink-wrath's boat (Stink-wrath was what Madge called the giant riverman Stigrath) went over the falls, don't you remember? And they don't have another one. And try landing anywhere near that Pyramid city in the Goodcheer and those Skomiar fellows would be swarming all over us like ants."

"So you intend just to sit here and do nothing?"

Madge looked at him sternly. "I'm working on it, Tom, believe me. I've been talking to one or two people here, friends of Quenrie's."

"You've seen Quenrie?"

"Mm, he was here last night, when you'd gone off to petition Lord Whatsisname about organising a search party... How did you make out, by the way?"

Tom shook his head. "He looked at me with those big frightened eyes of his and said: 'Only the Knights can do anything now.' I felt angry with him first, then just very sad. He really has taken Pageya's disappearance very badly..."

Tom stopped suddenly. "Actually," he said, "that isn't such a bad idea!"

Madge looked up at him. "What idea?"

"Ask those Silver Knight guys to help..." Tom was looking out of the window towards the mountains on the far side of the lake, beyond whose snowy summits lay Tekram, the city of the High Towers and capital of the Yenomi, or Silver Knights. "If we went back in ourselves, to Teivos I mean, we wouldn't have a chance. As you say, we wouldn't have time to land and moor the ship before they'd be on to us. But if we went in with the protection of the Silver Knights? You remember how they made short work of the Skomiars in the battle at Wesomethe..."

Madge was horrified. "You mean invade the Skomiars' territory with an army of knights! There'd be terrible bloodshed."

"No, no. I mean if we were to go into Teivos itself, as part of a delegation..."

"You think the Skomiar are in the habit of receiving Yenomi delegations? They'd probably slit their throats as soon as they were inside the gates of that awful pyramid! And ours as well..."

"Yes, that's the bit I haven't worked out yet, I have to admit. But it wouldn't do any harm to go to this Tekram place to test the idea..."

Madge looked at Tom incredulously. Was he serious?

"Look," she said. "To go to the Yenomi Knights' supposedly impregnable citadel, this stupendous city of high towers, would be a risky business in itself. But to then persuade them to go and plead with the Skomiar to let us find our friends, just like that... It's just not on, Tom. Anyway, it's my duty to get at least one of you back over that mountain to safety."

But Tom wasn't listening. "We could offer the Knights the use of the airship to take them to Teivos on the pretext of some sort of parleying mission, while pointing out to them the possibilities of aerial reconnaissance of Skomiar territory... Anyway, we can't just leave Bridget here. We brought her here too, and it's up to us to take her back safely! You know that as well as I do..."

Madge said nothing. She was still searching for something to say to Tom when there was a brisk rap at the door. Quenrie came in, followed by a decidedly mournful Yentsilbor. The Skomiar officer, while grateful to escape the clutches of Xaram's priests, was missing his homeland. He had confided in Tom, who seemed to be his only friend here, that he had a large family of seven children and his wife was expecting another.

Since their return to Nirei, a firm bond of friendship had grown up between Tom, Quenrie and the burly Naisur. It all dated back to the perilous ride they had shared on the rope ladder trailing from the belly of the airship. Neither Tom nor Yentsilbor had been able to make much progress up the wildly swinging ladder, and the heavily built Naisur had experienced particular difficulties because he had to go on supporting the dead weight of Quenrie as well as his own. They had been forced to cling on to the rope for dear life while Madge manoeuvred the *Goodcheer* back across the wide valley of the Traa to the forested slopes on its further side. But finding nowhere suitable to land on the tree-covered mountainside, Madge had been forced to fly some way up the valley in search of a clearing which might offer a landing site.

Finally, when Tom was certain he could hold on to the rope ladder not a minute longer, the Goodcheer had started to dip down, and he spied a small clearing approaching fast from below. Here their luck had held. It turned out that the meadow they had located was furnished with a suitably thick covering of wild grass, and Madge's exhausted, stressed and windblown passengers were able to drop into it with little more than a jolt.

Tom had risen unsteadily to his feet and seen to his alarm that a number of shadowy figures had materialised out of the forest undergrowth.

But they were in luck. Tom recognised the newcomers as a group of the local inhabitants, the Ineals, and though at first surprised and a little frightened by the unexpected arrival of the 'flying ship', they were friendly enough. They had heard something of the mysterious 'flying horse' from their relatives down the valley near Teivos, and of its occupants. And when they had recovered from their initial shock, they seemed eager enough to help.

They had no news, however, of their friend Bridget and her companions Stigrath, Pageya and Perorin. Indeed, they had had no contact with the Ineal communities near Teivos for some weeks.

"This wind's a real stinker," Madge had declared. "It's blowing up the valley at a rate of knots, back towards old Lake Nirei and the great Lord Could-you-Tell's castle. ('Could-you-Tell' was the one of the names Madge had coined for the Lord of the Green Vale, Curutel.)

And so they had decided that the wisest move for the moment would be to return to the Green Vale and the island castle of Nirei.

"Ha! And what are my friends plotting now?" said Quenrie as he entered. "For plotting is, I suspect, what you are engaged in!"

Madge smiled. "Only plotting, friend Quenrie, how to bring Bridget and Geya back here to the castle."

"Not to mention Stigrath and Orin," added Tom glumly. "Don't forget them!"

"Be not so gloomy, friend Tom," said the weather-beaten sage robustly. "I, Quenrie, have been thinking. And when Quenrie thinks, the world should take note!"

"Why's that? Is it such a rare event?" asked Madge innocently. Quenrie ignored her.

"I have been thinking on what my friend Yentsilbor here has been telling me."

"It is most essential," the broad-faced Yentsilbor butted in, "that we go to the Yenomis' city, Tekram!"

Tom and Madge looked at each other.

"And we must go in your ship that flies!" Quenrie affirmed. "It is the only way we can reach Tekram in time…"

"…Though I personally do not look forward to such a trip," Yentsilbor put in, looking distinctly ill even at the prospect.

Quenrie smiled. "You mean you did not enjoy the sensation of floating over mountains and valleys?" he asked solicitously. Yentsilbor's face turned a pale green.

"But why must we go to Tekram?" asked Madge, frowning.

Yentsilbor glanced expectantly at Quenrie, and the Lord of Nirei's adviser simply nodded. "Captain Madge and the boy are to be trusted in all things," he said. "They have an essential role to play in what we have discussed and deserve to be fully informed."

"Very well, then…" said Yentsilbor, looking a little dubiously at Madge. Clearly, the idea of discussing state secrets with a woman was somewhat alien to him. "Our trip is necessary because the Guardian Deonil is planning a campaign…"

"Against Tekram!" exclaimed Tom in disbelief.

"No, against Orotworm… His plan is to seize the Mother City itself."

"But there's no way the Silver Knights will accept that!" said Tom.

"Exactly," put in Quenrie. "It would mean war, a war so totally destructive and awful that it does not bear thinking about."

"So let me get this right," said Madge. "You, Yentsilbor, want me to fly you to Tekram to warn the Yenomi leaders, and then – am I right? – from there to Teivos for you and them to parley with this crazy Deonil fellow."

Yentsilbor nodded vigorously and muttered:

"By the winds of the desert, this woman has the vision of a sorceress!"

Tom caught her eye and she winked at him.

"There's only one problem," said Madge.

"What is that?" asked Quenrie, frowning. Obviously, he was keen on the trip to Tekram too.

"I don't have enough fuel."

Yentsilbor and Quenrie looked at each other perplexed.

"Fuel?" asked Yentsilbor.

"Liquid, watery stuff that smells bad and looks like very runny honey – it's what makes the airship fly," Madge explained to him.

"It burns very vigorously and spins the wheel that drives the airship," added Tom helpfully.

There was a puzzled and rather despondent silence.

Then Quenrie said: "Perhaps I have an answer…"

Madge raised one eyebrow.

"If this yellow water that burns is what I think it is, then Tekram may be the very place to go to seek it…"

"Really?" said Madge, intrigued.

"On the far side of their territory is a mysterious region where fire spouts from the ground."

"More and more interesting."

"Only… I think the stuff that makes these fires burn is black, not yellow…"

"That's possible," Madge encouraged him. "But it sounds as if it could, in principle, be the right sort of stuff. The problem is I need a particular sort of burning liquid. My engine only takes a certain type… It has to be, as we say, refined…"

Quenrie nodded. "It is our belief that the Yenomi, and some others too, have for many years been experimenting with this burning material… for their own purposes!"

Yentsilbor muttered angrily in agreement. "They are inventing some devilish war machine with it, according to our spies."

Quenrie pursed his lips. "Of course, the Yenomi say their experiments are quite peaceful. They have been trying to make use of pioneering work with burning liquids which were first developed by a sinister figure called Shoderim…"

Tom glanced up at him sharply.

"But he's mentioned in…"

"…In the story of Kalmom. Yes, it is the same man, the one that the woman Vencengea – whom you call Retsinis – went to join. He used to live and work in a wild and bleak castle overlooking the marshes of Niur, a nasty, unhealthy part of the Realm… When he disappeared, the castle was taken over by the Yenomi, who persuaded his remaining servants and collaborators to work for them…"

"But what had Shoderim been doing with these inflammable liquids?" asked Tom. "Was he also making weapons of some sort?"

"No, not weapons… He had discovered that he could use different sorts of burning liquid to create colour and sound and enliven religious ceremonies."

"Religious ceremonies!" Tom couldn't believe his ears. "With burning petrol!"

"It appears so. The Yenomi, of course, have quite a different use for the liquids…"

"Ah," sighed Madge. "It takes all sorts… But if what you say is true, Quenrie, then it might indeed be worth taking a spin over to this Tekram place… I'll have to find fuel somewhere in this prehistoric wonderland of yours. I just don't have enough to get us back over that great mountain we crossed on our way here!"

Quenrie looked thoughtful.

"There may be another reason for going to Tekram," he said after a few moments. "You remember how Bridget decided that the next clue or 'keyword' for deciphering Kalmom's document might be found in a library, or possibly a library with a shrine?"

Tom nodded doubtfully. He was still a bit sore that it was Bridget who had

17

thought of this.

"It seems," Quenrie continued, "that there is more than one such keyword for Kalmom's manuscript. So there must also be more than one library or chapel."

Tom nodded again. Then his face lit up.

"And there's one at Tekram!"

A curious little smile crossed Quenrie's wrinkled features.

"At least one, if I'm not mistaken. But if there is, it will be well hidden and will not exactly be *in* Tekram."

"But somewhere in that direction?"

"Yes."

"Wonder of wonders!" exclaimed Madge. "Everyone has finally admitted that I was right!"

"Right about what?" asked Tom.

"About having to go to this Tekram place. It's what I was telling you only ten minutes ago!"

Tom couldn't help laughing.

"What's happened to you, Madge? It was you who **didn't** want us to go back to Teivos. Said it was too dangerous and you should be getting us back to parents and all that. Now you want to take us somewhere that sounds even more dangerous!"

Madge screwed up her face and shrugged.

"Perhaps I'm jealous of all the fun you had down there in that Nilmerk place and don't want to miss it this time… Anyway, I suppose I'd better go and get the GOODCHEER ready for another trip!"

Chapter Two
Through the Ravine

The glittering surface below appeared to shudder for a moment, then, as the vibration in the cabin rose in pitch and intensity, the water began to slip away beneath them, faster and then faster.

A single white bird slipped in below the gondola, skimming over the surface of the water, following their course until it was no longer able to keep up with them and dropped behind. Tom's eyes followed it, until it arched away to one side, and there was nothing left beneath them but the rapidly shrinking walls of the ivy-clad castle floating uneasily on the shimmering expanse of the lake.

They were off again, and Tom was glad, because he was beginning to be oppressed by the feeling of utter helplessness that had settled on him as they sat in the castle and did nothing. Maybe they were doing totally the wrong thing by going to Tekram. His early enthusiasm for the idea had given way to many doubts. Part of him said they should be going back to Teivos as soon as possible. But there was, he had to admit, a certain sense in Yentsilbor and Quenrie's arguments, and Madge had fallen into line with them.

At least now they were doing something!

He turned his eyes shoreward, towards the green slopes which were slowly coming nearer. His gaze rose up the wooded sides of the mountain to where the dark green of the trees gave way to the lighter shades of pastureland. Then he looked beyond that to the point where the green gave way to patches of grey rock, and finally to the higher slopes where the grey gave way to the whiteness of snow.

They would have to rise a lot higher if they were to climb over all this to reach the plateau which Quenrie said lay on the other side. Tom searched for some gap in the immense wall of rock before them but could see none.

Madge consulted with Quenrie and slowly turned the airship to the right, up a river valley that ran parallel to the one they had come down on their arrival in the Green Vale. For half an hour or more they hugged the side of the valley wall, climbing ever higher, then veered out a little so as to get a better view of the forbidding slopes to their left.

"There it is!" cried Quenrie above the cacophony of the engines. "The Gap of Efra – the gateway to the Land of the Knights."

Tom looked to where he pointed and his jaw dropped. There, still some way above them, was a huge cleft in the rock. A road or pathway zigzagged up towards it over the grass-covered slopes, then suddenly disappeared into the dark chasm that split the mountainside.

"We still have to climb much higher, Ont-Maj," said Quenrie, "for we dare not brave the winds in the lower reaches of that gloomy chasm. They would be sure to dash your frail craft against the rocks on either side of the Gap."

Madge nodded grimly, then turned the airship's nose away from the mountainside in a wide arc and steered it round again to face the formidable wall of rock. They were climbing fast, but Tom saw that as yet they hadn't gained nearly enough height to enter the sinister cleft, which still lay well above them.

Madge took the craft round in another arc, and another. The two small engines laboured away noisily, making the gondola throb with their efforts. Tom found himself taking deeper and deeper breaths, though he couldn't tell whether it was from the rarefied atmosphere or from pure tension, as they climbed closer to the awesome black gash in the mountain wall. He glanced at the broad-shouldered Skomiar officer Yentsilbor, standing beside him in the cramped cabin. His pockmarked face was as pale as it was possible to be.

Finally, they were close enough to the Gap of Efra for Tom to look straight into it. The sun shone brightly down, showing up every wrinkle and outcrop of the great tumbling cliffs on either side of it, the rocks glistening in places where water oozed out of the mountainside. But the Gap itself seemed to be filled with an impenetrable darkness, a texture of gloom which seemed more than just an absence of light. Tom shivered.

"I know the Gap," said Quenrie. "I have passed it several times. I shall guide you, have no fear, my friend Ont-Maj."

Madge nodded again, but her face was becoming ever grimmer.

Now they were at the very entrance to the great chasm, and inside it was every bit as black as before. Not a chink of light, not even some dull gleam of rock could be seen within its gaping jaws.

The wind had risen, blowing in sudden gusts down the broad valley from their right, and the airship bucked wildly as it headed towards the jagged cleft. The dark chasm was now directly in front of them. The bright, almost luminous, greys and greens of the sunbathed mountainside were sliced in two by the absolute blackness of the sinister gorge beyond.

Then they were in, and for one heart-stopping moment it felt as if they had been swallowed by some great animal. They were literally sucked into the chasm by the wind. Tom could hear, above the steady roar of the engine, another sound, the shrieking of the wind rushing into the chasm as it tore past the rocky pinnacles on either side.

"Rise, rise, we must rise," shouted Quenrie. "The Gap climbs and climbs past rocks… like those ahead!"

As he pointed, they made out dimly ahead of them shapes so tangled and weird that it was hard to tell that they were rocks. The airship shot past one great pinnacle, its sharp, damp edges gleaming evilly as they caught the light from high above.

"You must climb… but go straight. There is a sharp bend to the left up ahead, but I shall tell you when you must turn."

Madge was struggling with the controls, trying to steer the madly swinging craft as it sped onwards through the half-dark. On either side, Tom caught sight of vast towering walls of darkness, with here and there a thin line of white that indicated a waterfall tumbling into the maze of rocks and crevices beneath them.

Tom looked ahead once more, and he saw the bend. There was now light, light flowing from beyond an enormous buttress on the left of the gorge. If they could only make it to that light…

"Now, turn sharply! Now, now… More, you have to turn more!"

Madge did her best, but their frail craft was flung by the rushing wind over to the right-hand side of the gorge.

"You must pull it round more!" cried Quenrie, for the first time losing his calm. "Or we shall perish on the rocks!"

Chapter Three
The Towers of Tekram

There was a lurch, and for a moment a horrible slithering sound.

And then the airship was free again, floating on through the air.

Their flight was smoother now, and there was more light. They flew on, and the chasm turned slowly back to the right. The sides of the cliffs were no longer so close, and they were covered now in greenery, grass with the odd little tuft of bushes.

"Pfff!" Madge exhaled in evident relief. "Well, we're through that one."

"Do you think we may be damaged?" Tom asked. "We must have touched the side when we came round that bend."

"The envelope touched the rock, but we don't seem to have hit anything sharp. The skin clearly wasn't punctured. Pure luck, but I think we're OK!"

Quenrie, however, was still looking grim. "I fear, my friends, that we are not through all our trials yet. No, not by any means."

They had emerged from the gorge and were now flying across what appeared to be a broad grassy bowl in the mountains, surrounded by steep slopes that led away upwards into the clouds. The clear skies and bright sunshine which had blessed them on the other side of the chasm had completely disappeared, and above them now was a sullen blanket of grey cloud. What unseen peaks and crests lay hidden above them? For a while Tom looked round for a way out of the circle of enormous hills that surrounded them, other than the narrow defile through which they had come. He glanced back at the evil dark cleft in the side of the mountain and shivered. Surely, there had to be some other, less terrifying way back to the Vale?

Quenrie pointed. "There is where we must go, and it looks as if we are not in luck."

They followed his pointing finger and once again Tom's heart fell. The grassy sides of the mountain on the far side of the vast amphitheatre sloped gradually upwards to a fringe of rocks which seemed to circle the whole of the great natural bowl… except at one point. At that point, the rim of the bowl dipped, and they could see that the road, which they had seen earlier entering the Gap of Efra, now snaked upwards to that dip. Clearly, they had to negotiate a second pass, this one not quite as terrifying, perhaps, but higher than the first and again quite a challenge for their frail craft.

But what dismayed Tom most was not the gap itself but the fact that it disappeared very abruptly into a thick, silvery and very solid mist – a mist that totally obscured whatever lay beyond.

"We're never going to make our way through that!" muttered Madge. "We'll have to stop somewhere this side of it!"

Quenrie shook his head. "That would be madness. The weather in these mountains is never kind. They are prey to fierce and unexpected storms, and there is no shelter whatsoever in this bleak place."

It was obviously true. Tom looked round the great bowl, and there wasn't a tree, nor even a rocky outcrop which might give them shelter.

"Quenrie, my friend," said Madge, "what have you got us into? You clearly overestimated the abilities of my 'ship that flies'!"

Quenrie looked rather sheepish. But he simply pursed his lips and said:

"I am sorry. But I'm afraid we must go onwards. And I shall have to try and guide you again as best I can. The one good thing is that the upper pass may be high, but it has none of the terrors of the gorge we have just come through."

Madge muttered under her breath something which to Tom sounded like *'mad egg-heads'*.

They went on, climbing again up towards the dip in the crater-like amphitheatre's rim. As they advanced, the fog appeared to be coming to meet them, slipping imperceptibly down the mountainside in their direction, as if anxious to enfold them in its wispy embraces. Since their adventures in the Vale, Tom had developed an irrational fear of mist or fog of any kind. He tried not to look ahead, preferring instead to look down at the slopes of grass beneath them and follow the hazardous track from Nirei to Tekram which wound its way from one grassy knoll to the next. But it was no use. The tension only increased, and an icy fear suddenly took hold of his heart.

What if the dense cloud above them was no ordinary cloud but the same horrible greyness which brought with it the corrosive falls of sludge? How could the poor Goodcheer possibly survive that?

Then they were suddenly enveloped in the cloud, and in an instant the world became a world with no colour.

From below, the cloud had looked white. When they were in it, it was grey, nothing but grey. All the colour disappeared, even from the brightly coloured sweater that Tom had pulled on that morning in the castle, so far below.

But at least, for the moment, the greyness around did not seem to be attacking the fabric of their ship.

"Keep on a steady course," Quenrie advised. "This pass cuts straight through the mountains. Then, as far as I remember, we go over some small hills and… then we should be at Tekram."

"As far as you remember…" muttered Madge sourly.

But she stuck to her task, easing the airship steadily onwards. At least now there was no wind pushing them in directions they didn't want to go. Madge more or less had control over the airship's movements. But would that help if they came up against a sudden outcrop, or worse still, some great wall of rock that Quenrie had not remembered…?

They went on and on through the mist…

There was no relief from the threatening darkness around them, no welcome lightening of the cloud ahead.

Then suddenly to their left, in an instant the cloud became very dark. A solid mass loomed out of the mist… and passed away just beneath them.

And all of a sudden, just for a moment, they could see the ground, fifty to a hundred feet beneath them. Then once again the fog blotted it out, and the cloud became so thick they could see no more than ten feet on either side of the cabin windows…

On and on they went, the engines droning busily behind them. Tom drew comfort from their familiar, steady sound. Well done, o good and faithful engines…

He heard Madge ask Quenrie a question, but he could not hear what they were saying…

And then the engines faltered, and their pitch changed.

Tom looked round in panic at Madge.

"We've been going for twenty minutes," she said, "without seeing anything below or on either side. I'm going to risk taking her down a bit, to see what's beneath us. It could be we're over the pass and are floating round some snowy mountaintop. The sooner we find out where the ground is, the happier I'll be."

As long as we don't locate the ground too suddenly, thought Tom, but he kept his thoughts to himself. Quenrie, meanwhile, looked uneasy. He peered through the windows at one side of the cabin, chewing on his bearded lower lip in worry and frustration, conscious that he had not proved a very successful guide. Yentsilbor had retired to somewhere at the back of the cabin.

They began to drop slowly, maintaining the same direction, edging down through the mist, which grew thicker and thicker as they went.

"We can't see anything at all, Madge," Tom said hoarsely. "Might it not be better to go up again?"

Madge muttered something to herself and kept the airship heading downwards. Now the mist on either side began to eddy and swirl, and the craft was shaken by light tremors.

Once again, something dark and solid loomed out of the mist ahead of them and slipped rapidly past the left-hand window of the cabin. Another gloomy shape quickly materialised to their right. It passed even closer.

"Madge, I don't like this," said Tom tensely. "We just don't know where we are!"

At that very moment, they emerged from the cloud and saw exactly where they were.

Right in front of them, looming tall and straight out of the damp atmosphere, was an impossibly tall thin structure. Tom thought at first it must have been a natural formation, some incredible freak of nature which had left a pinnacle of rock soaring hundreds of feet into the sky. Then he realised it was no natural pinnacle. It was made of stones, one set on top of the other. He realised that it was…

"A tower," he breathed. "One of the…"

"Towers of Tekram!" whispered Quenrie behind him, his voice hoarse with awe.

Chapter Four
A Hot Reception

Then they plunged back into the mist. Madge cut back the Goodcheer's throttle so that they were hardly moving at all. At least, thought Tom, the mist outside seemed to be calm. They were no longer being buffeted from side to side, or swirled about in directions they could not control.

But then the cloud ahead darkened again, and Tom realised that they were heading straight for another perpendicular band of darkness, one of the impossibly tall, thin towers. Only just in time Madge swung the craft away to the left. This time they passed so close to the stone pillar that Tom could make out individual stones and the cracks between them.

Just below them, on the side of the tower, was a kind of platform or balcony, and on the balcony Tom saw two figures, pointing up at them and gesticulating.

"Theologians of Thifa!" Quenrie muttered in disbelief. "I have been many times to the High Towers! But I have never seen them in this way!"

Madge was now weaving her way through the enormous, stalk-like towers as best she could, veering from one side to the other as each new pillar of masonry loomed out of the mist.

Then, quite suddenly, they were out of the mist again and gazing down to the ground far below – for so high were the towers that the gondola was still several hundred feet above ground level. As they drifted out from among the last towers, Madge steered her airship in a broad loop, and they looked back at the extraordinary city they had just come through. It was like a thicket of tall beanpoles, nestling in a broad valley entirely surrounded, as far as Tom could tell through the patches of mist, by snow-capped mountains.

Tom was overwhelmed with wonder. All the towers were exceptionally tall, but each one of them had its own individual shape and design. Some were round, with balconies jutting out at irregular intervals from their sides. Some were four-sided, some looked as if they were hexagonal and some octagonal. Some had staircases running up the outside, or slender bridges of stone linking them with the next tower. Some were plain grey, the colour of the stone from which they were built. Others had been decorated on the outside, with various heraldic images – bears, lions, shields and so on – as if to designate that they belonged to this or that lord or guild or company of knights. Some stood in clusters, as if in sign of mutual support, while a few, larger and prouder, stood in defiant isolation.

The Goodcheer was now circling over an open plain or field, situated between the cluster of towers, on one side, and a steep mountainside that climbed abruptly back up into the mist. This wide grassy space was a startling shade of deep emerald green, made all the more vivid by a few tentative rays of sunlight which had begun to penetrate the bank of cloud above.

The field was swarming with small, ant-like figures. Some, Tom noted, wore the familiar silver armour that they had seen when Pailtac's band came to collect the young people from the Vale. These armour-clad figures were gathered mostly round either end of a long avenue marked out by two parallel wooden palings. The ground in between the fences had been trampled heavily either by man or beast, he couldn't tell which. Tom came to the conclusion that this was some sort of jousting arena and that the knights at either end were preparing to do battle with each other. A crowd of onlookers milled round outside the palings, most of them dressed in dull greys and browns.

As the airship descended, the crowd of onlookers, evidently taking fright, scattered in confusion towards the protection of the towers, several hundred meters away.

The knights, on the other hand, reacted in a totally different way. Those knights who were not already mounted rushed to their horses, grabbing their lances as they went. Then the two groups, one from either end of the jousting arena, rode purposefully out of their respective encampments, converging rapidly on a single point just underneath the airship.

"Hm, they don't look altogether friendly," murmured Madge. "Might be better to find another landing place."

Just then the first arrow arched upwards from the nearest groups of riders. It fell some way beneath them, but Madge nonetheless held the airship at the height they were at and turned its nose away from the field. Quenrie nodded his approval. "Yes," he said, "I agree we should find another landing place. The knights are prone to act first and think later."

They were now heading straight for one of the towers, a much lower, dumpier tower than the others, which stood slightly apart from the main clusters, close to the jousting field. It could not have been more than a quarter the height of the other towers, and was broad and low with a flat top.

"I wonder," said Madge, "whether the people on that roof would oblige us."

There were at least twenty people on the broad roof of the tower, not knights, but the dully-dressed people who were obviously their servants.

Madge circled a couple of times above the tower roof, checking that there were no armed men among its occupants, and told Tom to release the mooring ropes. The people on the roof understood her intention and organised themselves into small groups, as if preparing to take hold of the ropes.

Madge eased the Goodcheer down to roof level and shut off the throttle. The airship glided slowly towards the people on the tower. Nothing happened. The people just stood there without making any attempt to catch the ropes, and the airship passed straight over their heads. But when Madge had managed to turn the cumbersome ship around to make another pass, they saw that one of the figures on the roof was beckoning to them to try again. They were almost past the tower roof when they felt the airship lurch gently and then moved ever so slowly backwards.

27

Madge opened the cabin door and looked down, then threw out the rope ladder. In less than a minute, she and Tom had clambered down and stood among the admiring 'ground crew', who had by now secured the airship to four massive metal brackets in the middle of the roof.

One of the people on the roof, a stocky man with a bushy beard, stepped forward proudly.

"Tom! Ont-Maj! It is you!" he called.

"Thedin!" exclaimed Tom. "What luck! So you made it to Tekram?"

Their friend Thedin, Ferthedin by his full name, stumbled forward and embraced them both warmly.

"I have been here a week," he said, beaming. "You remember, do you not, that the Lord Pailtac commanded that I leave Wesomethe within a week for Tekram? Well, when you disappeared so mysteriously with Stigrath and the honourable Quenrie" (he gave the latter a rather disapproving glance) "and did not return within the allotted time, I had no option. I came here alone."

"And did the Lord Pailtac understand?" asked Quenrie a little sheepishly. He had just climbed down the rope ladder, and Yentsilbor was struggling down after him.

"No, he did not!" answered Thedin heatedly. "I am having great difficulty in placating him. The only reason he did not order an immediate new levy from Wesomethe was that I blamed someone else…"

"Who did you blame, Thedin?" asked Tom innocently.

"Why, the guilty man, of course, who's standing here with us!" And he wagged his finger at Quenrie.

Quenrie raised his hands to acknowledge his guilt. "You have reason to be angry, good Ferthedin. Please forgive me! I would, of course, explain it all to the knights personally, but…"

"But?"

"But, as you know, I am obliged in their presence to adopt a form of disguise…"

Tom had noticed that Quenrie, that day, was wearing a particularly long and drooping cloak with a hood which hung down his back. And he now drew the hood up over his head…

"You've brought your Boatman costume!" exclaimed Tom, watching Quenrie transform himself in front of them into the mysterious figure who had rowed through the mist on the Lake of Nirei to parley with the Silver Knights, soon after their arrival at Wesomethe.

"Of course, I have, boy," said Quenrie in a strange, hollow voice which Tom did not recognise. "The knights are always impressed by mysterious, slightly grotesque figures… and not very much by moderately sized, unshaven and unarmed old men! They think I am some ghoulish presence from the Underworld when I play my little part as the 'Boatman' or, as they prefer to call me, the 'Stranger'…"

Several of the roughly clad people surrounding them began to chuckle. They obviously knew already of this little deception.

At that moment a young boy came scampering up the flight of steps that led on to the roof.

"Honourable Ferthedin, the knights are coming! They are armed to do battle and they seem very angry!"

"It would be better, honourable Ferthedin," said one of the men in Thedin's group, "if the knights did not find us here and discover that we had helped the strangers."

Thedin looked troubled, but Quenrie patted him on the shoulder.

"Your friend is right, good Thedin. Leave us here. We shall be able to look after our own interests. We have something to offer the brave knights of Tekram!"

Reluctantly Thedin left with his group, hurrying down through a broad wooden trapdoor which gave access to a flight of steps.

"Are you're sure you will be all right?" he asked anxiously as his head disappeared.

Quenrie waved him on his way. "I am sure, honourable Ferthedin. But I think it advisable to delay our meeting with the noble knights, at least until they have cooled down. It would be foolish to try and bargain with them while they are in such an unreasonable mood."

He lowered the heavy wooden trapdoor into place behind their departing friends.

"We now need to delay the knights' progress a little while we parley with them," said Quenrie. Yentsilbor nodded and pointed to some repair work which was in progress on the low crenelated parapet that surrounded the roof platform. A number of heavy stones had been left there.

"Those should do," agreed Quenrie. With a little help from Tom, Yentsilbor dragged several of the stones over and deposited them on top of the sturdy trapdoor.

"That should keep them out, for a few turns of the clock at least," murmured Quenrie. Then they went back to the side of the roof to watch for signs of the knights' approach.

Ferthedin and his companions had managed to exit the tower, and not a moment too soon. A group of knights were riding up to the squat tower's only entrance. They dismounted and began running with drawn swords towards the entrance, clearly determined to lose no time in dealing with this impertinent incursion into the very heart of their stronghold.

Some of the servant-class had also emerged from nearby towers and were gathering in groups to watch.

Quenrie stepped right up on to the rampart, the hood still covering his face. He looked for all the world like some spectral monk come to haunt the Yenomi for their past sins.

"Ho, knights!" he called down loudly in his eerily hollow voice. "Why do you attack those who would be your friends?"

The knights stopped abruptly, and one of them pointed up in awe at the hooded figure. Quenrie took advantage of their hesitation.

29

"We would speak with your leaders, knights of Tekram. We would particularly like to speak with the knights Pailtac, Erash and Kotz, who are of our acquaintance."

There was a murmur from the assembled company down below, and the knights, whose numbers were growing by the second as more rode up from the jousting field, huddled together for consultation. Some of the more headstrong, however, were clearly annoyed by the delay and broke away from the main group, heading for the entrance to their tower. Several of them were gesticulating angrily. Among them, Tom noticed, was a knight who looked remarkably like Kotz, the surly knight they had met at Wesomethe.

As they disappeared inside, one of the main group stood forward and said:

"I am Erash. Why have you come here, unknown one, in this devilish sky-machine, and what is it you want?"

"A, Lord Erash!" Quenrie intoned. "You were one of those, were you not, who recently rode to the Green Vale on an expedition to find Thedin, lord of the village of Wesomethe?"

The tousle-haired Erash was clearly unnerved by the fact that the ghoulish figure of the Boatman had singled him out for attention. He looked round uneasily at his comrades and shrugged, before turning back to Quenrie.

"Aye, I was one of those who stayed… and fought… at Wesomethe… Is that to be held against me?"

Quenrie ignored the knight's question and went on: "Perhaps you do not wish to hear something to the advantage of your sacred and indeed much-honoured city? So then, we shall take our flying machine and depart. We had wished to put this powerful machine at your disposal…"

Erash was silent, but there rose a murmur from among his comrades. Then Erash was pushed aside by another knight. Tom immediately recognised Pailtac, the leader of the expedition to the Green Vale to requisition young people.

"So it is you, Stranger. What have you come to demand of us now?"

"You will remember, perhaps, foreigners who were in our midst – strangers you would have taken with you, had the servant of the Lord of Nirei not come to summon them to his castle?"

"I remember," Pailtac called upwards. "Why? Have you now brought them with you?"

"These are the strangers, or two of them." Quenrie indicated Tom and Madge, who had come to stand on his either side. "And this is the wonderful flying machine in which they crossed the high mountains from the unknown lands. They have decided to ignore the rather harsh way in which you spoke to them back in the Vale, and they have a proposal to make. They wish now to offer their services to the noble knights of Tekram, the Silver City."

This was greeted with an excited burst of noise from among the knights, and Pailtac summoned his comrades into a huddle. Then he turned and shouted upwards:

"How can they possibly help *us*, the army of the Invincibles? We have no need of their magic flying machine… We think, in any case, it is some illusion.

A trick of the eyes that is created by some magic. Who ever heard of a ship that flies?" And some of the knights around him began to laugh, though there was a certain nervousness in their laughter.

At that moment there was a loud thud, followed by a heavy hammering on the trapdoor in the middle of the roof. Kotz and his comrades, it seemed, had reached the top of the tower.

For several tense moments Tom and his friends stood and looked nervously at the wooden frame of the trapdoor. Would it hold out? Might the knights not be able to push it open? Or hack it away with their swords? Or perhaps set light to it?

"If they look like breaking through, I suppose we can always just get back into the Goodcheer and leave," Tom suggested to Quenrie.

At that very moment there was a crunch, and the point of a sword shot out through the boards of the trapdoor.

Chapter Five
The Knights' Council

Yentsilbor was clearly feeling vulnerable, aware that he, as a Skomiar officer, would be a particular target for Yenomi wrath were the knights to penetrate the trapdoor. Muttering to himself, he lifted another large stone and crashed it on to the point of the sword, driving it back through the wood. There was a sharp cry of surprise and anger from below and a clattering and cursing, as of mail-clad bodies falling on top of each other down a flight of steps.

Within a few moments the angry thumping re-started, but Tom and Yentsilbor had rolled several more heavy stones on to the sturdy trap door, and the knights beneath it soon realised that there was nothing they could immediately do to move it.

Quenrie went back to the parapet and hailed the knights at the foot of the tower.

"Knights of Tekram, why do your comrades try to attack us when we have something we would willingly share with you? We have also some highly important information about the plans of your great rivals, the Skomiar."

There were angry shouts and snarls from below at the very mention of the hated enemy. Quenrie ignored them and went on:

"Even if your friends do break through the trapdoor, they'll bring half a ton of stone down on top of themselves… and we shall simply fly away, unharmed, and you'll never know how useful we could have been to you."

The knights below were again in conference. Quenrie looked down at them and smiled. "I think it's time I brought a bit of bargaining into play. The knights never could resist a good bargaining session." He raised his voice and called:

"We also need to strike a bargain with you… The strangers' flying machine will eventually need feeding, with a special sort of liquid we think you can provide. We shall put it, and ourselves, at your service if we can strike a bargain about the burning liquid that the machine drinks. We want to negotiate a contract."

This obviously caused a great stir down below. Quenrie chuckled. "What did I tell you? They always get excited when it comes to drawing up and signing a contract. Other than jousting, it's their national sport!"

The group of knights quickly ended their discussion and one of them, neither Erash nor Pailtac, shouted up:

"We think, fellow, that you are merely playing for time. What you have offered so far is hardly worth considering. We think it is you who need us, because you are short of this burning liquid you speak of!"

"Ha, good! They are beginning to bargain!" Quenrie muttered. Then he shouted downwards in his hollow, booming voice: "Oh but you are wrong. We can easily fly off and find this liquid elsewhere... Besides, I think we have something you should be especially interested in. We have an envoy here straight from Teivos...."

This provoked the greatest uproar yet. Quenrie let them shout and rail for several minutes, then called down again.

"And this special envoy has important news of secret plans which the Guardian Deonil has put before the Council of Priests in Teivos... Would you not like to hear about them?"

An animated conversation was now going on below. The debate was clearly heated, with voices raised against each other, and at one stage a scuffle broke out, though order was soon restored. Finally the unknown knight who had spoken before stepped out from among the others and called, in his sharp, strident voice:

"Ho there, Fellow from the Vale, and you, strangers from beyond the Snows! I am Reknab, president of the Council of Knights, Defender of the Treasury, Upholder of the Laws. Who is this envoy from Teivos whom you claim to have with you? Let us hear his name."

"His name... is Yentsilbor, Captain of the personal guard of Gybor, the Younger Guardian!"

Quenrie's words were greeted with a stunned silence. But it soon gave way to cries of indignation and anger. Reknab had some difficulty in calming his comrades.

"Stranger, whom they call the Boatman, wise and powerful as you are... or at least that is what we have always heard... you have angered us by bringing to our sacred city such a one, if he is indeed who you say."

"Nonetheless," Quenrie replied in his lugubrious voice, "I have always heard that it is your tradition, here in Tekram, to grant a hearing to all those who seek to do business with you..."

There was a sullen silence from below.

"Indeed, that is our tradition," Reknab confirmed.

"And are you willing to listen to our arguments about the flying ball and how it can help you?" asked Quenrie.

This time there was a long consultation among the knights. Finally it was Pailtac who spoke on their behalf.

"Boatman, we have set a time for your audience with the Council. We shall hear you in the Grand Chamber, in this very building where you stand, at two hours before sunset. That is, in an hour's time."

"And how do we know you will not simply arrest us and put us in your dungeons, Sir Knight?" called Quenrie.

Reknab's voice came back, with a hint of annoyance and offence. "You have the word of a knight, sir, and not just any knight, but the President of the Council. What more could you ask?"

Quenrie chuckled into his beard again. "They get so irritated when you question their word... As if they were the most honest people in the world. Yet when they give their word, you can usually trust in it… for a while, anyway."

"Indeed, Sir Knight," he continued aloud, "we accept your pledge and your offer. But can you tell your comrades to desist from breaking open this trapdoor? If they do, you can tell them, they'll avoid giving themselves a big headache!"

There was no answer to this message.

*****

The meeting took place, as arranged, an hour later in the Grand Council Chamber.

Yentsilbor and Tom cleared away the stones from the stairway entrance and Quenrie, with a strangely sinister stooping stance and the hood drooping low over his face, led the way downward. Pailtac and Erash were waiting for them on the floor below, remonstrating with Kotz and a group of young knights who stood aside only very reluctantly to let them pass. There was an audible hiss when they caught sight of the hated Skomiar officer descending the steps behind the others. But none of them dared disobey Pailtac, and the order had clearly gone out to treat the Skomiar envoy correctly, if not with warmth. Pailtac led them down a winding stone staircase to a large room below, hung with tapestries like the ones Tom had seen in their apartment back at Nirei. Here they were met by a delegation headed by Reknab.

The knights had by now discarded their jousting mail and were dressed magnificently in ceremonial splendour. Over shining suits of silver armour they wore the brightly coloured tunics of their fraternities, emblazoned with lions, eagles, griffins and all sorts of creatures that Tom did not recognise.

The Yenomi knights stood in a wide circle, glancing uneasily at Yentsilbor, clearly suspicious of the claim that this hunched and untidy figure was an envoy of the Younger Guardian. The Skomiar officer, in stark contrast to the magnificent costumes of the Yenomi knights, was dressed in the same brown-grey uniform in which he had been rescued from the pinnacle of the Nilmerk pyramid, and it had been made even scruffier by his labours in lifting the heavy stones on to the wooden trapdoor above. Still, he did his best to give himself an air of dignity, constantly wiping specks of dust from his apparel and adjusting the one garment he wore which had any colour, the crimson robe that hung limply over his shoulders.

The newcomers were offered – in a somewhat surly manner – some bread and ale (an old Knightly custom, Quenrie murmured to Tom) – and then escorted downwards another floor.

It transpired that the broad, flat-topped tower Madge had chosen for their landing was no less than the Tower of Elstertwal, the Seat of Power in Tekram, and the wide circular hall into which they were now led was known as the Grand Chamber. Here the tapestries which lined the walls were even more magnificent.

Reknab and Pailtac joined the other members of the Grand Council behind a wide semi-circular table. The Council – Quenrie whispered – consisted of the fifty Gonvurs, or leaders of the knightly fraternities.

Erash led Tom and his companions to a row of seats facing the Council and took his place beside them. Tom was no longer so sure he trusted the severe-faced Reknab, or the pledge he had given them. But it was too late to go back now.

Quenrie still had his face covered by his ample cowl, and Tom began to realise that the knights were not just in awe of the Stranger, as they called him, but of himself and Madge as well. They kept gazing at Madge in particular. It was her ginger hair, he concluded, that impressed them most, and Madge had put on one of her severest expressions, her mouth set in a disapproving grimace and her eyes stern and challenging. Tom felt a sudden urge to laugh, but controlled himself, aware that if he did so it might have fatal consequences.

Reknab began to speak.

"I am sure you will appreciate the honour being done to you, strangers. It is very rare for the full council to be summoned at the request of outsiders, men – and women – who have no knightly status."

Quenrie rose slowly to his feet and, after a pregnant silence, spoke from beneath his hood, in the deep and solemn voice he had used from the start of their parleying from the battlements. "I beg your indulgence, noble Reknab, but in that you are not entirely correct. For as I have said, we are accompanied by a senior envoy of the Younger Guardian of Teivos, the Lord Yentsilbor himself…"

There were angry mutterings from among the audience of knights and their retainers as they gazed malevolently at the Skomiar officer. Nor did Reknab make any effort to conceal his hostility.

"We do not understand at all why you have brought with you this Skomiar. Nothing could be better calculated to anger and insult us. Especially as you say he is some mere servant of one of their chieftains!"

Yentsilbor understood the intended insult and sprang to his feet.

"I have come here very much against my better instincts," he declared loudly in his guttural accents, "because I thought the noble lords of Tekram would be grateful for what I had to say…"

There was another angry murmur around the crowded room and Tom noticed that Kotz and a number of knights standing with him instinctively reached down and fingered the handles of the knives protruding from their belts. Reknab held up his hand for silence.

"And what is it you have to say to us, Skomiar?" he said imperiously. "The Skomiars are not known for passing the time of day with idle chit-chat!" A ripple of ironic laughter passed through the knights' ranks.

"I come to warn you of a common danger that hangs over our two nations," Yentsilbor stated grandly, "though since you doubt even my identity I do not see why you should believe any of it…"

There was a rumble of agreement among some of the knights.

"Nevertheless," said Reknab coolly. "Tell us what you have to say."

Yentsilbor took several deep breaths. Then he said:

"Deonil intends to seize Orotworm."

There was a moment's silence, then some voices expressing amusement and disbelief, finally a burst of excited, angry voices.

"Silence!" shouted Reknab. He leant forward and addressed Yentsilbor.

"When do you predict this will take place?"

"Within three turnings of the moon."

Another outburst of anger and incredulity.

"That is why I appeal to you, noble knights!" Yentsilbor cried above the hubbub. "You and I, Reknab, we must go there together, to Teivos. With any other knights who care to come with us. And we must parley with the Younger Guardian Gybor, and persuade the Council of the Star... our equivalent of this assembly... that this is folly, that Deonil is mad!"

Chapter Six
Agreement

The meeting now broke down into a series of seething arguments, with Reknab struggling to keep control. Tom and his companions could do nothing but sit there and listen.

Tom noticed that in their arguments the Knights liked to refer to a thick leather-bound book which they called 'the Codex'. Some of them even carried a copy with them. It seemed to be some compilation of apocryphal stories about legal arguments. Now the quotations from it were coming thick and fast.

"There is not just one, but three chapters relevant to this case," shouted the black-bearded Kotz, who was one of those who carried the book. "Chapter Sixty-Three, clause fifteen, for example, illustrates how it is important to resist evil, and promptly, rather than allow it to fester…"

"So you agree with the Skomiar," said Reknab disapprovingly, "and think we should parley…"

"On the contrary," cried Kotz. "We should not believe a word he says! We should try him immediately and administer the relevant punishment…"

"But of what is he guilty?" asked the mild-mannered Erash. "Of trying to warn us of his overlord's treachery…? No, friend Kotz, I think if you look in the ninety-seventh chapter of the Codex, you will find a very interesting story…"

"The story of the Sacred Moss that covers all foul things! Of course I know this story… It is the most misquoted part of the Codex, often used to justify inaction even against the most virulent evil! I say we must act quickly to unmask this Skomiar spy…"

"My lords, could I interrupt?" Quenrie suddenly boomed, rising to his feet.

The hubbub died down a little and was followed by a suspicious silence, as all eyes turned to the hooded figure.

"It strikes me that you have not given sufficient attention to what our friend Yentsilbor is actually saying… It is your custom to refer everything to your laws, and it is a good custom, which I deeply respect. But laws are a tool, gentlemen, a means to an end. The laws should not become more important than the realities of life. So can you apply your laws correctly if you have not first studied the facts of the matter before us?"

There was a short silence, then a nervous laugh, and finally more shouting.

"The Skomiars never give facts!" one knight shouted. "It is well known. This is some concoction, a crude trick to put us off our guard!"

"But why?" cried another. "Why has he come here? That is the point."

"Do we even know he is who he says he is?"

Quenrie laughed, a strange, hollow laugh. "Why do you not question him?" he said.

This was greeted by a storm of noise, with some of the knights shaking their fists, others waving their black-bound copies of the Codex.

Reknab rose imperiously and held up his hand for silence. Then he made a gesture towards Tom and Madge.

"Most Honourable Stranger, we shall indeed question the Skomiar in a moment... But it strikes me that you have not yet properly introduced the other aliens in our midst... And what they have to do with the Skomiar. "

Quenrie inclined his head and turned to Tom and Madge.

"These are the Lady Ont-Maj and Prince Tome-Maas, who are very considerable people in their own country beyond the sky and sea. They have only recently escaped from Teivos..."

There were expressions of astonishment, tinged with sympathy, and perhaps even respect.

"...With the help of the noble Yentsilbor. They were in very severe danger there from the mad Deonil, who..."

The murmur of voices died down expectantly.

"...Wished to feed them to the Prophet, the august Xaram-Ninel!"

There was a roar of throaty laughter, and some of the knights started to slap each other on the shoulders with mirth.

Quenrie, who now had their total attention, appealed for quiet.

"The Lady Ont-Maj, you understand, is one of a very small elite in her country who ride in the sky in such machines – which they call Sky-ships..."

"But what are they for?" called one of the knights at the back of the hall.

Tom could almost see Quenrie's brain working in over-drive.

"Why, well, for example... to..."

Tom caught his breath. Quenrie's inspiration, for once, seemed to have dried up.

Tom jumped to his feet. "To keep order when the peasants are restless..." he said, in the best Tachalyne that he could muster, and in as loud and commanding a voice as he could muster.

All eyes turned towards him.

For a moment the faceless figure of Quenrie seemed taken aback. But only for a moment.

"Indeed," he said, "as the Lord Tome-Maas says, to keep order when the peasants are, well... restless!"

The members of the Council looked at each other in perplexity. But some of them were clearly impressed. Obviously this was an activity of which they approved.

Quenrie now warmed to the theme.

"Indeed, the Sky-ship is a machine uniquely equipped for such a role. It can disperse a troublesome crowd in a few moments, quite easily, by raining down missiles or boiling liquids." (*Don't overdo it, Quenrie!* Tom thought to himself.) "These sky-ships spread fear and terror among the masses of their lands... or so the Lady Ont-Maj tells me."

Reknab looked curiously in the direction of the Lady Ont-Maj. "A curious role for a woman... Has this lady no voice of her own? Can she not speak for herself?"

Madge had apparently understood. Tom heard her mutter something which could have been slightly blasphemous. But Quenrie continued unperturbed. "The Lady Ont-Maj speaks little of our local dialects. Besides, she is a woman of action, of deeds not words. She does not normally deal in diplomacy or bargaining."

Again this brought a murmur of grudging approval. Another member of the Council rose to speak. It was Pailtac. Tom had noticed that he had become rather less hostile than the other knights, almost as if he was taking a protective interest in the newcomers. But his manner was still sceptical.

"These missiles that you say they rain down on the peasants... and the boiling liquids... Could you perhaps show them to us? What sort of missiles are they?"

There was a sudden silence. Again Tom heard Madge mutter something inaudible. Quenrie, however, was equal to the crisis.

"My lords," he protested, "you don't think we would actually dare come to your honoured land with our craft equipped with weapons of war! That would have been unthinkable, a hostile act against your noble selves. No, we have come unarmed. We have come in peace..."

"But what sort of missiles?" insisted Pailtac.

"All sorts..." Tom broke in. His intervention once again caused a stir. The alien prince had an impressive command of the common tongue! Again, most of the knights were clearly impressed.

"They can be throwing spears," said Tom, warming to his task, "or bows – which can be mounted on the cabin beneath the great balloon. Or sometimes just small spiked balls... Those are the most effective. It doesn't really matter – the mere appearance of the sky-ship is enough to strike absolute terror into the heart of the cockiest peasant rebel!"

There was a rumble of approving laughter from the Council. Clearly, they enjoyed the idea of terrifying the despised peasantry. Tom, for his part, was also beginning to enjoy himself.

Quenrie's hooded figure turned to him. "Well done, my boy," he muttered, "but don't overdo it. Leave the talking to me!"

Tom felt just a little aggrieved. Who was Quenrie to talk about overdoing things?

Reknab, meanwhile, had gone into a huddle with the other knights around him at the table. After a few minutes, he turned back to Quenrie with a knowing look on his face.

"So, as I understand it, you wish to offer us in some way the use of this flying sphere... But you did not come here out of the kindness of your hearts. You need something from us..."

Quenrie bowed in acknowledgement. Then, with support from Tom when he felt it was needed, he explained that the remarkable Sky-ship had an enormous appetite for burning liquids... the same burning liquids which they thought lay in certain parts of the Knights' Realm...

One of the Gonvurs began to protest, but Reknab quickly silenced him with a sharp motion of his hand.

"I am not sure of which 'burning liquids' you speak, and am certainly not sure that they exist in our lands... But tell us more of the uses you think your floating ship can be put."

Quenrie explained how he thought the ship that floated in the sky could be used to check on trouble in far-flung corners of the Knights' territory, to reconnoitre territory before a battle, carry messages at unbelievable speed, and so on, and so forth... He explained the advantage of looking down on an enemy from a height where he could not assail you; of moving rapidly from one part of a battlefield to another; of keeping track of the foe's own movements from afar, when he sometimes wasn't even aware of your presence; and so on.

The negotiations had now begun in earnest...

Just occasionally Madge, still sitting rigid and unsmiling, added a word or two in a gruff voice which she clearly thought sounded authoritative. The knights looked at her curiously. Surely, thought Tom, they had sensed that she had no military experience whatsoever!

But the negotiations seemed to be going reasonably well. Reknab went on to ask more about their request for material to feed the sky-ship. What exactly was the liquid they needed to make it fly in the air? He was sure they knew of no such liquid in their domain.

"But yes, the Lady Ont-Maj is convinced that the dark liquid that you pump from the ground in the marshes of Niur is just what she needs. You may consider it a secret still," Quenrie gave an apologetic laugh, "but most people in the Realm know about the work of the Brethren of Niur to develop these liquids... for religious reasons, of course, and for use in feeding lamps and lanterns..."

Reknab immediately struck a pose of indignation.

"But the holy liquids are not for use by strangers!" he said in a shocked voice. "These are the very juices of mother earth! They are to be used only for sacred purposes, in praise of the Good Fates!"

"And they will be put to a very sacred purpose, my Lord Reknab, you will see!" replied Quenrie quickly. "What more sacred purpose could there be than the protection of your mountain homeland?"

Reknab and the other knights sat is stony silence. Once or twice the other members of the Council glanced at Reknab, as if waiting for him to give a lead.

Quenrie also stood and said nothing. Had the sage's luck run out? Tom wondered. Had his confidence in their mission been misplaced? He recalled what Yentsilbor had told them, of the Skomiars' belief that the Yenomi were preparing some deadly weapon of war from the burning liquids of Niur... They clearly did not want any outsiders, particularly not a despised Naisur, to know anything about that. Clearly, it was considered some sort of state secret here in Tekram...

To Tom's surprise Reknab suddenly burst into laughter.

"You mean you want this stinking liquid from the marshes! Why, this is the least valuable commodity that we control in the name of the Broadlord. We earn little money for this stuff, amusing as the coloured flames it produces may be… and the marshes where it comes from are treacherous and unhealthy. I doubt if the product from such a foul place would make anything fly…"

There were murmurs of agreement from several of the other knights. When Tom glanced in the direction of Kotz, however, he saw that his face had turned black as thunder.

Quenrie, meanwhile, with great deliberation and care amid the scoffing, explained that the burning liquid did not actually make the craft fly. That was a secret gas contained in the great balloon. But by burning the oil in a small container called an engine, he explained, a wheel was turned which drove the sky-ship forward. He invited a small delegation – no more than three, he said – to inspect this wonderful machine and see how it worked with the burning liquid that they already possessed… They had enough of it to fly for some time, but eventually they would need more. That's why the lords from the outer world had decided to make their generous offer.

"Of course," he concluded, "if the noble knights were not interested in making use of the sky-ship, then we would simply leave and trouble them no more…"

"No, no," interrupted Reknab hastily. "We have an interest in your strange sky-ship. When can we organise the visit to inspect the driving mechanism?"

Quenrie looked at Madge, as if asking for her approval. Madge shrugged and said: "Whenever." Quenrie turned back to the Council.

"Immediately, if you like… But which three noble lords shall we have the honour of welcoming on board?"

For once the knights were caught off their guard. None of them seemed keen to inspect the mysterious sky-ship. At the same time, however, none was willing to admit any weakness of resolve or courage. Could it be, Tom wondered, that some of these noble knights were actually not quite as valiant as they tried to appear?

Finally Pailtac spoke. "I, for one, would welcome the opportunity to inspect the strangers' claims. You too, Lord Reknab, should come, I think. And I propose that Lord Kotz, who is always ready to question what others do… (there was some muted laughter at this)… I propose that he too mount with us onto this remarkable steed of the skies!"

Kotz rose angrily to his feet and started to protest.

But Reknab, a grim smile on his face, said: "I shall not go on this test flight, thank you. But I agree that Kotz can go with you, Pailtac, and maybe Erash too, since we know his boyish interest in everything new!"

This time everyone laughed.

"Tomorrow was to be the jousting tournament," Reknab continued. "In the circumstances, I think it will be wise to postpone that… indefinitely. We may have another form of jousting to entertain us. We must prepare for the new situation… You strangers, and the Skomiar chieftain, will enjoy our hospitality

41

for this night. Pailtac and his team will visit your sky-ship and report back to the council on whether they think it is capable of what you say. Depending on what they say, we may permit you to travel to the blacklands surrounding Niur – in search of the required flame liquid… In the meantime, we shall begin preparing for the worst, in case what the Skomiar says has some truth in it."

His voice became grave. "If the treacherous Skomiar are preparing to move against Orotworm, we must be ready to stop them. We shall of course give due consideration to the suggestion of… of the Lord Yentsilbor… about a mission to impress on the Skomiar the madness of their ways… We shall have to decide, however, what sort of mission that will be."

Chapter Seven
Can There Really Be No Books?

Tom, Madge, Quenrie and even Yentsilbor were assigned sumptuous quarters at the top of the one of the tallest of the towers. Each had a room and a servant – except Yentsilbor, who was given four – strapping fellows who looked as if they had just been in a pub brawl. Clearly, they were meant to look after the Skomiar officer in more than one sense.

That evening the mists parted and a bright sun shone on the gleaming peaks around the city. Yentsilbor's resentment at the knights' suspicious reaction to his message had been increased by the imposition of his unwanted bodyguard, and he locked himself in his room and refused to speak even to Quenrie. The others wandered down several sets of stairs and, finding a bridge at this level which connected their tower to the next, they started to roam among the forest of tall buildings. Most of them, they discovered, were linked to their neighbours by one or more of the narrow, arched bridges. The bridges had rails on either side, but the gulfs beneath them were so vertiginous that Quenrie, who clearly had no head for heights, closed his eyes each time they had to cross, before asking Tom to lead him over.

They climbed to the top of a particularly tall tower in the centre of the city, where they looked out over the curious clusters of similar pinnacles around them, and down at the tiny figures bustling about at the feet of the great towers. Though the sun was now sinking towards the line of mountains to the West, the city was preparing itself, and this time not for the jousting tournament.

"All this activity!" Quenrie muttered from under his cowl. "Clearly the Yenomis' preparations are not merely defensive."

It was true. Everything was in turmoil. Though Yentsilbor and Reknab might both still be talking of a peace mission to head off an out-and-out conflict between their nations, the majority of knights seemed to assume that it would sooner or later come to war. And they did not seem too upset by the prospect.

Within the space of a few hours Tekram had become a large military camp. The knights were lining up at the local smithies, mostly located in the lowest floors of the towers, to have new swords forged or old ones sharpened; or were charging up and down the nearby jousting ground on their horses practising various manoeuvres with their favourite weapons. Others were standing in small groups in between the buildings, or on the many balconies and landings, evidently discussing strategy and tactics.

The friends left the top of their tower and crossed to another one, where they found some of the knights' living quarters. Here, for the moment, there were only women and some – though not very many – children. The womenfolk seemed neither excited nor disturbed by the possibility that their menfolk might once again be going to war. They could be seen through the doors of the apartments washing or mending their warriors' best clothing, ready for it to be torn and stained once more by the blood of battle.

Tom, Quenrie and Madge descended several more floors and crossed several of the connecting bridges. Now they found themselves in altogether shabbier surroundings. Evidently they had stumbled on one of the towers which was reserved for the servant class. Only here did Quenrie finally push back the hood from over his face and blow a sigh of relief.

"Whuff! I was suffocating under that thing… I have never worn it over my face for so long!"

Just at that moment they heard some shouting and arguing, and looking out over a balcony they saw, at a slightly lower level on a neighbouring tower, a small group of men pushing and shoving each other, with loud and angry cries.

Two of the men were knights, and as Quenrie and Tom watched, they drew their swords and held them high over the heads of the other, unarmed men. But at that moment an authoritative voice rang out from further along the balcony.

"Ho! Hold your swords! What is the matter here? Why the violence, my friends?"

The sturdy figure of Ferthedin appeared.

"These men are thieves!" shouted one of the knights. "We caught them stealing clothes from our quarters. Look, they are carrying the evidence even at this moment."

Thedin looked severely at the alleged thieves.

"Believe us, honourable Ferthedin," one of the men said. "We were told by one of the knights' wives that they were cast-offs and that we could take them. We are not thieves, just men who have to clothe their families!"

"That's what you thieving rogues always say," growled the second knight. "We will have you before the tribunal. If you didn't spawn so many brats, you wouldn't have to steal to clothe them, would you?"

Another shouting match ensued, until Ferthedin interposed himself between the two groups and held up his hands.

"Enough. Enough!" he shouted. "Brother knights, put away your swords. And you, with the garments, you will give them to me. Then you will tell these knights your names and where in the towers you live. The matter will indeed go before the tribunal, so that both sides can have their say. Until then we shall have no rough justice here, thank you!"

The two knights slunk away, clearly resentful at not being able to mete out punishment on the spot. The others turned to Ferthedin, still pleading their innocence.

"Good old Ferthedin!" Madge exclaimed. "He seems to be earning his keep, all right, keeping the order…. Hey, Ferthedin – wait there for us, we're coming down!"

Ferthedin, looking upwards, opened his arms in surprise and happiness.

"Dear friends!" he called up. "Yes, do come down. We shall walk together."

So they continued their tour of the stalk-like towers in Thedin's company. They had also acquired a following, a gaggle of fascinated, chattering young Elonyms.

"I meant to ask you when you arrived, but we had so little time... Where is the Lady Bridget?" asked Thedin. "Did she not come with you?"

"Alas, the lady Bridget is somewhere in the vicinity of Teivos," Tom replied. "We do not know exactly where. Quenrie and I escaped from the Skomiars, but..."

"You have been to Teivos and returned safe!" exclaimed Thedin, clearly finding it hard to believe. There was a gasp of admiration also from the small group of people who were following them. Then Thedin's face suddenly clouded over. "And did you find out...?"

Tom looked appealingly to Quenrie. The little man took Thedin by the arm and said gently: "We did locate Pageya and Orin in Teivos, and the last time we saw them they were well. The good news is that we freed them from the Skomiar and they are now, as far as we know, being looked after by friends who live in the caves outside that dread city..."

Thedin clasped Quenrie's hand gratefully. "And the bad news?" he asked nervously.

"We ourselves were captured by the Skomiar and only the intervention of the Mistress Ont-Maj and her flying ship saved us... And I am afraid we lost touch with Bridget, Pageya and Orin. Captain Stigrath is also with them. We can only hope they are safe and well..."

Thedin nodded, though the uncertainty of Pageya's fate clearly troubled him.

"But the Skomiar chieftain Yentsilbor is here with us," Tom added, hoping to cheer Thedin up, "and we hope to go to Teivos along with him and some of the Gonvurs, to negotiate. While we're there we shall also try to locate Bridget and Pageya..."

"You are going with the knights?" exclaimed Thedin, incredulous.

"We shall join them near the Slave City," explained Quenrie. "Before that we shall go with some of the knights to find some fire-fuel for Mistress Ont-Maj's floating ship."

This news was greeted by a burst of excited conversation among the listening Elonyms.

After a pause, Thedin said gravely:

"There is much peril in your venture. The knights are troublesome friends."

"Yes, we understand that, friend Ferthedin," replied Quenrie. "But we must find Bridget and Pageya, and we cannot do that without the fire-fuel."

Tom suddenly had an idea.

"Ferthedin, is there a Teaching House in Tekram, like the one we visited at Widmos?"

The old man looked at him in surprise. "Why no," he replied, "the Yenomi do not practise their religion in the same way as the other peoples of the Realm. They do not have houses of meditation, and the Order of the Balance does not have many adherents here…"

"So… do they not have chapels… or altars? Like the one that Quenrie has in his tower?"

Tom noticed that Quenrie was frowning at him and shaking his head. But Ferthedin merely gave a small laugh.

"The Yenomi knights do not have much time for private contemplation…"

"But Quenrie told us they are very superstitious and influenced by signs and omens and that sort of thing…"

"Oh yes, they are deeply influenced by spiritual things, in many ways. And they have large gatherings – sometimes in the open air, sometimes in the large assembly halls at the bottom of each tower. They spend long hours discussing, and often disputing, the writings in the Codex…"

"The black book I saw some of the knights holding at the meeting in the Central Tower? But I thought that was a book of laws, for sorting out disputes and that sort of thing…"

"Yes, it is," it was Quenrie who responded. "But at the same time they give it an altogether religious significance… They allow it to rule their lives. Which is good in some ways, because it means they do have a strict moral code. But the Codex contains not just rules of conduct, but also quite a few rather obscure mystical writings, which ordinary people… and even many scholars… find quite difficult to understand. And some of the knights interpret it in a rather strange and… belligerent way."

Tom found this all quite frustrating and disappointing. He needed to locate another of the little shrines with the Symbols of the Balance if he were to find another code word, and it didn't sound as if the Yenomi had that sort of thing.

"So, no chapels or shrines in Tekram?"

Ferthedin and Quenrie shook their heads. Then Tom had another thought.

"And no library?" he asked.

Quenrie smiled to himself, but Thedin looked astonished at the question. Then his face broke into an ironic smile.

"Library!" he laughed. "Here in Tekram? The knights, I'm afraid, have little time also for reading!"

There was a ripple of laughter from the other Elonyms.

"But there must be a library!" protested Tom. "We have good reason to believe that there may be a book in it which will guide us in our search…"

"Your search?" asked one of the Elonyms. "What, my lords, are you searching for?"

"For the cause of the Greyness!" Tom announced grandly.

There was a general murmur of interest and sympathy.

"Can there be no books at all in Tekram?" Tom persisted, finding it hard to believe that absolutely nobody was interested in reading in Tekram.

"Well, the knights do have some people who tally the wealth from the mines," murmured Thedin, clearly trying to be helpful.

"But they are mostly slaves," said another of the men. "I mean 'paid helpers'… from other parts of the Realm, mostly from the plains of Tworm."

"But have they no books?" asked Madge.

"Only simple ledgers…"

Tom turned to Quenrie in disappointment. "But you said there was at least one library in Tekram!"

"Not IN Tekram, Tom… I said there was a library… in this general vicinity. But I fear we shall have to leave the city to find it."

Thedin looked at him sharply. "You do not mean, surely… the vanished library?"

"The vanished library?" Tom was confused. "If it's vanished, it's hardly going to be much use to us, is it!"

Quenrie ignored him. "That is exactly the place I mean, Ferthedin. Have you seen anything of our disreputable friends Elbevire and Durbote recently?"

Thedin laughed. "Not since I returned here among the towers. But I have heard they are still somewhere about, in the hills, causing trouble for our friends the knights!"

"What!" exclaimed Tom. "There's a resistance movement here too, like the one at Teivos? They must have quite a following, to hold out against the knights!"

Quenrie and Thedin both laughed heartily.

"They have no followers at all," laughed Thedin. "And they survive only by their wits."

"And they are still in the vicinity, you say?" asked Quenrie. "That means that they must still dwell in the same place…"

"Yes," Thedin replied, furrowing his brow, "though as you know, it is almost impossible to find. Folk say that its inhabitants have put a special spell on the country around it to make it always seem different to the unwelcome visitor… In any case, the Yenomi can never locate it."

"But you could help me to find it, good Thedin, could you not?" Quenrie asked.

Thedin pondered a moment.

"I could take you in the right direction, at least. Then you would have to use that special knowledge and power only you possess, noble Quenrie… But may I ask why you want to visit Elbevire and Durbote?"

Quenrie smiled.

"Because they have books," he replied.

Chapter Eight
Under the Stones

Early the next morning a young man from the Green Vale came and fetched them from their quarters. Along the corridor, Yentsilbor was busy arguing with his four 'bodyguards', and their own servants had gone along to enjoy the amusing spectacle of this confrontation, so Tom, Madge and Quenrie slipped out without any problems. When they finally reached the bottom of the tower, they checked to see if there were any knights in the vicinity. When they were sure the coast was clear, Quenrie led them towards a maze of low wooden buildings nestling under the 'servant' towers. These contained kitchens and workshops where the working people mended tools for the silver mines. At the end of one of the long buildings they found Thedin, with several sturdy mules.

"We have some climbing to do," he said with a smile.

They set off through the workshops and were soon out from under the high towers and climbing a path which rose steeply into the hills. Their departure, it seemed, had not been observed.

"The knights should not bother us," Thedin told them, "Those who aren't busy gazing up at the flying ship are preoccupied with preparations for whatever expedition it is their leaders are planning. Whatever it is they mean to do, most of the knights are sure it will involve real, active fighting with the Skomiars! And many undoubtedly hope it will…"

"So where are we going?" Tom asked eagerly, unable to suppress his curiosity any longer. "Who exactly are these Elbevire and Durbote people?"

The towers were now well behind them. Quenrie threw back the cowl and exchanged a wry smile with Thedin. But annoyingly all he would do was chuckle and say: "Oh, you'll find out soon enough, young lad!"

Their path passed along a broad valley, with well-tended farmland on either side, and then climbed into the mouth of a gully and rose up through it, zigzagging between ridges of sharp black rock. Mist had descended once more on the higher slopes, and they were now swallowed up in it again. The air grew colder and colder, and increasingly they came upon patches of hard-packed snow trapped in clefts in the hillside.

Finally they emerged out of the gully on to a stony slope that climbed even higher into the mist. Thedin led them ever upwards. Soon the patches of snow began to merge into larger sheets.

Thedin stopped.

"This is where it grows difficult," he acknowledged. "I was sure there was a gully somewhere here…"

Tom was freezing, and he was sure Thedin was lost.

"Perhaps if we go just a little way further into the mist…" Quenrie suggested.

Tom groaned inwardly. But Quenrie and Thedin were off again, their sturdy mounts climbing ever higher up the snowy slopes. They were now totally enveloped in a cold, clinging mist.

"Yes, here we are!" Quenrie's voice rang out through the fog. "I recognise where we are now! Thank you, Thedin. You have done it… But we must keep close together. Tom, watch my every move now. It is easy to lose one's way!"

Tom looked at the high wall of rock before them and could not understand what Quenrie was talking about. Surely there was no way through. But the hooded figure of Quenrie spurred his mule eagerly forwards, turned sharply just before the blank wall… and disappeared! Thedin did likewise. Tom was left alone in the mist and snow.

In a sudden panic, Tom urged his mount forward to the spot where their two companions had disappeared. To his enormous relief he saw that there was a hidden gully cutting at a sharp angle into the rock, very narrow and visible only when you were right beside it. Signalling back to Madge, he plunged into the gully. It twisted this way and that between incredibly high walls, so that at every turn the figures of Thedin and Quenrie, which he could barely make out in the gloom ahead, constantly kept disappearing. Without prior knowledge of the route, Tom reckoned, and the assurance that it led somewhere, there was little chance that anyone could either find it or follow it.

The gully, what's more, was almost blocked at several points by thick snow. Even the sturdy mules had great difficulty in ploughing their way over the hard-packed drifts. But they struggled onwards and eventually the rugged walls of the narrow cleft fell away and they emerged into an open space. How broad the space was, however, it was impossible to tell, so thick had the fog become. They moved cautiously onwards, into what appeared to be a flat, boulder-strewn wilderness.

The path began to descend. And to Tom's relief, they finally emerged from the mist.

Before them lay a hollow in the mountains, perhaps half a mile across, surrounded by rocky walls on all sides. As far as Tom could see there was only one exit, the gully through which they had passed. And on the far side of the hollow Tom saw a dwelling. At least he presumed it was a dwelling. There was no sign of any doors or windows, only a small wisp of smoke which rose from the middle of an untidy heap of stones, suggesting a fire and warmth. As they approached down the snowy path, Tom saw a figure appear out of the pile of stones and stand staring in their direction. When they drew closer, he could discern that it was a small person, dressed in rough clothes, a homespun cloak draped over a heavy shirt and thick trousers. The person wore no hat, in spite of the cold, perhaps because its head was amply protected by an unruly mop of golden hair. But Tom could not, for the moment, tell whether it was man or woman.

The newcomers dismounted and led their mules up the last few metres to the rough stone cottage, for that is what it apparently was. The small person stood motionless until they had reached the top.

"Thedin son of Fer, what brings you to this remote spot in such inhospitable weather? It is many turnings of the moon since you deigned to visit us. And now that you have, you've brought an army with you!"

The voice was low and gruff and reproachful, though Tom still could not tell whether it was male or female.

"Durbote, greetings!" said Thedin. "I have indeed brought friends to see you, some of them from beyond the Great Divide."

The small person stared suspiciously at the mounted figures behind Thedin. Quenrie had once again covered his face in the ample hood of his dark brown cloak, but now he threw it back with a flourish and gave the small person a strange, warped grin.

The small person's face creased into a puzzled frown.

"I do not think this one came over any Divide," it said.

Quenrie, meanwhile, slid off his mule and, to Tom's astonishment, rushed forward to the small figure with the unruly hair and went down on his knees.

"Durbote Ro Kernith!" he breathed with emotion.

The small figure signalled to him impatiently to get up and peered at him almost angrily. Next, it turned to Tom and Madge, and gave them two a cold, suspicious stare.

Then, quite unexpectedly, the features softened and formed the beginnings of a smile. It was a curious face. Tom was sure he had never met this person before, yet there was something very familiar about her – for he was now tending to the view that this was a woman, despite the rough voice and nondescript clothing.

"Well, you had better come in then out of the cold," Durbote said finally, with just a glimmer of good grace. "Take the mules round to the back, Thedin, where there may, or may not, be some hay left for them!"

While Thedin led off the mules, Durbote led the way to a door which was almost hidden in the middle of the pile of stones in front of them.

Inside they found a pleasant surprise. They had entered a dim but delightfully warm room. The first thing Tom noticed was the merry fire burning brightly in an open fireplace some distance from the doorway. It provided the only light, and for a while Tom had difficulty focussing on the objects in the room. When some of them did gradually take shape before his eyes, he saw that it was a complete mess of a room. There didn't seem to be a single straight wall, or any level patch of floor or ceiling. An odd assortment of crazily shaped furniture lay scattered round the room in apparently random disarray. Boots and leggings lay here and there, and boxes and crates cluttered what floor space there was. But the room had a warmth to it, with the walls draped unsparingly with thick curtains and tapestries, and the floor well protected by animal skins. You could not see the whole of the room from any one place in it, with various nooks and crannies leading off from the main space at a variety of unpredictable angles. But as Tom advanced into the misshapen chamber he slowly began to realise that the dimly visible walls all round him were filled with something he had not seen since they left Nirei…

Books! An enormous collection of books!

A second small figure, short and raven-haired, but in almost every other detail identical to the one that had greeted them outside, rose from a chair by the fire and came to meet them.

"This," said Quenrie in a strangely subdued voice, "is Elbevire. Durbote is his twin sister!"

"So that means…?"

"Yes, yes," said Durbote a little tetchily. "I'm a woman, he's a man! We get so tired of explaining to everyone!"

Elbevire seemed to be of a much less cantankerous nature than his sister. He greeted them warmly and offered them something hot to drink, which they gladly accepted.

"Excuse me for asking," said Tom tentatively, as they sipped a mug of hot liquid with a bittersweet taste like that of wild honey, "but your faces somehow seem rather familiar!"

Durbote scowled, Elbevire beamed.

"So you had noticed!" Quenrie said.

"Noticed what?" asked Madge, as if she felt she was being left out of everyone else's secret.

Quenrie smiled an enigmatic smile. "Can you really not work it out, Tom?" he said quietly. "For with such special skills in working out riddles and puzzles, you are sometimes very slow to see what is plain to the naked eye!"

Tom stared at the twins, and his mouth suddenly fell. "Are you…? You are! You're Quenrie's brother and sister, aren't you?"

Elbevire went on beaming. Durbote simply snorted, but there was now a kind of twisted smile on her face. "Took you long enough to see the obvious, didn't it?" she quipped.

"So was this your home too, Quenrie?" asked Tom.

"One of them," cut in Durbote. "For a while."

"It is where we lived when we were children, yes," said Quenrie.

"And it is where he returns when he needs rest," added Elbevire, patting his brother gently on the arm.

Tom's brain had been working furiously.

"Forgive me again," he said tentatively. "But did someone called Kalmom ever come here?"

There was a sudden silence. Then Durbote snorted again. Quenrie had turned away from both of them. Elbevire looked down at the floor.

"The Honourable Kalmom," he murmured. "A most upright man…"

"A righteous nuisance, you mean," said his sister. "Always sure he knew more than others…"

"He usually did, Durbote," Elbevire smiled. "He usually did…"

"But he didn't have to let us all know so clearly what he thought of us, did he?" For some reason she was looking towards Quenrie, who remained with his back towards them all, pretending to examine a bookshelf.

51

"He really was a much kinder man than you give him credit for, sister Durbote. He did not, shall we say, suffer fools gladly... But he never, ever considered you a fool, Durbote."

Durbote said nothing, thus accepting her brother's last statement.

"So Kalmom also lived here!" Tom said eagerly. "He lived with you?"

"Yes," said Quenrie dreamily, "a long, long time ago."

Chapter Nine
The Myth of the Maiden

Tom and Madge looked at each other. Madge whistled.

"So Quenrie, you clever old fox, that's another reason why you wanted to come to Tekram. I thought there must be some other reason. But why didn't you tell us?"

"I have my own quiet ways of doing things," said Quenrie evasively. "And I rarely offer information unless asked directly."

Durbote chuckled and smacked her thigh – a gesture, Tom noticed, which many of the locals indulged in. "Ha, yes, that's my little brother, all right!"

Tom felt a little annoyed with Quenrie, but hid his feelings. Elbevire meanwhile was explaining something.

"The fact that Durbote and I are twins has been hugely helpful to Quenrie in his career. According to our lore, twins are very auspicious. They signify the closeness of one human being to another. It is often said that twins understand each other particularly well, even when there is no visible communication between them..."

"Hm, yes, that old ESP theory...," mumbled Madge.

"... So they are seen as models, examples of what brotherly love should be like..."

"Or sisterly love," added Durbote.

"Indeed. Twins are also said to be part of the natural Balance in life... They complement one another, to make up for each other's weaknesses and deficiencies. So when one is strong, he or she can help the weaker one. When one is wiser than the other, she or he helps the less clever, and so on."

"And when one is good-natured," said Elbevire, beaming...

"... The other is crabbed and cross," added Durbote, smiling her naughty smile.

"And when the twins are of opposite sexes," Elbevire continued, "as in the case of myself and Durbote, it is seen as especially auspicious in a family. Twins from opposite sexes are said to symbolise what is highest in humanity..."

Durbote snorted.

"... symbolising the basic need of male and female for each other, their essential dependence on each other for procreation and..."

"... Other things!" Durbote hastily completed the sentence.

"Extraordinary!" said Tom, though he felt a bit bewildered by what seemed a very complicated way of looking at twins.

"Dubious!" muttered Quenrie under his breath. "There are equally popular

53

fables about single strong men and extraordinary women…"

"Ah!" said Durbote, "you refer no doubt to the most famous of them all, the Myth of the Maiden!"

"The Myth of the Maiden?" queried Tom.

"There is a belief that at a time of great hardship and disaster… a bit like now, in fact… a quite remarkable maiden, a girl of no particular background or importance, will come to save the Realm."

"A variation on other, similar legends," commented Quenrie drily. For some reason he had suddenly become very grumpy.

Durbote raised her eyebrows. "Yet a story that you in particular, my brother, have long been fascinated by!" And the little tousle-headed woman gave another of her snorts.

"Indeed," confirmed Elbevire. "It is one that you… and Kalmom before you… spent many years studying… I remember Kalmom in particular had bitter arguments over it with Vencengea…"

Madge leant forward in her chair. "So you know Vencengea too. Tell us more. We have had some dealings with this woman, as Quenrie will tell you. But we really know very little about her."

Durbote gave her now familiar snort. Elbevire smiled and began to explain.

"Vencengea was a member of the Order of the Balance, like Kalmom. Indeed, they at one time studied together at the White Palace, the great teaching house at Orotworm, and then again at Lusedion. Some say they were close friends…"

"Hm, we know what 'close friends' means…" interjected Durbote.

Elbevire ignored her. "…Close friends and the best pupils of the Order. But then, Vencengea became obsessed with strange theories involving the occult and the dark powers. Kalmom quarrelled with her, and by the time he came back here they were bitter rivals… Vencengea was eventually dismissed from the Order…"

"Yes, and look what harm that did her!" commented Durbote. "Now she has taken over one of the cults, the so-called Order of the Raven, and made it her own. In recent times, it has become much more popular and influential than the pathetic remnants of the Balance!"

"That, sadly, is true. Vencengea's cult has gained many acolytes in recent years."

"What does it teach?" enquired Tom.

"Noise and Fire!" answered Durbote, flinging her arms wide and rolling her eyes dramatically.

"Yes, and enjoyment and merriment and immediacy…," continued her twin. "Not in themselves a bad thing."

"But I thought this Vencengea was obsessed with the occult?"

Elbevire nodded. "Yes, there's a dark side to her religion too. The Noise and Fire my sister referred to are part of the elaborate ceremonies which the 'Ravenites', as their order is popularly known, like to stage. They draw enormous crowds, especially in these times of despair, with the Pestilence playing more and more on the minds of the people."

54

"The Ravenites claim they are the true successors to the Order of the Balance. They try to attract people away from the other sects and have started to build their own temples in all the towns, where they dazzle their audiences with extraordinarily loud music and magnificent displays of different-coloured lights – flashing and banging before the eyes of these simple ones. You can imagine what an effect it makes on the minds of people whose lives are lived normally in the drabness that has increasingly spread over the Realm. Oh, yes – and there is often great drunkenness towards the end, or the taking of hypnotic substances."

"And then, at the climax of this great spectacle," Durbote continued, "there will be something quite unexpected – maybe a great bang and silence. Or a deep sinister voice will ring out with some dire warning. And then a picture will appear on a big screen hung at the back of the hall or temple, and some horrific or lewd or, above all, frightening image will play on to the screen. There will be a picture of a wild cat about to pounce on a lamb, or a giant spider creeping slowly towards an unsuspecting bird, or an enormous snake slithering through a forest towards a child… Horrible, terrifying images… And all the disciples will depart, frightened to the core at their own mortality and vulnerability."

Tom shivered. Though the fire still burned brightly in the stone fireplace, he had felt a finger of cold creep into his soul.

Outside, an icy darkness had begun to gather around their small haven of warmth.

Chapter Ten
Another Clue

"I think Tom has a request to make," Quenrie told their hosts. He seemed to have returned from his little sulk. "It is a request which may have some connection with Vencengea and her cult."

"Really?" said Elbevire. "How very exciting!"

"I hope it's not going to be a nuisance," said Durbote grumpily.

Tom looked round the uneven, cluttered room for some sign of a shrine or chapel, with a tapestry like the one they had found in Quenrie's library. But he could see nothing even remotely similar.

"We would like to look in your library," he said, "for some message, or at least a clue with which to decipher a message," said Tom.

Both Durbote and Elbevire had the same bushy eyebrows, and these shot up in surprise. Then both of them burst out laughing.

"You're very welcome to try!" laughed Durbote ironically, indicating the piles of ill-sorted books and manuscripts crowded into every corner of the many-cornered room.

"You're very welcome to try!" repeated Elbevire invitingly. "But I fear you would have to spend quite a time sorting through this little lot!"

"What sort of book is it you are looking for?" asked Durbote, her eyes narrowing.

"Well I don't know exactly…"

She snorted. "Well how do you expect to find a book if you don't even know what it is!"

"I'm actually not looking for a book, only for a word…"

"A word! Well we have only a few million here. Take your pick!"

"A word!" said Elbevire eagerly. "How fascinating! Do you know what sort of word it is? I mean, is it a noun, or a verb, or an adverb…?"

Tom shrugged. "A noun, probably, but it could be anything…"

"What complete nonsense!" said the impatient Durbote. "Completely hopeless, some people. I haven't the time to spare… I'm going to go back to work on my 'Basic Logic for Yenomi and Naisur'. Tell me when you've decided what it is you're looking for!"

She wrinkled her nose, adjusting the round-rimmed lenses perched on it, and then, sniffing grumpily, she waddled off behind one of the many piles of assorted junk into a remote corner of the room. Peering round the corner of an over-laden bookcase, Tom saw her sit down at a rickety old table illuminated from above by candles in a very lopsided bracket hanging from the wall. Perhaps sensing she was being watched, Durbote picked up a heavy leather-bound volume and ostentatiously pretended to lose herself in it, sniffing loudly as she did so.

"What did I say?" asked Tom, bewildered.

Quenrie chuckled.

"She is by no means as bad-tempered or intolerant as she pretends to be," he said. "She just likes people to think she is. Oh, and also she does actually like people to be precise…"

"Now this word you are looking for?" asked Elbevire, who was clearly trying to be as helpful as possible. "Is there any subject it might be related to?"

"Well, er, possibly philosophy…or morality…or religion…" Tom was having great difficulty sorting out exactly what sort of word he *was* looking for.

"Ah, that is a start!" said Elbevire enthusiastically. "Do you perhaps have an example of the sort of word it might be?"

"Well, the only one we have found so far was 'mercy'," he said hopefully, encouraged by Elbevire's positive attitude.

"Ah! Very good! So the word we want might be something like 'love' or 'compassion' or something like that?"

"Yes… I think it would probably be something positive. But it probably wouldn't be 'compassion', because that has two 'S's and two 'O's."

Elbevire did not stop to ask why this mattered. He went on: "Might it be a word you would find in a religious book?"

"Yes…"

"Or a religious building?"

"Yes, yes! Is there a religious building near here, a chapel or a sanctuary?"

Durbote looked up from her table. "Certainly not!" she snapped. "There's nothing up here but snow… oh yes, and a little rock!"

Elbevire, however, had risen and signalled to Tom to follow him. They went to the far side of the merrily burning fire and turned round a corner which Tom had not previously even noticed.

At the end of a narrow passageway cluttered with boxes and little cupboards they came to a large chest with a circular lid. Elbevire gently opened the chest and began rummaging round inside. After a minute or two, he pulled out what appeared to be a folded cloth.

"Is this the sort of thing that might give you your word?" he asked, unfolding the cloth and holding it up.

A sudden surge of wonder and gratitude came over Tom. What Elbevire was holding up was a depiction of the red and blue flame, just like the one hanging in Quenrie's upper room in his tower at Nirei! And it had words at the four corners of the diamond formation and in the centre of the flame.

"Durbote does not like me to use it," Elbevire whispered. "But when I am feeling a bit… out of sorts, or if I have a particular problem to resolve, I come here and hang it by this little window up here… and I meditate!"

"Could you," asked Tom in a husky voice, "translate the word there in the middle?"

"The one by the flame?"

"Yes."

"Why, it is my own favourite word of all words! It says: RAHMOYN."

Tom frowned for a moment, but then his face lit up with excitement. "Could that be," he whispered, "the Tachelyne word for… Harmony!"

Elbevire nodded.

Tom turned to him and stretched out his hand.

"Elbevire!" he said, "After Quenrie, you are the greatest person in the world!"

Elbevire looked taken aback, but he accepted Tom's proffered hand nonetheless, and allowed it to be shaken vigorously.

Back before the fireplace, Tom pulled out of an inner pocket of his anorak a wad of crumpled papers, copies of the Kalmom's coded manuscript which he had made back at the Castle of Nirei. And with his trusty ballpoint pen he set to work.

Chapter Eleven
Kalmom's Story 5
Deception

"That ceremony was the last time we saw Thirdrol. The following day he was gone, as suddenly and as quietly as he had come. Where he went, and how, we learned only much later.

Vencengea was still confined to her sick bed, high in one of the many towers of the fortress. Thankfully she was in the care of goodly people, faithful servants who had stayed on from the days when the castle was ruled by Thirdrol. One in particular, a woman called Kyndil, we befriended. She made it clear to me that she neither liked nor trusted Shoderim or his confederate Alim and would do all in her power to protect both Vencengea and her twins from them.

How I would have loved to leave that dreadful place. But I could not. Had I not been charged with the safety and welfare of one of the twins? Shoderim, meanwhile, had locked himself up in a distant part of the castle and never now appeared before us. And when I sent a message to him suggesting that Maaniriv and I depart to Orotworm with the babes, to protect them from the dangers that lurked in the foul swamps so close to the fortress, he replied with a blunt and cursory "No". I was not at all sure by what right he thought he could refuse us this request, but his reply was so vehement that I thought it impolitic to go against it, for the time being at least.

In any case a period of terrible storms had set in, making the roads from Niur back to the nearest town of Tatellis well-nigh impassable. I occupied myself during this time with studying some of the learned books in Vencengea's not inconsiderable collection. For it was in her quarters that Maaniriv and I were now confined, while she herself was under the care of Thirdrol's healers. This meant that I tended to ignore Maaniriv, and this was a mistake for which I still rebuke myself, all these years later. Because it gave our host, the new master of Niur, Shoderim, the chance to work his ways with him...

I came down to supper one day, having engrossed myself in reading in Vencengea's study and found that Maaniriv was not there. The servant who was due to serve the meal told me that he had gone with Alim and Shoderim to the nearby town of Tatellis, to attend 'a special event'.

I rose from the table immediately, throwing my fork aside.

"Why was I not informed of this?" I demanded angrily.

"We could not find you, master Kalmom," the man lied, barely bothering to conceal his smirk. He had known perfectly well where I was.

I called for a horse and when one was belatedly saddled for me, I rode off as rapidly as I could along the rough track that led over the escarpment to Tatellis.

That evening the rain, for once, had held off and though the sky was darkening fast, over to the West from where the weather was coming the evening star twinkled brightly between the lingering clouds. The sun had already set, leaving a reddish tinge to the clouds which reflected on the trees and bushes as I rode on as fast as I dared. But I had no eyes for the beauties of the evening. My mood was dark, because I feared what I would find in Tatellis.

Finally the lights of the town came in sight, more lights than one would expect from a small provincial town in a remote region like Niur.

There were carriages on the road now and people on horseback. Family groups were making their way by foot from the surrounding farms to the town…

When I rode up the street leading towards the main square, it was already clear that I would not be able to reach it on horseback. I had to dismount and pay a local lad to look after it, with the promise of a rich reward if he kept it well.

"Well now, I might just be here when you come back," he said cheekily, "though I'm sore tempted to go myself to see and hear the great Maani!"

So I had been right. Shoderim had taken charge of my protégé and persuaded him to give one of his addresses – without a word of consultation or permission from me.

I climbed a small hill topped by an ancient fortress and looked down on the brightly lit market square. They had erected a stage at the far side, near what looked like the local temple of the Old Religion. And I was only just in time. The 'show' was just beginning…

And it was a show!

No plain and simple introduction by myself, leading to an address by Maaniriv. No, that would have been much too dull and ordinary. The stage was lit in a pale green, which gradually changed to yellow and then to orange… And then the music came, a low and doom-laden music, growing louder and louder…

And then the voice. I was sure it was Shoderim's. I would have recognised that deep and mendacious voice anywhere. It boomed out with a false solemnity, preparing the audience for a momentous revelation from one… who had appeared in the Realm from 'the Beyond'. Listen, the voice said, and learn… for there is a message for each one of you in the words of the Maani…

And only then did Maaniriv appear. The lights suddenly went white, and the music stopped. For several dramatic moments there was silence, and I thought that my good and simple friend had been too overcome with fear to speak… This had happened before, and he had only been able to start speaking when I encouraged him… Good, I thought, the great 'show' will be seen to be a sham…

A moment later, however, he began, hesitantly at first, but then growing more and more confident… more and more eloquent.

I have to admit I was impressed. Impressed by what he said that night and by the presentation, the colours and the sounds. They made those simple people really believe that they were listening to a prophet… and that he had spoken to each one of them personally.

But I was also jealous and bitter. I slunk away long before my friend had finished speaking and found my horse abandoned, tied to tree. The lad had not waited for his reward. He had forfeited it for the sake of the seeing the 'Great Maani' and listening to his words.

✶✶✶✶✶

For several days, in the fortress of Niur, I pretended that nothing had happened. Nor did Maaniriv speak to me about the 'event' on Tatellis square. I was aware he kept glancing at me nervously, and I knew he felt guilty that he had not told me in advance about his involvement. Finally, one night at dinner, he began to blurt out to me some excuse about not being sure himself what Shoderim's intentions were; that he had only found out himself an hour or two before he was taken there and that he could not find me to tell me... But I was so angry I refused to answer him.

And then he disappeared again, also – I discovered – in the company of Shoderim, and this time they were gone for several days. After they had returned, I overheard two servants talking in the corridor, evidently knowing that I was listening, discussing the 'huge successes' of the Maani... under the tutelage of his new master, Shoderim.

In the meantime, I had been practising. To my own surprise I had become interested, no fascinated, in the theories and experiments that Vencengea had been involved with here at Niur. Her own field had become the psychology of expectation... **If you expect to see something, you often do!** *That was the sort of thing. But she had also experimented with what she called 'residues' or 'echoes' – the imprint which people and events leave on a particular locality. I discovered that she had been delving into ways of recreating these 'echoes', of bringing people and events back days, weeks, even months later to the locality where they occurred...*

It was done with what Vencengea had termed 'atmospheres', a combination of sounds and colours and smells, so that the senses were brought into contact with the 'echoes' of events which had already taken place in a certain place. I will not go into all the details. One would light a candle, or a stick of incense, intone a tune... even the sound of laughter or of weeping could invoke a 'residue'...

I began to experiment, in a small room that nobody seemed to use, not far from the main 'test rooms' that Shoderim and Vencengea had used for their experiments. Late one night I was following one particular incantation I had found a few days before in one of Vencengea's notebooks, burning on a small dish some of the strange blue-green grass that Vencengea had evidently gathered somewhere in the nearby marshes and intoning words in one of the ancient dialects which even I barely understood...

Quite unexpectedly the room around me seemed to change. It had the same walls, the same floor, the same chairs and table... but it **felt** *different. It had a different* **atmosphere.**

Then there were voices... One of them I recognised instantly. It was that of Shoderim. I would recognise that booming, totally self-confident voice anywhere. The other, I was fairly sure, was that of Alim – a thin, reedy whine of a voice. Then I began to see them, faint, ghostly images sitting at the table on the other side of the room. Shoderim's massive frame was restless. He strode backwards and forwards, his bald head bending forward to emphasise his words in that characteristic way that was his. Alim was sitting crouched over a table, his thin, wiry body swaying from side to side in an obsequious way... They were deep in discussion.

'So you intend to take them?' Alim was saying. 'But what will you tell the mother?'

'That is the point,' Shoderim's bass replied. 'I must take them soon, before she recovers sufficiently to sense their absence.'

'And will you allow her to follow? After all, she is not yet acquainted with the Way to the Opening...'

'I shall have to ponder that carefully. It depends on how much she seems ready to accept their destiny...'

'You mean accept what it is you plan for their lives?'

The images became blurred, and at the same time the voices began to distort and become inaudible. I tried to concentrate harder, but their words were becoming fainter and fainter. Then, just as I had given up trying to make out what they were saying, I heard one last exchange.

'What of the idiot prophet and his would-be mentor, the failed priest?'

'They will be no problem. But we must deal with them fast. We must make use of the forthcoming event...'

'Event? Do you mean...?'

Then the images blurred again, their voices weakened, and finally died altogether. The 'atmosphere' which I had felt simply dissolved, and I was back alone in a nearly empty room at the top of a weird and frightening castle...

I awoke the following morning with a heavy head, in the room where I had conducted the experiment. The air was still thick with the acrid smoke of the blue grass. I remembered the vision of the two plotters, how vivid it had been and how clear the words spoken... No, I concluded, I must have become intoxicated with the fumes... This must have been mere fantasy, the product of my prejudiced and over-suspicious mind.

As the days passed, I became more and more convinced that this was the case. Only a few lingering suspicions remained... until the day of the Great Ceremony...

It was the custom in those days, as it still is in some parts of the Realm, to celebrate the third month after a birth with an outing of some kind, a visit to a nearby temple or shrine to give up thanks for the successful birth and the preservation of the child. So it was no particular surprise when one day Shoderim announced an excursion to the Shrine of the Secret Waters, to celebrate the three moons of the lives of Pageya and Pathemy. The only surprise was that he appeared in person in our apartments, for the first time since the twins' birth, and that he was in such a jovial mood. He even approached and clapped me on the shoulder in a comradely sort of way.

'You must be bored here in our dreary provincial backwater... It will be a pleasure for you, no doubt, to take in the fresh air for once...'

'But this shrine...' my friend Maaniriv stuttered, 'is it not amidst the marshes... where the air is full of unknown and harmful gases? Surely it will not be healthy for such young and vulnerable babes to go there?'

But Shoderim only laughed. 'The Shrine of the Secret Waters is a famous place of well-being, much visited because of its healing powers.'

'Indeed,' I concurred, 'but Maaniriv is right. It is set among the marshes, and we will have to pass through places where there are not only dangerous water creatures but also highly toxic vapours...'

'Then you had better wrap your faces in linen sheets,' said Shoderim dismissively, turning his back on us abruptly and leaving the room.

So we were being given no option, it seemed, but to go on this perilous expedition. At once I was on my guard and began to rack my brains for some way to avoid it, or at least prevent the two tiny children from having to go...

I found a willing collaborator in Kyndil, their nursemaid. As I have said, she had no liking for her new master. But she could think of no way of evading the trip to the shrine.

'When the master Shoderim sets his mind on something,' she said bitterly, 'he makes sure he is not thwarted. And this Shrine of the Secret Waters is indeed a remote place, which only the most experienced boatmen can locate among the many branches of the long river which descends through the swamps. The journey there will indeed be full of danger, and not just for the babes..."

Indeed. But how could I protect us all? My brain worked frantically to think of some way of warding off the evil which I felt looming over us all, myself and my friend Maaniriv, the mother, Vencengea, and above all, the two babes.

I questioned Kyndil in detail about the Shrine in question, about the building itself and the lie of the island on which it stood. She had been there several times and told me what she could...

The appointed day arrived. The expedition was to consist of two flat-bottomed boats, known locally as 'marsh-boats'. They were each propelled by two men, at front and rear, armed with long poles. On the first of these Shoderim would travel, together with several of his servants, plus Maaniriv, the twins and their nursemaid Kyndil. I was told to take my place in the second boat. The only other occupant of this boat, apart from Alim and half a dozen or so of Shoderim's armed retainers, was the priest who would perform the ceremony, a dry stick of a man with no humour or character.

As I stepped warily on to the vessel, Alim leered at me unpleasantly. This was not going to be a trip which I enjoyed.

We set off, winding through a bewildering maze of channels, zigzagging among a wilderness of reed beds and marshy islands covered in low, stunted trees. Shoderim's craft took the lead. Ours followed at a short distance.

I kept feeling for the handle of the small dagger which I had concealed under my cloak. I had also supplied one to Maaniriv, though he, poor innocent man, looked at it foolishly, as if to ask what possible use someone like himself could make of it. If only we were allowed to reach the shrine, I told myself, I would be able to do something. If Alim and his thugs acted before then, I knew we were lost... Alim had not said a word to me since we set off, but the look of smug anticipation on his face made me feel distinctly uneasy.

Finally we turned a corner in the channel and saw ahead a low grassy mound which rose above the surrounding swamp. On the top of the mound was some sort of rough stone building, surrounded by a copse of low, wizened trees.

"The Shrine of the Secret Waters," Alim announced with grim satisfaction. He looked like a gigantic spider, sitting there crouched at the stern of the boat, as if ready to pounce at any moment.

I felt once more for the handle of my knife.

But he still made no move. We landed and made our way up the broad grassy slope. Shoderim led the way, followed by Kyndil carrying the two babes, and then the rest of us at some distance behind. Maaniriv and I were hemmed in on all sides by Alim and his toughs.

We entered the shrine, a small, rough structure which barely housed the whole company. Shoderim's men stood at the rear, near the entrance, and made sure that any exit that way was impossible...

The ceremony began. I shall not describe it because it was long and boring. Every so often the priest would place some herb or incense on the small brazier which he had lit on the altar, and clouds of pungent fumes would rise up and surround us all, as he called down blessings of purity and long life on the twins. Through all this the babes, though they coughed and spluttered once or twice in the fumes, made no wail or whimper of protest.

At long last the ceremony began to draw to a close. The priest made his final invocations and started to gather up his sacred implements.

I knew this was my last chance to make a move.

'Lord Shoderim,' I said quietly. 'Allow me now to pay my own special homage to the twins. For it is our right, mine and the Maani's, to honour them with our own particular little ceremony..."

Shoderim, who all this time had stood watching with rare good humour, frowned. He was immediately on his guard, suspecting some stratagem on my part.

'The sun will soon be at its highest point,' he said. 'It is the most unhealthy time of day in these swamps...'

But the priest, unexpectedly, came to my aid.

'It is the tradition,' he said, 'that anyone present at the ceremony, particularly a relative or guardian, should add their own invocations or prayers...'

Still Shoderim hesitated.

'It will take a mere five minutes,' I said, pulling from my cloak a pouch that I had been carrying with me. 'Look, I have brought this health-giving incense

from their mother Vencengea's own workshop. All I wish to do is burn a little, on her behalf and ours, in the same manner as the good priest has done…"

Shoderim looked extremely displeased, but the priest nodded his approval and Shoderim obviously did not care to go against him. I moved forward towards the brazier on the altar, bidding Kyndil, with the twins in her arms, and Maaniriv, to come with me. I told Maaniriv to take one of the babes, while Kyndil kept charge of the other, and then I asked them both to kneel before the altar, with the babes in their arms and their heads bowed. And as I did so, I whispered to them to take a deep breath and cover their faces with part of their cloaks…

Then I opened the pouch and poured its contents on the brazier…

Shoderim barked a word of warning to his men, but it was too late. The powder's effect was instantaneous. There was a blinding flash and the small sanctuary was immediately filled with the most acrid, stinging fumes I have ever experienced. Indeed if I had known beforehand how powerful they were, I would have hesitated to use them…

I pulled Kyndil to her feet.

'Where is the exit, good woman, that you said was at the rear of the sanctuary?'

She was not only a good woman, that Kyndil, but also quick-witted and practical. She knew exactly what was happening. She ran at once to an exit which was barely visible in the stonework behind the altar. Around a sharp bend we came to a doorway which by good fortune lay wide open. We were through it in a flash, and I slammed the heavy wooden door shut behind us.

Two of the boatmen were there, and they heaved a heavy block of wood against the door, wedging it shut.

"We have done the same at the front, master," one of them assured me.

"But where are the other two boatmen, brother Kyndefrin?" Kyndil asked anxiously. "Are they not with you?"

"Unfortunately, my sister, we could not persuade our comrades to help. But neither have they tried to stop us. They have allowed themselves to be bound hand and foot, as if we were forced to overpower them."

"But have you disabled the other boat?" I asked anxiously, as we hurried round the side of the sanctuary and began our descent of the hill.

"We have loosed it to the current, so that it will float away and be lost."

I nodded with grim satisfaction. It was not what I had ordered Kyndil's two brothers to do, but it should be enough to allow our escape.

"And your families have all left the vicinity of Niur."

"Yes, master, they are already on their way to a place far distant where we shall join them…"

I hoped that this would be far enough for them to escape Shoderim's vengeance.

By now we had reached the remaining boat, passing the two men bound and gagged and fastened securely to a tree. I felt sorry for them and tried to persuade them to come with us. But they would not. They thought, poor fools, that they would be able to protect their families better if they stayed.

The boat had a small sail, and my plan had been to unfurl it and allow the prevailing south-west wind to sweep us slowly upstream, to the headwaters of the river Niur, to the place where they descend from the plateau of Tekram. I had no particular fondness of the Yenomi knights who ruled that domain, but they did have their own rather warped sense of honesty and honour, and I reckoned that we might be relatively well received there. I hoped that my status as a priest of the Balance, albeit a humble one, might carry some weight. And if the worst came to the worst I could also reveal the identity of my companion, the stranger from beyond the high snows, the Maani. I had reason to believe that his fame, in the short time since he began his public rallies, had made some impression even among the high towers of Tekram.

But at this point the Good Fates deserted us. We had not been on the water more than half an hour before the wind, which from the start had been fairly feeble, died out altogether.

Our two boatmen, Kyndefrin and Kynbor, struggled boldly to steer us in among the shallow channels which wound through the low trees and reed banks. But it was now the hottest time of day and we made little progress.

And then the wind stirred again and grew stronger. But instead of blowing us up the valley it was now coming straight into our faces. If we unfurled the sail again, it would drive us back down the way we had come, towards the shrine, and Niur, and the wrath of Shoderim.

And yet there was no alternative. We did not have the strength to punt our vessel all the way up to the plateau. Our sail was our only hope. After a quick discussion with the two boatmen, we made our decision. We would unfurl the sail and head back downstream, hoping to find one of the branches of the river which bypassed the shrine and the fortress of Niur.

The wind was strengthening all the time and fairly swept us along. It was all we could do to keep the shallow boat on an even keel. We made rapid headway, steering all the time to the right, to avoid the island of the shrine, until eventually we rushed out into a stretch of open water, a league or so wide, a lake in the middle of the swamps.

And there, to our horror, far across the lake to our left, we saw the other boat. And at its prow the tall figure of Shoderim himself!

How had he retrieved the boat? Later we discovered that it had floated only a few arrow shots away from the island of the shrine before becoming ensnared in a reed bed. And when Shoderim and his companions had freed themselves from the sanctuary, and found the two remaining boatmen, they had little difficulty in recovering it. One of the boatmen had been forced to swim across the treacherous waters and punt it back to the island.

Luckily, Shoderim's boat was still some distance away from us. We searched madly for an exit to the lake. Luckily, Kyndil's brothers knew the waterways well, and they guided us into a broad and easy channel between the marshland scrub. But Shoderim and his followers had seen us and were now in hot pursuit. And they were hardly half a league behind!

The weather was also getting rapidly worse. A cold rain began to fall, blown *down on us by the squally wind. We rigged a makeshift shelter for Kyndil and the babes, which kept the worst of the elements at bay. But we ourselves rapidly grew colder and number.*

On and on through those dismal swamps we plunged, dodging down side channels, through gaps in the reeds, trying to throw off the pursuit. But Shoderim's pilots knew the marshes as well as our own did, and they were rarely fooled by the ploys we used.

Slowly they were gaining on us.

It was now growing dark, and Kyndefrin called to me from his post at the stern of our craft:

"Master, it will be madness to continue in the dark. We must find refuge on one of the few inhabited islands. In this way we may at least survive the night. If we continue onwards in the dark, we shall go aground and not be able to float ourselves again. What's more, there are creatures in the swamps, wild and fierce things that even we who know the marshes fear…"

"We must go on," I called back to him. "If we fall into the hands of Shoderim, we shall know fear which no dark monster of the marshes could inspire!"

And so we ploughed on as best we could.

I thought of hiding among the reeds, so that our pursuers would pass on without seeing us. But Kyndil's brothers cautioned against this course. The reeds, they said, harboured terrible monsters with scaly body and enormous jaws, able to tear a man in half in a second. We could not land anywhere here, they said. We must go on, keeping to the open water.

It was now almost totally dark. If we had not heard the cries from behind us, the deep booming voice of Shoderim and the angry or frightened voices of his crew, we might have thought we were alone in this appalling, empty wilderness. How we avoided going aground in the reeds or the drowned thickets of thorn trees, I shall never know. It speaks volumes for the skill and courage of our two helmsmen, Kyndefrin and Kynbor. Now and again we would hear close by some sinister rustle or gurgling splash, as some heavy body launched itself into the water, though whether it was in pursuit of us or of some other helpless prey we could not tell…

Oh how that night was dark! Never have I known a time or a place where the least spark or glow of light was so totally absent…

Now our vessel had begun to rock and sway alarmingly. We were being born upwards, then deposited down again until the water began to dribble in over the sides.

"What is happening?" I cried. "Kyndefrin, what in the name of the Evil Fates is happening?"

"I do not know, master," came the reply, tired and hopeless.

Then Kynbor's voice cut through the dark.

"We have reached the lake, the Lake of Crystal. We have been swept down into the lake. And the storm is upon us! We are doomed… for this frail vessel will never withstand the anger of the waves!"

Chapter Twelve
Devastation

Bridget had been thinking. She wondered if there was any significance in the similarity between the names Tom and Tim. Had Retsinis and her associates, the faithful Stitgoe and Lulby, perhaps got the two mixed up, and kidnapped the wrong boy?

The heave of the oars and the rush of the water past the boat's hull was as regular as the beating of a heart. The river and the night seemed endless. How long had they been going? Five hours? Six? Maybe ten?

Bridget and her friends had left Lusedion with the Ineals and clambered back up the slippery chute to the network of caves high in the mountainside. But they had not stayed there long. After a day's rest, they had set off again, down along the banks of the Traa, over difficult paths, rocky and overgrown, for what seemed an age, until they came to the first settlement. There they waited for one of the boats which, their friends informed them, regularly plied these waters, trading between the upstream villages and the great city of Orotworm.

The Skomiars, their friends assured them, would not bother them on the boats. The desert men had an almost superstitious dread of the water and never sailed in ships if they could help it.

As it happened, a riverboat was already tied up at the village's rickety landing stage when they arrived. It was not much of a craft. The captain looked as if he had spent far too many nights carousing. He leered at them suspiciously from behind bushy eyebrows and a straggling, unkempt blond beard. The crew too were surly and unfriendly. But Bridget persuaded her friends to take the chance. She felt sure that with Stigrath as their companion they would be safe.

So they bade a fond farewell to their Ineal friends and set off. Very soon into the voyage Bridget became even more convinced they had made the right decision. She had translated the whole of the next section of Kalmom's message with the help of the new keyword HEART. And she noticed that in this section there was a mention of only one place where you might expect to find a tapestry like the ones on which they had so far found their keywords. And it was in Orotworm.

Bridget read Kalmom's account to her companions and asked for their views. But Orin had much too restless a mind to give it much thought. In any case, he was always too willing to accept whatever Bridget thought about things. As for Stigrath, he was too baffled by the intricacies of even simple sentences to attempt a guess at any hidden meanings behind Kalmom's convoluted sentences.

Bridget, however, was firmly convinced that Kalmom's account was deliberately drawing them to Orotworm, the capital of the Broadlord, the very place towards which their dilapidated vessel was now heading…

She lay on the narrow bunk and listened to the sound of the water rushing past, only a few inches from her head. She pulled the single thin cover back over her head. She didn't want to wake up properly and have to think about what they would do when they reached the great city.

But now it was growing light, and sleep was no longer possible, no matter how closely she wrapped the blanket over her eyes. She heard Stigrath stir and then clamber down from the lower bunk. A moment later the wooden panel that served as a porthole slid back noisily. The big sailor took a deep breath, and then there was sudden silence.

"No, by… holy… Adiro, not… believe…!" she heard him mutter after a while.

"Yes, it is indeed so," said Orin's melancholic voice. He was perched on his own high bunk on the other side of the cabin from Bridget, looking down at Stigrath with sad, worried eyes. All the mischief had disappeared from his demeanour. He had obviously been looking out at the countryside beyond, through his own little slit of a porthole.

Bridget joined Stigrath on the lower bunk and looked out.

The sun was rising somewhere far away over the endless plains of Orotworm. The light was slowly gathering again for a new day, but the fiery globe itself could not be seen, for everything was shrouded in a grey mist.

"What is it? What is wrong?" asked Bridget.

"Everything…! Look!"

Bridget peered out at the landscape sliding slowly past them. At first she could see very little. A great spreading tree loomed out of the mist, and then a whole line of tall poplars. Then there was a farmstead, nestling on the riverbank under its small copse of willows and oak, its outbuildings huddled together, as if for comfort. Bridget heard the clucking of hens and grunts and squeals from one of the outhouses, and the clanking of some machine or bucket. Though she sensed there was something not quite right about the scene, she could not immediately define what it was. On the surface it all seemed reassuringly normal and peaceful.

"Grass… at grass! And trees. Their leaves!"

Bridget looked again. In the grey twilight of the misty dawn, the grass seemed fairly normal. And the leaves.

But then, as the sun rose higher and its rays began to pierce the thick, suffocating mist, it slowly dawned on her what was wrong with the countryside around them.

What she had taken to be the greyness of the morning light was not disappearing as the rays of the sun gathered strength. It was still as grey as when she had first looked out of their cabin. Now and then they saw a patch of sickly green. But the trees, the leaves, the grass, the hedges, all were virtually colourless.

All were the same drab, dreary, lifeless grey.

"It's awful," she breathed, "truly awful. Much worse than in the Vale."

As the sun rose still higher, they saw the full extent of the devastation which the Pestilence had caused. The fog through which they were ploughing had nothing in common with a normal damp, refreshing mist of early morning – it was a permanent cloud of dust that hung over the plain like a disease. Even here, on the river, it entered the mouth and nostrils, filling them with the taste of ash as from an extinguished fire. The plains around them had obviously once been lush and prosperous, rich with pastures and croplands. Now their fields were bare and worn, the great spreading trees bore only wizened, colourless foliage, and the animals hobbled around feebly searching for some escape from the oppressive ashen dust and the growing heat.

The river seemed to afford the only relief, and here and there along the bank they saw mixed herds of thin cattle and strangely apathetic pigs and sheep crowding along the bank or wallowing in the water where it was shallow enough.

As for the people, they seemed mostly to be hiding indoors from the scourge of the Greyness. Only occasionally did they see a lone yokel trudging wearily along the bank, and he would turn to stare with sullen indifference at the silent vessel that swept on down the river, the only part of this blighted landscape that showed either purpose or movement.

One thing puzzled Bridget in particular. Near every farmstead or settlement she noticed a series of small hillocks, shaped roughly like small pyramids. She wondered what they were. Were they, perhaps, some sort of open-air ovens, or limekilns? Strange, then, that they appeared to have no entrances.

The sun rose slowly in the sky, but brought no relief. On the contrary, as the day wore on and the heat became more intense, the dust in the atmosphere grew gradually thicker. And as it did so Bridget and Stigrath both began to feel increasingly listless and found it more and more difficult to breath. They closed the shutters over the square portholes and stretched out on their bunks. Only Orin seemed to have any energy left. For some reason he seemed to thrive on the heat, leaping round the cramped cabin impatiently, peering out of the small porthole as if soaking up the details of every passing scene.

They saw little or nothing of the crew and were not sorry for it. The captain had been a surly man, blond and muscular, with thick curly hair and a nasty scar on his left cheek. Most of his crew were equally sombre and unfriendly, except for one, a wiry young man little more than a boy who brought them regular meals of thin gruel and water. Towards the middle of the day he entered again, pushing the door open with a heavy wooden tray and set it down with a bump on the small table between their bunks.

"How near are we to Orotworm?" asked Bridget. "Shall we be there by nightfall?"

The youth shook his head. "Probably not. As the bird flies, it is not so very far. But the river meanders a lot here, so the journey is slow."

"Cabin… a minute longer… cooked," Stigrath grunted.

"Yes," Bridget agreed. "And my throat is so dry from this dust that I'll never be able to swallow again!"

"Come, come, dear passengers," said the young sailor, "be of good cheer! We are on our way to the great metropolis, where every form of consolation… physical and spiritual… awaits you. And people there…" (he winked mysteriously) "…will certainly be interested in you! Here, let me pour you some of this water. It will revive you."

But the water was tepid and tasted of rust. Bridget wasn't sure it didn't make things worse.

The young sailor left them, smiling broadly and muttering to himself. Bridget wondered what his words had meant. Why should people in Orotworm be interested in them?

Surely nobody in Orotworm even knew they existed…

Chapter Thirteen
Orotworm!

The boat ploughed onwards, turning bend after bend in the long, meandering river, driven by the steady beat of the oars. The boat's dark sail, which they had glimpsed in the torchlight as they boarded in the river-port, was useless, since there was no wind to fill it. They passed villages, grey and drab as everything here, and a few towns, with their small clusters of fishing boats tied up to deserted quays. One of these towns, among the first they came to, had been larger than the others, and the tiled roofs of its houses huddled round the bottom of a high rock topped by the grey walls of a castle.

"I recognise this place," Orin exclaimed, "from pictures I have seen in the castle at Nirei. It is the famous fortress of Donogorm, where the wild prophet Xaram-Ninel once signed a treaty with the Broadlord, that is, the father of the present one."

Bridget found she was not the least bit interested in this story. *Perhaps,* she thought, *the apathy of the Grey Dust is having its effect on me too.*

Finally, to their immense relief, the sun began to sink in the sky, curving down towards the haze-hidden horizon away across the flat dusty plain. The youth brought them an evening meal, of the same gruel and tepid water.

"We have passed the citadel of Argud, so it is not so far now to Orotworm, the capital of the Broadlord. The captain says you can come on deck to watch our approach to the city, as long as you go quickly below deck again if one of the Broadlord's patrol boats challenges us."

Bridget wondered vaguely whey they should want to hide from the Broadlord's patrol boats, but was so overjoyed at the chance to leave the stuffy cabin that she did not think to ask. Out on the deck there was still a heavy, parched feeling in the atmosphere, but at least she could breathe with relative ease. The searing heat of the middle of the day had passed.

As the young sailor led them up towards the deck, he turned to Bridget. "The captain said to tell you that when we arrive he will smuggle you off the ship dressed as simple village people from up river. But after that you are on your own. The Skomiar have their spies in Orotworm, and since the captain suspects you have escaped from the mines at Teivos, he does not want them to find out he has transported you. He depends for his livelihood on trading with the Skomiar…"

Bridget nodded. "We understand," she told him. "As long as he brings us safely to Orotworm, that is all we ask."

The mist seemed to have thinned just a little, and in the reddening glow of the sinking sun they found they could see some considerable way across the wide plain through which their vessel was winding.

High, poplar-like trees divided the dusty fields, and here and there the horizon was lined by thick woods. But there were fewer villages here, only the occasional hamlet clustered round what appeared to be large mansions, pillared and elaborate. Even these richly decorated residences, however, showed the wear and tear caused by the pestilence. The plaster on their walls seemed to be pealing in many places, and the paintwork on the shutters and doors was dull and tired.

The sun was now beginning to set on the western horizon, in a blaze of glory.

Suddenly, the young sailor pointed.

"There! Now you can see it…"

The angry red glow of the setting sun had caught on something, maybe eight or ten miles from them. The fog seemed to be growing thinner and thinner, and as it receded a curious red glow was gathering in intensity through the gloom. At first Bridget did not understand what it was. Then she realised that the rays of the sun were reflecting off the white walls of houses, of many, many houses. More and more of them appeared as the vessel wound closer to the great metropolis. And the city, the great white city of the Broadlords, was literally shining out at them through the mist and the gathering gloom.

Here was the fabled city set on a hill, and what a city it was! Soon it seemed to fill the whole of the horizon, with multiple gleaming white walls, and a countless number of towers and pinnacles and domes of every shape and size.

The great dome in the middle, the young sailor told them, was the Vysou-Salem, the White Palace, the original centre of the Order of the Balance. This, he said, was an old religion, now in decline because it made too many demands of people. And the temple, in any case, had been taken over 'after the Maani', as he put it, by a group of elderly and reclusive priests who hardly spoke any more about any 'Balance' in life, but seemed to preoccupied with trying to postpone their own deaths.

"They seem to think they can save themselves from dying by fleeing across the Crystal Lake to somewhere in or around Fles," the young sailor said contemptuously. "Their religion is only for old people!"

Right beside the Vysou-Salem was another dome, smaller but higher, and this, their informant told them, was the New Temple or Ellektys, the Central Sanctuary of a new Sect which was spreading like wild-fire across the land and was called the Order of the Firmament. "Its symbol is the Raven, which soars in the sky! The Ellektys is a much livelier place than the old White Palace," said the young sailor. "People like it because they do not have to think or feel gloomy. There's plenty of bright lights and entertainment, and the people who lead it, they're called Orchestrators, can sing and tell jokes and keep simple people like me and you… well, me anyway… amused until it's time to go home."

"But don't they have to do something in this religion," asked Bridget curiously. "I mean, like meditate or study or… do things to help other people?"

The boy shrugged. "I don't know," he said. "I don't go very often. But they have a lot of games. And it takes people's minds off… well, all this!" And he waved his hand towards the devastated countryside all round.

They were advancing ever closer to the great white city. Again their guide pointed. Not far from the Vysou-Salem and the Ellektys, on a great rocky ridge, stood an imposing fortress. That was the Mephadore, he said, the citadel from which the Broadlord reigned. It was a city in itself, he told them, with high battlements and numerous shady courts, cut off from the rest of the city by a deep ravine spanned only by one or two narrow bridges. And at its centre was a high pinnacle. That, said their informant, was the Calletorne, the Tower of Forbearance.

The river seemed to cut right through the centre of the city. Bridget saw they were now approaching a series of quays along the riverbank, and the nearby buildings – warehouses she imagined – towered above them, blotting out the fine skyline of the City centre. Orin had never been to the great city before, and he stared in wonder at the enormous, six-storeyed houses of the merchants along its waterfront, and at the crowds of people who flocking along the bank. Crowds of them, yes… and yet… here too the people appeared to be stricken by a curious listlessness. The heat and dust of the day had waned, and Bridget had the impression the people must have emerged from their homes to enjoy the relative cool of the evening. Yet they were all, or almost all, moving about with such languor that they appeared almost to be in a trance.

Bridget heard the surly captain bark some low orders across the deck and two decidedly intimidating sailors came and stood over them. Their friend, the youth, spoke to them in a low voice.

"You must descend now. There are a patrol boats which ply the river… to prevent pirates from waylaying innocent travellers. Our captain says we should not let you be seen on deck, because he does not have a permit to carry passengers…"

Stigrath looked at the two heavies and muttered something under his breath. Bridget thought for a moment that he was going to resist the invitation to go below decks, but finally he decided to comply.

As their new and unfriendly bodyguard led them back below deck, the last rays of the sun were disappearing behind the myriad spires and domes of the city. Bridget's anxieties, which had lifted with their approach to the city, were beginning to return. Lights had begun to spring up along the wharves on the riverbank, and as she left the deck she was suddenly sorry to see them disappear. They had somehow brought comfort and reassurance.

But there was nothing they could do about it, and soon the three of them were back in the cramped cabin, now lit by a single candle on a shelf. The tiny porthole, they found, had been jammed tight and even Stigrath could not open it. As the door closed heavily behind them, they heard the wooden bolt on its outer side being drawn across.

"If soldiers come," came the rough voice of one of the crewmen outside, "remain silent! If you do not, you will not live to discover why!"

The words came as a shock to Bridget. She looked at Stigrath, and then she called through the locked door:

"Why do we have to stay below? We have nothing to fear from the Broadlord's men... We want to see the Broadlord..."

The reply was a low, guttural laugh from both of the men outside the door.

"There's no way you are going to see the Broadlord," one of them muttered, "not on this trip or any other!"

Stigrath swore an oath and fell on the door, hammering at it with his giant fist.

"What... do with us!? Villains! Who... sell... captivity? Break out! Not rest here!"

But there was no answer. The villains had gone.

"Is that it?" asked Bridget in horror. "Are they planning to sell us into captivity? Who would want to buy us?"

"Skomiar... Yenomi... Bandits... Any of these!" growled the enraged Stigrath. He paced up and down the cabin like a caged lion. Then he hammered on the door again and tried to force it open. But their captors had chosen the cabin well. Even Stigrath's great strength was not enough to budge it.

They were prisoners. And their vessel gave no appearance of stopping at Orotworm. They were sailing on down the river, to goodness knows what destination!

Chapter Fourteen
Rescue

The three companions sat and looked at each other glumly. None of them spoke. There was nothing to say.

Then Stigrath beat his fist against the bulkhead and uttered some incomprehensible oath.

"Why so stupid… agree to come below…? Stupid, stupid, stupid!"

And he began hammering on the bulkhead again.

But Bridget laid her hand on his arm and said: "Wait! Listen!"

There were other thumps and bumps coming from a different part of the wooden vessel. Then they heard frantic shouts from above and one single gigantic thud. All three of them were catapulted forward on to the cabin deck, and the candle was knocked from its shelf. The cabin was plunged into total darkness.

There was more shouting from above and heavy steps thudding on the deck. Now Bridget thought she heard the clash of metal against metal.

They heard a voice hailing the crew from a distance, possibly from another vessel. In reply there were only oaths, more shouting, and the sounds of a desperate struggle above them on the deck. Then a man screamed, and something fell with a splash into the river.

After that there was silence. They could hear the water gently lapping against the side of the boat, but nothing else. The friends picked themselves up off the cabin deck.

"Are you all right, Orin?" asked Bridget anxiously.

"Right as a feather, light as rain," answered the little fellow.

"Stigrath?"

There was silence. Then the boards creaked as Stigrath pushed himself upright, and he said:

"Top of head… Much pain… big bump. Other ways… right as Orin's rain!"

Now there were muffled voices, from above and also below deck. Someone was coming near. A door was thrown back noisily. And another. A few more words were exchanged.

A light appeared under their door. For several moments Bridget did not dare to breathe. Stigrath tensed himself. Lifting a chair which was the only moveable implement in the cabin, he positioned himself behind the door.

Then in a single movement, it seemed, someone tore back the wooden bolt and threw open the door.

A very strange figure stood there in front of them.

He was dressed in a red and silver tunic which was clearly a uniform. And he had a neat moustache and long hair. On his head was a strange pointed cap and at his side he wore a short sword. Behind him were two figures in a similar uniform, though with fewer trimmings, each holding aloft a burning torch.

The man with the moustache took a step forward into the cabin and raised above him something that looked like a small plaque.

"I am Commander of the Broadlord's Seal," he declared imperiously. "You are now my prisoners!"

"Oh thank you!" said Bridget in enormous relief. "It's so good to see you."

"We also... humble... servants... of Broadlord," murmured Stigrath, emerging from behind the door. "Stigrath... of Nirei... captain... "

The newcomer's moustache puffed out in a way which suggested indignation, but Bridget quickly realised he was smiling.

"Stigrath, my friend! Do you not remember Eclopis, whom you met many years ago when the Broadlord visited the Vale?"

Stigrath stared. Then his bearded features lit up.

"Eclopis... Also captain... very fancy ship... Our river... too narrow for you!"

And they both laughed.

"So how come you to Orotworm?" asked Commander Eclopis, becoming more serious. "And on board a vessel of brigands!"

"We were taken prisoner by these cut-throats, further up the river," Bridget explained eagerly, embellishing the truth for the sake of effect. "We are on our way with an important message for the Broadlord..."

Eclopis frowned. "A Message for the Lord himself...? I hope you are endowed with much patience... I fear not many people gain access to the Broadlord these days. Even those of us who are his most loyal servants are denied entry to the Mephadore... Strange things are happening here, my friends... but I have said enough already. You say you have an important message for His Highness. From whom does it come?"

"From Curutel, Lord of Nirei," lied Bridget. "It concerns that lord's adopted daughter Pageya... She has been kidnapped by Retsinis... or rather Vencengea the sorceress and is in mortal danger... "

"Stop, stop!" cried Eclopis holding up his hand. "Not so quickly, young lady who speaks the Broad Tongue with so strange an accent... The name of the woman you mention is not uttered lightly in this city. She is a figure of some importance in this Realm and any criticism of her must be well justified, or it could have serious consequences... "

Bridget bit her lip. She was not doing very well. "But can you take us to the Broadlord?" she asked. "We do need to speak to him urgently."

Eclopis looked enquiringly at Stigrath. The big sailor nodded emphatically.

"Important message... very!" he said.

"Very well," said Eclopis, still frowning, "I shall do my best, though I guarantee nothing... As it happens, I must myself report to the Mephadore, the Broadlord's stronghold, before the morning... I have submitted a report on the increasing laxity of our river patrols. It will do no good, because it will not get past the Moktimete... That is the body of self-appointed courtiers who have thrown a screen round the Broadlord, so he is cut off from his most loyal servants... But I shall submit it nonetheless. In any case, I am happy to lead you to the Mephadore, and you can try to gain access... I wish you luck. Though I am of a certain rank, I have not spoken directly to His Highness for over six months!"

Eclopis and his men escorted them out of the cramped cabin and up to the deck. Here they found a scene of turmoil. Somehow in the struggle for the ship someone had set light to one of its two sails, and by the lurid light of its flames Eclopis's men were disarming the last of the ship's crew and herding them into one corner of the deck. Here they stood in a crouching knot, dark and defiant, glaring at their captors as if outraged that anyone should dare to interfere with the shady business they had been pursuing. When Stigrath, Bridget and Orin appeared on deck, there was a low snarl from some of the prisoners, including the bearded blond captain, as if Bridget and her friends had somehow been the cause of the crew's downfall.

Bridget was glad to see that the young sailor, the one who had been nice to them, was being led away separately from the rest. He waved to them cheerfully.

"I too am no longer prisoner!" he called. "I go back to my village."

Eclopis's patrol boat was fastened securely to one side of the pirate vessel by what appeared to be grappling hooks, and Eclopis personally escorted them past the hissing knot of river pirates on to the deck of his vessel, and from there down into a rowing boat manned by four of his uniformed men. Soon they were pulling away across the calm, ink-black water, leaving behind them the bright circle of light thrown by the blazing sail.

They were now enveloped by one of the darkest nights Bridget could ever remember. She had been sure they were still close to Orotworm, but there was no sign of the great metropolis, no sounds, no lights, nothing.

Eclopis saw Bridget staring into the darkness and seemed to read her thoughts.

"The city is there all right," he said. "It's the dust. It soaks up light as well as everything else. In the day it makes everything grey and dull. In the night it swallows up every trace of light and leaves the world in complete darkness. A great assistance to villains of all types. But you'll see the city soon enough."

And indeed, as he spoke, there emerged out of the blackness a row of dim lights. Bridget perceived that they were close to a wharf area which must have lain downstream from the city itself. The lights on the bank were braziers set at regular intervals along a ramshackle wooden quay. Several boats were loading or unloading their cargoes in the relative cool of the night.

Yet there were only a few vessels and though there were plenty of people engaged in rolling barrels or dragging crates off and on to the vessels, the work was proceeding at a very slovenly pace. Further along the quayside there were even more people, walking here and there, apparently going about their business now that the heat and dust of the day had subsided. But what exactly their business was did not seem at all clear, and whatever it was, no one showed any great enthusiasm for doing it.

They tied up beneath one of the braziers and climbed up a rusty metal ladder on to the quayside. A few people turned and stared at them impassively. But no one seemed really to care what the story was behind the burning ship, still just about visible as a dull glow out in the middle of the river. Nor did they seem capable of mustering the slightest interest in the fact that Eclopis and his soldiers had arrested a group of somewhat bizarrely dressed strangers.

Eclopis led them through the crowds along the quay and then turned into a dark maze of streets beyond. The houses were mostly of two or three stories, very solidly built in stone or brick, with decorated cornices and fine, large doorways sheltered by ornamental portals. Everything, however, was dilapidated and dirty. The occasional torches at the street corners showed up the stained and peeling plaster and the broken-down casements around the windows. Hollow-eyed women and men stared at them out of the gloom, their faces pale and haggard, their eyes lifeless and indifferent.

And everywhere there was dust, horrible grey, clinging dust that reminded Bridget of that first morning in the Vale when the village of Wesomethe had been covered by the stuff. Here it seemed thinner and more powdery, but all the more malignant for that. Some attempt had been made to wash the grey matter off the streets, but evidently without much conviction or purpose.

They emerged into a broader, better-lit street, and Eclopis hailed a passing four-wheeled carriage with open sides, pulled by two emaciated and heavy-footed horses. Several citizens who had evidently been using the carriage as a taxi climbed out wearily but without protest. Eclopis ushered his wards and their guards into the clumsy conveyance and gave some brisk orders to the driver, who urged the horses back into motion with an indolent flick of the reins, uttering not a word to beast or man.

They now entered a more prosperous quarter of the town, where the buildings were no longer quite so shabby and the broad streets were lined by a double row of trees or shrubs. The people were better dressed too, though there were not many of them out at this time of day, the hour now being, Bridget reckoned, close to midnight.

At every other corner, it seemed, stood buildings markedly different from the residences which lined the boulevards. At first Bridget thought they must be shops or places of entertainment. In contrast to the plain-fronted residential buildings, these were highly ornamental, often with coloured glass windows and fantastically carved façades and towers.

Bridget suddenly realised that these must be temples, or places of worship, the Teaching Houses about which they had heard so much. She looked at them with growing fascination. Some, it was true, looked fairly abandoned, almost derelict. This type generally had one or more domes on their roofs and were symmetrical, the same number of windows, doors and towers on each side. They were also decorated in pale, unpretentious colours, pale blue or green, or sometimes just a thin white, while the roofs and verandas, she noticed, were painted black.

The other type, which seemed better kept and still at this hour showed signs of activity, were very different in appearance from the domed temples. There was no symmetry or balance about them. They had fantastically shaped towers and spires, of various forms and sizes, and at various levels. Their architects seemed to have done their best to make them as irregular as they could. Some had walkways rising diagonally up one side towards the roof. Others were extremely tall and thin, with turrets and pinnacles protruding at different levels in a chaotic profusion of architectural whimsy.

The broad boulevard they had been following finally opened out into a giant square. Their carriage turned to the right, allowing them an unhindered view of two enormous buildings standing at the far side of the wide plaza they were crossing.

"The two great Temples of Orotworm," Eclopis said to them, not without a note of pride in his voice, "the Vysou-Salem or White Palace, seat of the Old Religion… that is the one with the great dome… and the Ellektys, or House of Images, centre of the New Faith… or faiths…"

Bridget gazed in awe at the two gigantic buildings.

Chapter Fifteen
The Two Temples

The two great buildings were breathtaking for their very size, if nothing else. Above the square, the dusty atmosphere that obscured all light in other parts of the city seemed to have thinned. They could even see above the rooftops the pale rays of an almost full moon. Its steady light shimmered dimly on the vast dome of the White Palace or Vysou-Salem. The blank, unwindowed walls of the great edifice looked down coldly on the cobbled surface of the city square. Not a light was to be seen anywhere on its colossal frame. There it lay, for all the world like an enormous, crouching white toad, overpowering, intimidating, imponderable. From its massive walls... or was it just Bridget's tired imagination...? There seemed to issue a deep, long-drawn-out groan of slow, mournful but strangely haunting music...

To its left, separated by a gap of only a couple of hundred yards, stood the other Temple. In startling contrast to the Vysou-Salem, the House of Images or Ellektys was a hive of activity. Light poured from all of its many orifices, bright, coloured, flashing light accompanied by a swelling and fading of jangling, discordant music. From its roof, in light-hearted profusion, rose pinnacles and towers of every shape, size and colour, topped by a single, steep dome like the top of a pear. While the gloomy temple to the right seemed, at least to the casual observer, deserted, this was clearly not true of the Ellektys. People were constantly entering and leaving through the numerous doors along its side...

Bridget wanted to ask all sorts of questions, but Eclopis, as if anticipating her queries, turned to them and said:

"You shall no doubt have ample opportunity to hear of the differences between our two great temples and their followers... It is a subject in which, to be honest, I personally have little interest... like a growing number of our citizens."

But Bridget was fascinated and could not wait to find out more. "Oh please," she said, "can we go and have just one look inside each of them?"

Eclopis looked a little put out and Stigrath muttered into his beard:

"Urgent... message... for Broadlord..."

Nonetheless Eclopis called to the driver to stop and they climbed out of the open carriage. Only now did Bridget notice the small structure which stood in the gap midway between the two great Temples. It was a tiny octagonal building with darkened windows and a cone-shaped roof. A chapel of some sort, Bridget concluded. But to which of the two temples did it belong? That was not clear.

Eclopis led them across the smooth paving of the vast square. It was broken here and there by what once had clearly been a tasteful selection of trees and shrubs. Now their leaves had almost all been eaten away – obviously by the Pestilence. Only bare branches or the last remnants of yellowing foliage remained. This, and the eerie glow of the moonlight, gave the square an utterly desolate appearance, and the few shadowy figures that still inhabited it gave the impression of wandering souls who had lost track of their original purpose and destination.

That illusion was increasingly dispelled, however, as they drew closer to the giant temple on the left, the Ellektys. The cacophony of music and voices they had heard from the other side of the square was now much louder, and several of the entrances along the side were emitting a throbbing rhythm, accompanied by pulsating, multi-coloured lights. *It's almost like one great, gigantic disco,* thought Bridget, *or an oversize version of the amusements arcade back at Havenmouth!*

It was a roughly circular structure, surmounted by the strange, pear-shaped dome she had seen from a distance. Now she saw the building was made up of segments, like those of an orange, spreading out from the centre. There seemed to be a separate entrance to each of the segments. And as they arrived at one of these entrances, the throbbing beat and flickering lights increased in intensity.

They entered. The long room before them, tapering to a point in the shape of a V, was full of people. They seemed to be ordinary working citizens of Orotworm, dressed in plain, often shabby clothes, though some of them had clearly put on their best tunics or dresses. They were sitting at tables, pouring over sheets of paper inscribed with words. Bridget strained to look over a few shoulders, and although she found it difficult to read the writing, she saw the words were clearly short and simple ones. A man on a dais at the point of the V was calling out words, like 'butter' and 'cream' and 'drainpipe'. Occasionally, he would pause and then read out, with great dramatic emphasis, a word like 'garbage' and everyone would burst into laughter.

Every time the man read out a word, some of the people would stroke out a word on their sheet of paper. Then, as Bridget's party moved silently along the back of the hall, a man jumped up in excitement and yelled: 'A to Z! A to Z!' and everyone began cheering wildly and clapping. The man came forward and was presented with a small prize, a kitchen knife of some sort on this occasion, and returned to his seat amid further applause.

"The activity itself is of course harmless," whispered Eclopis. "It can even be seen as useful, spreading literacy among the people. The problem is that the people who run this place have more in mind, I think, than helping the level of literacy. They are interested in influence and, in the long run, control."

Bridget noticed that after the applause had died down and those present had settled down to another game, two smiling attendants approached the man who had won the prize and spoke in his ear. The man, seeming pleased, rose at once and followed them to a door near the dais, where all three promptly disappeared.

Bridget wanted to draw Eclopis's attention to this occurrence, but found that he and the others had already passed through a dividing door into another segment.

Here they were greeted by strangely sporadic bursts of laughter. The hall was brilliantly lit, but at first they could see nobody because the centre of the room was occupied by a series of screens and curtains. They discovered that within these screens was a maze of narrow corridors which, once they entered it, explained the laughter. The screens each bore a mirror, but not a normal mirror. They were distorting mirrors, just like the ones back at the funfair in Havenmouth, and people were wandering among them, gazing at their outlandish reflections, and laughing their hearts out!

It all seemed to be good, innocent fun, the most heartening thing that Bridget had seen since she arrived in the Realm. But Eclopis, unsmiling, led them on to a third room.

Here the scene was different again. It too was full of people, but the lighting was much dimmer. And the people were standing, their attention fixed on a stage where a man was gesticulating and talking in a dialect Bridget found difficult to understand. The audience would stand rapt in silence for several minutes and then spontaneously burst into laughter and applause, evidently at something the man on the stage had said.

"It's a stand-up comic!" Bridget exclaimed.

"A what?" asked Orin, straining to hear above the babble of voice.

"A stand-up comic, a man who stands and tells jokes."

The little Elonym boy was silent for a moment, then said:

"I find it sad. His jokes are not very funny…"

"But the people seem to be enjoying them!"

Orin sighed. "It is all about people being rude to each other and cheating each other. These people's lives must really be very dull and empty to enjoy such jokes…"

Eclopis was waiting for them at the door into the next hall or segment.

"All the rest is the same," he said. "Entertainment of a vulgar sort, but entertainment with a purpose…"

"What purpose?" asked Bridget. "It all seems harmless enough to me…"

"Dependence," said Eclopis. "It is like a drug… These people lead such dreary and pointless lives that even the tawdry companionship of these low-level pursuits brings them joy."

"I think you're being a bit harsh…" Bridget began to protest, but Eclopis had already disappeared through the outer door and one of his soldiers invited Bridget to do the same.

Eclopis was already heading back towards the four-wheeled coach, but Bridget called after him.

"What about the other temple?"

Eclopis turned slowly. "You want to see that?" he asked unbelievingly.

"Yes, of course. Since we're here. Who knows if we'll get another chance."

"But after the break-up of the Order, the Vysou-Salem was taken over by the most reactionary and gloomy elements in the Old Religion. They said that the age-old doctrine of the Balance was too difficult for people to follow. Their founder, the first Prelate of the Raven, Ysterym I, said he had had a new revelation. Only certain chosen ones had the power to interpret the Balance and make it understandable to the masses. He and his followers founded their own Order, with the symbol of a bird of prey, the Raven... The Vysou-Salem, which was once a temple of light, is now a dark and frightening place!"

"The very opposite of the Ellektys, in other words?"

Eclopis frowned. "In some ways, yes... though in others the two temples are allies!"

"Allies? But they seem so different..."

"Allies in the sense that they both detest the Balance, and those few people who still try to uphold it... And they are interested principally in influence... for themselves."

This statement definitely weakened Bridget's interest in seeing the second temple. But after a moment she said:

"I'd still like to take a look, if only for a minute or two?"

Without another word Eclopis set off towards the great white building across the square.

When they arrived under its shadow, he walked round one side and rapped on a small door in a darkened recess. For what seemed an age they waited in silence. Then, when Bridget was beginning to give up hope of an answer, the door suddenly opened. Eclopis ushered them through.

Who had opened the door was a mystery. Bridget could see nobody in the corridors into which they stepped, except Eclopis and his soldiers. But Eclopis seemed to know which way to go and led them off down a dim passage which seemed to follow the outer wall.

They walked in silence, and Bridget soon became aware of the same dismal chanting she thought she had heard before. It was coming from behind the inner walls of the corridor they were following.

Suddenly, as if out of nowhere, a tall figure appeared before them, blocking the corridor.

He was a grey and grizzled old man, with piercing, frightening eyes and he looked down on them with obvious displeasure. Then he spoke, in a deep, croaking voice, in a language which Bridget could not understand at all.

Eclopis answered him in the same dialect, uttering what appeared to be a rehearsed statement, some form of password, perhaps. After a few seconds, the grizzled old priest bowed his head slightly and addressed them all in the common language:

"You will please respect the sanctity of this place and remain in silence, whatever you see."

He then went to an arch in the inner wall which was hung with thick dark curtains. The tall man pulled the curtain back a little way to allow them to pass through.

They found themselves in an enormous sanctuary. The domed roof high above their heads was barely visible in the dim light of a number of candles that flickered feebly around a great central altar.

Then Bridget became aware of the bodies. They were everywhere, lying on litters all round them and on all sides of the altar. At first she thought they were dead bodies, but suddenly – to her horror – the one closest to her moved and a thin arm stretched out to touch her. She recoiled, but as she did so she saw the face, the face of a gravely ill person, appealing to her for help.

She tried to overcome the instinctive horror she felt and summon up some kind word or gesture. But she could think of nothing and was forced to turn away in confusion.

The mournful chanting she had heard earlier came from the altar, on a raised dais in the centre of the vast sanctuary, immediately under the dome. Here another priest, this one even older and greyer than the first, stood intoning some reading from what was evidently a holy book, set on a lectern in front of him. On and on he chanted, amid the flickering candles and the fumes of four incense-burners hanging from the ceiling far above.

"These souls will soon depart from us," the grizzled priest murmured. "We are preparing for the visitation."

Bridget did not ask what sort of visitation he meant. She was so dumbfounded by the sheer tragedy and horror of the scene.

Then, high up in the dome of the building, something caught her eye. At first it was nothing but a blue light, like any other.

But then she realised with a start that she had seen this particular steely blue glint somewhere before.

And more than once.

She had seen it from Ferthedin's cottage, back in Wesomethe, as she looked out towards the Fortress of Nirei on their first evening in the Vale.

And then again from the windows of the castle itself, as she watched the eerie, darting shapes that seemed to be looking for something or someone below them…

The icy blue light grew stronger and took on a form – the form of a flying figure, a creature of evidently supernatural design – fierce and awful and yet, at that moment, with a strange look of pity on its haggard features.

It was the same contorted face that Bridget had seen from her sleeping chamber above the lake back at Nirei. Neither then nor later could she make out what the figure was – only that it had a face and a wild, staring look, half-compassionate, half-horrified.

Without warning the figure appeared to swell, and at the same time the blue light, which now suffused the whole vast space of the sanctuary, also grew in intensity. It grew stronger and stronger, until suddenly there was a bright flash… and the figure, and the light, were gone. The temple was left once more in semi-darkness.

The onlookers, dazzled by the momentary glare, were left rubbing their eyes with shock and – in Bridget's case at least – disbelief.

Their guide, the elderly priest, seemed himself shaken and moved by the experience.

"You have witnessed," he said in a hushed whisper, "the recording of the souls. These poor mortals may now prepare themselves for the end in peace. "For they know now that they shall be transported."

"Transported?" Bridget asked in a hoarse, timid voice.

The priest frowned at her. Clearly, he was not used to being questioned about the faith. He also seemed annoyed that she had not been awed into silence by the sight they had just seen.

"Transported to the Great Beyond, to the other side of Fles!" he said curtly. "To the blessed Garden at the Centre of Being where all faithful souls, those who die in the Care of the Faith, go."

Bridget was bewildered by this statement and wanted to ask more. But the priest had already turned away and disappeared amid the grotesque tangle of bodies. Eclopis, meanwhile, was heading back towards the curtain-hung arch. One of the soldiers indicated that Bridget should follow at once. The man's face showed clearly that he wanted to leave this gloomy place as quickly as possible. She had no choice but to comply. Reluctantly she stepped back through the curtain and hurried along the corridor after the others.

"But what was it, the thing in the roof and the flash?" she whispered to Stigrath as they went. The big man merely put his finger to his mouth, as if to indicate he preferred to be off the premises of the temple before he discussed such things. Eclopis, on the other hand, evidently not so reverent in his attitude to the Temple, said over his shoulder:

"The priests offer no logical explanation. They explain it as a miracle, some hidden thing which is beyond mortal man's comprehension. Increasingly, people have begun to doubt and suggest that it is some conjuring trick, designed – like the games in the Ellektys – to win control over simple people's minds…"

"And what do you think, Eclopis? Is that all it is?"

They had reached the outer door, and Eclopis paused before opening it.

"That would be the easiest explanation," he replied.

"But you're not totally convinced?"

Eclopis thought carefully before replying.

"I would like to investigate what there is, up there, in the dome of the Vysou-Salem… I would like to see for myself whether it is a man-made phenomenon… or something else."

With that Eclopis opened the door on to the street, and they walked back towards the carriage.

They passed close to the strange little chapel Bridget had noticed earlier, standing alone in the square between the two great edifices.

"I'm sorry to bother you with all these questions, Eclopis," Bridget asked a little timidly, sensing that the patrol captain's patience was growing thin, "but what is this little building on our right?"

Eclopis glanced at it. "Oh that, that is what the people call jokingly 'the In-Between Temple'… Others have nicknamed it the 'Gateway to Paradise'. I think the name is supposed to be ironic. It leads down to an underground chapel of some sort, but to reach it you have to find your way through a maze of corridors. It used to be open to the public… but so many people got lost in it, and were never seen again, that it was closed as a public hazard…"

Bridget looked at the small building with a new fascination.

"Would it be possible, do you think…?"

"No, I am afraid not!" replied Eclopis curtly, finally losing his poise and politeness. "I must take you to the palace or I shall myself be late."

Chapter Sixteen
The Mephadore

The carriage was now back among the high, unadorned houses typical of the city, but the street they were following had begun to rise sharply. Soon it became so steep that the driver stopped the horses and called back to Eclopis in a surly, complaining voice that he could take them no further. Eclopis appeared to accept this without argument, paid the man off and led them on foot up the cobbled slope.

The street began to wind one way and then the other, and it grew steeper and steeper. Finally the houses on either side ended, and Bridget saw only the cobbled slope leading on upwards. She was suddenly aware of a great dark mass looming up in front of them. In the darkness it seemed to be just an immense featureless wall, though here and there a lone lantern or torch flickered bravely, barely penetrating the gloom. As her eyes adjusted, she saw that they illuminated a winding path that led upwards from the end of the cobbles. Presumably this was the way up to the great fortress, the Mephadore, residence and stronghold of the Broadlord himself.

They trudged wearily up the winding path until they came finally to a small level platform lit by a single lantern. Some twenty or so metres beyond it was a strange little square tower, built over an archway housing a solid wooden gate. Eclopis stopped them with a sharp word of warning.

"Be careful! There is an unguarded drop between us and the gate!"

One of Eclopis's men hung his lantern out over the edge of the platform. Only then did Bridget realise that between them and the gatehouse lay a narrow gorge, so deep that they could not see the bottom, though after a few seconds she caught from its depths the faint and rather unnerving sound of flowing water.

"The Gorge of Scolipti," breathed Stigrath. "Divide people from Palace of Broadlord! This bridge only way over…"

"Or at least," Eclopis corrected him, "the only one the people know about."

Bridget now saw that the wooden gate was in fact a drawbridge waiting to be lowered from the other side of the ravine. There was no sound, however, from the gatehouse. The guards, if there were any, appeared to be asleep. But after Eclopis called loudly across the gulf, they heard a creaking, then a slow clanking, and the massive drawbridge began descending slowly and painfully towards them.

It dropped with a resounding thud on to the paved platform where they stood. Beckoning to them to follow, Eclopis advanced across its wooden planks towards the cavernous black hole that had appeared on the other side.

But their progress was halted abruptly. From the gloom ahead of them there suddenly appeared a large and shadowy figure. Bridget let out a small cry of surprise and alarm.

The figure stood still for a moment, then shuffled laboriously on towards them. As it came closer, Bridget saw that it was a stocky, padded figure in some sort of rough uniform, a livery which might once have been grand and showy, but was now tattered and faded, covered in an uneven layer of grey dust. In one hand the figure trailed a halberd, whose butt clanked passively along over the cobbles and then the planks of the drawbridge.

This, it seemed, was one of the palace guards.

The man's bloated face peered at them suspiciously, but after a moment he gave a surly nod to Eclopis and stood aside. The party proceeded into the darkness under the archway. A second guard appeared in a doorway, holding high a lantern, and his coarse, twisted features glowed unpleasantly in the reddish light. But neither guard spoke a word or made any attempt to stop them.

They entered a small courtyard, dark except for the meagre light of the thin moon above them, and Eclopis led them up a broad, but crumbling flight of steps on its further side. He hammered with his fist on the solid wooden door at the top.

A shutter in the door slid slowly open and then, with an equal lack of urgency, was drawn shut again. After a pause, the door was opened by an unseen hand to reveal a dingy antechamber, lit by a single lantern on a table. At the table sat a man, around whom there stood, or lounged, several more of the indolent palace guards. They appeared to be in the middle of some sort of game involving cards and dice.

"Friend Eclopis!" said the seated man in a lazy, mumbling voice. "What brings you to the palace of the Broadlord so late in the evening? Surely you know that His Highness will have retired hours ago. Do you really think I can give you permission to enter?"

Eclopis went up to the table and placed his hands on its rim.

"I think His Highness may forgive me this one time," he said, glaring defiantly across the pool of light thrown by the lantern. "We have important visitors, with important news – and I suspect he will be none too pleased if we fail to report to him immediately."

The man behind the table raised his eyebrows. "Important visitors?" he said with a hint of sarcasm in his voice. He nodded towards Bridget and her friends. "These?"

Bridget stepped forward and glowered at the man. "I am a royal princess from the realms beyond the high mountains," she declared as pompously as she could. "My friends and I have come here to Orotworm on a mission to help His Highness. We demand that we be allowed to see the Broadlord immediately. We have important information to communicate to him."

The man was evidently some sort of official. His dress was gaudier and just a little cleaner than that of the soldiers, and his face was both proud and cunning. A man, Bridget decided, with an exaggerated view of his own importance. He eyed Bridget for a moment, the corner of his mouth twitching. Then he burst into loud laughter.

"My dear young lady, I have had people come here and tell me that they were the prophet Xaram-Ninel himself, and one said he was Aruterys, the legendary Silver Knight who founded Tekram. I didn't let them in, so I am hardly likely to permit entry to some fictitious princess from another world. We have a theatre for clowns down at the Ellektys. I suggest you go there!"

"You will allow us to enter, Niradnam, or it will be you who suffers," said Eclopis coldly.

Niradnam's demeanour changed in a flash. He rose to his feet, his face disfigured by anger. "You dare threaten me, the Broadlord's most trusted servant!"

"You lost the Broadlord's trust long ago, and you are well aware of it," Eclopis retorted. Let us through, or we shall force our way through." Eclopis's men drew their swords.

The guards surrounding Niradnam suddenly came out of their torpor and also reached for their weapons. For a moment their commander stood there scowling. Clearly, he had at his command a much larger body of men than Eclopis. For several moments Bridget feared the worst.

But Eclopis had evidently judged his man well. Niradnam's body suddenly relaxed and he sank back into his chair, his arm draped lazily over the table. Clearly, he was not prepared for the hassle a fight might cause. His face creased into a humourless smile and he waved his hand vaguely in the direction of a door in one corner.

"Go in then, if you must. But don't blame me if the High Lord isn't pleased to see you."

With a wry smile, Eclopis led his party through the door indicated.

Clearly, he knew where he was going. He led them across another forbidding, unlit courtyard, this one surrounded on all sides by galleries, several tiers of them, stretching upwards to a rectangle of star-strewn sky high above. Then they climbed more steps and entered what seemed to Bridget a veritable maze of corridors and galleries, all of them deserted and lit only by the pale moonlight filtering in from outside.

Here and there, framed in a window or archway, she would catch sight of a small garden or courtyard bathed in the moon's pale rays. And on the walls of the galleries themselves there hung paintings and tapestries, dim pictures of epic or idyllic scenes, images of a lost age before heroism and happiness had faded. Clearly, this had once been not just a great palace, but a beautiful one.

But why, thought Bridget, *is the palace of such a great and mighty lord so empty of people?*

At last they came to a great wooden door, outside which there flickered a single torch in a metal bracket. The door itself was carved with rich, intricate designs. Eclopis struck it with the hilt of his sword and it gave out a deep, booming noise that echoed back through the darkened corridors of the empty Mephadore.

They waited for what to Bridget seemed an eternity before suddenly there was the sound of bolts being drawn, and one side of the great door moved slowly aside. Standing in the light of the brazier stood a tall figure in a long white robe.

It was the whiteness of his beard that made the most impression on Bridget. That and the equally white mane of hair, framing a face which wore an expression of deep and inconsolable sadness.

"Greetings, my Lord Onu," said Eclopis quietly. "I was not expecting to be received by the Broadlord's Chancellor himself! But so much the better! I have brought strangers who request your protection from the Mistress of the dark arts, Vencengea."

Lord Onu's eyebrows narrowed just a fraction. His expression betrayed a momentary spark of anger. Then it set in an expression of resolve. He said:

"Anyone who needs protection from the wiles of the sorceress of Iprades is indeed a friend of the Broadlord. Enter and be welcome!"

And the Broadlord's Chancellor stood back and bade them step through the great doorway.

Chapter Seventeen
The Broadlord's Halls

Beyond the carved door was another world.

Not only was there light – a gentle, yellow light provided by four large candles, each on a high stand in each corner of the anteroom which they had entered. There was also colour. Bridget suddenly realised how much she had missed the colour of everyday life. It had been almost entirely missing from the scenes they had passed through in the last few days, as if it had been bleached from fields and faces, animals, trees and buildings by constant washing or exposure to the sun.

But here there was colour, and colour in its richest form. The antechamber walls were mostly of a delicate lime green, with darker green drapes at each corner. And when they passed through a gap in the curtains into the room beyond, the colouring suddenly changed to a tasteful mixture of blues and yellows. This new chamber was broad and airy, furnished with plain but comfortable divans and armchairs, and hung with curtains similar to those in the antechamber. Here and there in recesses in the walls were paintings – simple landscapes for the most part, country scenes, some with high mountains or wide lakes, and in one case a valley that looked very like the Green Vale of Nirei.

Below the paintings were bookcases, full of ancient volumes, charts and documents – piled in an untidy jumble which reminded Bridget a bit of the shelves in Quenrie's tower or the old bookshop back in Havenmouth where her whole adventure had begun.

In the farthest corner of the room stood a desk, also covered in papers. But apart from that the room was empty.

Onu invited them to sit. "You look hungry and tired," he said gently, looking at Bridget and Orin in particular. "I shall go and see if I can find some refreshment."

He left them to return a few moments later, carrying a tray of cool drinks and small, tasty cakes.

"All that we can manage at this time of night," he said apologetically.

"We thank you, Lord Onu," said Eclopis politely. "And His Highness, is he available?"

Onu seemed not to hear the question. "I see," he said glancing at Stigrath, "that you have come from the Green Vale. Tell me, how is the Lord Curutel?"

Stigrath bowed his head stiffly in Onu's direction.

"Lord Onu recognised... humble servant... great honour. The Lord Curutel... well in body... much disturbed in mind."

"I am sorry to hear that. But it is understandable. We all live in troubled times."

Onu's gaze rested on Bridget. For several moments he was silent, as if he didn't know what to say.

"And you, young lady?" he said finally. "Is it correct what I hear from my informants, that you are one of a group that came from beyond the white mountains of the Great Divide? Possibly from the same place as the great seer Maaniriv? Could this be true?"

Bridget wondered how it was that Onu was so well informed. But what she really wanted to know just at that moment was where the Broadlord was and why he had not yet appeared. She was impatient to speak to someone with real authority. Nevertheless, she answered Onu as politely as she could.

"We certainly came over the high mountains, and I *have* heard of a... a teacher called Manny Reeve."

The chamberlain's eyes lighted up. "Aha! This is good... As you have seen for yourself..." (He looked vaguely towards an open window in one corner which Bridget had not noticed before and which she guessed looked out over the city) "our once noble Realm is in a very sorry state. It would be of great interest to His Highness the Broadlord... and encouragement too, if he could talk with you about our troubles... and discuss possible solutions..."

"But where is His Highness?" Bridget took the opportunity to ask.

Onu looked down at the floor and cleared her throat.

"He is, er... unfortunately absent at the moment."

"Absent?"

"On one of his periodic visits to the provinces, you understand... The life of a monarch is always very busy... as you can imagine."

Bridget's heart fell.

"But we were told that he rarely leaves this great palace!"

"Hm, well, that is not exactly true... He actually spends much of the time away from the Mephadore... and from Orotworm."

This was not what Bridget had hoped or expected. She didn't even try to hide her disappointment.

"And do you know when he will be back?"

"No, no, he never announces his departure or his return," said Onu.

"But is that not very strange for a ruling monarch?"

Onu's patience seemed to be becoming just a little frayed. He squirmed a little in his seat. "You must understand, young lady, that the times are very dangerous... The Broadlord has many enemies. He must slip away as he can and return when he is least expected... But come, it is time for you to retell your story, how you came to our humble Realm and how you escaped the clutches of those most intolerant of the Broadlord's subjects, the Skomiars..."

Bridget's disappointment was such that she did not feel much like recounting all they had come through to get to the Mephadore. But reluctantly she sat back on a divan and began recounting their adventures as best she could.

The effect on Onu was astonishing. At first he sat engrossed, saying nothing, but as the story progressed he grew more and more animated. From time to time he would utter an exclamation of wonder, or pleasure, or at some parts of the tale unrestrained anger.

He became quite agitated at the point where Bridget described the abduction of Pageya.

"Vencengea took her, you say?" he said shaking his head. Then he looked at her in a strange, coy way, as if he wanted to probe for more information, but was wary of revealing too much himself. "You say you think the girl may be the daughter of someone important? But who, pray?"

"We do not know," Bridget answered honestly. "Perhaps you can help us." She hesitated a moment, wondering if she should voice her own suspicions. "We thought that possibly she might be a lost daughter of the Broadlord himself…"

Onu sat back, as if in surprise. Then he let out a small laugh and shook his head.

"…Or possibly," piped up Orin brightly, "of Kalmom, the mysterious man who was the friend of Maaniriv and wrote many very difficult riddles!"

"And who is also the enemy of the sorceress Vencengea," added Bridget.

Bridget saw Onu wince, as if with displeasure at the very mention of Vencengea's name. And he seemed to pointedly ignore the mention of Kalmom.

"Your Lordship," Bridget was not quite sure how to address their host, "you obviously know Vencengea, or know of her. Could I be so bold to ask who exactly Vencengea is and why she might have brought us to your Realm? And… do you think she could have something to do with the Pestilence?"

Onu held up his hands, as if to stop the flow of questions. He smiled, shaking his head, and seemed to be searching for something to say. But then his expression changed, and an ironic little smile spread over his face. After a short silence, he spoke again, in a weary, resigned voice.

"Vencengea is a former devotee of the Sacred Inspiration of the Balance. But she forsook the ways of wisdom and moderation, and is now generally known as a sorceress. She certainly does have a very passionate interest in the Pestilence and tries to give the impression she knows a lot about it and its origins… But I think she pretends to know more than she really does… Nevertheless, if she is not actually involved in the creation of the Pestilence, she would certainly like to be. This lady has a great love of power, especially if it is destructive power. She never seems satisfied with the uncanny influence she already possesses over people's minds… And in the Pestilence she scents further power. A quite phenomenal power!"

As Onu was speaking, Bridget had caught sight of what looked like a map on the wall on the other side of the room. She rose and walked over to examine it.

"I sometimes suspect," Onu continued, "that Vencengea's ambition is somehow to master and control the Pestilence, for her own ends… But something, I don't know exactly what, is blocking her efforts. And that is making her very frustrated and very dangerous."

The wall map was a beautifully drawn chart of all the Broadlord's domains.

As far as Bridget could see, it was an almost exact copy – though much larger – of the map she had found in Manny Reeve's notebook. There were the great snow-covered mountains they had crossed in the airship; the Green Vale with its lake and its river; then the dark mass of the gloomy city of Teivos, at one extremity of the great plains. And in the centre of those plains stood the Broadlord's capital, Orotworm, where they now were. To the north-west of the plains on the map was an area of hills, mountains and forests, in the middle of which was marked the city of Tekram. And beyond the city of towers was an area of greyness, marked: 'Desolation of the Mines', and off to one side a low area, criss-crossed by rivers, identified as the Marshes of Niur.

Bridget's eyes turned to what was south of Orotworm, in the area they had not yet reached. The map depicted a large blue mass, marked as the 'Crystal Lake, otherwise known as the Lake of Mystery'. And finally, right at the bottom of the map, a great oval shape marked 'Fles, that creates yet also kills all joy'.

Onu had joined her beside the map.

"At one time the Realm was a land of content, "he said. "People did not know how happy they really were. Now there is unhappiness and discontent. Local rulers struggle to keep order in their cities. And the Broadlord's authority over the provinces is weak. The fiefdoms go their own way, and more and more they quarrel and fight among themselves, to no purpose."

"But surely you… or the Broadlord… will be able to find enough good and loyal people like Captain Eclopis," exclaimed Bridget, "and rally them to help you re-establish authority? And surely… the Silver Knights will help you. Though they are selfish and hard, they are powerful."

Onu sniffed dismissively.

"The Silver Knights have indeed many times offered their help and sometimes given it. But their methods are brutal and destructive. They act in the name of order and peace, but they kill and destroy more than they build. And their price is high… They demand freedom for themselves, to do as they please throughout the Realm… Yet because of their lawless acts, the authority of Orotworm is diminished, the lords of the plains and the hills reject both the rule of its Lord, and the doctrine of the Balance it has long promoted… And the people are left in despair, not knowing whom to believe or trust."

"Then it is absolutely vital," said Bridget, "that we find Kalmom, or the Broadlord… or, preferably, both."

Onu heaved a great sigh.

"That is a matter we shall not resolve tonight," he said. "Come, it is late and you must be tired after your latest adventures. I shall show you to some quarters which, though humbly furnished, are at least relatively safe from intruders…"

'Intruders?' though Bridget, as they followed Onu through some curtains and down a tastefully decorated corridor. 'We are in the greatest fortress in the land, and the Broadlord's chancellor is still afraid of intruders!'

Chapter Eighteen
Frustration

The night was frighteningly still. Yet Bridget was sure she had heard voices outside her room, in the corridor.

She slipped from her bed. Orin was asleep in a little cot near the door of her room. He had refused to sleep alone. Stigrath she could hear snoring deeply from the room next door.

She tiptoed to the outer door of their apartments, cautiously pulled back the bolt and peered out into the corridor.

It was deserted. Moonlight and shadow. But no other light and not a sound nor a soul.

Outside the door where she stood was a line of columns giving on to one of the palace's many open-air courtyards. Beyond the moonlit rectangle of withered plants and flowers lay a similar colonnade, and beyond that she could glimpse more courtyards and corridors, with here and there a shimmer of moonlight among the shadow…

But there was no one to be seen…

Yet she was sure she had heard the murmur of voices, at least two of them. Guards, perhaps, passing on one of their fitful wanderings around the palace? But the voices had not had the coarse edge of the men they had met in the guardhouse when they were entering the palace…

Then a flicker of movement caught her eye, the faintest of shadows stirring in the darkness, beyond the colonnade opposite, in among the patchwork of moonlight and shadow. She saw it again, a dark robe catching a glint of moonlight as it moved slowly along a cloistered walk. Then it was gone.

Bridget went and slipped on her anorak, then padded back out into the corridor. Cautiously, keeping to the shadows, she crept along the tiled passage and round the corner leading towards the colonnade where she had seen the mysterious figure. She went down a set of uneven stone steps into a sort of atrium, in the centre of which there had once been a circular pond with water plants. There was no longer any water, and only the pathetic dried up remains of the plants.

This was the colonnade where she had seen the movement, she was sure. She started to skirt round the open space, keeping behind the columns as far as she could. She was now on the side where the mysterious figure had walked…

She turned a corner and found she had a clear view along a lengthy passage lit by the moon's silvery light, flooding down from unseen openings above. And there, right at the other end of it, she was just in time to see a distant figure disappear round another corner.

She hurried along the passage. The next corridor was shorter and there was no one in it. Or in the one that followed. She continued her search, but soon realised that she had lost track of the person, if person it was, and was herself lost in a labyrinth of passages and colonnades…

At last she turned a corner and pulled up abruptly. Glancing up, she saw that she was now right under the tall white tower in the centre of the Mephadore which the boy sailor had pointed out from their boat as they approached the city. What was it he had called the tower? Something like Calletorne… which she thought meant something like… Forbearance. That was it. It soared high above her, looking out over the wide plains that surrounded the city. Why, she wondered, was it called Forbearance? Had it been built in the old days when the Balance reigned supreme to appeal for patience and peace to all those in the Broadlord's Realm who could see it?

And then she saw the dark form again, a tall, slightly stooping figure. Was it a man or a woman? She could not tell. But it appeared from behind a column and glided towards a small, arched entrance in the base of the tower. The tall person dipped its head and entered.

Bridget waited a moment or two and then approached the arch. Behind it she could make out in the dim light some steps, leading upward.

Tentatively she began to climb.

The tower was circular, and the steps went round and round as it spiralled upwards. What, she wondered, would she find at the top? Clearly, the steps were leading right to the top of the tower. There were no doors leading off the circular staircase. Just occasionally there was a square, open window giving a view of the city below, with its dim, sparsely lit streets, and the countryside beyond, bathed in an eerie mist which glowed faintly in the moonlight.

Eventually she caught sight above her, where the steps ended, of a low doorway. The wooden door lay open. A warning voice inside her mind told her she should be wary of stepping beyond it, but her curiosity got the better of her, and she tiptoed straight through.

She found herself in a large, circular room, with windows all round looking out over the city. At one side was a simple desk, with some papers on it. It was unoccupied. Where had the tall figure gone?

Then she saw it. And she saw clearly that it was a man. He was standing on the far side of the room with his back to her, facing a small alcove in the gently curving wall.

For a moment she thought it was Onu, but a moment's reflection told her it was not. Onu's figure was much more stately and well groomed than this one. The man stood staring into the alcove for a good five minutes or more. Bridget could not see what he was staring at, because the interior of the alcove was obscured by a slanting ray of pale moonlight which fell across its entrance from the nearby window.

Bridget thought for a moment of calling out to the figure, but something told her not to.

Finally the man began to turn. Instinctively, Bridget slid into the shadows near the entrance. The figure moved past, apparently without seeing her, and began to descend the steps.

Bridget waited a few moments, then moved out of the shadows and approached the alcove where the man had been standing.

It was nothing more than a small rectangular hollow space built in the stone. She could now see into it, bathed as it was in the bright glow of moonlight. On the plain stonework at the back of the alcove she saw that there was some sort of a plaque or inscription.

She leaned forward to examine it more closely. A sudden, exciting thought flashed through her mind. Was this, perhaps, the shrine which she needed to furnish her with a new keyword? But almost immediately she saw with a certain disappointment that it was not at all like the shrines at Nirei or Lusedion. It was a plain tablet, with nothing but a few carvings of small woodland animals and flowers.

But its very simplicity moved her. It seemed to be some sort of memorial. And it did have the familiar symbol of the coiled flame. And underneath it an inscription.

She bent over to read the words.

NY RYMEOM YM DOVELEB YFIU DAN NOS ASTIRIAL

The two names Yfiu and Astirial rang a bell, though for the moment Bridget couldn't remember where she had seen them…

But there was definitely no keyword. No single word inscribed in or around the coiled flame. This could not be the sanctuary she was looking for…

There was a faint sound behind her and she whipped round. The tall man was standing a few feet away, looking down at her.

She froze with fear.

He was thin as well as tall, with a stooping posture and wispy, unkempt white hair sticking out at various angles from his over-large head. He had long, mournful features with large, suspicious eyes which were now fixed on Bridget as if he were trying to penetrate and read her thoughts. For a moment she felt a vague tingle of recognition, but after a moment's examination of the man's grey features and his untidy appearance she decided she had never seen this face before.

She suddenly remembered who Yfiu and Astirial were.

"You are Kalmom!" she breathed slowly, her voice trembling.

The tall man went on staring at her, then threw back his head and gave a curious, cackling laugh.

"No, no… you are quite wrong there!" he said in a hollow, strained voice.

Then, abruptly, he stopped laughing, turned away and walked back towards the stairs.

Bridget ran after him.

"Please, don't go!" she called. "If you are not Kalmom, you must be the Broadlord… Or you must know one or both of them! Please stop and speak to me!"

But he continued down the stairs, without turning. She followed as best she could, but found that this strange, ungainly man was moving at a terrific pace, apparently hurrying away from her as if he should never have approached her.

When she came to the foot of the stairs, she looked one way and then the other but could not see him.

"Please come back!" she called. "I want to talk to you about Kalmom... and Vencengea... and Pageya, my friend Pageya.

She hurried to the nearest corner and ran round it. And suddenly there he was again, standing stock still, framed between two of the columns. Out beyond him she could see the dim lights of the city and the eerie, frightening mist that hung over it like a pall. The man was staring back at her, his features pale and ghostly in the moonlight and his body arching like some giant cat. Again, Bridget froze in terror.

"Were there not others with you, when you came to the Realm?" he asked hoarsely. "A boy... and some wise man from the Upper Vale? I was expecting him to be with you..."

"We were parted from them," Bridget stammered. "They were captured by the Skomiars in the city of Teivos..."

"Ah!" the haggard man caught his breath. He was obviously disturbed by the news. "So that is where..." His words tailed off into a murmur and she could no longer make any sense of them. Then he fell silent altogether, staring mournfully into the grey mist which hung over the city.

Who is this man? she asked herself.

"Please, I'm sorry to ask you again, but if you are not the Broadlord, then you *must* be Kalmom! Or at least someone close to him..."

He looked up at her, his eyes dark pools in his ashen face, and he began to nod his white, dishevelled head..."

"Close to him?" he said nervously. "Close to Kalmom? Yes, yes, I suppose..."

And then he turned away again and seemed to lose himself in thought. He leant his huge head, on its frail, spindly neck, against one of the pillars and said:

"You are not far... not far away."

"Not far away from what?" she asked, puzzled.

"Not far away from finding Kalmom... and the Broadlord, for that matter," he replied and gave a funny little chuckle. "No, you are much closer than you think..."

Bridget began to lose her fear. Now she began to feel only irritation at the man's vagueness. But she tried to suppress her annoyance and humour him.

"You see, we want to help Kalmom, and the Broadlord, against the Pestilence," she said, hoping to draw him out. But he merely began to swing his heavy head from side to side.

"What you would be best advised to do," he said, "is return the way you came. Go back up the Green Vale and over the High Mountains to your own much-blessed land. There is no longer anything you can do here! All is lost, and no one can save us... No, no one," he went on, and a small gleam came into his eyes, "unless you can find Kalmom!"

"But that's exactly what we're trying to do!" cried Bridget, becoming increasingly vexed. "But we need some help. Can't *you* help us to find him?"

The frail figure, however, abruptly pushed himself away from the pillar, as if he had just made a firm decision, and strode off at an enormous rate back down the gloomy corridor.

"Wait, wait!" she called again, running after him. "Please stay and help us... It sounds as if you would like to find Kalmom too. So we can help each other..."

The man hesitated just for a split second. Then he resumed his rapid march back into the shadows.

"How can we get in touch with you again?" Bridget called after him.

But there was no reply. The man was already turning one of the many corners of the Mephadore, and when she arrived there, he was nowhere to be seen.

*****

"And you can say nothing, Onu, about who this strange person was?"

They were at a table near the window of the Broadlord's apartments, looking out over the city. Away to the East the sun was just rising over a bank of cloud on the horizon. The rose-grey light of early morning was barely managing to filter through the murky air, and Bridget could just about make out the dim outlines of the streets, palaces and temples of Orotworm the Great.

Far off to the left Bridget could see the quayside where they had landed, a small island of light on a sea of greyness. Other than that the drabness was relieved only by isolated patches of clarity and colour, most of them around one or other of the many temples. Some of these had a decorated dome, or a steeple, or some symbol of their sect rising above their roofs and painted in an ostentatiously cheerful colour.

"No, I can say nothing, except that it certainly was neither Kalmom nor the Broadlord... Of that I am sure."

"How can you be so sure?" Bridget asked. "Where is the Broadlord, anyway? Can't you even tell us the general direction he's gone in? The name of a village? A town? A district?"

Onu shook his head again.

"So what are we supposed to do now?" Bridget turned tetchily to her friends Orin and Stigrath. "The whole point of coming here was to get help from the Broadlord... at least to get us back to Nirei!"

"You are of course welcome to stay in the palace," Onu said, looking very uncomfortable.

Perhaps, thought Bridget, *now is the time to ask for a favour.*

"Onu..."

"Yes, my young lady?"

"Is there a chapel or a sanctuary in the palace'? Other than the one... to Kalmom's wife and child, which I found in the tower?"

The chamberlain looked at her for several moments with his grave, sad eyes.

Then he beckoned to her to follow him across the room to one of the long curtains which covered the wall on that side of the room. Beyond the curtain was an alcove. And facing them was what appeared to be a small shrine.

With a thrill of excitement, Bridget recognised the familiar symbols of the mingling flame surrounded by a diamond shape.

"What is the word in the middle?" she murmured, her voice strained with anticipation.

"The one in the middle is… RECYM."

"But that…"

"It means MERCY in our language."

"Yes, I know," said Bridget in deep disappointment. "But it's not the word I want. I've used it already… There has to be another shrine somewhere here."

Onu shook his head. "No, there is only this one. This was the Broadlord's personal prayer place. I know of no other in the palace."

Another dead end, thought Bridget. *Another disappointment. But she must go on looking! Surely in the great city of Maratworm there must be another shrine and another keyword.*

Kalmom's story was not yet complete.

Chapter Nineteen
The Gateway

Bridget had an idea.

"The two temples… The Vysou-Salem and the Ellektys. They must have shrines like this one, and plenty of them… Can we go back there and look for the key word we need?"

Onu still looked puzzled. "What is this key word you talk about?"

Bridget explained that it was a special word that unlocked the writings which they hoped would lead them to Kalmom's whereabouts. The tall official looked doubtful.

"The devotees of the Ellektys have done away with shrines of this sort. I doubt if there are any left at all in their temple… As for the keepers of the Vysou-Salem, they do not let any but their own enter their shrines. We would have great difficulty gaining access to them."

"But we could try!" said Bridget eagerly.

Onu shook his head. "It would take weeks," he said, "maybe months. And even then I'm not sure that their High Council, the Yesheol, would give permission, even to the Broadlord's representative…"

Bridget was downcast.

Then Orin piped up in his small voice.

"That little chapel in the Temple Square, I think Eclopis called it the 'Gateway to Paradise'. There must be a shrine in there! Would it be possible to go and visit it?"

Onu shivered visibly and shook his head in horror, as if she had uttered some terrible blasphemy.

"You do not want to go anywhere near there!" he said with a look of genuine terror on his face. "It is a place of very ill repute indeed."

But Bridget somehow liked Orin's suggestion.

"Why not? It has such a beautiful name – 'Gateway to Paradise'!"

"I fear it is a very bad joke. No one ever reached paradise that way… though perhaps…"

"Though perhaps what?"

"Though it was the way, people say, that the Priests of the Vysou-Salem in former times took dead or dying people through underground passages to the river, from where they transported them to Fles."

"To Fles!" said Bridget in astonishment. "Why to Fles?"

Onu sighed and went to sit down on one of the chairs near his desk.

"The legend was… or so the Order of the Raven would have it… that those souls who died near Fles, or were taken there shortly after departing this life, would be saved for eternity if they were committed to its fires…"

Bridget shivered. "So all those people in the Vysou-Salem…"

"…In former times would have been prepared for transportation down the river and across the Crystal Lake. Nowadays, of course, they are merely cremated outside the city, here at Orotworm. You may have seen the small hillocks in the form of pyramids?"

Bridget nodded. She remembered them from their journey down the river.

"They are built so as to look like miniature replicas of Fles itself."

"And why are they no longer taken to Fles?"

Onu looked at her dolefully, shaking his head.

"It is impossible now to go to Fles – because of the great storms on the lake. What is more, all the monasteries on the further side of the lake which were built there to receive the Departing have been destroyed, by lava… and by the hot ash we call the Pestilence… "

"So the Grey Pestilence does come from Fles!"

"Oh yes," said Onu. He seemed quite surprised that she did not know this.

She thought hard for a few moments, then said: "So you would not recommend exploring the 'Gateway to Paradise'"?

Once more Onu shook his head disapprovingly. "Beneath the chapel structure there is a maze, which became known as the 'Maze of Madness'. Many people went in there, looking for adventure, or for some hidden secret, and never came out… or if they did, as in one or two cases, they were found to be suffering from a painful and hideous madness… from which they never recovered."

"How awful! Are these people still alive? Might it be possible, maybe, to talk to them…?"

Onu replied, yet again, with a shake of his head.

"So how long has it been there?" asked Orin. "Who built it?"

"It is said that it was devised many generations ago by Ysterym II, one of the prelates of the Old Religion. Incidentally, all the Prelates used to be called Ysterym. They were up to Ysterym IX when Thirdrol was elected. It was Thirdrol, as you may know, who revolted against the elitism of his predecessors and attempted to swing it away from mysticism and centralised power, and back towards the original idea of Balance, which in his opinion had always been the way towards bringing fulfilment to men and women's lives. And when he disappeared the traditionalists said it was because he had been punished for having broken with tradition…"

"But that sounds like nonsense!" exclaimed Bridget.

Onu nodded. "I agree. But there you are, that is what some people are like… Anyway, Ysterym II apparently decreed that only those souls who were worthy should be taken to Fles. It was not something for everybody. So only those whose relatives or friends could find their way through the Maze should earn the right of being transported to Fles."

"Hm." Bridget did not like this story at all. "So he favoured a sort of elitist religion… with room in paradise only for super-souls!"

Onu smiled.

"Yes, you could put it like that," he said quietly.

*****

Bridget spent the rest of the day exploring the colonnades and corridors of the Mephadore. But she found neither a shrine with a keyword nor any trace of the strange figure who had talked to her about being close to Kalmom.

By midday she had grown tired and was left sitting on the narrow balcony next to their quarters, looking in dejection out over the gloomy, dusty city beneath. In spite of what Onu had said, Bridget was now very keen to go back and explore the Temple Square, particularly the small chapel at its centre. Onu clearly would not agree to such a scheme and would probably do everything possible to prevent it, for the best possible motives. So her mind turned to ways of defying his opposition. Who else could possibly help them?

Her problem was resolved quite unexpectedly.

Bridget had started off again to wander through the dry, empty corridors, in the forlorn hope of coming across some niche she had not yet explored. She was trailing aimlessly round a gallery looking down at one of the courtyards near the castle entrance, when the courtyard gate opened to admit a group of newcomers. She recognised the familiar red and silver of the river guard. And among the newcomers, to her delight, she saw their rescuer of the previous day, Captain Eclopis.

"Eclopis! Eclopis!" she shouted, searching wildly for a way down into the courtyard. "Don't go away!"

The group of officers stopped, clearly surprised, even a little shocked, by the unexpected sight of a girl trying to summon one of their comrades. Eclopis looked extremely embarrassed.

"I cannot come now, young lady. I have to make my report…"

"Then come and see us this evening, or tomorrow. I absolutely must talk to you." Then she added, to save Eclopis's blushes. "And Stigrath will be glad to swap river stories with you."

Eclopis waved his hand noncommittally.

But he did come, early that evening. The friends had finished a meagre and rather tasteless supper when they heard a gentle knock on the outer door of their apartment. Eclopis slipped in, glancing over his shoulder. The first thing he did was rebuke Bridget for approaching him so directly.

"You were maybe not to know it, young lady, but it is not acceptable manners here in Orotworm for officers of the palace guard to associate in public with young women, especially… one as young as you! I have been much mocked since this occurrence."

"Oh Eclopis, don't be such a stuffed shirt," she said to him. "We need to talk to you. You're the only person in this tired and tiresome place who shows any sign of life… And I have to ask you something!"

She explained her plan in a few excited sentences.

As she outlined her plan, Eclopis's eyebrows rose higher and higher, and he began to object. But she persisted, and as she went on, he became more and more interested in her story of keywords and coded messages and the trail left by the mysterious Kalmom, who was supposedly the Broadlord's Chief Adviser. Eclopis knew of the existence of such a person, but said that he had never actually met him, in spite of having been in the Broadlord's presence on frequent occasions. Bridget thought this was rather curious, but she didn't question him any further, so keen was she to finish explaining her plans.

The more she spoke, the more it became clear that the Captain of the River Guard was warming to what she had in mind. A strange little smile began to hover around his lips.

When she had finished outlining her plan, Eclopis reflected for a while.

"Hm," he said. "I have to say… it's a chance to get away just for a little while from detaining river pirates and arguing with tiresome courtiers, and all the other dreary chores that make up my life. It might even be a bit of fun!"

He looked enquiringly across at Stigrath.

"And what have you to say, my friend?" he asked. "Do you fancy another adventure with your old companion?"

Stigrath grunted. "I… too many adventures these last days! Would like a rest!"

"Oh come, my good fellow!" said Eclopis, clapping him on the arm. (He could not reach the big man's shoulder!) "The Greyness must be getting to you! You're as bad as that dreary Niradnam and his boring officials."

Stigrath did not like that.

"Hm," he growled. "Stigrath is honest man… but never boring! Maybe go with you… Will think."

Chapter Twenty
The Maze of Madness

That night a low knock came on their outer door, and there was Eclopis again, this time dressed in a long, dark cloak and with a supply of similar clothing for Bridget, Stigrath and Orin. Stigrath's cloak was far too short for him and Orin's far too long, but Bridget managed to tuck it up into the cord around his waist so that he didn't trip on it.

Eclopis also carried two lanterns.

"We shall have to try the side entrance to the fortress. It is not quite true, Stigrath, that the Gate of Scolipti is the only way into the palace. There is another way across the ravine. It is less well guarded, and I am on good terms with the officer in charge there."

They descended through the labyrinth of halls and courts to a part of the Mephadore that Bridget, for all her earlier wanderings, had not yet discovered. They came to an open courtyard where several small trees had managed to keep a fair bit of their foliage. Eclopis made them wait under one of the trees while he went ahead. A few minutes later he was back.

"Follow me," he whispered. "And please, do not say anything, any of you!"

They followed him through a narrow passage and found themselves unexpectedly beside an enormous wooden gate. In front of the gate stood a uniformed officer of the guard. As soon as they appeared, he pulled back a bolt and opened a doorway in the frame of the gate.

"Good hunting, Brother Eclopis," said the officer. "I hope the girls are in a good mood tonight!"

Eclopis murmured something inaudible.

They were now on a small cobbled terrace high above the Mephadore's moat. The sleeping city lay far beneath them in a grey twilight, only partly visible amid the pall of dust that enveloped its boulevards and streets. The pinnacles and domes of the various temples seemed to be floating on a thick layer of colourless mist.

Out across the moat from their terrace stretched a narrow wooden bridge, only wide enough for them to cross one behind the other. To Bridget it looked perilously fragile, but without hesitation Eclopis led them out on to it.

"If you do not like heights," he murmured over his shoulder, "do not look downward!"

Bridget stepped out on to the bridge as quickly as she could, following Eclopis's advice. But the wretched man seemed to take a perverse pleasure in going as slowly as he could. And behind her, as Stigrath's great bulk moved out across the flimsy structure, she heard it groan under the burden and could have sworn that it was beginning to sway.

Right over the middle of the gulf, there was a particularly loud groan from the boards beneath her feet, and an ominous crack.

Eclopis stopped. *Go on, man, go on*, Bridget thought to herself desperately. *The last thing you want to do is stop.*

"Hm," she heard Eclopis mutter to himself, "have to get this bridge seen to in the near future."

Then he went on.

Finally they reached the other side. The path passed through a copse of stunted trees. Ahead, they could just make out some blurred buildings and a dark, narrow alley leading off between them. As they crept through the sparse undergrowth, Bridget threw fearful glances at the deep shadows on either side, remembering what had happened the last time they had ventured into a copse at night.

But soon they were through and into the alleyway, which plunged down into the maze of steep, narrow streets which formed the old town. Every so often, Eclopis called a halt at a corner and checked they were neither being followed nor likely to meet anyone in the next street. Evidently he was keen to keep his part in their escapade a secret.

Then they emerged into the broader, richer streets and finally came to the great central square.

The two enormous temples lay there as they had on the night of their arrival, the one massive, hunched and resentful, the other almost indecently open, inviting and accessible.

In between, barely visible in the mist and darkness, lay the little conical roof of the 'Gateway', the entrance to the ill-famed 'Maze of Madness'. A tingle of excitement, and also of fear, passed down Bridget's spine.

They walked across the square as nonchalantly as they could, a line of robed figures which must have looked like a procession of ill-assorted monks heading for the Vysou-Salem. *We must make rather a strange sight*, Bridget thought to herself, as they advanced across the square. Eclopis's slim figure was followed by the mountainous bulk of Stigrath and then the dwarf-like form of Orin, with Bridget bringing up the rear. But there were very few people about, and those that were showed little interest in the odd procession of pilgrims.

They reached the squat building in the middle of the square without interference. Its only door was an iron grill set in the stonework. Through the metal bars they glimpsed a cobbled floor and nothing else. The grill was locked with a giant padlock covered in a thick layer of grime and dust. It looked as if it had not been touched for decades.

This was no barrier, however, for the resourceful Eclopis. Taking a small dagger from his belt he wrestled with the padlock for only a minute or two before there was an alarmingly loud click and the chains fell away on either side.

"Bingo!" whispered Bridget.

"What did you say?" asked Eclopis.

"Oh… I meant… 'A to Z'! 'A to Z'!"

"Aha, yes… We have indeed won this part of the game," he said, smiling.

They entered the small space under the conical roof.

Bridget had expected some sort of altar or religious decoration, here in the chapel-like structure. But as her eyes adjusted to the gloom she saw to her disappointment that the 'Gateway' was entirely bare and empty. She had begun to think it was a complete dead end when she spotted the dark opening in the floor on the opposite side of the round cobbled space and the steps leading down into it.

Still not daring to light their lanterns, for fear of being seen by some watchful temple guard in the Vysou-Salem, they made their way gingerly to the head of the stairwell.

"As you see, young Bridget," said Eclopis, "there is no sanctuary here in the gateway. If there is one, it is down below. So shall we go further? You have not changed your mind?"

Bridget shook her head, though her heart was in her mouth. She felt for the spiral talisman round her neck, and gripped it tight for a moment. The feel of the stone and the thought of her friend Pageya, who had worn it for so long and now wore hers, brought comfort and courage.

"No, I want to go on… definitely."

"Here now… May as well… go on," Stigrath agreed.

"We must bring light to this terrible dark place," Orin chipped in bravely, though his small voice quivered slightly as he spoke.

Bridget smiled gratefully at her two friends, then walked confidently to the top step and started to descend, feeling her way down the circular wall at her side. Eclopis shrugged and followed.

After two complete circles, they felt bold enough to light the lanterns. The small flames took an age to catch, as if some evil force of darkness, resentful of the intrusion, was trying to suppress the timorous probing of the light.

The air here was foul, and the walls around them were black from the dampness, glistening in places with moisture. Somewhere beneath them they could hear faint and indefinable sounds. A whispering sound, or was it the sound of water dripping? And a very faint and distant groan… or was it only some subterranean movement of air? Yet before they entered the Gateway the night had been still, with no trace of wind.

They restarted their descent.

After several more spirals, the steps ended and they found themselves in a second circular chamber. But here again there was no sanctuary and no altar. On one side was the stone staircase they had just descended. Opposite it stood a large doorway which looked as if it was made of solid metal. It appeared to be embossed with carvings so old that they, like the walls around them, were black with accumulated grime.

Above the doorway, carved in the stonework was a huge scowling face, pale and bearded, with eyes that seem to penetrate your very soul. Beneath it, in classical Elonym letters which Bridget could now decipher with ease, were the words:

TREEN EHRE, WOY WUH VEHA SLOT LAL EPHO*

Bridget shivered again as she read the words. But Orin came to her rescue by piping up in his elfin voice:

"If we have lost it, perhaps we can find it again on the other side of the door?"

They all laughed, and the laughter echoed eerily round the little chamber. And there was also – or was it only Bridget's imagination? – a faint echo from behind the door, down whatever endless corridor it was that lay beyond.

Bridget, nonetheless, felt better. The laughter seemed to have pushed back the gloom that was trying to close in round them.

With a grunt, Stigrath went over to the door and, putting his shoulder to it, gave a great heave. Immediately there was a horrible grinding noise which brought more hollow and sinister echoes from the darkness beyond.

Stigrath gave another great shove, and the door moved backwards just enough to reveal a vertical line of blackness. This time, Bridget thought, the metallic echo sounded like a sinister laugh, taken up by unseen spirits of malevolence, and repeated over and over again, on into the distant gloomy depths of the Maze, as if in mockery of their recent good humour.

They glanced nervously at each other. But there was no going back now. Several more pushes, and the gap between door and stonework was wide enough for even Stigrath to pass through. Anxious not to be left behind, Bridget followed him as quickly as she could, with Orin and Eclopis in her wake.

They were now in a dismal corridor faced with worked stone. The damp on its walls caught the light of their lanterns and seemed to glow menacingly. The corridor curved gradually to the left, away from the door, and Stigrath had already set off along it.

"Hey, Stigrath, don't walk so quickly! Wait for us!" called Bridget. "We mustn't get parted from each other. Remember that this is a maze where hundreds of people have got lost!"

"Yes," Eclopis concurred, "and we would be advised to approach it methodically. If we want to retrace our steps, we should think of a way of marking them as we go."

He took from one of his pockets several large lumps of chalk.

"We shall make regular marks on the wall... I suggest arrows pointing in the direction we are moving. And numbers beside them. Then we know which way to return if we find them again!"

This seemed a good idea. They all nodded their agreement. Bridget was glad they had chosen this eminently sensible and practical man as their guide.

The corridor continued to curl slowly to the left. Bridget was still finding it difficult to keep up with Stigrath, who had one of the lanterns. He seemed like a man possessed as he strode off into the darkness.

"Please, Eclopis, tell your friend that little Orin here can't keep up with him. His legs are simply too short."

Stigrath was persuaded to go more slowly, though he grunted and grumbled every time he had to stop and wait for them.

109

Then they came to the first opening.

It was a simple round hole in the left-hand wall. They stopped and Stigrath thrust his lantern through it. On the other side was a corridor identical to the one they were in and running parallel to it.

"Which way do we go, Eclopis? Any idea?" asked Bridget.

Eclopis shook his head, but Stigrath seemed to be in no doubt. He grunted and pointed down the corridor they were already in, in the direction they were already moving. He seemed to be suggesting they completely ignore the hole in the wall. Eclopis merely shrugged and made an arrow on the wall opposite the hole, pointing the way they were heading. Beside it he wrote a number One. Then they followed the big sailor down their original corridor.

After fifty metres, it came to a dead end.

Orin giggled nervously and Bridget smiled to herself.

"Hm," said Eclopis, "it looks as if we are going to climb through that hole after all."

Stigrath raised his great shoulders in genuine bafflement.

"Instinct... I follow instinct...," he said with a silly smile. "But this time... it is wrong!"

Bridget laid her hand on his arm. "I think we're going to need a bit more than instinct, Stigrath, to get us through this maze."

They went back to the opening and stepped through it. This time Eclopis chose the way. They turned right. This second corridor went on rather longer than the first. Then, to their dismay, they saw another blank wall ahead of them.

"Alas, this is a maze of no exits!" said Orin.

Stigrath, however, went on walking towards the blank wall.

"He is an obstinate person, is he not?" said Eclopis, shrugging his shoulders and looking at Bridget.

But Stigrath, when he had reached the wall at the end of the corridor, beckoned to them to join him. When they reached him, they saw why. On the left-hand side of the corridor, beside the dead-end, was another opening in the wall. Stigrath beamed at them in triumph.

"Instinct!" he said triumphantly.

Eclopis was also smiling as he drew another chalk arrow on the wall and the number Two.

They continued in this way for some time. Bridget had brought with her the faithful rucksack with the coded manuscript from Manny's diary. In fact, she had not let it out of her sight since leaving the Ineals' cave above Teivos. And it also carried plenty of spare pages of the paper Quenrie had given them. She grabbed a sheet and began hastily sketching a rough map of the way she thought they had come. And as they followed its windings, she attempted to record all the twists and turns that they took. Several times she reckoned that they should have re-joined their previous route. But it didn't work out that way. She decided after half an hour or so that if they had to rely on the map they would become completely lost. Nevertheless, she persisted.

Then what she had feared from the start happened. They came across one of the arrows Eclopis had inscribed on the wall. Their numbered arrows had reached as far as number 42, and now they were back at 26!

They all stared in dismay at the chalk mark on the wall. There was no question that it was the one they had made only fifteen minutes or so before. Bridget tried to work out on her map how they could have gone in a circle, but it just did not make sense.

"This maze has a mind of its own!" she exclaimed.

"Or a madness," muttered Eclopis grimly. Stigrath simply uttered a rumbling oath. In the circumstances Bridget found it strangely comforting.

"We shall just have to try this other way," she said in as decisive a voice as she could muster, for Orin's sake. Without a word, Eclopis inscribed his 43, with an arrow pointing in the opposite direction from 26!

Their new route brought them back to number 15.

None of them said anything, but they set off on a third route. It led them to 34.

"We are lost," said Orin in a small, quivering voice.

"Lost," Eclopis concurred, "in the Maze of Madness."

* ENTER HERE, YOU WHO HAVE LOST ALL HOPE

Chapter Twenty-One
The Harbour of Tears

"We should extinguish one of the lanterns," suggested Eclopis, "just as a precaution. That way we can wander in these tunnels for several more hours."

They had already been in the maze for at least two, Bridget reckoned. She studied her map again, checking every turn. She was trying desperately to suppress the first tinglings of panic.

"We have a number of options," she said finally. "The first of them is just a little way up this corridor and to the left."

They trudged off after her and took the turn she indicated. After a couple more turns, they came to a flight of steps leading upwards.

"Ah... much better!" muttered Stigrath.

"What is that smell?" asked Orin. "I have sensed this smell, I believe, somewhere before."

He was right, thought Bridget, there was a heavy, musty smell that she too found very familiar.

"Let's climb the steps and see," she suggested.

The steps led up to a short gallery, from which rose a second flight of steps. They climbed these and came to a curtain.

Behind the curtain there were now muffled sounds, a vague whispering, echoing eerily round what appeared to be a wide space. There also came an intermittent groaning and an occasional muffled bang as if something were being lifted and set down again. Even before they parted the curtain Bridget knew where they were.

Stigrath drew the curtain back a little way and with a sinking feeling in her heart she saw she had been right. Beyond the curtain lay rank upon rank of stretchers. The relatives and carers of the afflicted walked among them, ministering to their charges in whatever way they could.

They were back in the great temple of Vysou-Salem, among those who awaited 'the Passage Beyond'.

Stigrath hurriedly let the curtain fall back.

"Do not want... to be here," he said tersely. No one disagreed. Soon they were back down at the bottom of the two flights of steps.

With the help of Bridget's jottings, they tried several other routes. *At least,* Bridget thought to herself, *we now know there are at least TWO exits from this awful place, which doubles our chances of finding a way out in an emergency!*

On a whim they followed a route similar in pattern to the one that led to the flight of steps, only on the other side of the maze. Bridget was not totally surprised when they found a second flight, in almost every regard similar to the first.

"Any guesses as to where this will lead us?" she asked. But none of the others seemed in the mood for guessing games. They climbed the steps, and the second flight above, and found themselves, as before, behind a curtain. Only this time there was no musty smell, no whispering. They had all heard the laughter from halfway up the first set of steps. And when they opened the curtain they found themselves in the Hall of Mirrors in the Ellektys.

"I don't think we want to be there either," said Bridget firmly. And though Orin pleaded passionately to be allowed to stay just for a little while and 'look at the wicked mirrors', she remained firm and was supported by Stigrath.

"Many times… Orin… you can go. But not now!"

There was a great temptation, nonetheless, just to slink out through the Hall of Mirrors to the open air and freedom beyond. But Bridget felt that they had not tramped round the sinister maze for hours just to give up now.

"I vote we go back down into the Maze and explore it to the end. We don't have to be so afraid of it now that we know there are at least three exits. And I'm sure there is something else to find down there. The Maze can't just link the two Temples with the Gateway between them. It must lead somewhere else as well…"

Stigrath grunted his assent, and after a moment's reflection, Eclopis nodded too. Only Orin seemed unhappy to be going back down into the gloomy, frightening passages beneath them.

Stigrath laid one great hand gently on the boy's shoulder.

"No fear, Orin… Ugly old Stigrath will let no harm to you…" And the giant's face warped into a grimace that was supposed to be a reassuring smile.

The corner of Orin's mouth flickered in an attempted smile, but he did not look happy at all.

"This dark place is full of bad humours," he whispered. But he followed them nonetheless back down the steps.

So they were back in the Maze, and had found no sanctuary or chapel, and no clue to a keyword for the next part of Kalmom's story. Nor had there been any sign of what exactly might lie at the maze's heart – if it had one.

They continued their search. Several times they reached a point which, according to Bridget's calculations, should have been at the centre of the maze. But there seemed to be absolutely nothing there. So they went on.

Several times, however, they came back to one particular spot. It was simply a short passage off the main tunnel which, when they shone their lantern down it, showed a blank wall after about twenty metres.

Then, on the fourth time they passed it, Bridget stopped and said:

"Let's explore this passage a bit more thoroughly."

"But it's a dead end," protested Eclopis. "We've looked several times already."

"Perhaps not closely enough," replied Bridget. She had caught a glimpse of something glinting in the rock wall at the end of the little cul-de-sac.

This time she took the sole lantern they now had lit and walked right up to the end of the passage. She gave a little cry and disappeared.

The others rushed down the passage in alarm.

"Bridget, Bridget!" called Orin. "Where have you gone so we cannot see you?"

Bridget popped out from the wall right in front of them.

"I thought so! We should have learned from Stigrath's experience right at the beginning. Never think you're at a dead end until you've actually arrived there… You see, it's all an illusion…!"

She indicated the wall at what they had thought was the end of the passage.

"Look, it's a mirror, carefully angled to show us this dead-end to the right! What we saw down at the other end of the passage is a reflection of a dummy passage at right angles to the main passage. Sure enough, it's a dead end. Meanwhile, however, cunningly concealed around this U-turn… yes, I'm right… is a perfectly normal continuation of the passage! Whatsisname, Ysterym or whatever, who built this maze certainly had a few tricks up his sleeve when he designed it!"

Excitedly, they turned the corner into the carefully hidden passageway.

"Yeugh!" exclaimed Orin. "This is not a passage that has been washed!"

A veritable curtain of cobwebs hung before them. "Yes, it is obvious that nobody has come down this way for a very long time," commented Eclopis.

But he pulled out his sword and took the lead, cutting his way into the curtain of cobwebs and grime. The others followed, somewhat reluctantly. Bridget found that even after Eclopis had passed through, cobwebs would fall down and slide across her face, making her shudder at the thought of what might be hidden in their folds…

After a few twists and turns, they came to a small circular cave.

"We have done it!" cried Orin. "We have reached the centre of the maze!"

They looked round the small chamber.

If this really were the centre of the maze, it was rather disappointing. The walls were grimy and bare, the domed ceiling likewise. Its only notable feature was a roughly hewn block of stone projecting at one point from the wall.

"What have we here?" asked Eclopis approaching the stone slab. Like the rest of the stonework it was covered in a thick layer of encrusted dirt. Bridget's first reaction was to leave it be, but Orin, inquisitive as ever, began wiping off some of the dirt with a rag he had produced from somewhere in his tunic.

"Look, there are some picture-writings beneath!" he exclaimed.

Bridget needed no further invitation. She too began rubbing off the filth from the surface of the stone slab.

Soon the wall's secret was revealed.

"Why, it's just what I'd hoped for!" cried Bridget. "Another altar, like the one in Quenrie's tower. Only it's a stone instead of a tapestry! Are there any words written on it…?"

"Yes," answered Eclopis, "here is something… **'What is Unique'**."

"And here is another one… **'What is Familiar'**," read Orin.

114

"Yes, and '**What is Irreplaceable**' is on that side and '**Life Never ending**' at the top... But where is the Flame, and what's written inside it?"

The centre of the stone slab was encased in a particularly stubborn layer of filth and it took them some time to rub and scrape it off. But finally, to Bridget's growing excitement, she saw the outlines of the familiar motif of the coiled flame slowly emerge...

Oh please let there be a word there! she said to herself.

"Here it is," said Eclopis finally. "It is in very small letters, but it is quite distinct..."

"And what does it say?"

"The word in our language is **Cegoura**," said Eclopis. "Do you understand that?"

Bridget thought for a moment and then said: "A yes, I have it! I think we may have our next keyword!"*

She was so excited that she took Orin by both hands and performed a little dance round the circular chamber. Then she skipped up to Stigrath and tried to do the same with him. The big man had seemed baffled by all the word games, and now, though he smiled down at her in his awkward way, said anxiously:

"Perhaps... time to leave?"

They looked round the little chamber for the entrance through which they had come, but for several moments no one could see it.

"I'm sure it was here, opposite the little altar," said Bridget.

"No, it was at one side of the altar, I am certain," said Eclopis.

"Yes, but not that side... this one!" Orin contradicted him.

In the end, they found not one entrance, but two, one on either side of the little altar, both difficult to see because of the uniform griminess of the walls. No one, however, could remember which of the two openings was the one through which they had entered.

"If we knew which one it was, there would be no problem," said Bridget. "I still have my map of the way we came."

"Let us try this one," suggested Eclopis. "If it is not the correct one, we should know it soon by looking at your map."

So they chose the exit to the left of the stone altar. For the first few turns it seemed to conform exactly with Bridget's map, which was reassuring. But it was so filthy and clogged by cobwebs that it was difficult to believe that it was the one they had just passed through a few minutes before.

"Should we turn back?" asked Bridget. "I'm not at all sure that this is the way we came."

"Hm, you may be right," answered Eclopis, "but now we have come this far, let us continue a while on this path... Who knows? It could lead us to some new discovery!"

Bridget admired the young officer's enthusiasm, but she wondered if they had not had enough discoveries for one night. And she had already found what she had been searching for, a new 'keyword'.

This passage now began twisting and turning at very short intervals. This was definitely **not** the way they had come, and Bridget sensed that they were still very close to the heart of the maze. There were no longer any side-passages, so there was no need for any more chalk arrows, even if they could have found a clear space on the walls to write on…

Bridget was beginning to feel very tired. The damp and dark passage was also beginning to smell dreadfully. She had to breathe as little as she could so as not to be sick. But she was driven on by the sheer anticipation of what they might find at the end of this unexplored part of the maze.

They stopped from time to time for a rest, and Bridget took the opportunity to sketch out on her piece of paper the latest twists in the tunnel…

Finally they came to another set of steps.

These steps, however, led downwards.

Cautiously Stigrath began to descend. Half way down Bridget heard the first faint murmur of lapping water. And was it her imagination, but did she also catch the faintest glimmer of light reflecting on water far below? Could they have been in the maze so long that dawn had already come?

As they descended, the walls opened out on either side, and they found themselves on a broad platform. Slowly, they moved towards the sounds of water and found themselves on a long stone quayside overlooking a pool of the blackest water imaginable. Opposite where they stood the water lapped gently against a blank wall. To their left the pool came to a dead end after twenty or so metres. To their right it continued for a hundred metres or more, then disappeared round a corner. It was from this direction that Bridget sensed rather than saw the faintest suggestion of daylight.

"This must be the Tropora, the Harbour of Tears!" breathed Eclopis in awe. "This was the old underground harbour from which they took the bodies of the dead or dying for transportation to 'the Other Side', as it was called. For some that meant another world, to others it just meant the other side of the Crystal Lake…"

"In other words," said Bridget, "to Fles."

Eclopis nodded. "The harbour was built underground, it seems, partly to avoid upsetting the grieving relatives, partly to give the whole exercise an aura of mystery… The departing souls were transported on the so-called 'Boats of Evening', dark, mournful vessels with black sails. I remember there still were some on the river when I was a boy… But the practice of transportation of souls ceased years ago, after the lake became too stormy and its further shore was devastated by the volcano."

They wandered along the quay towards the corner beyond which Bridget had thought she had seen daylight.

"This pool gives on to the River Traa, presumably?" she asked.

"Yes, by an underground channel that emerges in the grounds of a monastery, so that idle eyes could not observe too easily the dark vessels' coming and going."

They had now reached the corner.

On the other side, another surprise awaited them.

The pool continued for several hundred metres until it disappeared into a dark tunnel. There was no sign, however, of daylight. The source of light was a single lamp, hanging high on the mast of a curious dark vessel moored to the quayside. The ship was painted, it seemed, entirely in black, and black was also the colour of its folded sails. Between its two masts was strung an awning, also of the deepest black.

"One of the Boats of Evening!" exclaimed Eclopis. "They must have left one here after the transportation ended... This is really interesting."

But Stigrath held up his hand, as if in warning.

"What's the matter, Stigrath?" asked Bridget sharply.

"Instinct!" he growled. "Feel... Evil forces... not far!"

"Evil forces?" Eclopis laughed. "What are you talking about, man? Let us go and explore this relic of the past!"

He strode forward, and since he was holding the only lantern they were forced to follow him.

"If it's a relic, Eclopis," Bridget called after him, "why is there a light on its mast?"

Eclopis stopped in his tracks. They were now no more than a score of paces away from the gloomy vessel moored by the quay.

"You have a point," he replied, now clearly worried. At that moment they saw something stir on the deck and within the awning.

"Hoa, who is there?" Eclopis called. "In the name of the Broadlord, what is your business here?"

Several dark figures now moved across the deck. And then, ever so slowly, they emerged from the shadows and stepped on to a gangplank leading down to the quayside. More were emerging from beneath the awning.

"Who is it that asks?" asked a voice, deep and hollow. One that Bridget had definitely heard before. She shivered.

"I am Eclopis, captain of the Broadlord's river guard. And who are you? And what are you doing in this unused place?"

"Eclopis," said Bridget quietly, "would it not be better to summon help?"

Stigrath had placed a hand on her shoulder, evidently to reassure her. But it merely showed that he too was not happy with the situation. She thought for a moment of trying to light the second lantern, which she held in her hand, and turning to flee. But she sensed that any attempt at flight would soon be cut off. And even as she spoke, other shadowy figures emerged from the darkness on the quay itself and took up a position behind them.

"Welcome, Eclopis!" said the man with the hollow voice, and he detached himself from the group now standing on the quay near the boat. With curious sliding and jerking movements, he approached. Bridget no longer had any doubts as to who it was. "Do come on board! We have nothing to hide. And please bring your companions with you."

He stopped some five metres away and pushed back the dark hood which had covered his head.

"Stitgoe!" Bridget whispered.

Eclopis turned to her, frowning. "Who did you say?"

"He is, I think you will find, an assistant of the sorceress Vencengea."

"Ah, so our mistress has now been officially branded a sorceress!" said Stitgoe. "She *will* feel honoured, will she not, Lulby?"

Lulby had appeared as if by magic by Stitgoe's side. His rough, misshapen features wore a frown. "Oh, I am not sure about that, Brother Stitgoe. I think she might take it in quite the opposite way…"

"What are you doing in these waters?" demanded Eclopis. "Have you a traders' warrant? That is necessary, you know…"

Stitgoe's initial smile had faded and now he fixed the Broadlord's officer with a look of withering disdain.

"We are not traders," he said coldly. "We have other business here… and neither the Broadlord nor anyone else will prevent us from pursuing it."

The robed figures now formed an almost unbroken circle around them. Eclopis glanced nervously around him, but persisted with his challenge.

"Pray state what business it is, then," he said quietly.

"We have come, as it happens, for this young lady…" (he indicated Bridget) "… and her companions. The Lady Vencengea desires her presence on her island in the Crystal Lake, the Isle of Iprades."

Bridget's heart sank. She had thought they were free of Vencengea and her dark plans.

"And what if I do not want to go to this island?" she asked defiantly.

Stitgoe shrugged. The sickly smile had returned to his face. "Then I have orders to tell you that it is by the request of the Lady Pageya that you have been summoned."

Bridget was caught off guard. Her immediate impulse was one of suspicion. Then she felt a surge of anger that they should try to snare her by talk of her friend. She gulped hard and tried to suppress her emotions.

"How do I know what you say is true?"

Stitgoe shrugged again.

"Why should you doubt me? The Lady Pageya is… very fond of you, it seems. And the Lady Vencengea is extremely… but extremely… fond of the Lady Pageya and wishes to comply with her every request. Pageya, I believe… well, shall we say, finds life somewhat tedious on the Isle of Iprades. She wishes for some company."

Bridget hesitated. "I could still refuse to go," she said.

"Then I should leave you in no doubt that we shall take you anyway, my spirited girl. You see, though it is true what I say about Pageya wishing to have your company, it is also true that the lady Vencengea has thought twice of her decision to leave you at Lusedion… She thought that Pageya alone could guide her to what she seeks, and that she no longer needed your help. The Lady Pageya has now disabused her of this notion. Vencengea needs you and, if we can find him, the boy as well…"

"What, myself?" asked Orin in a timid little voice.

"No, not yourself!" snapped Stitgoe. "The boy from the Beyond, the one who dressed like an animal! Unfortunately it seems we may have to go all the way up that tedious Green Vale again to search for him!"

Bridget felt Stigrath becoming ever tenser and sensed that he was weighing up the possibility of breaking out of the ring of monks and making a break for it. She put a restraining hand on his arm and said:

"It would be no good, my friend Stigrath, there are too many of them. You might simply be injured on my behalf, and I don't want that. Besides, I can believe that Pageya is rather lonely on this terrible island where they've taken her. Perhaps our best course of action will be to go with them."

Stitgoe inclined his head and said: "A wise counsel, if I may say so."

"But you cannot abduct an officer of the High Realm!" protested Eclopis.

"Oh, you are welcome to stay here, my friend," Stitgoe replied. "We have no need of you."

"Eclopis," said Bridget, "we thank you for all your help and kindness. Go and tell the Broadlord of our plight, and see if you cannot persuade him to do something. He is, after all, the supreme ruler of the Realm…"

Stitgoe's hollow laughter suddenly echoed round the vaulted ceiling of the Tropora. Lulby joined in with his whimpering giggle. The other monks remained silent. They, it seemed, had no sense of humour.

"By all means, tell the Broadlord," laughed Stitgoe. "Maybe he will launch an expedition to rescue you!"

And he burst into a new fit of laughter.

* **Cegoura** = courage

Chapter Twenty-Two
Kalmom's Story 6
The Chase

"There are obviously some pages missing!" Bridget exclaimed in disappointment. "And it seems to be a really interesting part of Kalmom's story too! He's explained about the two stones…" Bridget stopped herself before she said too much. "I wonder if he's going on to talk about the disappearance of the Messengers! Or when the Pestilence started to fall…"

Stigrath grunted. Orin moaned. He was curled up on a bunk in the cramped cabin they had been confined to in the gloomy black ship. The little Elonym had again lost his sparkle. He was dejected at falling once more into captivity and frightened by the sinister figures he called the 'Men of Darkness' who were their captors.

"It seems that in this part of the story Kalmom and Manny are now back at Orotworm, with the twins. They must have escaped Shoderim's clutches at Niur and got back to the Mephadore!"

This time there was no reply at all from her companions.

Bridget read on.

"…rally was a failure exactly. But it attracted only modest crowds by comparison with the earlier meetings. And the Maani, though still held in awe by some, did not have quite the magic that he showed at those first great rallies.

It was an irritation, too, that at this particular moment a new crop of Sectarians appeared, peddling a cheap message of cheerfulness, with the usual sectarian techniques of light-hearted songs and clapping in rhythm… This batch, of course, claimed something new. They heard Voices! And what's more, they could talk back, and send messages to the Life Force itself…

Well, of course it was a highly fanciful interpretation of the Life Force and its workings inside of men and women. But like all these sectarian waves, it took hold of many simple minds, filling them with cheap emotionalism and diverting them from the serious problems they had to face up to… like what to do about the Pestilence!

By this time all Eight of the Messengers had disappeared, vanished! One day Messenger Thirthims would be working as usual in her library and presiding at the regular offices. The next day she would be gone. Messenger Thirastu would be on a visit to a teaching post up country, and one morning he would not turn up for the early morning prayer readings. His things, including all his clothes, would be in his room. The only thing missing would be Thirastu himself…

And so it went on.

It was some time, however, before the first falls of the Pestilence came. That only started a year or more after the last of the disappearances. I am talking, of course, of the disappearance of Shoderim.

Shoderim was not a Messenger, but when he too vanished it was assumed that he had gone to join the Eight. People pointed out that Shoderim had been a convert of Thirdrol, the Master Messenger himself. And they presumed that he was still a loyal and active servant of his old patron...

It was only after Shoderim disappeared that the first falls of the Greyness began. Do I emphasise this point too much, out of prejudice against Shoderim? No, I am merely stating a fact.

After the first coming of the Greyness, when all its noxious effects had become obvious, it was all the more important that Maaniriv should re-establish his old influence, to lift the spirits of the people. Prince Voel also underlined to us how essential it was to galvanise the people into action against the Greyness.

And so at the rallies we would sign people up to go and wash the grey matter off trees and shrubs after the next fall... And this activity would in turn, we knew from experience, strengthen their morale and help them regain a healthy interest in life...

Oh, some of the sectarians copied us, of course. But in reality they were too obsessed with their blessed voices, and their laughable interpretations of what they meant, to care much about people's real problems!

It was at this time, just as I was beginning to launch the Maani's campaign again, that the blow struck!

Vencengea came to Orotworm.

All this time she had remained in Niur. Indeed I had heard that once Shoderim had gone she virtually became the mistress of the castle at Niur and the whole district round it. I had long expected that she would come to Orotworm eventually to reclaim her children. But we heard nothing from her. We heard only that her illness was a long and debilitating one. And I have to confess that I did nothing to get in contact with her. For some reason I felt that the twins were safer here at Orotworm than in that unhealthy and malodorous marshland...

It was also not clear to me how much Vencengea knew about Shoderim's disappearance and where he had gone. Or what he might have told Vencengea about the hasty departure of her two children from the fortress.

We had expected him to make some attempt, open or otherwise, to have the twins brought back to Niur. And indeed the palace guard, who were on a special alert to detect such efforts, uncovered two separate plots to infiltrate the ranks of those who served in the Mephadore as soldiers or courtiers. But there had been no formal request from Shoderim, nor was one received from Vencengea.

Then she came herself.

It was a sunny day and I was working at some new speech for the Maani on the balcony of my apartment in the Mephadore. I turned and saw someone standing in the shadows, partly hidden by a curtain that billowed gently in the morning breeze.

"Who is it?" I asked, slightly alarmed by the appearance of the stranger.

She advanced into the open and I recognised her at once. It was the same Vencengea, tall and vivid and beautiful. But she had changed. I saw in her eyes, her stance, her whole manner, a harshness, a coldness that had not been there before.

"Where are they?" she said in a voice that was little more than a whisper.

I set down my pen. "If you mean the children, then they are away from Orotworm, escaping the summer heat in the mountains, with Maaniriv. But they will be back in a few days…"

"Why did you not return them to me?"

"You did not send for them."

"They are my children."

I stood up and took a pace towards her, but stopped. Something warned me that any friendly advance would not be welcome.

"You must understand, my dear Vencengea, that the circumstances of our departure from Niur… We had reason to believe… that Shoderim…"

"That Shoderim what? Wanted to harm them?" she said, and for the first time there was a sign of her old fire, in the sarcasm of her words.

"Yes, and harm us too. I mean myself and Maaniriv."

Her mouth twitched with disdain.

"And that, of course, was the most important consideration… You and your precious Maani."

I was stung. "He was once your friend too."

She was silent and looked away.

"We must organise some accommodation for you, some rooms," I said.

"I shall not be staying," she answered curtly as she turned to leave. "I shall be going back to Niur as soon as I can, with my children…"

"And are we allowed to come with them too?" I asked a little coldly. "After all, we have been declared their guardians, by Thirdrol. We have given them all our care these last three years. And Maaniriv is quite devoted to them…"

"You are not to come to Niur," she cut me off. "Neither you nor the man you call the Maani. Neither now, nor ever…"

And she turned abruptly and left.

I was incensed. My mind was in turmoil. She could not simply take the children like that. We had been enjoined by Thirdrol himself to look after their interests. We had devoted ourselves for over three long years to their care and upbringing. And she… she was still in league, as far as we knew, with Shoderim, a man whose powers and intentions left me with a deep foreboding of evil.

Somehow I had to warn Maaniriv, and prevent Vencengea from taking the children!

I decided I would have to go myself.

Alas, I had not reckoned with Vencengea's exceptional powers. Why oh why did I underestimate her so completely? Had I not read enough into her own library of the occult and the semi-occult back there in Niur to know that she had special techniques for reading into one's thoughts and intentions? What a naïve fool I was.

That very evening, after I had organised apartments for Vencengea in an isolated part of the Mephadore and impressed on the captain of the guard that she was under no circumstances to be allowed to leave them that night, I crept to the stables and had a horse saddled. I departed by the narrow bridge which spans the moat at the rear of the mighty fortress and headed with reckless speed down through the cobbled streets of the sleeping city.

Soon I was out on the plains, riding as fast as I could towards the distant foothills and the rambling old house in its narrow valley where I knew I would find Maaniriv and the two small children fast asleep, in comfort and safety.

I had covered only half the distance when I became aware that I was being followed. At a village on a slight mound above the plain I reined in my mount to take a gulp of water from my flask. Glancing back towards Orotworm I saw, not a league behind me, clearly visible in the bright moonlight, a rider thundering across the dry moonlit plain, pursued by a plume of dust...

Could this be one of the guards, trying to catch me with an urgent message? Or someone else, with a less welcome mission?

I did not wait to find out. I turned my horse and plunged down the slope and on towards the hills.

At every rise in the road I paused to look back. But I saw no further sign of the pursuer.

Now I was in the valley, following the track up alongside the winding, chattering river. Soon the old house, on its several overhanging levels, would show white in the moonlight ahead of me.

And then I heard the pursuer again, or rather I imagined I did. I became aware of a low hungry panting, almost like that of a wolf which senses it is close behind its prey. And I imagined I smelt the foul odour of such a beast, as I spurred my brave horse onwards up the valley...

There was the house, its high gables looking down on the stream and the little stone bridge below it...

The gate was closed and barred for the night. I banged frantically on it, until a bemused and sleepy soldier, a member of the Mephadore guard, drew back the great wooden bolt and let me enter.

I clattered up the stairs to Maaniriv's apartment. There was a light. He must have been wakened by my banging.

I burst into the room.

She was already there. She was standing alongside Maaniriv, looking down at the two small beds and the sleeping children.

Chapter Twenty-Three
Kalmom's Story 7
Flight

"How she had got there before me I still do not understand. But that was
Vencengea! Things which were beyond the powers of other people she seemed
to manage with ease…

As I say, she was standing with Maaniriv, looking down at the two babes.
She turned as I entered, and instead of the hostility and venom that I had
expected, she actually smiled at me. It was a coy, ironic smile, but without the
venom I knew she was capable of.

'So, the midnight rider has come to join us! A strange time to visit your
wards, my friend Kalmom… But I am glad that you care so deeply about their
welfare!'

Her old teasing, mocking self! I could not speak. For a start, I did not know
what to say.

Maaniriv stepped forward. 'Vencengea… desires to take the twins back… to
the Fortress of Niur,' he said, in his endearing, hesitant way, that had won over
so many hearts and minds.

I nodded grimly, but still said nothing. Vencengea continued to smile at me.

'Will you not bow gracefully to the inevitable, my dear Kalmom? After all, it
is not as if I am going to forbid you access to them… You will be welcome to
come to Niur any time…'

This was not what she had said at the Mephadore. What was she playing at?
Was this show of gentility for Maaniriv's sake? I was thinking furiously.

'Will you assure me,' I said hoarsely, 'that these children, our wards, will be
well protected from Shoderim and his plans, whatever they may be…?'

Vencengea looked astonished.

'Shoderim? But he is long gone. Had you not heard? We have seen nothing
of him for these nine months or more…'

But I detected in her voice just a tiny hint that she was not as totally ignorant
of Shoderim's whereabouts as she claimed.

'You will stay at least and eat before you leave,' I said, recovering my
composure just a bit. It was just beginning to dawn outside and the birds were
beginning to stir in the forest.

She nodded. 'We shall leave when the twins awake and have eaten.'

The children duly awoke and were amazed and overawed by all the people
who had come to visit them, especially this tall woman with the long black dress
and the strange eyes. I forced myself to eat, though I had no appetite. During our

brief and silent meal Vencengea seemed on the point of asking me something, but each time she hesitated and held back.

In the meantime, I was still desperately trying to think of some way I could outfox this vixen of a woman. By the end of the meal I had come to a firm decision. Now was the time to put to the test what Vencengea's true intentions were...

'You seem preoccupied,' she said, scanning my features with amused interest, as if trying to read my thoughts. For all I knew, that was well within her capabilities.

But I shook my head. 'Soon you will be gone... and three, no, four of the people I have loved best in this life will depart from it.'

'You are not coming with us?' she asked in surprise.

'No, I shall stay here and be alone for a while. I need a rest from all the plotting and planning of the Mephadore...'

She nodded sympathetically, though I could see she was on her guard...

And then it was time for them to leave. Maaniriv was to accompany them, at least as far as Orotworm. He would decide there, he said, whether he would go further, as Vencengea invited him to do.

'Before you go,' I said, 'allow me to spend just a minute or two in meditation, in my private shrine upstairs.

Vencengea had not let her eyes leave me for a moment since she arrived. 'May I join you in your meditation?' she asked. But I shook my head. 'I would rather be alone for these few moments,' I said with emotion.

But in the small chapel I had no time to meditate. I took the two small boxes which lay before the altar, side by side, and from each one of them I removed the pendants which had been their gifts from Thirdrol on the occasion of their 'Day of Blessing.' Then I knelt before the Diamond of Life depicted on the altar tapestry, and stayed there for a few moments before finally I stood up, made a last obeisance and, taking the two boxes, left the chapel.

I found the others ready to depart. Solemnly I approached Maaniriv and handed him the two boxes.

'You almost forgot these,' I said to him. 'They cannot go without their precious pendants.' I looked at him with as weighty and meaningful an expression as I could muster. 'Look after these treasures with your life!' I said.

*Vencengea looked on, a strange glint in her eye. She, evidently, had **not** forgotten about the pendants and would have enquired after them if they had not been produced.*

'Can I see the pendants?' she said, as if all she wanted to do was satisfy her curiosity.

I took one of the boxes back from Maaniriv and opened it. Vencengea gazed down at the delicate pendant, with the strange, misty gem at its end.

'And the other? Is it exactly the same?' she asked.

'It is,' I answered, my throat dry.

'May I see it?' she said, looking at me coyly.

I turned back to Maaniriv, in order to hand him the first box and take the one he had been holding.

We had come to the crucial moment. Maaniriv and I had often discussed the question of magic. It was one of the things which fascinated him most in life, whether there really was such a thing as magic or whether it was all done by sleight of hand, by an illusion, by tricking the eyes of the beholder. And we had dabbled in cheap conjuring tricks, he and I, to amuse ourselves.

But would we be good enough to fool Vencengea, with her exceptional perceptiveness? And did Maaniriv understand what was required of him? I would find out in a few seconds.

I took the box offered to me by Maaniriv and, turning back to Vencengea, opened it.

'They are exactly the same,' I said. 'As you see.'

She looked at the pendant in the box. Her eyes flickered for a moment, with uncertainty. I thought she was going to ask me to open both boxes at the same time, but at the last moment she decided enough was enough. She nodded and smiled.

I stood on the veranda of the old house, with the servants, as the small open carriage with Maaniriv and the two small children, laughing and chortling, disappeared over the stone bridge and into the trees on the other side, accompanied by Vencengea on her horse.

As soon as they had disappeared, I turned to the servants.

*'My friends,' I said. 'I too am leaving, but in another direction. 'If anyone would have you tell them which way I went, indicate this forest track, which leads down through the forest towards the hamlet… And if perchance you do **not** see me take that road, be assured that it was because you were not attentive enough!'*

I re-entered the house and plunged through its now-empty rooms to the back entrance, which led to the stables. My horse, I knew, would have been taken there for grooming…

Alas, it had little rest that day, the poor steed. I re-saddled it as rapidly as I could, mounted and set off, not in the direction Vencengea and the carriage had taken, but uphill, towards the mountains, and the pass high above the valley.

And as I urged my good horse up through the trees at as swift a pace as I dared, I felt inside my cloak for the cloth in which I had carefully wrapped the second pendant. I had sensed that Vencengea had been as interested in the infants' pendants as in the infants themselves. Something about the two trinkets, and the way that Thirdrol had entrusted them to us, Maaniriv and myself, had alerted her to the fact that they held some special force within them, some special power.

And power was, above all, what Vencengea and her mentor Shoderim sought after!

But if the pendants were ever separated, would they retain the same power? My guess, and my fervent hope, was that they would not. Without each other, I prayed, the pendants would be useless.

*****

How long it would be before Vencengea discovered my ruse I could only guess. I hoped, though I did not expect, that it would not be before Orotworm that she would find that one of the two boxes was empty.

In the meantime, I must reach a place which would afford me adequate protection from the special skills which I knew gave her the power to locate and hunt down any quarry on which she set her sights.

I continued for a goodly distance up through the trees. The path now cut back diagonally along the slope to a point not far above the old mansion, as the crow flies. When I reached a gap in the forest, I looked down, making sure I was not easily visible.

I could see the house and a thin line of smoke rising up from its chimney. But there was no sound, other than that of the birds, and no sight of anything untoward astir in the forest. So far, so good.

I urged my mount on up the hill. Now the trees were thinner, and the track was becoming rougher and rougher. My poor steed, already exhausted by the breakneck ride from Orotworm, was tiring fast. But I must go on. I had a long, long way to climb, and an even longer journey to make if and when I reached the high pass.

Now I was out of the trees, on a bare slope. Above me rose the mountains, the first outcrops of the majestic line of peaks that divides the Green Vale from the Plateau of Tekram. Even in summer the higher slopes still wore part of their white winter garment. And I must reach a place almost as high as that...

The track was climbing steeply now, zigzagging across the bare mountain slopes.

I looked back towards the dark line of the forest, now far beneath me...

And I saw her!

The long black cloak was unmistakable. She was alone, on the first open stretch of ground above the trees, forcing her mount to climb at an incredible speed.

My heart sank. For the first time I seriously asked myself whether Vencengea's powers were of this world, or whether she would catch me as much by sorcery as by sheer force of character and will.

But I did not tarry long to ponder on it. I urged my poor beast onwards, up the slope. Soon Vencengea was hidden from me by a shoulder of the mountain...

Had she seen me? It did not seem to matter. She seemed to know with an unnerving certainty which route I had taken and would take from now on.

I struggled round another corner and at last I saw it, the high pass. It was still several leagues away, at the top of the valley I had been following, which all the time had been narrowing. The track was not so steep now. I was even able to coax my steed into a lumbering trot. It was a valiant beast, I have to say that. Not once did it stop or show any unwillingness to carry me on up that desolate gorge.

I prayed for some divine intervention, a sudden mist, a rock fall behind me across the path. At one stage I even considered stopping and waiting to send a boulder down on top of my pursuer from some hidden spot on the hillside. It was

127

nonsense, of course. Vencengea was no fool and it would simply have aided her search.

And the day was sunny and bright, without a cloud anywhere to be seen.

Finally the poor horse ground to a halt before the last, steep ascent. I jumped off and led the animal by the reins up the rock-strewn path. We were making very slow progress, I realised. Fearfully I glanced down the valley... At first I did not see her, and my heart leapt in panic. I remembered how she had reached the old mansion ahead of me, without having seemed to pass me! But then I spied her, not a league off, trotting steadily and relentlessly towards us.

We came to the last few metres, and we were over the top.

And here my luck began to change. And for the better. In the valley on the other side, just a few hundred metres below the saddle, lay a thick blanket of mist!

I rode almost joyfully down into it. I had no fears, for I knew these mountains well, and was sure I could negotiate the way to my final destination even in the thickest of fogs.

Yet when I was in it, and it enveloped me in its cool, clinging waves, I began to have doubts. It was dark and grey down here in the mist. And darkness and greyness I somehow associated with Vencengea and the more sinister side of her character...

Also I could not travel so quickly. There were precipices near, I knew, and I had heard many stories of how even mountain men had lost their way in the fog and ended up at the bottom of some terrible abyss.

But there was nothing I could do but go on. I knew I had to travel the length of this valley, and then up another one, to the plateau of Fytanas, the place where I hoped I might find sanctuary.

I must have wandered through that dreary mist for hours, with only the vaguest of notions of where I was and whether I was heading in the right direction. Finally I came to an even patch of ground, where the mist seemed lighter. I thought I recognised it. If it was where I thought it was, then the valley I was seeking should be over to the right...

I headed off in that direction, half expecting at any moment to meet the black figure of Vencengea looming out of the mist...

But my luck held. My horse now seemed a little fresher and picked its way almost cheerfully through the rocky terrain. The ground began to rise...

Soon I was ascending a broad slope flecked here and there with the last snow of the winter. The slope climbed and climbed. I was now so tired that I almost did not care whether Vencengea caught me up. What could she do to me? Tear me limb from limb?

No, I said to myself, but she would certainly take the pendant, and so the fate of the Twins would, I felt certain, be at the mercy not just of their unbalanced and fearsome mother, but of even darker beings and forces...

This slope did not seem familiar any more. Had I taken the wrong way? If I was in the right place, then there should be a narrow gully just over here, one which was almost impossible to find if you did not know it was there. That was one of the secret defences of the sanctuary which I sought.

But I could not find it! For what seemed an eternity I probed the wall of rock to the right of the slope. But there was no opening, no gully, no refuge.

I looked nervously down the slope, through the mist. Was it my imagination, or did I hear the clink of harness somewhere below…

I took off my cap to wipe my over-heated brow. Then a voice came out of the mist.

'You fool of a man! Why didn't you show us your face before? Come, the opening is just to the left, behind that rock that looks like a goose! Though you're the goose, if you ask me…'

Thankfully I followed her instructions, and sure enough, behind the said rock was the narrow gully I had been searching for.

Durbote appeared on top of a rock just beside me.

'Well,' she said, 'are you going to offer me a lift or not?'

And without asking my leave, she plonked herself on the saddle in front of me.

'Ride on, brave knight who cowers in the mist! And as we go you can tell me what brings you to these parts, and why my brother Elbevire will have to stay out here all night, probably, trying to deflect your dark pursuer from the true path…'

Chapter Twenty-Four
Kalmom's Story 8
Hiding from the Darkness

"I stayed over two weeks with Elbevire and Durbote, my kinspeople. I saw nothing of Vencengea, though they did. Every day for a week she came prowling around the barren slope where she had last seen me, searching no doubt for some cave or tunnel into which I might have disappeared. But either because the gully was so cunningly hidden, or because Elbevire and Durbote were such artful illusionists, even the great Vencengea was unable to find the entrance to their little hollow in the mountain, or their house hidden under the stones...

Finally, however, she seemed to give up the search, and when I judged it safe I bade a sad farewell to the good-natured Elbevire and the acid-tongued Durbote. I had enjoyed their company and would gladly have stayed longer in the comfort and security of their lair... But my concern was for Maaniriv and the two babes. What had happened to them all the time Vencengea was seeking me out? Had Maaniriv found the little message which I had placed in one of the boxes, written in the code which only he and I could interpret?

My kinsfolk accompanied me out of the gully under cover of a new mist, and downhill to a place where a barely visible path, no more than a sheep track, cut off round the mountainside.

'This, good Kalmom, is the path you must take if you want to go direct to the Vale,' said Elbevire. 'Take care, for there are many perilous places along it...'

'He would not have reached this far if he had not been careful, brother!' the sharp-tongued Durbote cut in. 'Do not waste your breath with useless words...'

But she too embraced me fondly as we parted.

I shall not retell all the adventures which befell me on that track, because they have little to do with my story. Let it be enough to say that I did not meet Vencengea or any of her creatures or spies... though I did come across some very good and honest people, who helped me with food or a night's lodging.

As I went on, a curious change came over the weather. Dark clouds descended and covered the mountaintops. I am not over-imaginative, but it seemed that these clouds were no normal clouds. They were tinged with a faint purple glow, and I felt that they were looking down on the land beneath them, scouring it, searching it... for what? For me, perhaps?

Also a terrible wind arose, tearing at my clothes and the harness of my horse. The wind always seemed to be against me, driving me back, trying to dissuade me from my mission...

I struggled on, and eventually I came to another high pass and found myself *gazing down through the bizarre, purple-tinged light into the deep and beautiful Vale. This was where I had first met the Maani, and this is where I hoped against hope I would find him again.*

I had suggested a rendezvous in the old, ivy-covered castle of Nirei, where we both knew the kind-hearted but over-anxious lord, Curutel. The people of Nirei had always been loyal to the Broadlord, though they had long struggled to ward off the influence of the proud city of High Towers, Tekram, and the growing ambitions of its rival, the slave city of Teivos. So it was thither I bent my way, hoping to find Maaniriv and the babes unharmed. As I descended into the valley, the weather finally relented. The wind died, so that I was able to persuade some villagers to venture out across the lake to ferry me to the fortress. As I approached those ancient walls, however, I realised at once that something was wrong. The sun was now shining again, but the gay and noisy company of young people who habitually frequented the battlements was not there ... Nor were they in the small harbour where the boats tied up. In the broad and luxuriant gardens where I had passed so many happy hours listening to music and poetry there were only a few down-at-heel courtiers and even fewer ladies. And there were far more armed men than usual, guarding each gate and door, questioning me about who I was and by what right I sought to enter ...

Finally I found Curutel in the great hall of Nirei, sitting sadly alone on his throne, staring into space ...

At first he did not seem to notice me. And when he did he gave a start, and rummaged through his cloak for a dagger, which he finally pulled out as I approached ...

'Do not ... do not come any closer,' he stammered. 'I shall not tolerate any more messengers of the devil who come to play tricks on our minds and ruin our lives ...!'

Just then another figure, huge and sinister, stepped out from behind the throne and loomed above me. I heard a rumble like that of Fles on an angry day ...

'Fear not, my lord,' it said. 'It is ... it is but ... your friend Kalmom. The one who ... who amuses you so much ... with his jokes.'

It was Stigrath, the Lord Curutel's captain, a worthy fellow and by no means as rough and stupid as he looks ... But what had happened to his speech. He had always spoken with a thick and heavy accent, for he was by origin a native of Naisur, in recent years renamed Teivos. But now he stammered, as if he could not find what the next word in his sentence should be!

'G-greetings, Lord Kalmom,' he stuttered. 'Excuse ... excuse our lord Nirei. He has had ... we all have had ... a terrible shock.'

He told me the story.

The Maani, as he called him, had arrived at Nirei as planned some ten days previously. And with him the babes. Maaniriv had been in a terrible state, frightened out of his wits, so frightened indeed that he was unable to relate to Stigrath and Curutel what the matter was. They understood only that it had something to do with Vencengea.

The Lord Nirei was indignant. He had heard of this Vencengea and was determined she would not frighten or intimidate such a holy man as the Maani and such innocent creatures as the two babes... even if they were her own. He took them in and promised to protect them, should Vencengea discover where they had taken refuge. Hopefully, he said, the Maani's good friend Kalmom would arrive before she did and take matters into his own hands.

Alas, I did not arrive before Vencengea. She sailed up the Traa one wet and stormy evening, in a boat which apparently moved against the wind, not with it... This, at least, was the testimony of Stigrath, and he was an experienced sailor.

She stormed into the Great Hall, throwing wide the doors and knocking over the guards with a mere flick of her hands (this again was how Stigrath described it).

'Where are my babes?' she cried. 'You have no right to keep my children from me!'

Curutel had tried to appease her, reason with her, but this only incensed her the more. The storm could be heard howling through the eaves of the hall. Vencengea towered over him and issued such dire threats that the poor man cowered back in his throne like a small boy.

'She produced pictures,' Stigrath recalled, 'pictures out of nowhere, which hung in mid-air... and showed him what she would do to him if he did not give up the children.'

'And then I... stepped forward... and stood before her...'

That is all Stigrath managed to say. He just could not drive himself to utter any more. Clearly, I thought, whatever Vencengea did to him has caused his disorder with words... She has addled his brain and put some wicked spell on his tongue...

'But what of Maaniriv and the Twins?' I asked in horror, anticipating the worst.

'One of the babes was ill when they arrived... with the fever. We gave it over to the carers... in the far side of the castle... And it is still there. We did not... betray it to Vencengea.'

'And the Maani?'

'He took the second child and fled,' Curutel took over from his tongue-tied servant. 'They fled as we held Vencengea at bay...' He looked down at the floor, clearly embarrassed and ashamed that he had not been able to do more.

'So they escaped!' I said, almost laughing with joy. 'They escaped her clutches...'

Stigrath and Curutel clearly did not share my joy.

'She went after them,' said Stigrath. 'We were unable... to stop her. We delayed her no more than an hour or two...'

My heart sank. 'How long ago was this?' I asked with foreboding.

'Yesterday,' muttered Stigrath in his deep voice. 'Yesterday in the evening. I would have followed and tried to protect them... but I was lying in a swoon. She... she laid... evil affliction on me! And... I still cannot speak... with sense.'

'Come, man!' I cried. 'You seem well enough recovered now. We must follow *and prevent her from seizing them!'*

He nodded and suddenly seemed to throw off his despondency. 'You are right… We could still catch them before…'

'Before what?' I asked, my whole body suddenly seized with fear.

'Before they reach… the high passes over the Snowy Mountains,' he replied. 'That is where they were headed. Maaniriv had some idea to… to return to his own world… across the Great Divide…'

Yes, I said to myself, that was the last thing left open to him.

We took a dozen of Stigrath's most trusted men and, taking one of the fleet riverboats which still plied those waters at that time, we sped as fast as we could across the lake to the upper shore. The night was already falling, the second night since Maaniriv had left Nirei, with Vencengea in pursuit. Though the storm had calmed down for a while, the wind had risen once more and was blowing in violent gusts down the valley in our faces. Our small craft was buffeted by huge and vicious waves, unnaturally high waves for such a small lake… I imagined somehow that these were emissaries from Vencengea's evil world, doing the utmost to hold us back on our sacred mission…

We landed near a village called Wesomethe and there hired some mules, the only beasts available to the villagers. We began to climb up the upper valley. For the first few leagues there was a broad enough path between the trees and it was easy enough to follow even on that dreadful night. But as the night wore on the track became narrower and several times we lost it altogether, so that we were forced to clear our way through the undergrowth with the short swords that Stigrath's men had brought with them.

We fought our way onwards through the whole of that night…

The day dawned, bleak and cold, though the wind had abated a little. Above us and ahead the clouds were low on the mountains, and soon we were climbing towards the ceiling of mist.

All that day we climbed. I drove them on, with Stigrath's help. I was obsessed. I had only one goal: to stop Vencengea from overtaking Maaniriv and bringing the innocent babe back to our Realm, and into her power… her power and that of Shoderim! For I was convinced that he had never really vanished! I was certain that Vencengea knew where he was!

And the weather was once again deteriorating. As the day wore on, the clouds thickened, and the first ominous rumbles of thunder began to roll and echo once more around the mountains, all the time growing louder.

Late in the afternoon the storm finally overtook us. A startlingly vivid flash illuminated the air of the deep valley we were ascending, and suddenly sheets of rain, heavy, drenching rain, came tumbling down on top of us.

We looked for some rocky outcrop under which to shelter. Just ahead of us, where the track rounded a bend in the hillside, there was one such place, which might give us some respite from the viciousness of the elements. We were no sooner installed under it, however, when Stigrath tugged urgently at my tunic and pointed up ahead.

Further up the mountain, barely visible through the driving rain, the track reached a point where it curled round the side of the mountain under a massive precipice. Along this part of the track we made out some shapes moving slowly and painfully up the steep path. One was clearly a man, tall and bent. He was trudging forward, leading behind him a small horse or mule. And on the mule was perched a small bundle. Maaniriv and the second twin!

But where was Vencengea?

I froze when I saw her. Her lone figure, dark and sinuous, moved out from behind a rock. She was barely half a league behind them, and she was on horseback, urging her mount forward with unhurried movements, confident that her quarry would not now escape her.

I ran out into the deluge. I had no particular plan in mind. All I knew was that I must distract Vencengea' attention. And I called at the top of my voice:

'Vencengea! Maaniriv! For pity's sake, we must stop this madness... Let us all return to Nirei and talk together. Have we not been comrades? Are we not friends?'

At that moment there was a blinding flash, and my last words were drowned in a tremendous crash of thunder almost above our heads. I was thrown back from the edge of the road and fell on to the hard unyielding ground.

Stigrath helped me back to my feet. I peered again through the rain towards the darkening mountainside. The light was now fading fast. For some time I could not locate the figures on the road above us. But then I saw them again. Maaniriv and his charge had almost reached the corner of the perilous track that led beneath the precipice, and Vencengea was now closing on them fast.

I am still not entirely sure what happened next, or how. Did Vencengea really have the power, as I inclined to believe at that time, to force the elements to obey her? I have grown more sceptical with the years...

But what I did see I can tell. Vencengea suddenly stopped her horse several arrow shots away from Maaniriv and his charge. She rose tall in the saddle and flung out an arm, as if commanding the forces of nature to obey her.

A huge, jagged bolt of lightning forked out of the sky and hit the lofty crag high above the corner of the road. There was another deafening boom, and we all shielded our faces from the blast.

When I looked again, I saw something moving high up above the helpless Maaniriv, who was standing transfixed beside the mule with its precious load. Only a few stones came at first, but then they dislodged other, larger boulders, and soon a whole section of the mountainside was sliding down towards the pathway.

Maaniriv saw what was happening and urged the mule desperately onwards.

Vencengea was still moving forward towards them, but now she checked. The landslide, she saw, would not only block the track, as she had intended. Maaniriv had continued to move onwards and was now in danger of being swallowed up in the avalanche of rocks! She saw it would also envelop her if she continued. She wheeled her horse round, but as she did so it took fright and reared up on its hind legs, unseating its rider. Vencengea fell heavily on the stony track.

The landslide fell with a sickening crash across the path. The whole valley seemed to reverberate with the deafening roar of the rockfall.

Then slowly the noise subsided... A minute, two minutes later, and the wall of sound could still be heard, rolling off into the vast emptiness of the mountains that surrounded us... Now there was almost total silence, broken only by a sharp clatter of individual stones as they came to rest on top of the rockslide. Somewhere far away, it seemed, there was a low rumble sent back by the fleeing storm.

Stigrath and I rode in panic up the stony track round the great bend in the mountain to where it had all happened. Stigrath's men were close behind. As we struggled upwards, a large dark form materialised out of the gloom in front of us and rushed past. It was Vencengea's horse, fleeing in terror down the mountain.

Finally we reached the motionless body of Vencengea, lying beside the track.

'She still lives, she still lives!' grunted Stigrath, though he did not seem overjoyed at the discovery.

'But what of Maaniriv and the babe?' I muttered, frantic with anxiety, and rushed on.

I reached the place where the landslip had blocked the road. There was no way round it! The rock fall continued downwards on the lower side, towards the bottom of the valley. I began to clamber out on to the mass of boulders and loose stones, trying to find some way over it. But the stones began to slip from under me, and I was pulled back rudely by a massive arm.

'Do not even try it, Master Kalmom! Very dangerous... Also kill yourself...
'

Yet I was beside myself with anxiety. I had to know what had happened to my friend, and to the child who had been in his care. Stigrath despatched some of his men down the mountainside to try and by-pass the rock fall.

They came back some time later. They had climbed round the bottom of the landslide and reached the track on the further side. There was no sign of the Maani, or his mule, or of the child. There was no sign of them in the upper valley, they said. There was only one conclusion. My friend and the precious child had been engulfed by the terrible crush of rocks from above.

We returned down the valley, carrying the prostrate form of Vencengea. When we reached the forest, we made a rough litter for her and bore her back to Nirei.

*****

Two days later I found myself standing in a large room in the Castle of Nirei, with windows which looked out over the waters of the lake, calm now in the evening sun.

On a long bed beside the window lay the motionless figure of Vencengea. She had not regained consciousness since we had brought her back here. But she was no longer in danger, the carers told us.

So I knew that now was the time for me to depart. The child, the second twin, was still seriously ill. I was told it would be dangerous to move her, to take her with me. But I knew I could not leave her. I could not give her up to Vencengea; this wonderful but wild and unpredictable woman that the Fates had decreed should be her mother. I must take her with me, and the sooner the better for both of us.

And yet, as I gazed down at the pale and troubled face of Vencengea, I tarried. Did something remain of our old friendship? Was I still forcing myself to believe that perhaps, given the events on the mountainside, there might be a reconciliation between us? Yes, I wanted to believe this. But cold realism intervened and told me it would not happen that way. The die was cast. There was a bottomless gulf now between me and Vencengea, however much I had once loved her.

I took my silent farewell and went to find the child.

Chapter Twenty-Five
The Marshes of Niur

The great army was preparing for war! Out across the green meadows before the city of Towers men were loading food and equipment – tents, weapons, bedding – on to crude wooden carts. Over to one side, one of the tallest towers was belching smoke from all its upper windows. This, explained Pailtac, who had become their guardian and guide, was the Smiths' tower. The master smiths were busy sharpening the army's swords and other weapons.

They were atop one of the nearby towers, the tower of the Efcanin clan, of which Pailtac was the Vonrug. Pailtac, like a majority of the other knights, seemed excited and elated by the prospect of another campaign against the despised Skomiars – this time they would have an even greater advantage than in previous wars, thanks to the wonderful flying machine and its spying capabilities!

"We shall mass in the hills on the near side of the River Traa… then sweep down on the Skomiar filth when they are least expecting us. Thanks to our new 'Eyes-in-the-Sky' (he nodded down to where the Goodcheer was tugging gently at its moorings on the Broad Tower) we shall know exactly where they are and what they are doing, while they will have no knowledge of our whereabouts or intentions!"

Tom felt a little nervous about their becoming participants in the forthcoming battle.

"Isn't there a risk that some of the slave workers at Teivos will get mixed up in the fighting and could be killed or injured?" he asked tentatively.

Pailtac snorted through his large moustache. "In war, my young friend, many innocent people suffer. That is why it is our responsibility to wage it as efficiently as possible. Short and sweet, as they say… Get it over and done with. Drive the Skomiar scum off the lands of civilisation, back to lick their wounds in the desert where they belong!"

"But won't they just gather their forces again and come back?" Tom persisted.

"Ha – we shall give them such a hiding that they won't dare come back for a long time! And all the civilised world, all the domains of the Broadlord will thank us. And the Broadlord himself will finally be forced to recognise us as the true… and only defenders of civilisation."

All this time Madge was standing stiffly just behind them, saying nothing, as if trying to preserve her new image as an important expert on military strategy. *I wish she'd relax just a little*, thought Tom, *and not look so pompous. Sometimes she makes me want to laugh, and that would expose us as the frauds we are!* Yentsilbor was also standing on the tower, a little way off. Tom hoped he had not heard what Pailtac had said. He could not be very happy with the sight of the Yenomi preparations for war against his country, even if they had held open the possibility of peace talks.

"We should go now," Pailtac announced, and beckoned to his companions Kotz and Erash. Together with Tom, Madge and Quenrie they descended their tower and crossed the open space to the Broad Tower.

They arrived beneath the Goodcheer. Tom noticed that all three knights were showing distinct signs of nervousness as they surveyed the swaying bulk of the airship. He took the opportunity to show off to them, catching the rope ladder with one hand and tripping lightly up it towards the cabin.

"Who's next?" he shouted down to the hesitant knights beneath.

Yentsilbor clambered slowly up the ladder. Then it was the turn of the three knights.

Madge had explained to the Knights' Council that the airship could carry only a few of their number. The knights wanted at one point to send Quenrie with the land army, but Madge absolutely refused to set off unless all three of them, herself, Tom and Quenrie were together in the airship. Reluctantly, the Knights agreed and also accepted that only three of their number could travel in the flying machine.

Erash tried first, but found that his dangling sword soon became entangled with his legs and with the irritatingly disobedient rope ladder. Madge had the knights take off their weapons – which they did very unwillingly – and gave them some basic guidance on how to steady themselves before mounting each rung. After some time and effort, all three knights, and Quenrie, had struggled up into the small gondola, and Yentsilbor was hauling up their swords, tied together on the end of a rope.

The knights were even more uneasy now, peering nervously out the windows at the ground far below them. Yentsilbor sat on one side, keeping to himself, but clearly enjoying the Yenomi trio's discomfort.

Madge started the engines and Tom signalled to the men on the tower to release the mooring ropes.

Part of the Grand Army, under the command of Reknab, had already left earlier that morning. The knights would have to climb all the way to the forbidding Pass of Tekramkotz, high above the plateau, before passing into the valley of the River Wolfshak, which would take them most of the way to the group of peaks that overlooked Teivos and the valley of the Traa.

The airship was to take a different route. Their destination, Pailtac explained, was a region called the Black Fields. This, apparently, was where the burning liquids were pumped out of the ground and refined. Some members of the Council were still unhappy that the flying machine was not going with the main army to the battlefield. But he, Pailtac, had won them over eventually by pointing out that Skomiar spy bands had been reported in the vicinity of the Black Fields, and the flying ship would help him to investigate.

"I hope he doesn't forget that we're desperately short of fuel," Madge grumbled as she set her course westwards. "We can't afford to take any crazy detours to look for these imaginary spies!"

As they rose above the high towers, they flew in a wide curve round the green plateau surrounding the city, and at one point passed over a long line of armed men snaking up a track on the mountainside. Tom waved and saw that several of the mounted knights waved cheerily back. The army was in good heart, confident of victory, of new glory and new spoils.

Then the airship turned and headed off in the opposite direction.

There was no mist, as there had been on the day they arrived, and they had a broad view across the undulating countryside beyond Tekram. The City of Towers stood on a high plateau between two lofty snow-tipped ranges. At one end of the plateau the ground rose gradually towards a ragged line of hills. That, Tom reckoned, must have been the route they had followed on their way from the Green Vale. At the other end of the plateau, in the direction in which they were now moving, the land was not so high. It broadened out into a region of broken countryside, a series of bare hills, wooded dales and stretches of rough pasture. Occasionally, they would pass over an isolated village or fortress, though for the most part it was an empty country, inhabited mainly by sheep and wild goats.

The plateau eventually sloped down into a broad valley. Soon they were approaching a line of lush green vegetation. But this was no jungle. When they reached it, Tom saw that there were comparatively few trees, only a maze of thick and tangled undergrowth, through which Tom caught the frequent glint of water. The place was clearly marshland. Some might even have called it a swamp.

As they turned down the valley, they caught sight in the distance of a number of open stretches of water, long thin lakes divided from each other by patches of lush green reeds and undergrowth. The lakes were in turn linked with each other by watercourses threading their way through the whole wide expanse of marshland.

"Unhealthy looking country," murmured Madge.

Quenrie nodded. "The Marshes of Niur," he said. "Many a good man or woman has perished there, trying to escape from…" Then he stopped, aware that some of their knightly companions were within earshot.

On the far side of the valley, barely visible from this distance, they could just make out two great scars in the landscape, where it looked as if some giant had taken a great bite out of the side of the hills.

"The silver mines of Retupmoc and Nocilis!" This time it was Pailtac who spoke, and it was with pride in his voice. "When we have won the war, you must return and visit them. You will be impressed by the orderliness and efficiency with which they are run."

Tom glanced in the direction of Yentsilbor, but the big Skomiar commander did not react to Pailtac's words. Tom and Madge said nothing, and Quenrie's

139

mouth was set even more firmly than it had been before. He had told them of the evil reputation of these mines, so close to the swamps, where many of the workers did not survive more than a few years.

At about noon, the valley broadened further, and the hills on either side fell away, to leave an amazing view across the great central plains…

Tom was not sure whether his eyes were deceiving him. The day had grown misty again and when he looked towards the southern horizon he thought that maybe the darkening of the sky in that direction was perhaps a gathering storm. But then he saw that the borders of the dark mass were too definite and clear. And as they flew closer its outlines became ever more solid. There could no longer be any doubt – the dark mass he was looking at was a mountain.

And what a mountain! It was huge, dominating the whole horizon in that direction. It rose imperiously from the mist, looking down on the world at its feet with something that Tom could not help but feel was disdain.

Fles again! But now it was much closer than when they had seen it from above the Green Vale. Its enormous conical mass, shimmering slightly through the haze, had a powerful effect on Tom, a sort of mesmeric hold on his senses which he could not easily explain. The overall impression was that the giant mountain, with the wide smouldering crater at its top, hid some malevolent intention, held some dark secret stored in its bowels. It seemed to be taunting them, challenging them to come closer and delve into its very entrails to discover what malign secrets were concealed there.

They might indeed have to do that, Tom reflected, if they were ever to solve the enigma of Kalmom's messages, the mystery of the Grey Pestilence and the secrets of the dark mistress Vencengea and her sinister plans.

Away across a wide plain, below the mountain, Tom made out what he thought must be a lake, glinting faintly in the watery sun. Was this then the enigmatic Crystal Lake, the lake of the philosophers where Kalmom had spent so many years? And where Vencengea dwelt on her mysterious Isle of Iprades? Tom hoped that they would manage to get a closer view of the still distant lake.

The river they had been following down the valley now split again into several branches as it spread across the flatlands. Tom had expected that when they reached the plain there would be more dwellings, villages or even towns. But he now saw that the countryside below them seemed almost totally deserted. The only buildings that Tom could see were a number of hovels, scattered thinly over the plain, surrounded each one by some derrick-like structures which Tom at first took to be water-pumps.

Trees there were too, and grass and bushes, but blighted, it seemed, though not in the same way as the greenery in the Vale of Nirei had been blighted. In that unhappy valley, the Grey Pestilence had somehow deprived everything it settled on of its colour. But here the trees and grass were, if anything, darker than they should be. It looked as if they had been smeared by a film of some oily substance. And the waters of the river itself were black, he saw.

"The Black Fields," murmured Quenrie. "Where they dig in the ground for the foul liquid that lights their lamps."

Tom suddenly realised what the dark slime was which covered the surrounding country. It was oil, oil which had escaped and polluted everything around it.

All his previous doubts about the wisdom of their stratagem rose anew in Tom's mind. Could it really be possible that the rough, unrefined oil that the Knights apparently used to light their towers and halls could in any way be suitable for the airship's engine? If it was not, then that was that. They would not be able to continue their journey.

Pailtac told Madge to start descending. Looking downwards, Tom now saw they were passing over regular clusters of the crude stone buildings, each one surrounded by a whole forest of the derrick-like pumps.

He suddenly became conscious that Quenrie had said very little in the last twenty minutes or so. He glanced at the little philosopher's face and saw that he was staring fixedly in front of him, out of the forward window of the airship's gondola.

Tom followed the direction of his gaze and saw what it was that had so riveted Quenrie's attention.

They had been following, on their left, a low line of hills which marked the edge of the desolate swampland of Niur. And on a rocky outcrop at the very end of these hills stood a building. It rose high above the marshy plain, dark and grey, its jagged outline making a sharp contrast to the smooth contours of the land around it. The roof of the distant castle was a series of pointed towers and pinnacles, like nothing Tom had ever seen. What crazed architect had built this sinister stronghold? He was suddenly glad of the bright sunshine bathing the gently undulating landscape around them. On a different day, the dark building they were fast approaching would have been the stuff of nightmares.

Yet this was obviously their destination.

"The Fortress of Niur," murmured Quenrie grimly, "a place with a sinister history and a black reputation… for some more than others."

Chapter Twenty-Six
Fire, Noise and Colour

"A creepy place, to put it mildly," muttered Madge as they walked towards the forbidding complex of buildings on the ridge.

They had moored the Goodcheer, with some help from a group of bemused sheep farmers, by a copse of stunted trees in a clearing in the low scrubland that bordered the marshes. They were now crossing a soggy stretch of open ground towards the castle itself. Though the sun was bright, an atmosphere of gloom and depression hung over its confusion of steep roofs, jagged towers and narrow windows. The grim edifice seemed to glower down at them suspiciously. They were now close enough to see that it was built of rough dark grey stone, and that at one point amid the irregular and pointed towers there lay an incongruously smooth dome. From a distance it looked as if it were made of something like plastic.

The path left the marshy ground and began to ascend past some ragged thorn trees. They followed it up to the windowless lower walls. These were broken only by a single immense gateway where a wide track swept in under an elaborately carved arch only to be blocked by a huge wooden door. It looked like the entrance to some sort of cathedral or temple rather than a castle. Tom gazed at the carvings around the rim of the archway, trying to read some of the lettering.

Before he could decipher anything, however, Pailtac led the way to the one side, to a small door in the flat grey wall of the castle. To Tom's surprise it was both unlocked and unguarded. They passed through unchallenged and found themselves in a dimly lit corridor. Here they met their first human being. A thin, haggard man, clearly a servant, came scurrying round a corner, evidently alerted by the sound of the opening door. In his astonishment, he uttered a cry and dropped the bowl he had been holding. The man literally fell to the floor in a mark of grovelling submission to the knights.

"Get up, man," ordered the surly Kotz, "and go and inform Tisnectis at once that Pailtac is here from Tekram, with some very important business."

The man rushed off and was at once replaced by another, dressed like the first in course and rumpled clothes. He bowed and ushered them along the corridor into a rough, dimly lit room that appeared to be some sort of refectory. Here he showed them to a table and hurried off, returning a few moments later with a simple meal of goat's cheese, oatcakes and buttermilk. These the knights ignored, but Tom fell on them with relish. He realised they had not eaten since early that morning in Tekram.

As they were finishing, a door at one end of the room opened and there entered one of the most bizarre figures Tom had yet seen in this land of strange and wonderful people. He wore a long robe of what appeared to be blue silk, though Tom noticed that here and there the material was spotted with dark stains. His face was flat and severe, like that of an angry bulldog, and he wore a double beard which hung down in front of him in two untidy twirls. On his head he wore a circular cap of the same blue material as the robe. He surveyed them for a few moments, frowning and saying nothing. Then he beckoned to them imperiously.

"Tisnectis evidently wants us to follow him. He is one of the Keepers of the Secret," said Pailtac, clearly referring to the newcomer. "We are being invited to make obeisance."

"Make obeisance… to *him*?" asked Tom.

"No, no. To the Great Secret themselves," replied the knight, with evident reverence.

"Themselves…?" Tom was mystified.

"The Secret is Man, and Woman, and also the Essence of the World Itself!" said Pailtac stiffly, as if annoyed that this alien boy should question such self-evident truths. He said all this with a perfectly straight face.

Quenrie made a strange noise. "This seems to be some deity that's grown up since I was last in these parts," he muttered.

"You shall see the proof of the power of the Secret, in the Sanctuary," Pailtac went on. "If you wish for the aid of the secret, you will have to do it honour!"

"Hmph!" Madge murmured suspiciously as they trooped off after Pailtac and the blue-robed priest. "It depends a bit on what 'doing honour' means."

They climbed a plain stone staircase and then another, and passed through several more of the dingy, irregular rooms, until they came finally to a large wooden door, surrounded by an arching stone portal, which looked like a much smaller version of the great gate into the castle. Above the semi-circular arch over the door a crude picture was carved in the stonework. It appeared to be a scene depicting a great fire – with people fleeing from buildings which were being consumed by flames.

And over this dramatic scene the mason had sculpted an ominous and very familiar shape: the cone of the great volcano, Fles.

Tisnectis paused dramatically at the double wooden door under the arch, then rapped on it with his bare knuckles. Immediately it was flung open from the other side. Tisnectis ushered them through.

At first Tom thought the space beyond the door lay in total darkness. He had the feeling that they were in a large open area, but for several moments he could see nothing. Then gradually objects began to take shape in the dim light. He made out columns, circular stone pillars supporting an unseen roof. They must surely be in a temple or church. He remembered that Niur had originally been a teaching house for the Order of the Balance, and so was a monastery rather than a castle.

Gradually he began to distinguish, in niches along the walls, shapes which looked like statues or altars of some sort. The only light in the sanctuary came from the far end, near what must be the main altar. There three tiny flames were flickering gently. There was a blue one on the right, a pink one on the left, and between them, one that was golden. This, Tom thought, was an interesting variation on the theme of the coiled blue and red flames.

Tisnectis moved them forward towards the centre of the sanctuary, closer to the three glowing lights. Tom sniffed the air, sure he had caught a whiff of a pungent smell which he couldn't for the moment identify.

Tisnectis now spoke for the first time. In a curt, clipped voice he told them to stop where they were, and so they stood there, Tom, Madge, Yentsilbor and Quenrie with the three knights of Tekram behind them, in the semi-darkness. For a while all was silent, but Tom then began to feel a growing tension in the air, an electricity which he was sure was due to more than the sense of waiting.

Tom glanced at the three coloured lights, and slowly he began to make out some sort of cloth or tapestry behind them. Soon he started to recognise a familiar pattern…

A diamond shape surrounding a picture of the coiled flame…

The silence was broken for a moment by what sounded like the opening of a door, deep underground, somewhere behind the altar. Then there came a hissing sound, and a trembling, which gradually grew into a rumbling and continued to grow louder until the very walls and pillars around them seemed to tremble.

Then the three tiny flames in front of them shivered momentarily and suddenly, accompanied by a terrific roar, they swelled dramatically to become massive burning lights, the red and pink and yellow vying with each other for supremacy.

To their right and left, between the pillars of the temple, in what seemed to be side-chapels of the main sanctuary, there now appeared smaller flames, but all of them in the same combination of colours – blue, pink and gold…

Tom had always loved colours. At primary school he had always drawn his pictures in as many different colours as he could find in the box of crayons. Now he found himself almost hypnotised. He just could not tear his eyes away from the dancing, hissing flames. And when the three knights beside them bent down on their knees, he felt an involuntary urge to do likewise. Yet something inside him, perhaps the inborn stubbornness he had grown up with, refused to let his limbs comply.

A mighty voice boomed out from behind the flames.

"The Man, the Woman and all the Things that are in and on and under the Earth. Bow yourselves, unbelievers, prostrate yourselves in wonder, for the Power is before you and demands obeisance."

More flames appeared in front of them, behind the three magnificent fountains of colour at the end of the sanctuary. To the left was a sinuous line of pink flames rising from the darkness, while on the right there rose a twisting line of blue. And in the middle, just before what had seemed to be an altar, there appeared several strands of golden yellow, gyrating and twisting upwards to form changing shapes.

The whole thing now slowly fused into a single picture. Tom could have sworn that when they entered, while he was peering into the gloom trying to adjust to the darkness, there had been nothing at the end of the sanctuary except a plain cloth curtain. Now this curtain began to glow. Colours began to take shape on it and coalesce into recognisable shapes.

It was a picture, a beautiful, lifelike picture, of a peaceful, sparkling lake, and on its further shore a giant slumbering volcano.

The volcano of Fles!

"What have we here?" Tom heard Madge say from behind him. "The temple of the volcano-worshippers?"

"Strangers be silent! And beware!" boomed the voice, which appeared to come from behind the curtain. "Bow yourselves! Throw yourselves on the floor and beg mercy. The Mighty Power of Fles does not forgive insolence and disobedience!"

"Kneel, strangers, kneel!" Pailtac urged them. He and his fellow knights had not just gone down on their knees. They were lying flat on the floor, arms stretched wide. "For the sake of your mission and your safe exit from this place, kneel and give obeisance!"

Tom glanced to either side and saw that Madge, Yentsilbor and Quenrie had all been stubbornly refusing to do anything but stand. Now Quenrie, very reluctantly, went down on his knees in a not very convincing show of respect. And then Yentsilbor, to his surprise, followed suite, falling clumsily on to his knees. Shrugging, Tom followed suite. Only Madge remained standing defiantly, hands on hips, glancing around her as if not at all impressed by the proceedings.

With growing unease, Tom noticed that dim figures had begun to appear in the side-chapels among the pillars, and he gradually began to make out that they were all robed in the same long blue garments that Tisnectis wore. They took up position just behind the glowing flames, staring fixedly at the small group of infidels in the centre of the temple.

Then Tisnectis himself suddenly appeared from behind the roaring flames on the 'Volcano' altar and pointed an accusing finger at Madge.

"Seize her!" he cried shrilly. "Seize the one who desecrates the sanctuary!"

The robed priests rushed in from all sides and grabbed the unfortunate Madge, pulling her away into the shadows beyond the left-hand row of pillars.

Tom immediately jumped up and ran after them. One of the priests turned and tried to block his way, but he easily dodged past him and ran on, following the dim ripple of billowing blue robes just ahead.

Beyond the row of pillars, Tom glimpsed yet another arched doorway and figures disappearing into it, so he ran as fast as he could towards it. But just as he got there a stout wooden door slammed shut in his face.

Madge had been abducted!

Chapter Twenty-Seven
The Keepers of the Secret

For several moments Tom stood there, banging on the door. A moment later he was joined by Quenrie, Yentsilbor and the three knights.

"What foolishness!" said Pailtac glowering down at Tom. "Your captain is a foolish and arrogant woman! The priests will never forgive her blasphemy!"

"All she did was just stand there," protested Tom.

"And if you wanted her to worship their Flame-gods, you should have warned her!" said Yentsilbor testily.

Pailtac grunted, scowling. Then he lifted his mailed fist and banged on the door. Behind them, the flame-show had ended. The sanctuary was once again in virtual darkness.

Finally the door opened just slightly and the grumpy face of one of the priests appeared. Pailtac pushed impatiently past him, followed by his comrades.

"Where is Tisnectis?" he shouted angrily at the priest. "How dare he drag off the Emissary from beyond the White Snows? He will pay for this when the Council of Knights next meets!"

As they pushed their way past the priest, Tom spotted through a doorway to their right a large room which lay directly behind the altar. He had little time to take in what he saw there, but there appeared to be some sort of device on a table, a collection of mirrors with, at their centre, some sort of tiny glass ball. An array of candles had been placed to one side of this assembly, which presumably had created some of the light and colour which then reflected from the glass in the direction of the hanging curtain. But that was all that Tom saw. Suddenly, the grumpy little priest rushed past him and hastily slammed the door shut.

The others, meanwhile, had swept down the passage straight ahead, with Pailtac continuing to utter threats and bang on doors. Tom followed as quickly as he could. He had no desire to be left by himself among the seemingly demented monks in blue robes.

They burst into the room at the end of the corridor. A number of the blue-robed priests were there, busy cleaning what looked like some sort of scientific apparatus, thin metal pipes and glass beakers. Across this room was another door, only this one, unlike anything else in this ramshackle building, was neat and compact. And made of metal.

"Sir knight!" shouted one of the priests, trying to block the way. "You cannot go in there!" Other priests rushed to join him in blocking the doorway.

"Then where is Tisnectis? Take me to him or I shall break down this door with my bare hands!"

The priests all started to gabble angrily at Pailtac and his companions, gesticulating wildly and pointing to the metal door and shaking their heads as if it were blasphemy even to look at it.

Finally Pailtac drew his sword and striding over to the metal door, hit it with the sword's butt. There was a loud, resounding clang, which echoed alarmingly in the hidden space behind.

"Take me to Tisnectis!" Pailtac roared.

There was complete silence for a few seconds. Then an ugly little priest stepped forward.

"He is this way," he said meekly, indicating a side door to the left. "We shall take you to him immediately… But you do understand that it is sacrilege to enter the Inner Place, where the Holy Shoderim himself worked!"

"A plague on your inner places and holy shudderers!" growled Pailtac angrily. But he followed the priest as he led the way through the side door. Tom and the others hurried after them.

They came to a large room, evidently some sort of recreation or common room. There, to their surprise, they found Madge in apparently earnest but amicable conversation with her recent accuser, Tisnectis.

"You mean you achieve the different shades by slightly altering the refinement process?" Madge was saying.

"Indeed," replied Tisnectis, obviously warming to his subject, and to the woman who had so recently defied the demands of his religion. "We have a number of differing methods of refining the liquid that we pump from the earth – what is it you called it – oil? And each one of them produces a fuel which gives a different colour of flame. We have thirty-two different shades, but only three are what are considered 'pure' – the blue, pink and yellow that you saw in the sanctuary. These are our 'sacred' colours."

"And do the different types of fuel have differing qualities in other ways, as well? For example, do some burn more fiercely than others?"

"Yes, as a matter of fact they do…"

"Tisnectis, remember yourself!" barked Pailtac. "Remember that these people are strangers!"

Tisnectis looked up at him with innocent blue eyes. "But friend Pailtac, did I not just hear you say a few minutes ago that these were our honoured guests from beyond the Eternal Snows? And that they must not be ill-treated?"

"Yes, but that was when I feared you might try to do some evil experiment on her. We have every interest in keeping Captain Ont-Maj in good health. She operates the flying machine on which we came to your depressing swamp, and which can be of great service to our cause."

"Really!" said Tisnectis, his blue eyes flashing with genuine interest. "I have always been fascinated by the possibilities of flying machines. Tell me, friend Ont-Maj, on what principles is your invention based?"

And he and Madge launched into a technical conversation on the principles of flying. Pailtac interrupted them in irritation.

"Captain Ont-Maj did not come here to discuss your theories, Tisnectis. She is interested to know if your holy liquids might be able to feed her flying invention… Do you think that possible?"

Tisnectis suddenly became very serious. He scratched the wispy strands of hair on the side of his head as if perplexed, muttering to himself in some incomprehensible language. Finally he turned to Madge.

"It is a most unusual request. We do not normally allow the use of the sacred liquids for anything but the highest purposes. Since the departure of the Holy Shoderim… who had his own plans and uses for the sacred liquids… we have devoted ourselves entirely to the honour and adoration of the Great Secrets. However… since your invention seems to be of so miraculous a nature, I feel sure it has a lot of sacred merit too. Indeed, who knows, it may be one of those new revelations of the Great Secrets Themselves which we have been told to expect. Pray, how is it that you think the holy liquids can serve your machine?"

Madge explained as best she could. Tisnectis listened gravely, clearly engrossed.

"This is indeed extraordinary!" he exclaimed at last. "Such a fascinating and practical use for the liquids would, I feel sure, be profoundly pleasing to the Great Secrets, in all Their manifestations. It would also greatly expand our understanding of Their ways and Their will for us, Their servants. It seems to me," he said, turning towards Pailtac, "that this is a use of the liquids much worthier than that which you, milord, have in mind for them!"

Pailtac was clearly taken aback by this public rebuke. But his embarrassment quickly changed to anger. "How can you say that?" he spluttered. "Can there be a cause more sacred than to combat the unholy infidel the Skomiar? In any case, Captain Ont-Maj needs the holy liquids to help us in our great crusade!"

Tisnectis looked at Madge, clearly a little disappointed. "Is this true?" he asked.

Madge pulled a face. "We *have* offered to help the Knights in trying to bring the Skomiar to their senses," she said apologetically. "But this is not the main goal of our travels – which is to expand our knowledge of the Great Secrets… though we call them by a different name…"

Tisnectis, perhaps fortunately, did not probe this statement any further. He seemed satisfied by Madge's explanation and without further ado rose and stepped to the door, signalling for them to accompany him.

They followed the strange blue figure back to the room with the metal door through which they had previously been forbidden to pass. The other blue-robed priests were still there, huddled in groups discussing the recent happenings. When they saw Tisnectis leading the strangers towards the metal door, their murmuring gave way to an astonished silence. But they made no attempt to stop the outsiders from approaching the door.

Tisnectis, apparently now convinced that Madge was a genuine worshipper of the Great Secrets, drew a strange, curved key from under his robes and opened the door.

"Please enter," he said. "This is the Testing Chamber."

The door gave on to a most extraordinary room.

It was filled with a row of what appeared to be giant vats connected by a complicated network of pipes. It all looked like part of some enormous illicit distillery. Some of the pipes were made of rough, unpolished metal, while others seemed to be of a surprisingly sophisticated transparent plastic. The plastic pipes seemed to be bringing some sort of liquid substance from beyond the far wall, which again was made of an astonishingly smooth material, totally unlike the rough stonewalls elsewhere in the building.

"Do you get the impression," Madge muttered to his companions, "that we've got several different levels of technology here?"

She indicated the rough metal pipes leading to a row of taps in front of the vats. They were as bent and uneven as the plastic pipes beyond the vats were smooth and regular, and in places the metal pipes were leaking, leaving heavy stains on the rough earth floor. The whole room was filled with a pungent smell, very similar, Tom decided, to the smell of your average roadside petrol station.

The room was lighted by a series of windows above the vats, again clean and regular, and through them Tom could see that the far side of this 'Testing Chamber' gave onto the smooth dome they had seen from outside.

"Does that smell seem familiar to you?" asked Madge, turning to Tom.

"Definitely!" said Tom. "I'd say it was… what do you think… unleaded 95?!"

Tisnectis went to one of the taps and poured some clear, glistening liquid into a rough stone tankard. He brought it back to Madge.

"Could this be the sort of liquid you are looking for?"

Madge took the cup and smelt the liquid. She raised his eyebrows.

"It could well be!" she said in astonishment. "You're right, Tom, it's certainly gasoline of some sort!"

"You mean we can use it in the Goodcheer?" asked Tom eagerly.

Madge frowned. "Well, I don't know about that. She's a bit fussy about what she drinks. But we've certainly got something here approaching her normal diet! What have you got in the other taps, Tisnectis?"

"The different varieties of the holy liquids. Some lighter than this, some thicker."

"Can I have some of each? I would need to test this fuel to see if it's suitable for my engine."

The elderly man thought for a while and then excused himself and headed for a door in the smooth wall on the far side of the room.

"He will have to consult with his colleagues, the specialists," said Pailtac. "They are the people who draw the pure liquid from the juice of the ground."

"Ah, so you have specialists. Well, why don't we consult them ourselves?" said Madge, setting off for the door through which the technician had disappeared.

At once Kotz and Erash leaped past her and drew their swords, barring her way.

"That is not possible," said Pailtac coldly. "Nobody consults the specialists except the Blue Priests. If you went through that door, you would automatically condemn yourself to death, or worse!"

Madge shrugged and accepted Pailtac's decision as final. Pailtac himself, obviously embarrassed by the brusqueness with which he had just spoken, suggested they retire to the crude blue priests' common room to await the verdict of the 'specialists'.

When they arrived at the shabby refectory, however, Pailtac excused himself and his two companions, saying they had to meet someone else in a different part of the castle – to discuss important matters which did not directly concern Tom and his friends. And off they went without further discussion.

Bridget and Quenrie exchanged glances. What, Tom wondered, could these 'important matters' be?

The taciturn but respectful servant who had served them earlier brought Tom and his friends drinks.

"What do you think?" asked Tom. "Will the stuff they refine here really fuel the Goodcheer?"

"I don't know," said Madge, "and won't know until we've tried it out."

"Do you get the impression," Tom asked, "that the Knights want something else from the liquids, quite apart from the fact it might propel the airship?"

"Indeed I do. Just what it is isn't clear, but I bet it's got something to do with war," Madge replied.

Quenrie gave one of his grunts. "There are rumours," he said, "that the Knights are developing some terrible sort of weapon, one that spreads fire over their enemy in battle."

"A flame-thrower!" exclaimed Tom in horror. "But those have been banned for a long time in the…" He almost said "real world", but then looked at Quenrie, found that he looked very real indeed and said no more.

"You could call it that," said Quenrie, suddenly seeming very weary. "But by all the fatheads of Fengwyn, whatever it is, I do not think it is very pleasant!"

The servant returned to say that both the Holy Tisnectis and the lord knights would be delayed in their discussions, and that he was to show them to a place where they could rest. Accordingly he led them to some simple accommodation near the refectory, equipped with crude bedsteads. Despite the roughness of the furniture Tom, exhausted by the day's adventures, soon went to sleep.

Was he imagining it, or was something or someone pulling at his sleeve and trying to wake him up.

"Tom, Tom!" came Quenrie's voice. "Wake up, I have something to tell you."

"Wodizt?" asked Tom, unwilling to leave the comfortable nest of his sleep.

"The word! The word in the flame…"

"Wotword? Wotflame? Wotcha talking 'bout?"

"The word key! The word you need to make known the writing! I have it! I went back up to the chapel and looked at the big cloth between the lights!"

"Mhm?"

"Do you believe? The word is called GLITH… It is our word for…"

"…Light!" mumbled Tom.

"Do you not think that is suitable for your reading the codes?"

Tom didn't reply. But he smiled with pleasure and fell back into his world of cosy dreams.

Chapter Twenty-Eight
Kalmom's Message 9
Pageya's Illness

"Hm, we're obviously missing a bit," muttered Tom as they pored over the text on the table in the refectory. "But this is the only bit that I could decipher with 'Glith' as the key word."

"The key word for the earlier bits must be in some other chapel or temple," said Quenrie.

"Whatever… let's get on with it!" said Madge. "What does it say?"

"I took the child to Thifa first of all, to that blessed isle where evil is kept at bay by the very goodness of its inhabitants…

But after a while I realised that I was bringing danger to those good people by my very presence. And by keeping the child with me. I knew I must move on, and keep moving, to try and outwit Vencengea, her growing number of associates and her totally unnatural power over the elements…

We moved from place to place, all over the Realm. Sometimes we stayed with Durbote and Elbevire, high up on the Plateau at Fytanas. And sometimes, as the child grew older, I left her in the hands of these my kinsfolk and other trusted friends to whom I confided her secret.

The child never complained. Indeed over the years she developed a quite remarkable aptitude for the principles of the Balance. She would always weigh things up carefully before giving an answer and showed a real talent for guessing other people's feelings or opinions.

That period of my life, despite all the endless wandering, I remember as one of the most blessed. I was happy with the child, though it was not my own. And a new Broadlord had come to the throne, my good friend Voel, who began, as the Grey Pestilence became more venomous in its poisoning of the land and the people, to combat its effects as best he could. It had become a real curse, laying waste the rich lands around Orotworm, and sapping both the people's will and their enthusiasm for life. For a while, under his guidance, the attacks of the Grey Matter seemed to be held in check, and then grow weaker, less threatening. And the people began, once more, to hope…

But how often, when things seem to be going too well, the Fates bring unexpected and unwelcome changes to our lives. In this case they worked through the Skomiars and their would-be prophet, Xaram-Ninel. It was at this juncture that Xaram and his hungry Skomiar hordes chose to invade the Plains of Tworm.

Pageya and I were staying at that moment in the Mephadore, which we did from time to time, disguised as a servant and his daughter. The Skomiar took the city's rulers by surprise. The Broadlord was on a visit to the other end of his kingdom, near the Crystal Lake, when it happened. The Skomiar cavalry moved swiftly across the plains, capturing one citadel after another along the banks of the Traa. Voel only just managed to get back into Orotworm with his bodyguard before Xaram and his rabble were at the gates, demanding its surrender.

There were those who would have acceded to their demand. Nightly the Skomiar brought before the city walls the heads of nobles and dignitaries whom they had slain, 'as a warning to all the Oppressors of the Realm', as Xaram's heralds proclaimed.

'They say, Sire, they will go on killing until we come to terms,' said the then Chancellor, Nechembril.

'And you think,' replied the Broadlord, that they will stop killing if we do surrender. It will be our heads then on those poles outside the walls!'

There followed a long and bitter siege, during which we were starved of supplies by the Skomiar rebels. There was a terrible hunger in the city, and we in the Mephadore also suffered from it. To make matters worse, the attacks of the Pestilence began with renewed vigour. Many citizens died of starvation and disease. Many more fell seriously ill with maladies we had never seen before. One of those was my beloved Pageya...

She stopped eating even what little food there was. At first I thought it was out of sympathy with those poor people in the city who had even less than we had. She had always been able to empathise with others, more than any other person I know. But if that is how it began, it soon became a real physical illness. She became very pale and would sink into deep reveries, from which it was difficult to rouse her. Sometimes, during the night, she would walk in her sleep, or during the daytime wander round in a daze... That is, while she still could walk...

And she started to say the most extraordinary things. She would talk in quite definite sentences about 'the Lost Ones' and how she had to find them.

'I have seen them, the dear and lost ones,' I remember her saying. 'I must find them again, and then we shall all be happy.'

And there were many more things, which seemed to suggest some deep and troubled message that she was trying to pass on to us, but I was not sure I understood her words. There was something about 'looking in at my little self'... I recall that phrase quite clearly. And she also said she wanted to 'make everything so that no one will worry'.

I thought again about her birth and whose child she was. I had always wondered about the identity of her father. But short of interrogating Vencengea herself, which clearly was out of the question, there was no way I could find the truth.

Sometimes I wondered whether she had not inherited some genetic illness from her father, whoever he was. At other times I was convinced she was in touch with some unseen force which was telling her things, inspiring these bizarre thoughts in her mind... Rather like the sectarians who claimed they heard 'voices'.

I dismissed this idea. In my more rational moments I simply did not believe it...

Pageya would have died had it not been for the Yenomi...

...Yes, I find it difficult to acknowledge it now, because I am no great admirer of these knights and their superior ways. But it was they who relieved the siege and put to fight the Skomiar...

And they never thereafter allowed Voel the Broadlord to forget it. From the time of the siege onwards the Realm, or at least the part of it which was not directly under the control of the Skomiar, was ruled in effect by the Silver Knights' Grand Council, not by the Broadlord or the Citizens' Convention which he had set up to advise him.

But I digress... Pageya, to my immense relief, recovered. With the help of ample food and daily nursing, she slowly regained her strength. I took her back to the Community on the beautiful Isle of Thifa on the Crystal Lake. There we would walk among the groves of fruit trees, which thanks to the care of the brothers and sisters of the Community were still not blighted by the Greyness. And on days when the weather was reasonable we would sit and gaze out towards the giant volcano of Fles, which was still visible looming over the island on occasional days. Or we would spend time in prayer and contemplation in the little chapel I had constructed near what I called my 'lair', overlooking the lake...

But she was never quite the same simple, unspoilt child again. There was something secretive and mysterious about her, hidden depths which I had not noticed before. She could still be very cheerful and affectionate, and was still very responsive to other people – to their kindness and also to their suffering. But she had become altogether more introverted and thoughtful. Also she suffered more...

And she had lost her memory.

At least, that is what seemed to have happened. She no longer knew my name, for example, although she seemed to relate to me as a familiar person. I can laugh at it now, so many years later... but we played a game to try and guess what my name was, and she usually got it wrong! So it came about that, for her, I had several names...

In the end, I came to the firm conviction that she was the victim of some witchcraft or sorcery, the source of which was probably her mother, Vencengea! What else could explain it, this total refusal to acknowledge my name?

I thought back to the project which Shoderim had started at the Fortress of Niur. It had all revolved around the projection of images, impressions and thoughts... Maaniriv had a word for it – he called it telepathy. Such a curious word. But it was more than just the projection of thoughts from one mind to another – that had been quite a common practice among the sages of the Realm, from time immemorial. What Shoderim and then Vencengea had sought to do was go one-step further. They wanted to READ other people's thoughts and also

CONTROL the minds of others. They said it was for the good of their souls, to prevent them from harbouring evil intentions…

But who was to judge when thoughts were evil or when thoughts were good? That was the question that neither Shoderim nor Vencengea seemed eager to answer…

Chapter Twenty-Nine
The Storm

Tom woke the next morning to find Quenrie once more tugging at his sleeve.

"Tom, Tom, come quickly. Ont-Maj and Tisnectis are going to test the fire jars!"

Intrigued by this news, Tom dressed quickly and followed Quenrie down to the main courtyard of the castle. There they found Madge and Tisnectis, with several of his blue-robed assistants. The specialists had loaded several bizarrely shaped canisters on to a rude cart pulled by a squat animal that looked like a cross between a pig and a mule. With a curious honking noise, it set off through the great entrance gate and down the slope to the watery plain beyond.

The airship was still moored where they had left it, tied to the sturdy boughs of some strange, white-barked thorn-trees half a mile or so from the Fortress of Niur (or the Tortures of Manure, as Madge had taken to calling it). They all climbed up to the gondola and hauled several of the jars up after them.

After some intricate procedure with the fuel feed into one of the Goodcheer's engines, Madge was ready to try the various types of fuel in the canisters.

"If the worst comes to the worst, we can always fly back on one engine," she commented philosophically. "It's possible, if slow!"

The engine was at first not at all happy with the mix fed to it and coughed and spluttered and wheezed in a most unhealthy manner. Madge sighed.

"This could take quite a while," she muttered.

The sun was rising higher in the sky, and as it did so, the wind picked up too. The gondola began to buck and sway in a most unpleasant way. Tom saw that Quenrie was beginning to look quite alarmed, so he helped the little man down the rope ladder and they went to take shelter in a grove of the stunted trees nearby. Madge remained in the gondola with Tisnectis and two of his helpers.

The wind was not a refreshing one. It was warm and carried a dusty grit down from the barren hills beyond the marshes. And its gusts and eddies whipped up the sand which was already plentiful in the bleak landscape around them. Tom and Quenrie lay with their backs against two of the gnarled trunks. From time to time their reverie was interrupted by a further attempt to get the port engine going on a variant of its new cough mixture.

Quenrie appeared to be dozing off.

"How far is it to this place Orotworm?" Tom asked suddenly.

Quenrie gave a small start and opened his eyes.

"Mm… ha… Probably at least two days. On horseback. Why do you ask?"

"Well it strikes me that if the Goodcheer doesn't take to any of the cocktails that Tisnectis is offering, then we may well have to get there by foot."

"Hm, yes… or on horseback. Not always comfortable, but less tiring than on foot. But why do you want to go there? I suspect that Pailtac and his friends would want to take us back to Tekram."

"Oh, I don't know. Curiosity maybe. It sounds rather grand, the chief city of the Broadlord."

Quenrie's eyes took on a dreamy expression.

"Yes," he said softly. "It is grand, and wonderful, and the last hope for us, I suspect."

Tom was going to ask exactly what he meant by this, but at that moment there was a shout from the gondola and they saw Madge waving at them through one of the cabin windows.

"I think we've got it!" she called triumphantly. "Listen! The engine sounds just right, doesn't it?"

And it did, Tom decided.

Madge descended from the gondola, wiping her hands on an old rag. She was humming contentedly to herself.

"We can go where we like now! My main worry has been overcome."

They heard quarrelsome voices and looking up towards the ragged outline of the castle they saw Pailtac and his comrades descending, clearly annoyed that they had not been informed of the morning's procedures. In spite of the heat, they were still wearing chain mail under their colourful tunics, and clearly they were not used to walking anywhere. When they arrived, hot and sweating, they appeared very disgruntled.

"Why did you not tell us you were doing the tests?" the irascible Kotz demanded.

Madge smiled sweetly at him. "I was told you were snoring away, peaceful as lambs and I didn't want to interrupt your beauty sleep," she said.

"Have you found the burning liquid that your air vessel needs?" asked Erash, who alone of the three seemed interested in the airship's technology.

Madge and Tisnectis smiled at each other and nodded.

Pailtac immediately took charge.

"Then if your machine is working again, we must move on as soon as possible. Reknab will want us to scout out the land for the coming battle."

"You're determined to have this battle, aren't you, Pailtac?" Madge commented drily. "It wouldn't do to try and actually negotiate with the Skomiars!"

Pailtac gave her a withering look, but he looked uncomfortable. There was clearly something else he wanted to say, but was reluctant to do so. Finally he leant over to Tisnectis and whispered in his ear.

"Commander Pailtac asks if your ship can also carry a special, er, appliance, to show to the other army commanders," said Tisnectis.

At that moment several more Specialists arrived from the castle on a cart which carried some sort of heavy machine draped in a cloth.

Madge frowned, and when the machine reached them, she went over to it and whipped off the cover. Beneath lay a metal canister, attached at one end to a flexible pipe which itself ended in a sort of nozzle. At the top of the canister, where it was linked to the pipe, was a lever.

"As I thought!" exclaimed Madge. "A flame-thrower! There is no way, Comrade Pailtac, that I am going to take this contraption in my airship."

Pailtac looked puzzled rather than angry.

"It's too dangerous," Madge went on. "If you tried to use it, you would burn a great hole in the side of my ship! And then it would simply come tumbling to the ground... Besides, it's a weapon, and my ship is a civilian ship. It's not licensed to carry weapons."

Pailtac looked at his comrades in bafflement.

"It's against the Geneva Convention!" Tom put in, hoping this would impress the Yenomi knights. Madge ignored him.

"If I were found carrying weapons of mass destruction like this," – *she does exaggerate sometimes,* thought Tom – "I would lose my licence to drive an airship. I'd be banned, forbidden for the rest of my life!"

The irascible Kotz now stepped forward, his right hand grasping the hilt of his sword. Pailtac had to hold him back. And then the Chief Specialist, Tisnectis, came to Madge's rescue.

"It really is not very safe, Commander Pailtac, to carry this liquid in such a canister on the flying craft. If it is thrown about by the wind, or becomes too hot..."

"But you carry a lot of it already, to feed the engine," retorted the red-faced Kotz. "Or are you telling me that we already risked being burned alive by setting foot in this foolish machine?" He waved his hand at the Goodcheer.

"The fuel for the engines is in special containers, made so that it cannot burn," explained Madge, more calmly, sensing that she might now be winning the argument. "This thing" – she indicated the flame-thrower – "could explode at any time..."

"Because of the altitude!" Tom added, trying to be helpful.

Kotz was furious. But Pailtac restrained him and finally he and Madge came to a compromise. They would leave the flame-thrower contraption behind on condition that they set off immediately for Teivos. It could be transported overland, and when the time came, they could discuss ways in which it could be carried by the flying machine, perhaps in canisters like the ones that carried the fuel...

Madge pointed out that they would not reach Teivos that day, since half the hours of daylight had already passed. They would probably have to stop somewhere even before they got to Orotworm, let alone Teivos, if the maps she had been shown were any guide. Kotz continued to swear under his breath, but Pailtac merely frowned and said he understood.

"There is a fortress at Derat, half way to Teivos if one takes a direct route. We can stop there. I know the Lord Retrab, who is lord of those lands..."

So it was decided. Some provisions were brought down from the castle, and Tisnectis arranged for several canisters of the new fuel to be carried down as well. It was with some difficulty that these were lifted up to the gondola and emptied into the Goodcheer's tanks, but finally, in the middle of the afternoon, it was done. They were ready to leave.

Tom was prey to very mixed emotions. On the one hand he felt elation that they had discovered a source of fuel and no longer had to feel they were prisoners of this strange and frightening land. The other side of the coin was that they were now committed to playing a role, however peripheral, in the coming battle.

They made their farewells with Tisnectis, who clearly would have enjoyed having them stay longer, such was his delight at meeting people who took such an informed interest in his work. But Pailtac was adamant. The three knights clambered laboriously up the ladder into the gondola, and Tom helped Quenrie up after them.

Madge set both engines running, the assistants on the ground undid their moorings and they were off again.

Madge guided the Goodcheer up and over the jagged towers and roofs of the Fortress of Niur. Tom was not sorry to see the last of the forbidding edifice. For some reason it filled him with a quite irrational dread.

Soon they had left the desolate area bordering the marshes and were sailing along over a fertile plain which stretched endlessly on all sides. Here there were frequent villages and small towns. There were pastures and ploughed fields, though not many of the latter. A lot of arable land seemed to have been left fallow, as if the farmers had lost the will to tend and cultivate them.

And there was dust everywhere! Or was it the remains of the apparently frequent attacks of the Pestilence which, they had been informed, plagued this region – so close to the Crystal Lake and the looming presence of Fles.

The wind had died down, but the atmosphere had become very misty. Tom found he could no longer actually see the huge volcano which he knew dominated the horizon to their right. But he was continually aware of its presence. The mist in that direction was ominously dark. The one thing he thought he did see from time to time, a seemingly a very long way across the plain, was the dull glint of water. That, Tom presumed, was the inappropriately named Lake of Crystal.

Tom became aware that Madge, at the controls, was not happy.

"What's the problem, Madge?" asked Tom. Pailtac and his companions were strapped in their seats and out of earshot.

Madge gave him a solemn look. "Are you looking forward to getting involved in this battle of theirs?" she said.

"Not exactly," Tom replied. "But we won't actually be in the thick of the fighting, will we?"

"No matter. We'll be giving one side the advantage over the other. And judging by what we saw back at Wesomethe, when the Knights made mincemeat of those hairy horsemen, the Knights don't exactly need many more advantages. I've an ominous feeling there's going to be a terrible slaughter, and we'll be partly responsible."

"It will not be your fault, Ont-Maj," Quenrie assured her from his seat just behind the controls. "This battle would have taken place in any case. And if it is all over very quickly, surely that will mean less killing, not more?"

But Madge was not consoled.

They were heading, the three Knights confirmed, in the direction of the great city of Orotworm, over which they would have to pass to reach Teivos. Tom felt his curiosity grow as they sailed closer to the metropolis.

But now there was reason for further concern. The horizon in the direction they were going was very murky, and to one side, to the southeast towards the lake, they could now see what appeared to be an enormous thundercloud. As they moved onwards over the plain, it seemed to grow in size and advance rapidly towards them.

Madge nodded in that direction. "Thunderstorm," she murmured. "Or maybe even one of those Pestilence things. Either way, we may be in for some dirty weather. I'll try to avoid it by moving further north.

But the knights detected the change of direction and protested. Kotz drew his sword and approached Madge menacingly.

"Lord Pailtac commands you will keep to the same course as before!" he barked.

"Tell Lord Pailtac that if we do we'll fly into a huge storm and my ship will be torn to pieces!"

And she stuck to her northerly course. But even with the change of direction the white cloud was still growing closer and very much bigger. Tom could see it really was a thunderhead, with great bulbous masses of cloud piling up high into the heavens, while underneath all the whiteness, at its base, was a broad band of darkness.

Pailtac himself came forward this time. Madge pointed to the cloud without a word. Pailtac looked out at it, and even his proud face seemed to blanch.

"Yes, do all you can to sail round it," he said, his voice slightly hoarse. "Or land if you have to."

The giant white thundercloud in front of them had now spread across the whole horizon.

"Better go down and look for shelter," said Madge, and she turned the Goodcheer's nose away from the threatening storm. They immediately started to lose height.

But it seemed they might already be too late. The wind was rising, and they were buffeted by a sudden squall which came out of nowhere. As they eased downwards, another sudden burst of wind came, and another, and now Madge was fighting with the controls.

"We're being pulled back towards the cloud," she muttered.

It was true. The menacing blackness which lay under the cloud was coming closer all the time, and though they were losing height, they were also being driven backwards, towards the massive storm which obscured the entire horizon.

"May the Lords of the High Palace have mercy on us," whispered Quenrie in evident terror.

Tom peered downwards. He could now see trees and bushes beneath them, tossing wildly in the wind. The Goodcheer was now bucking wildly as it struggled to make progress against the tempest.

Then Tom saw something that made his stomach turn. They were passing over a long, uneven line of broken sand and suddenly the turning, twisting trees below had given way to a grey, foam-flecked expanse of water.

They had been blown out over the lake!

Where now were they going to land? From what Tom had learnt earlier, the lake must be anything from twenty to thirty miles wide!

The fury of the wind was increasing all the time, and the airship shuddered and bucked like a wild horse trying to shake off some troublesome rider. All the time it was being driven further out over the angry waters of the lake.

And they were dropping. Madge seemed unable to take the airship upwards, out of the screaming wind. They were no more than a few hundred feet now above the water. They could see the lake beneath them, whipped into a veritable frenzy by the storm, its surface almost totally white from the driving spray.

Tom shivered and closed his eyes.

They were racing along now at an enormous speed, totally out of control. At least the terrible bucking motion had stopped, though the small cabin was still shivering and swaying. Heavy rain started to splatter against the windows.

"Where is it taking us?" shouted Tom above the tumult. "What is there in this direction?"

Quenrie simply looked grim and shook his head.

Pailtac was sitting, clutching at this seat, apparently petrified. Kotz was staring in horror out the window at the foaming waters. Erash was sitting forward in his seat, hunched, intoning some Tekramian prayer for salvation.

"There is nothing in this direction." Quenrie's voice was barely audible. "Only the Lake of Crystal Dreams with its islands… And the volcano… Fles."

"It is the evil spirit of Fles Itself that is taking us," moaned Erash. "It will devour us. It is the reward for all my sins! The storm is the fury of all the dead souls that I have killed!"

Pailtac, terrified as he was himself, would have none of this. He barked something harsh at Erash, who sank back into silence.

Tom peered out again at the wild fury of the elements beyond his window. The rain lashed against the glass, and he watched, petrified, as the waves tumbled beneath them, only a few dozen feet below, their crests whipped and scattered as they rose out of the inky mass of the lake water, as if trying to catch at the fragile airship speeding along above them.

Then he looked ahead and almost froze with horror. Dead ahead, not more than half a mile away it seemed, there rose a dark shape, a solid impassable wall. They were speeding headlong towards it!

He yelled out loud.

Madge saw the wall ahead too. Immediately she tried to swing the airship round to face into the wind. It shuddered and bucked, but slowly, very slowly it did come round. Then Madge opened the throttle to its full.

But it was useless to try and battle against the gale. Though the Goodcheer's engines slowed their advance towards the dark mass, they were still being driven irrevocably towards it.

They were now facing back into the wind, and Tom could no longer see the dark wall. When he looked out of his window, all he could see were the angry waves below. Then he saw they were still going backwards, passing over a ribbon of thrashing water which marked a coastline.

"Into your seats!" shouted Madge. "Into your seats, with your belts on!"

The impact came a few moments later. It was not the enormous crash Tom had expected, but a jolt, and then the sensation of hands, many strong and cruel hands, tearing at the bottom of their cabin. Then they were free again, and he saw that they were surrounded by long branches, bare, leafless branches closing over them like the arms of so many hungry, grasping people.

There was another jolt, the cabin suddenly gave a jump, then twisted sharply and slammed into something with a heavy thud. Tom was thrown head first against the cabin wall. Everything swam before his eyes for a few seconds. And then he passed out.

Chapter Thirty
The Isle of Thifa

When he came to his senses, Tom found he was in a room which was totally white. The ceiling, the walls, the small table near a window, the two chairs either side of it, the sheets and covers on the bed where he lay, even the sort of nightshirt that he was wearing – all were of the most spotless, vivid white.

For a few moments Tom felt a sharp fear. Where was he? Why was he alone? He peered over the edge of the bed and found, to his relief, that the floor was not white. It was of a greenish colour, and over to one side, under a chair – which *was* white – was a pair of slippers which were of faded red. The discovery came to him as a relief. He was not, after all, dreaming. Nor, probably, was he in heaven.

But he did have a splitting headache, and his movements in the bed seemed to have started some sort of physical disturbance inside his brain, as if a number of overcooked vegetables were now swilling about inside his skull – like Brussels sprouts in a saucepan. The objects in the room began to swim before his eyes. As he sank back into oblivion, the fear and the loneliness returned.

When he opened his eyes the next time, there was a face looking down at him. It was the gentle, wrinkled face of a man perhaps sixty years old, sympathetic and concerned, as if he had bad news to tell and didn't know how to start.

"How are you feeling, boy?" said the man gently.

Tom tried to speak, but all that came out was something between a grunt and a low moan. He tried again and found that he was talking gibberish.

"Never mind. Do not try to speak if it is difficult. You need more rest."

Tom closed eyes once more.

He woke for a third time when it was dark. He could barely see the outlines of the objects in the room. The only light there was filtered through the shutters of a window at one side of the room which he had not noticed before. As he lay there, his head still feeling heavy and dull, he heard music.

It was a music made by the voices of men and women, and maybe children as well, a harmonious, calm sound that immediately made the spartan room where he lay seem warmer, friendlier, more human. The voices seemed to come from some distance, and he could not make out individual words. But he felt sure, for some reason, that they sang of hope, of friendship, of understanding. He suddenly felt a deep sense of comfort, and his earlier fears seemed irrational and groundless.

He must have slept deeply for a long time after that, because when he next woke his head felt clear and his body rested. It was daytime, and the room was once again bright, clear and pure. He lifted himself slowly on to one arm and tried to lift his legs out of the bed. He wanted to get to the window, to open the canvass blind that covered it and find out what sort of place it was where everything was so white and pure and the people produced such heavenly music. But the effort was too much for him. His head fell back on to the pillow, and it was only at that moment that he realised that it was swathed in a thick layer of bandages.

At that moment the door opened and the man with the kindly, concerned face came in. His face immediately showed shock, almost anger.

"Boy! What are you doing? You must not move!"

"I wanted to open the window. I want to know where I am," Tom said weakly. But the words, though softly spoken, were at least words and not the grunting noise he had made previously.

"Let me do it!" said the kindly man. He was dressed in a long white robe, and on his feet he wore roughly made sandals.

He released a catch and hoisted the blind, taking care it did not bang or clatter against the wall. Then he came back to the bed and helped Tom lift his head from the pillow and look outside.

What he saw was the most exquisite scene. It appeared to be a gently sloping amphitheatre of grass, overhung by gracefully bending trees – some sort of willows, he thought. In the background, all round the circular hollow, were high banks of shrubbery, azaleas perhaps or rhododendrons, their deep green leaves making a pleasant contrast with the lighter, brighter green of the grass and the trees. At the bottom of this bowl was a small lake or pond, with several benches around its rim. The breeze rippled the surface of the water and the drooping branches of the willows swayed at its command.

"It's beautiful," said Tom. "So restful and peaceful. Where are we?"

"We are on the Island of Thifa, also known as the Island of Dreams," said the man. "And my name is Ecape. And I know that your name is Tom, is it not?"

His heart leapt. "So you've spoken to my friends! How are they? Are they well?"

The man's face darkened, and at once Tom feared the worst. But then Ecape smiled a slow, sad smile and said:

"Your friends are fine now – though our friend… Let me see, your name for him, is it Quenrie? – has damaged his arm. And…" And he looked troubled again.

"And what?"

"Your ship… your flying machine… it is completely destroyed."

Somehow this news, serious as it was, did not seem to upset Tom very much. Maybe it was because he felt that, after all their adventures, they had ended up among good and concerned people, and this time the prospect of not being able to leave immediately did not trouble him unduly.

The door opened again and in walked Madge. Behind her, with his arm in a sling, came Quenrie. Tom also caught sight of Yentsilbor, lurking awkwardly in the doorway. Quenrie smiled warmly when he saw that Tom was conscious.

"Ho, my lad. You're looking a lot better than when we last visited you."

"Aye, Tom," Madge put in, "you had us a bit worried there, you with your cotton wool head. But Ecape here (she pronounced it Ee-cappy) tells us he thinks you'll be all right now."

Ecape nodded. "A bit more rest and he should be able to rise – perhaps in two or three days."

"It was the singing," said Tom. Madge and Quenrie looked at him blankly.

"I woke in the night and there was singing," Tom explained. "And after that, well, I just felt a lot better."

Ecape smiled as if he knew exactly what Tom was talking about. "A healthy and hopeful mind is a great healer," murmured Ecape as he turned to leave. "We shall have more singing this evening. Make sure you wake and listen!" He said this with a twinkle in his eye.

"I shall!" said Tom. "I'll look forward to it!"

*****

There was singing every evening. And when Tom was finally able to rise from his bed on the third day, with the swathe of bandages now reduced to a thin, slanting ring of white round his head, he found out who it was that made the sweet melodies he had heard.

Outside the door of his room was a small patio and a path leading off through the shrubbery. Ecape led the way along the path, with Tom following, leaning on Yentsilbor's arm. Pailtac and his two Yenomi companions, Tom noticed, were nowhere to be seen.

They turned a corner and there before them lay another hollow, also surrounded by shrubs and trees, only wider than the first. And it was full of people, people of all ages, dressed mainly in white and sitting on the grass round a small platform in the middle. As Ecape's group appeared, several of these people rose and came towards them.

"Welcome to our island," said a middle-aged woman with a careworn but kindly face. "We hope you are feeling better now."

"Your wounds seem to be healing," said a man. "We were very worried about you at one stage. Ecape kept us informed of how you were faring."

"Yes, we held you in our thoughts when we gathered to meditate," said another woman.

Tom felt overwhelmed. "Thank you, thank you," was all he could say, nodding around to as many of these good people as he could.

Ecape led them to the platform, where he introduced Tom to some of the elders of the community. They all welcomed him warmly and invited him to sit in a soft chair at the rear of the platform. Then Ecape spoke to the people, giving a short formal welcome to Tom.

And then they sang.

Tom held that singing in his mind for many months, indeed years, afterwards.

165

It was slow and restful, and yet at the same time full of a deep emotion. In his fragile state, tears came quickly to Tom's eyes as he listened, and he had to bow his head to hide them. What it was they sang he did not know. But whatever the words were, it brought a new optimism to his spirit.

After the singing, there was a short, silent meditation. And then the meeting broke up for supper. Tom was asked if he felt up to sitting with the others, and he said he would be glad to.

The refectory was nearby, down another slope in a small cluster of whitewashed buildings just below what appeared to be a ridge stretching between two summits. Away to the left, a couple of hundred feet below, Tom saw the dark and forbidding waters of the lake. The Island of Thifa consisted, it seemed, of a single steep-sided ridge between two peaks, with a number of gentler, wooded dells and hollows on either side. Tom was painfully aware that somewhere beyond the southern, higher peak lay the sinister mass of the huge volcano, though it was not actually visible from where they stood, and on a gloomy day like today would probably be totally hidden by cloud.

Much of the isle was covered in vegetation. Here, round the community buildings, it was mostly the azaleas and willow-like trees he had seen round his room in the neighbouring hollow. Further down towards the water these seemed to give way to a mixture of small oak trees and hazels.

"How... how are the leaves so green?" he exclaimed.

Ecape smiled. "You mean, how are they not destroyed by the Grey Ash?"

"Yes. It's a miracle! Everything else, much further away from the volcano than this, has been totally destroyed!"

"Alas, that sadly is true. But the leaves here have us to protect them. After every attack of the Pestilence, we have to work very hard. We wash down every tree, every bush. Women, men and children, old and young, work very hard at this. And occasionally we are helped, when the real rain comes, not the grey ash. But that, unfortunately, happens less and less often..."

Tom saw that the appearance of greenery which the shrubbery gave from a distance was misleading. The leaves on some of the plants were spotted and blemished. A number had withered altogether and been cut from the branches, evidently by members of the community.

"Yes, we do our best to protect the foliage," said Ecape. "But it is a huge effort – we are so close to the volcano – and often it is too much for us."

They had arrived at the Eating-House or Refectory. Tom said:

"So is this really the... the Island of Dreams? That's surely where Kalmom lived, at least for a while..."

"Yes, the Isle of Dreams, also known as Thifa," Quenrie nodded, a dreamy look in his eyes. "It was indeed a favourite refuge for Kalmom..."

He and Ecape exchanged a quick glance, almost as if Quenrie was warning the old man not to say any more.

"So we've tracked him down as far as here!" Tom insisted.

"You mean we've stumbled on his haunts quite by chance," Madge corrected him, "and with some amazing good luck!"

"So can you tell us about Kalmom?" Tom asked Ecape eagerly. "When he was last here? Where he went after he left? Whether he had discovered the way to this Opening, this Hidden Place he was looking for?"

Again Ecape smiled his gentle, slightly ironic smile. "We can tell you something." He glanced across at Quenrie again, but the seer simply nodded and smiled, so Ecape continued.

"Yes," he said, "some of us remember Kalmom very well. But he never imparted much of his thinking to other people, at least, not in those days… We shall talk about this later, after we have eaten!"

Chapter Thirty-One
Pascomonsi

The Refectory was a small hall and, like everything else on Thifa, it was whitewashed. There were little tables for two people only, as well as round family tables with places for five or six, and then longer ones where larger groups could mix.

The food was simple, a gruel made of some sort of grain, mixed with eggs, it seemed, and eaten with a few raw vegetables.

"We have little or no meat, apart from some chicken," the man sitting beside Tom explained. Tom discovered his name was Melac and that he was one of the Community's Elders. "All the fish in the lake have long ago disappeared, though we manage to keep a few in our ponds... for eating on special occasions."

After the meal, Tom was still feeling quite fresh, so they walked along the path between the two peaks, with Ecape and Melac as their guides. Climbing up the southern summit, they came to a platform that looked out over the lake towards the further shore.

But there was no sign that evening of the great volcano. Fles was hidden behind a pall of yellow-grey mist. The wind was much less fierce than on the day when they had crashed on the island, and the waves now lapped apathetically on the shore far beneath them. But all round the island there hung a curtain of the seemingly impenetrable, clinging mist.

Tom could not see anything in the direction where Ecape said the volcano should be. But when he looked to the right, far away across the gloomy waters of the lake, he could vaguely make out a dark shape on the horizon, only dimly visible through the misty atmosphere.

"What's that over there?" he asked, shivering slightly, he couldn't think why.

There was a silence before Melac replied.

"That is the island of Iprades," he said quietly, "also known as Isle of Shadows."

Tom shivered again.

"Isn't that where... Vencengea... Vencengea the sorceress lives?" asked Tom softly.

Ecape nodded and gave him a curious look. "So you have heard of Vencengea?" he said pensively.

"Yes indeed. And we have crossed swords with her too."

"Crossed swords?"

"Just an expression we use..."

"Yes, I think I understand it."

Suddenly, Tom felt he didn't want to be there any more, looking out over the lake. He turned back towards the community. The others followed.

By the time they had reached the first buildings Tom had recovered some of his cheerfulness. "Isn't it rather strange," he asked Ecape, "to have a mixed community of men and women? I mean most religious communities tend to separate the sexes into different monasteries or convents. And you are a religious community, aren't you?"

Ecape smiled. "We think of ourselves rather as a contemplative community, rather than a religious one. We don't deny religion, and in a sense, yes, we are religious. We believe in a Life Force, which we call the Good Force, which is seen, for example, in the love people show to one another but which is outside of ourselves. But formal religion has gained such a bad reputation, hasn't it – a reputation for one group with dogmatic inherited beliefs fighting with other groups with different dogmatic inherited beliefs. Whereas for us, religion – or the contemplative search, as we call it – is about looking for new things within reality itself, new things which underline the good things given by nature."

Tom thought about that for a few moments.

"But what about this question of a mixed community? Doesn't it create difficulties – misunderstandings between men and women and so on?"

Ecape laughed. "Why no, why should it? We don't force people to live in the Joint Community. Only those who find no problem living in the same house as the other sex, do so."

"But… don't people sometimes want to marry and set up their own house, apart from the others?"

"Yes indeed," replied Ecape. "But they have their own community, called the Conjugal House, which is down near the shore on the eastern side of the island. They have their own apartments there, though the children are looked after communally. It is the largest of the communities."

"You know also, don't you," asked Melac, "that we also have communities for people who… well, prefer the company of their own sex. Those communities are situated on either side of the northern peak. They are smaller than the Joint and Conjugal houses, but we do not criticise or interfere with their way of life. They choose to live that way, and the whole community accepts that."

Tom suddenly realised that he still had not seen Pailtac and his two companions, Kotz and Erash, since he regained consciousness. He asked whether they had decided to live in one of the other community houses.

Ecape smiled a wry smile. "The Yenomi warriors have camped themselves at the end of the island, the point closest to the plains of Tworm. We have allowed them to cut down some of the remaining trees there, to build a boat."

Melac frowned. "Yes, I still regret giving this permission, my friend Ecape… I know you argued that the sooner these warlike men leave the island, the better. But we have so little timber left…"

Ecape laid a hand on his friend's arm. "Do not fret over the timber, good Melac. With time, when the Pestilence ends, as it must someday, the trees will grow again…"

But Melac was not convinced. "They should have waited until some vessel lands at our shores. As it is, it will take them weeks to build anything strong enough to withstand the gales that cut us off from the mainland…"

"And Yentsilbor?" Tom asked. "Where is Yentsilbor?"

"Your Skomiar companion seems very unhappy," Melac said. "He has taken to wandering round the island talking to nobody. He too, it seems, is very anxious to leave the island as soon as he possibly can."

Tom nodded. "Yes, I can understand why. He knows that his homeland is threatened with invasion by a well organised enemy, and he wants to be there to try and prevent it happening."

That evening, after Tom had slept for a few hours, they met with the Council of Elders in a small house halfway down the hill towards the lakeshore.

The Council was made up of five men and four women, drawn from all ages. They were told that the numbers always had to be five and four, though sometimes the five were women and the four men. And elders, in spite of the name, did not have to be old. At least three of the nine had to be under thirty years old. Every three months four new members were chosen by all the community in a free vote, with four serving members retiring.

Though Ecape and Melac had heard of the newcomers' adventures from Madge and Quenrie, the rest of the Council apparently had not. They listened to Madge's account of their travels with great attention and sympathy.

"So you do not know what has happened to your companions," inquired a young woman on the Council, whose name was Pascomonsi, "the girl Pageya and her brother, and the girl from beyond the snows… I think you called her Bridget?"

"No," answered Tom. "We don't know what has become of them. We believe they escaped from the dungeon under the Nilmerk, in Teivos. But we have seen or heard no more of them since. No news of them had reached either Nirei or Tekram while we were there… We think they may still be with the Ineals near Teivos."

At this there was a murmur of concern from the Council members. "Even if they are not in Teivos itself," muttered one of the Councillors, shaking her head, "the Skomiar are on the whole not very good neighbours. You must try to get them away from there as soon as possible."

"Indeed," said Quenrie, his melodious voice ringing around the small vaulted room. Quenrie was treated with enormous respect by the community members, though when he spoke Tom saw some of them signalling to each other, as if they were trying to conceal something. "It was our intention to try and re-join them and take them from the vicinity of Teivos. But the storm blew us off route and brought us here."

"It is unfortunate," Ecape murmured, "that we have little contact with the mainland and it may be some time before you can leave us to renew your quest. We are much closer to the volcano side of the lake, but all the territory there, under the volcano, has been totally devastated by the Grey Ash and is uninhabited. Even the villages on the shore furthest from Fles, at the edge of the

170

Plains of Tworm, have been emptying over the last years, such is the deadly effect of the Ash. The people just cannot grow anything there anymore. We tried to encourage them by training them in contemplation and devotion, but their spirits had already been eaten away by the Pestilence."

"But you must have a boat that can take us back across the lake," Madge interrupted him. "Even quite a small boat? According to my friend Quenrie here it's no more than fifteen or twenty miles across to the mouth of the river which leads up to Orotworm, and then on to Teivos."

Ecape shook his head. "Alas, as I've tried to explain, my friend Moj, we have no boats at all on the island."

"Boats used to come from the mainland, that's true," continued Melac. "The village people came to ask our advice and encouragement. And they brought visitors, and we were glad to receive them. But we have no boats ourselves. You see, we've always tried to be self-sufficient on the island, not expecting or demanding anything from the mainlanders."

"This is crazy," retorted Madge, jumping up and pacing about round the little room. "You mean to say we're stuck here forever! I'll never be able to repair our airship without help from the mainland. And we need to get to this Broadlord that everyone talks about, to persuade him to help us find Bridget and Pageya, whether they're still in Teivos or somewhere else!"

There was an embarrassed silence. Tom felt awkward about Madge's angry outburst. The Councillors really did seem sympathetic, but they simply had no means of helping their unexpected guests.

Tom turned to the Councillors. "While we're on the island," he said, "would it be possible to find out more about Kalmom, who called himself the Wanderer? You have confirmed that he stayed here for some time. But where, for example, did he live? And did he leave any books or writings?"

There was a sudden silence. The Councillors looked at each other, and he saw one of them put one finger over her lips, as if encouraging the others not to say too much. But no one said anything. Then the young woman who had spoken earlier, Pascomonsi, leaned forward. "It was interesting what you said earlier about Kalmom and his story. I hardly knew him, when he was here... earlier. But I have heard so much about him. In fact, I now live in his old home, what he used to call his 'lair', and I have tried to study in his extensive collection of books. He left so many..."

Ecape exchanged a meaningful look with Quenrie, who pursed his lips and nodded. What is it they're hiding, these two? Tom wondered. But neither of them spoke.

"Kalmom had a collection of books?" asked Tom, suddenly alert. "Where? Can you take us there?"

Pascomonsi smiled happily.

"But of course I can. It is up beyond the southern mount, near the point." And she indicated the end of the island they had visited earlier.

"You can go there tomorrow, perhaps," said Melac, clearly relieved that the community was able to offer its guests some form of entertainment during a visit

171

which threatened to be a long one. "It's late now and I'm sure our young friend needs to rest."

Ecape, who seemed to be the doctor among the elders, nodded his agreement. "Pascomonsi can come and fetch you tomorrow morning after breakfast and take you to her home."

"You go by yourself, Tom," muttered Madge, who was standing near the Council chamber door, arms folded, drumming nervously with her fingers on her upper arms. "I'll be working down at the Goodcheer. It's down at the other end of the island. And I'll need Quenrie's help. None of these people seem to have a practical skill between them. We may be able, at the very least, to turn the gondola into some sort of boat, to get us off this godforsaken place!"

Tom smiled and rose gingerly to his feet. He was indeed feeling a bit dizzy. He bowed politely to the Councillors and thanked them for all their hospitality. Ecape took him and his friends back to their quarters.

Madge and Quenrie were living in guest rooms just next door to Tom's. On their way back Tom began to scold Madge for her grumpiness towards the Council members. But Quenrie stopped him.

"Do not fret, young Tom," he said. "These are good and patient people. They have faced the ferocity of the great Vulcan of Fles for many years and can surely tolerate a bit of rudeness from a red-haired alien!"

Madge stopped in her tracks and Tom thought for a moment she was going to start an argument. But in the end she merely threw back her head and gave a loud laugh.

"Ha! Red-haired alien! That's a good one. I'll have to tell that one to the people back home... when I get there. Ha, red-haired alien! I like it!"

And she walked on.

172

Chapter Thirty-Two
Kalmom's Lair

Pascomonsi came for Tom as promised the next morning and together they set off along the ridge path towards the southern mount.

The wind had risen during the night, and the bushes and trees on either side of the path were now tossing and swaying like wild things. Pascomonsi, who was strangely subdued, clutched her robe tight to her and looked out in the direction from which the wind was coming.

"Another of the dreadful storms is brewing, it seems," she said. "Each time they get worse and do more damage."

Indeed, on the side of the island which faced into the wind Tom saw ample evidence of previous storms. Several of the small trees on the slope to their left had been uprooted and lay sadly on their sides, their branches in a tangle. In other places, there was merely a hole where a tree had been and had presumably been cleared away by the tidy-minded islanders after being uprooted by one of the ferocious storms.

Just before they reached the last stretch of the climb up to the southern summit, a path led off to the left, round the side of the peak. Pascomonsi took this one. As they turned a corner in the track, they began to feel the full force of the tempest, blowing straight in from the lake. It became difficult even to stand upright. But they struggled on. The path now began to descend slowly, until finally it disappeared round a pile of rocks. They made their way round these boulders and came face to face with a strange little construction, built into the rock itself.

Its circular front, which appeared to be a single wide window, looked out over the restless waters of the lake and on a clear day must have afforded an impressive view of the volcano.

Pascomonsi led Tom up a short flight of steps and in through a small door beneath the broad window. They first entered a tiny vestibule and then a rather bigger room. This appeared to be Pascomonsi's living quarters. In one corner stood a simple bed, and on the other side of the room, near a small round window, a little stove and some cooking utensils.

"This is where the great man lived," said Pascomonsi. "He had simple needs and felt no need to live otherwise."

Tom looked at her questioningly.

"And you took it over when he left?"

Pascomonsi smiled.

"Let's say I am keeping it for him until he returns."

Saying no more than that, she climbed a short wooden staircase at the far side of the chamber and, opening a small square door at the top, disappeared through it.

Tom followed and found himself in a spacious room lit only by the wide semi-circular window they had seen from outside. The walls at the inner end of this room were lined with shelves stacked with a disorderly jumble of papers and books. In between the book stacks, and also placed randomly out across the floor, were cupboards and chests, many of them with their drawers lying open, also stuffed with an untidy mass of papers and pamphlets.

Only some of the books had covers and bindings. Others were apparently manuscripts rolled up like charts, held tight by ribbons and marked by a seal. Others still were no more than piles of paper sheets, bound together with string or what looked like leather bands. The whole thing reminded Tom of another room he had visited in the not too distant past, but just at that moment he couldn't think where that had been.

In the middle of the back wall there hung a magnificent map. Tom went over to it and started to decipher the inscription above it. He found it read:

"THE KNOWN WORLD, FROM THE SNOWY MOUNTAINS TO THE FIRES OF FLES, FROM THE ORANGE DESERT TO THE LOST COAST."

Tom stared at it for a while.

"It's just like a map I already know," he whispered. "It's as if it were drawn by the same hand…"

"I have kept this room exactly as he left it," said Pascomonsi, indicating the cupboards and shelves that towered crazily above them. "You said you were interested in looking for something. Where do you want to start your search?"

Tom turned towards the jumble of cupboards and papers piled over the floor.

"It's quite simple," he answered. "I don't really need to look at the books. I just need to know where his personal chapel was."

She looked at him blankly.

"Well, I mean, the place where he prayed."

"I am afraid," she said, "that I do not understand."

Tom was taken aback. He had been so sure there would be a chapel or sanctuary in Kalmom's layer.

"Well… what I am really looking for is a word, the word in the centre of a tapestry… or a picture… with the emblem of the coiled flame." He was embarrassed now. He had meant to impress Pascomonsi with his knowledge and wisdom, by simply going up to a tapestry and saying: *'That's the word!'* Now he was beginning to feel foolish.

"I know the symbol of the flame," Pascomonsi said helpfully. "It is associated with the doctrine of the Balance, which we also honour here on Thifa… But there is no such tapestry or picture here."

Tom obviously looked so downcast that Pascomonsi came over and laid her hand on his arm.

"Be not downhearted!" she said. "Perhaps we can find some indication in one of Kalmom's books."

"Perhaps," said Tom glumly. "Where do you recommend we start?"

Pascomonsi laughed. "I do not know. But first, let me brew some herb tea downstairs. I still have some. Then we can get down to work. I think I know where those volumes are that may help us most."

They sat with their tea at a bare table on the upper storey, by the window looking out over the lake. This, said Pascomonsi, was where Kalmom the Wanderer had often sat, or so she had heard, because she herself had been a very small girl when he was on the island and barely remembered him.

"What memories do you have of him?" Tom asked, eager to know as much as possible about the elusive seer.

All Pascomonsi could recall was a distant, rather unsmiling man with a well-trimmed beard. He had seemed old to her, though she thought he might not in fact have been more than forty years of age at that time. There was a sort of aura about him, she seemed to remember, an aura of mystery and solemnity. But also of purity. It sounded silly to put it that way, she knew, but that was her childhood impression.

The moment she remembered most clearly was when she was playing with a group of friends and he had passed nearby. One of her friends, a small girl like herself, had run up to him and offered him a posy of simple flowers she had picked from the rocks nearby. He had looked down at the girl, and Pascomonsi thought for one terrible moment that he was going to scold her friend for picking the wild flowers. But he had smiled, a sad, rather bleak smile, accepting her present and thanking her. And then he had walked on, the smile still on his face.

Pascomonsi went to one of the cupboards against the wall and selected several large but ragged tomes which she carried over to the table by the window.

"These are books where he writes about his childhood. It seems to me that if we are looking for guidance about his search for the fabled 'Place to Heal All Ills' this is a natural place to start."

Tom had learned to read some of the alphabet the Elonyms used, but was still not very good at reading the ornate script. And his knowledge of the language was little more than rudimentary, so he needed a lot of help from Pascomonsi to plough through the books. Pascomonsi had to admit that she too was perplexed by some of the texts. Kalmom, she said, had often employed words which she did not understand. On further examination however, Tom found that he recognised most of these words.

"Why, they're just plain English!" he exclaimed. "Look, here he uses the word 'Compassion'. And in this sentence 'Consideration'... Kalmom must have learned these words from his friend Manny Reeve."

Tom half-expected Pascomonsi to react in some way to the mention of Manny Reeve, or Maaniriv as Kalmom had called him. But her expression remained blank.

Together, Tom and Pascomonsi worked through the text of the first stout volume. What one of them did not understand, the other usually did. Most of this first book, Tom found, was a more detailed description of Kalmom's childhood and early years: his home village, his family, his early education...

Outside, the storm was growing ever stronger. The small trees beyond the window were bent almost double as fierce gusts from the direction of the volcano tore at them. Far below them the grey waters of the lake were now specked and lined with foam, and mountainous waves came rolling ceaselessly from out of the misty horizon.

All that morning they toiled over the dusty volumes, looking for some indication of a message, some hint of guidance from the beautiful, flowing lines of script. Tom learned a lot more about Kalmom's childhood, his home village on the plains, his physical and spiritual development. But it all seemed to be straight narrative. No single word stood out from the rest.

Tom was still feeling the effects of the blow to his head, and as time wore on, he became increasingly tired. Towards midday, with the gale still howling round the small house in the rock, he lay down on a divan near the table to sleep, while Pascomonsi continued to transcribe passages from Kalmom's writings she thought might be useful or instructive, so that Tom could read them later…

When he awoke, she was still bent over the table pouring over some of the rolled parchments they had seen earlier. The light outside was fading, and she had lit a candle, which guttered constantly in the draught from the window. Pascomonsi looked over at him and smiled.

"I have copied all these," she said indicated a pile of neatly written pages. "I hope they are all correct."

She looked up as Tom joined her at the table and smiled.

"I think I have found something. I have finished his memoirs and these are some of his philosophical works… rather dry, I have to admit, and in some places almost incomprehensible. But here, right in the middle of a very complicated passage about the mysteries of existence I found this passage…"

Tom felt deep gratitude towards the patient young woman, and also guilt that he had made her work so hard, probably for no return. He looked at the passage Pascomonsi indicated and started to read. It seemed to be an explanation of the Religion or Philosophy of the Balance, for someone (Manny perhaps?) not familiar with its concepts.

"It is important to emphasise the meaning of the symbol of the Blue and Red Flame. This is the mythical flame popularly believed to lie at the heart of the Volcano of Fles. It is said to burn away all impurities and leaves the soul fit to enter paradise. In our places of meditation and Teaching Houses, the flame is usually depicted on a tapestry or altar, with the three 'Signposts to Eternity' inscribed around it.

*These are: **What is Familiar – What is Unique – What is Irreplaceable.***

*And above the flame is inscribed the Destination to which they lead, that is, **Life Neverending**.*

But these are not the only values or qualities of life which help in the search for the Destination. In our own lives we all come across truths, our own personal truths or insights, which help us on the Way. Such insights are frequently inscribed in personal altars or in the tapestries of individual communities or families.

For example, as you have seen, my own personal altar on the Isle of Thifa has a particular word inscribed right at the centre of the Spiral Flame.

Essential to the understanding of the Spiral Flame is the associated teaching of the Balance..."

Tom looked up at Pascomonsi, suddenly excited.

"He **did** have a private altar, and there **was** a word inscribed on it...!"

The girl smiled at him.

"Yes, but he doesn't say what the word is, does he."

"And he doesn't give any indication of where this personal altar might be!"

"No, he does not. I have searched through to the end of the paper..."

"And yet..." Tom was suddenly full of hope again. "And yet this DOES show that he had a chapel, with an altar, here on Thifa!"

"The only problem is," said Pascomonsi, half smiling, half-frowning, "that I do not know where it is!"

"But it cannot be that difficult to find, on such a small island," Tom insisted. "Think, Pascomonsi, think! Where could it have been?"

"I have been thinking all the time you were asleep... I just cannot imagine where it might be. And... and..."

"Yes?"

"Unfortunately so many places have been destroyed or damaged by the storms..."

Her frown deepened.

"Unless..."

"Yes?" Tom asked eagerly.

"When I think now... there was a place where he used to go a lot."

"Here on the island?"

"Yes, a bit further out on the promontory. I used to sometimes see him standing there, looking out towards Fles."

"He just stood there?"

"Yes, he would be standing... Gazing out over the water. But then he would sometimes disappear."

"Disappear? You mean... just vanish into thin air?"

"Well almost. I once went down to look where he had gone. But there was no sign of him. Just empty rock..."

"But he always came back again, obviously."

"Yes, but often he would disappear for quite long periods, and no one would know where he was..."

"As if," said Tom, "he had some little cave or private niche in the rock where he spent a lot of time in thought. Do you know where it is? Can we go there?"

"In this weather? The spot is very exposed to the storm. Some of the headland has crumbled into the sea!"

"But Pascomonsi, it is very important..."

"We should wait for the weather to calm down..."

"No, that may not be for days. And you said the weather was getting worse. Let's go there now while it's still possible."

177

Tom had already put on his anorak and was edging towards the door above the staircase. Reluctantly, Pascomonsi also put on her cloak and followed him. Before opening the outer door they braced themselves against the shock of the wind, then ducked out into the storm.

The wind had now reached horrendous proportions, with the bushes around Kalmom's windows tossing wildly and the waves hitting the shoreline amid huge clouds of spray. Further out on the lake the water heaved and plunged, and its surface was one terrible seething mass of foam.

Tom and Pascomonsi struggled out along the promontory into the teeth of the gale, clutching at the rocks around them to steady themselves.

They reached a point where the headland began to slope steeply down towards the sea, and for a moment Tom began to regret that he had forced Pascomonsi into this perilous mission. It looked as if what she said might have been true and that the angry waters of the lake had washed away the whole tip of the headland.

But Pascomonsi struggled bravely downwards, and just when it seemed they could go no further, they came to a cluster of rocks.

"This is where Kalmom was often seen standing?" she shouted above the roar of the wind and waves.

Tom looked at the jumble of boulders in disappointment. There was obviously no chapel or shrine there.

He stood and looked blankly at the rocks for some minutes, then shouted over the noise of the gale: "We should be getting back."

Pascomonsi nodded. But then, as if on an impulse, she turned back towards the strange assembly of stones. And after a moment's hesitation she moved towards it.

He was not sure if he dared follow. The rocks were right on the side of the cliff, and the spray from the waves was now regularly sweeping across them, so that they were extremely wet and slippery.

Then, quite suddenly, Pascomonsi disappeared.

For a moment Tom thought she had fallen and disappeared into the churning waves below. Horrified, he edged closer to where he had last seen her. At that moment an enormous wave hit the shore beneath and the spray came pouring over Tom and the stony ground all round him. A sharp fear pierced his heart. Why had he been so foolish to suggest this perilous expedition?

He was about to retreat in fear and consternation, convinced his new friend must have slipped and been taken by the waves. And as he turned, he saw it – the narrow cleft in the rocks. It was a dark slit about the height of a person, and just about wide enough to allow that person to enter. He realised that you could only see it if you turned round to climb back up the promontory.

With a quickening pulse he moved into the narrow opening.

It widened out almost immediately into a small grotto. It was very dark in here under the rocks, and for several moments Tom could not see Pascomonsi. But she was there all right, sitting on a natural stone bench along one side, staring intently at a rock wall opposite. She looked up at him as he dropped on to the slab beside her. Her face was wreathed in smiles.

"There!" she said simply.

He looked where she pointed.

On the rough rocky surface before them, barely visible in the gloom, he saw the all too familiar form of the twisting Flame. True, it was badly worn by time and half-covered by lichens. But Pascomonsi had already rubbed away a patch near the centre of the inscription, and Tom was able to make out a word. It was so worn, however, and the cave was so dark that he could not read it.

"Can you make out what it says, Pascomonsi?" he asked breathlessly. It would be too cruel if they had found one of the final keywords but were not able to read it.

"Yes, I think so," she answered calmly. "If I am not mistaken, the word is 'Tyrevi'."

Tom frowned. "And what does that mean?" he asked.

She told him*, and he smiled.

"That's what he was always looking for, wasn't it?"

*Tyrevi = Truth

Chapter Thirty-Three
Kalmom's Story 10
Desperation

'He has returned! The Maani has returned!

He has sent word to Nirei from high on the slopes of the Great Divide. He wants to meet me...

So the impossible has happened. My friend Maaniriv escaped the rock fall. In the months and years of hiding, my thoughts had constantly gone back to him. Had he really perished? Stigrath had told me that the stones and rubble were subsequently cleared from that road, but nothing at all was found there. Had Maaniriv and Pathemy been swept further down the mountainside and been born away by wild animals?

Or had the impossible happened? Had they escaped? Had they managed to cross the High Mountains?

Should I not go there, with Pageya, and be reunited with them, and also seek safety from the wrath of Vencengea?

Or persuade him to come back?

After all, there was still a mystery to solve...

Several mysteries indeed...

Now at least one question has been answered: he is alive! But what does he want? Does he want to return to the Realm and help us? Or does he want me to go there, to his blessed land in the Great Beyond?

I shall find out when I speak to him. But now I must make haste. I must go for the girl. For even if I do not cross the Divide, she must! She will be much safer there, far from the clutching hands of the one who claims her rights as a mother... though it is my view that she long ago forfeited all rights to motherhood!

In the meantime, I shall send two of my most trusted colleagues, to look after Maaniriv and make sure he does not disappear again before I have seen him. For who knows what dangers may lurk in the high snows, or what prying eyes may seek out the visitor from beyond?

I shall send with them this manuscript. If by some chance the girl and I are prevented from joining the Maani and journeying with him to his Other Realm, then at least let him have my story, so that he may make use of it to gather helpers – gifted people from that Realm beyond who may have some remedy, may be able to restore the goodness and happiness of this our own poor Realm...

But first I must bring my story to an end.

I am writing this in the Castle of Nirei, looking out on the lake. It is evening, but I must set off nonetheless and travel through the dark to find the girl and bring her back. As I sit here above the lake, I have the pendant lying in front of me on the table, the one I kept. Where, I wonder, is its twin?

Does Maaniriv still have it? Did the second twin also survive the rock fall with him? Is it still worn by a child in some distant land in a different world from ours? Or is it still buried somewhere high up on the mountain?

And what is the secret of the two pendants? Where did Thirdrol find them? Or did he perhaps create them himself, up there in the hidden darkness of Fles, by the skill of his hands or by some arcane gift received from beyond our knowledge...? And why did he then entrust them to myself and the Maani with such solemn words? Was it just a present for his two godchildren, the twins, or was there some hidden intention in his act of generosity?

If I am ever to solve these questions, I need the help and advice of my friend Maaniriv. **And I need the second pendant.**

And yet I know that if Maaniriv still has the second pendant, to bring it back to the Realm would be dangerous. If the two pendants have some special power when they are re-united, there are others beside myself who clearly have an interest in acquiring that power. More and more I am convinced that all this has more than a little to do with the experiments which Shoderim and Vencengea had been conducting at Niur and which Thirdrol knew about?

What I suspect is that they were close to some breakthrough in their quest for this supra-natural 'transportation' of sounds and images, and perhaps people as well, from one place to another?

That is a frightening thought. If Vencengea were to discover such a secret, what would someone like her, with all her ambition, be able to do with it? I shiver at the thought...

That is why I had resolved, even before I heard of his return, to try to make contact with my friend Maaniriv, out there beyond the High Snows, in the desperate hope that he had indeed survived the rock fall...

For even if the Maani no longer lived, surely I would be able to find someone else like him, in that other realm beyond the Snowy Mountains! And invite them... if necessary lure them... back to this Realm of ours, to help me solve, once and for all, the question that torments me. **Why is Vencengea (and Shoderim too?) so desperate not just to find her lost children, the Twins, but also to lay her hands on what they wore round their necks... their pendants?**

I know, however, that I must make sure that I bring back the right sort of people, people like the Maani himself, skilled in solving riddles but also well intentioned, good at heart. Would all the people in the Maani's realm be like that? I am not at all sure. And if I were simply to bring back people motivated solely by selfish ambition, what would be the point?

So I have hidden my message behind a series of riddles and puzzles which need to be solved if these people are to prove themselves... The Maani loved puzzles, he said it was what he missed most about his former home beyond the mountains, the puzzles they set in what he described as news-leaves, or something like that, for the amusement of the people... He said it was the highest form of intelligence.

So I know that if anyone ever reads this, they will be like him, Lovers of Riddles! They will have deciphered the riddles and puzzles and proven that they are among the wisest in that strange realm which gave birth to the Maani...

And would they be also pure of heart? Well, I would have to devise further tests to discover that too...!

Yes, it is to you I speak, those very ones who have solved the secret of reading my writings, who are my very last hope.

I say again to you strangers: Greetings! If you are reading this, it means you have come so far, you have solved many of the riddles I have set you, and passed no doubt through many adventures in order to find the answers.

Somewhere along the way you may also have found me! I may not be who you think I am. You may indeed already have met me, by some strange quirk of fate...

If, however, we have not yet met, I have left one last hidden clue for you to solve. It is a clue which will lead to the final key, the key which may unlock the last door...

The clues you have already found will help you. Consider them again, and then ponder a little more. Think of a place you may have heard of, or maybe have even been! A place of destiny where many struggle and face what seems a gloomy and terrible end. And use that name too. Mould them all together, words and names and letters...

*Then you also may follow where I think you will find the **Opening!***

For yes, I am now convinced I know more or less where it lies. But I shall wait for you, the unknown ones, to come. I shall not go through the Opening alone. I shall wait for you as long as possible. Come quickly! Our Realm has need of you!'

At this point in the manuscript there was a gap. Then, a little further down the same page, there was a hastily scribbled addition.

Now I must finally go! Farewell!

And that was all Tom could decipher. There was more text which Tom had not been able to decode. But this section seemed to bring Kalmom's story to a conclusion. He wondered whether Bridget might have been able to decipher those missing parts, if she had found other code words...

But where was Bridget, he wondered, as he gazed out over the storm-tossed lake.

Chapter Thirty-Four
Quenrie's Refusal

Tom was sitting in his room, busy reading through the last section of Kalmom's coded message again, discussing parts of it with Pascomonsi, when suddenly the door burst open and the Yenomi commander Pailtac rushed in.

"Thomas, you must hurry!" he cried breathlessly. "We have to leave. A vessel has come which will take us back to the mainland. But they don't want to wait."

"What! Someone's mad enough to want to sail in this weather?" exclaimed Tom. He was not at all sure he wanted to leave the island. In the few days he had spent there, he had become attached to more than one aspect of life there.

"And how did a boat get here in the first place?" Pascomonsi asked, clearly sharing Tom's reluctance to rejoice.

"It set out during the lull in the storm yesterday," said Ecape, who had entered after Pailtac. "And then when the gales came on again it had to shelter here. It doesn't normally stop at this island."

Pascomonsi frowned. "You're surely not talking of...? Where is it going, this ship?"

"Oh, some other island!" Pailtac replied impatiently. "What does it matter? The point is that after it's been there, it will return to the mainland. The captains say it runs regular supply trips up to Orotworm, and then on almost to Teivos. Exactly the direction we want to go."

It did seem too good an opportunity to miss, Tom thought reluctantly. But Pascomonsi seemed very doubtful.

"You know who this ship belongs to, don't you?" she said to Tom.

"No, who?"

"She calls herself the Mistress of Light and Dark, but among the people she's known simply as the Dark Mistress. She lives on the next island, the Isle of Iprades."

"The Dark Mistress?" asked Tom, his heart sinking. "She wouldn't be called...?"

"Yes, she is called Vencengea. She is the one you have spoken of in retelling your adventures..."

Tom stared at her.

"She is the self-appointed priestess," Pascomonsi continued, "of a cult whose symbol is the Black Raven, the bird of the after-life." Pascomonsi was clearly very agitated about the idea of Tom and his friends going on to Iprades.

Ecape laid his hand gently on Pascomonsi's shoulder and turned to Pailtac.

"I also would advise you to be wary of travelling on to the home of Vencengea. Our friends Tom and Ont-Maj have told us how they were glad to escape from her in the Green Vale."

But the islanders' doubts only irritated Pailtac.

"So what if her name is Vencengea?" he cried. "What if she *is* the head of some bizarre cult? Why should that worry us? She has no reason to do us harm!"

"I don't think that's the way she would see it, Pailtac," said Tom quietly, "if she found out who I was, for example. I have the impression she has a very specific reason for wanting to get hold of me and my friend Bridget, again."

Pailtac made an impatient gesture, uttering something that sounded like a Yenomi swearword, and hurried off with Ecape to wake Quenrie, who was asleep in the dormitory. Tom and Pascomonsi decided to go in search of Madge and Yentsilbor. They found the Skomiar officer sitting in the community prayer house in earnest discussion with the belligerent Kotz. Madge and Erash were looking on, a look of mild amusement on their faces.

"Your Skomiar bands have broken all the laws and treaties of the Realm," Kotz was saying angrily. "You are vandals and thieves…"

"But," Yentsilbor interrupted him, "if your knights will not allow the people of the plains to trade with Teivos, you leave us no alternative! We must take over what parts of the plains we can, just in order to feed our city and survive…"

They looked up as Tom approached. He explained about the arrival of the boat from Iprades and the dilemma it raised.

"This is grave news indeed," said Yentsilbor. "I have had some dealings with this Vencengea in my capacity as adviser to the Younger Guardian… Her cult has become popular in recent times with people who reject the old religion and say the last times have come… The Dark Mistress, it seems, claims to know the secret of what happens after death…"

"And does she?" asked Tom.

Yentsilbor gave a dismissive laugh. "She certainly seems to have certain sinister, hypnotic powers. But those who are not her followers consider she is a fraud, a mere soothsayer who dazzles people with mysterious talk and magic tricks…"

"And you, Pascomonsi, what do you think?" asked Madge.

"My friends," said Pascomonsi quietly, "be advised. There is danger in going to her island."

"But we do need to get away, back to the mainland, to look for our friends," insisted Tom.

"And leave the Goodcheer here?" Madge looked at him with a troubled expression on her face, "To the mercy of the winds and rains and pestilence and goodness only knows what? I don't think so. If we don't have an airship, we have no means of leaving this whole crazy place they call the Realm!"

"I'm sure Ecape and Pascomonsi and their friends will look after the Goodcheer, Madge," said Tom. "This just seems too good an opportunity to miss. Vencengea's boat, it appears, plies regularly between Iprades and the mainland, so it can take us back to Orotworm or beyond once it's delivered what it has to deliver to her island. Bridget and Orin and Stigrath could be in serious danger back in Teivos. Someone needs to do something to rescue them. Especially since there's a real danger of their getting caught up in a confrontation between Tekram and Teivos. And that's another reason for leaving. Our friends here, Yentsilbor and Pailtac need to get back there to stop the two sides from hurling themselves into a war…"

"A war which neither side would win," growled Yentsilbor. Kotz looked as if he was about to disagree, but for once managed to keep his mouth shut.

Madge was still frowning.

"Well, perhaps you're right… We could certainly try to play the role of 'strangers from the Outer World' again and help Quenrie and Pailtac and Yentsilbor to persuade a few people to do something to help us… And if we get to Orotworm, we might be able to send back help to repair the Goodcheer…"

Pascomonsi smiled sadly at her. "If you were to go, honoured Ont-Maj, you could certainly count on us to take care of your flying ship."

So Madge agreed to go. Yentsilbor also decided, despite his severe misgivings about travelling to Iprades, that it was on the whole preferable to staying indefinitely on Thifa. He still missed his large family, and something else was also preying on his mind. He turned to Kotz and Erash.

"My Yenomi friends," he said, "for friends I now feel you are… we left our two nations on the brink of war! Yet in talking with you, here on the Isle of Thifa, I have become ever more convinced that this war should not, must not take place. It is surely our duty to return and use our influence to put an end to this quarrelling over territory!"

Kotz frowned, and Tom thought the combative knight was again about to disagree, but then he nodded slowly.

"I love a good fight," he grunted. "But a good fight is one which has a good reason, and you have shown me, comrade Yentsilbor, that not all Skomiar are unreasoning fanatics!"

Erash too, though he hated going in boats even in good weather, was determined to get back home as soon as he could.

"If you are all going to leave," he said, "what would I do here by myself on this island of lamb-like angels?"

The others laughed.

"It is agreed, then, that we go!" Tom announced.

"No, it is not agreed."

The quiet voice from the prayer house doorway was that of Quenrie.

"There is no way that you should go to Iprades," he said. "The sorceress Vencengea is a person of evil, and evil will befall all those who find themselves in her hands."

Pailtac stepped in front of him in surprise and vexation. "But friend Quenrie, we *must* leave… and everyone else is agreed. What is it about this woman that you fear so much?"

Quenrie frowned at him. "I know 'this woman', as you call her, much better than any of you do… I have had dealings with her… many times, over many years, and I must assure you that it is highly dangerous to go anywhere near her island!" His mouth was set firm, his words astonishingly harsh and unyielding.

"Come, come, Quenrie," Madge put in, "aren't you being a bit extreme? You haven't spoken to us about her in such terms before."

Quenrie looked at her unsmilingly. Tom had never seen him look so grim.

"There has never been any question of going to her island before," he said coldly.

The others were silent, not knowing what to say. Then Pailtac said decisively:

"Well, I am not staying on this backwater island a moment longer than I have to. Kotz and Erash and I shall be going on the boat. What about you, Skomiar brother?"

Yentsilbor looked nervously at Quenrie, whom he obviously respected, but then nodded to Pailtac.

"I shall go," he said.

Madge went up to Quenrie and put her hand on his arm. "Dear old Quenrie, I understand that you don't like this Vencengea woman and are a bit afraid of her. But we need your brains and experience, **and** your influence in Orotworm, if we are to rescue Bridget and Stigrath and young Orin, and find help to repair our airship…"

Quenrie, obviously wrestling with his emotions, looked at her with troubled eyes, unable to put his emotions into words. But then he slowly took Madge's hand from his arm and moved away towards the door. When he reached the threshold, he turned and said emphatically:

"I cannot go! There are reasons which I am unable to explain. But I cannot go to Iprades. I shall stay here, honoured Ont-Maj, and do what I can to protect your flying ship. Yentsilbor and Pailtac are experienced and strong men. They will take you and Tom to Vencengea's isle and then, hopefully, back to Orotworm… But may the Good Fates protect you… You will need all the protection you can get!"

And he left.

Tom felt angry, annoyed with Quenrie that he was letting them down when they most needed him. He was sure that Quenrie was every bit a match for Vencengea, even when it came to occult powers…

It was only some time later, after they had left the blessed isle of Thifa, that Tom began to understand just why Quenrie had been so set against going with them. And only when it was too late did he understand the danger that was hanging over them.

Chapter Thirty-Five
The Island of the Forgotten

Bridget had missed the mouth of the river. Their only access to the open air was a tiny slit in the side of each cabin, with wooden covers on a hinge, and for one whole day she had peered through the one in her cabin, watching the dreary banks of the lower Traa slip past at the same monotonous pace. The countryside had grown dustier and more depressing as the journey continued. Then, on the second morning she opened the slit and there was water all round them. They were in the middle of a sea, or at least a lake so vast she could not even see the shoreline.

The previous morning she had awoken and for a moment thought she was back in the pirate ship which had brought them downstream to Orotworm. And her heart leapt, for that would mean they would again be rescued by Eclopis... But then she remembered that this was a different ship, with a different, even more sinister crew.

They had been kept locked up in their cabins near the prow of the boat ever since leaving Orotworm. Stigrath told her that the vessel, Vencengea's black-sailed ship, was known as the 'Maibiton'. They had not seen Stitgoe or Lulby again. Each of the friends had been given a tiny cabin or compartment, though happily they connected with each other. The wooden walls and floors gave off a strange, musty smell, which seemed to be a mixture of human sweat and incense. *Who or what had travelled in these compartments?* she wondered with a shiver.

They had been fed once during that first day, with a thin, foul tasting gruel. But Bridget had been so hungry that she managed to swallow it all in a few hurried gulps. She was glad in a way to be leaving the depressing, ash-laden plain behind them, though she soon found that the lake was not much of an improvement. Its waters too were dreary and colourless. The ash which had been washed into the lake or landed on its surface had turned into a sort of light grey slime, and Bridget watched as great lumps of it floated past their boat as they ploughed ever onwards.

At least she had managed to decipher the latest passage of Kalmom's message. She had had no problem finding the passage of the hieroglyphs which responded to the keyword. The latest section, describing Kalmom's stormy relationship with Vencengea, had been as absorbing and puzzling as the previous ones. And then, towards the end, it revealed the most astonishing discovery yet: Kalmom had known Stigrath. He had known this very same Stigrath who had been their companion since the beginning of the trip from Nirei.

Bridget had confronted the giant captain with this fact the night before. He had looked dumbfounded. Then he had said simply: "Cannot… not permitted… to tell the princess more."

"But Stigrath," she said angrily, "you know who Kalmom is! And it is vital that we find him!"

Stigrath had thought for a while and then smiled in an indulgent way at her.

"Maybe… we soon find Kalmom. Then he explains himself…"

Bridget was furious and for the first time lost her temper with the big man, banging the cabin wall and bursting into tears. Stigrath looked upset, but he remained adamant. He could not tell her anything about Kalmom. Now the giant man was asleep in the next cabin. She heard him stir and yawn loudly. She went into his compartment in time to see him lift himself on one elbow and look out of the slit beside his bunk.

"Going… to Vencengea's island… Iprades," he said gloomily. "Great Lords of Fate… be with us. Bad place… evil reputation."

"So this presumably is the celebrated Crystal Lake?" said Bridget.

Stigrath nodded.

"It is a very grey and sad crystal," commented Orin, who had come into the cabin when he heard the others.

"Once was indeed Crystal," grunted Stigrath. "Bright and cheerful… On one side, green Plains of Tworm. Other side, purple Volcano of Fles!"

"Yes, where is the volcano?" asked Bridget. "I can't see it, though it should, if I'm not mistaken, be on our side of the boat."

"Mist… mist too thick," said Stigrath. "More and more, they say, Fles covered in cloud, these last years. Often, no warning, fierce storms. Never so, in my youth. Used to watch great volcano smoulder on horizon. Deep mystery, dark secrets, Fles. But then peaceful. Last times, only storms and mist, or great clouds like thunderclouds. Lightnings up in the sky, over whole plains, to Orotworm, beyond. Loud thunder too…"

"But why have things changed? Is the whole climate here changing? Do you think it has something to do with the great Pestilence as well? Does the Pestilence arise out of the thunderstorms?"

Stigrath smiled at her. "So many questions!" But his face grew serious. "Yes, I think, pestilence, thunderstorms, same reason. But why? Who makes grey stuff, storms? Neither I, nor any man, woman knows. All we know, beautiful place now cursed, with terrible winds, storms."

As if to confirm the accuracy of his words, they felt a sudden gust of wind tear at the sides of the Maibiton, and it rolled heavily to one side. Above, men shouted warnings to each other and hurried footsteps beat on the deck over their heads. The water outside their window slits began to churn and fly into spray. There was a sudden thump and some water splattered into the cabin where they were sitting. Stigrath went and closed the slits in the other two cabins as tightly as he could.

"I think, one of storms come now," he said grimly.

Stigrath would have shut the slit in Bridget's cabin as well, but she stopped him. "I want to watch," she said. "I want to see just what one of these storms does."

"How far are we from the Isle of Dark Vencengea?" asked Orin nervously.

"Hundreds of arrow spans, boy. But not fear. Vencengea's sailors no fools. Sail Crystal Lake many times."

Soon the ship was rolling in a heavy swell, and the waves were breaking into lines of white foam. The wind could be heard moaning in the rigging above and soon the waves started to beat heavily against the hull of the ship. As the waves grew higher, the vessel began to rise and fall alarmingly, lurching unsteadily like a drunken man from wave to trough and then up again.

Orin had retreated to his cabin, looking green. Stigrath too decided to suffer the rest of the voyage alone. Bridget clung on to the sides of the slit in her cabin, staring out at the horizon. She had heard that if you did that you were less likely to feel ill. Every now and then she had to wipe spray from her face, as it blew in from outside, and soon her clothes were soaking. But she clung on determinedly, staring towards the horizon where she knew the great volcano lay hidden by the mist. What was the force, she wondered, that was generating these unnatural storms? For she was sure, from what Stigrath had told her, that they were not natural. From the dark and misty horizon, however, there came no answer, only line upon line of fierce, foam-flecked waves, bearing down on their boat with obviously evil intent.

The waves became ever higher, ever fiercer. "O Vencengea," Bridget breathed to her inner self, "if you do have superhuman powers, do something to stop this awful storm."

But Bridget felt no comfort in the thought that Vencengea might somehow have sufficient power to calm the storm. On the contrary, the thought only depressed and frightened her even further.

Two of the boat's black-robed crew, strange, misshapen and taciturn fellows, came in and closed all the slits.

"Waves enter boat," explained one of them in a dull, mechanical voice. He had strange, sunken eyes and his nose and jaw protruded well in front of the rest of his face.

Were all Vencengea's followers misshapen? Bridget wondered.

Bridget lay down and hid her head under the blanket on her bunk, trying to forget where she was and what was happening to her. But this brought her no relief. With each sudden lift of the ship, she felt her stomach sag downwards. Then the vessel would plunge endlessly into some great trough among the waves, so deep that Bridget felt sure they would never rise again. But they did, and as the boat reached yet another rolling crest, she and all around her in the cabin would seem for a moment to be floating uneasily on thin air… until suddenly everything began another sickening descent, ending with a giant thump, and the decks and bulkheads creaking and groaning, as if they were in pain and could stand it no longer. Bridget imagined the frame of the ship was about to burst and deliver them all into the clutches of the angry waters outside.

Bridget heard someone shouting above, and there were hurried steps on the rolling deck over her head. Gingerly, in the semi-darkness of the claustrophobic cabin, she moved back to her slit. She found she could peer through a crack at one end.

The waves were now enormous, line upon line of them, white-crested monsters frothing towards their fragile boat, stretching all the way to the horizon. The clouds above them tore across the grey, rain-laden sky, borne by the shrieking wind. For a moment her heart sank altogether. Surely they were lost in this seemingly endless maelstrom.

But then she saw, dimly, on the horizon before them, a dark line, a low, humped shape rising above the spray of the waves, visible only because it was greyer than all the other greyness round it. As their vessel was hurled upwards and then thrown downwards by the spite of the waves, she realised that the grey line was not moving, that it represented some sort of land.

For a moment her heart lightened. But then she realised that they were still a long way from the island, if island it was. Amid the creaks and groans of the protesting wooden spars around her she felt little confidence that their ship could make it that far.

The dull mass of the island, however, began slowly to grow nearer and clearer. It was a long, level ridge, which rose at one end in a cluster of jagged peaks. And as they drew ever closer, driven by the wind and waves, her heart slowly fell at what she saw. The flank of the island was an unbroken line of tumbling cliffs, a bleak, forbidding wall with no obvious bays or harbours. She could see no possible landing place, no possible shelter from the fury of the elements.

This could not possibly be the island for which they were heading.

Yet the black-sailed ship plunged on over the waves, heading straight for the blank wall of the island's cliffs. What were Lulby and Stitgoe trying to do? Prove they could pull off a miracle? Or were they trying to break the morale of Bridget and her friends, scare them out of their minds so that, when they finally reached the island, the 'Dark Mistress' could work on them again with her hypnotic powers, trying to extract from them whatever 'secret' it was she wanted?

No, that seemed too far-fetched. Perhaps it was simply that the vessel's helmsman had gone crazy and wanted to kill them all,

They were now right under the gigantic rock wall, which in places hung out in glistening dark slabs over the rolling waves. The troubled waters of the lake collided with the jagged, unforgiving rocks with towering bursts of spray and a continuous booming noise. Yet still their craft sped on, as it seemed, towards certain disaster.

They were a hundred metres… fifty… less than fifty metres from the nearest rock, a great misshapen lump of black stone, which reared up to the starboard of their prow…

Then, without warning, their vessel turned side on to the waves. At once it rolled over alarmingly to one side, so that Bridget thought it was going to capsize altogether. Slowly, however, it righted itself. Before the boat rolled again she saw that on the further side of the twisted black rock, between it and the cliff, was a channel of relatively calm water. As the waves bore their vessel sideways on towards a collision with the cliffs, the wind in its sails edged it forward past the giant rock… and into the sheltered channel.

It had all been a remarkably skilful manoeuvre, fraught with risk. But clearly Vencengea's helmsman was not so crazy after all…

Once they were in the channel the great black sail lost its wind and started flapping wildly above them. At once the robed crew were at their posts, pushing out the oars. There was barely enough room for them to deploy them on both sides, but slowly the boat gathered pace again, heading along the channel, the tortured line of rocks on one side, the huge sheer wall of the cliff on the other.

From time to time a huge wave burst over the rock to their right and drenched the boat. But the vessel pushed steadily up the channel, which continued for a hundred metres or so, and then took a sharp turn to the left, towards the cliff. As they rounded the bend, Bridget saw that the channel led into a gigantic slit in the cliff wall which had been hidden from view as they approached from the lake.

The opening of this cavern was too narrow to allow them to row in. Instead, the rowers waited for the boat's momentum to take them into its entrance, then proceeded to propel it onwards by pushing with their oars against the sides of the cave. Although Bridget had no optimistic expectations of what they would find on this wild, lonely island, she could not but feel glad that they were at least out of the wind and rain and safe from the danger of being drowned or crushed against the malevolent black walls outside.

They continued through the cavern for some while. They were now surrounded by total darkness. The crew of the *Maibiton* began to intone one of their low, baleful chants, though whether it was to keep up their spirits or, on the contrary, to give some expression of gladness at a homecoming, Bridget was not sure. Slowly the light grew stronger again. Through the narrow slit in her cabin wall Bridget could just make out an archway of light ahead. It seemed dazzling at first, but then, as they moved slowly towards the opening, she saw that it was the same grey, gloomy light of a rain-filled day they had left at the other end of the flooded cave.

They emerged into the open. Bridget did not know what she had expected, but what she did manage to see through her chink in the bulkhead left her amazed and speechless.

They had, it seemed, entered a huge bowl surrounded on all sides by tall cliffs, though perhaps not quite as sheer as those on the outside. This was evidently the remains of some vast crater, drowned by the lake thousands, maybe millions of years ago. The lake which filled it was as grey as the sky above it, though here the water was relatively calm, barely touched by the tempest that raged round the island. Alone on its rippling surface their vessel seemed lost, a forlorn scrap of flotsam in the midst of a massive grey amphitheatre of rock and water.

The crew unfurled the sail again and soon the boat was advancing across the surface of the crater lake. Despite all her fears and foreboding, Bridget could not help but admire the wild beauty of the place – the broad expanse of the lake itself, the dramatic sweep of the slopes that surrounded it, and finally the jagged rim of pinnacles above them, constantly disappearing into the flying clouds only to reappear a few moments later.

Someone was outside the door, jangling a set of keys. Bridget's door flew open and the Lulby's rubbery features appeared.

"You can come up on deck now, to admire the view," he said, and as he moved off to open the outer doors of Stigrath and Orin's cabins, he gave one of his familiar whimpering giggles. "We have arrived at Iprades... Come and admire what they call the 'Isle of the Forgotten Ones'!"

They emerged on deck, thankful to be out of the confined space of their cabins. The vessel was sailing on over the grey lagoon, towards its further shore. They seemed to be heading for an inlet that Bridget could just about make out among the grey hills that lined the shore. As they came closer, Bridget saw that the inlet was in fact a fjord-like ravine cutting deep into the mountain wall. As they rounded the promontory at the fjord's entrance, Bridget saw their final destination.

Along one side of the fjord was a small area of green, treeless fields divided by broken stone walls, with here and there a tumbledown grey building. Further along the inlet they could now see what appeared to be a small stone quay, evidently the final destination for the strange and forbidding craft which had brought them to the island.

But it was what she saw beyond the stone quayside and the green fields that caught her eye. Visible high above the landing stage, perhaps a mile or so away, there was an enormous cleft in the sheer grey wall of the mountain, and at its centre lay a dark cave driving deep into the mountainside. It was as if some giant had taken his sword and struck the cliff in anger, cleaving it from top to bottom, and then plunged his weapon into the gash to make it deeper.

"Behold the Sorcerer's Eye," said Stitgoe, who had moved up beside them without their noticing. "The mountain behind is called Cirorest, or the Sleeping Sorcerer."

Bridget now noticed that the great hill above them did resemble the head of a sleeping giant, with the slit-like cave forming the eye, and a ridge of rock nearby forming what looked like a nose. "The original sorcerer, whoever he was, is indeed asleep for all time," said Stitgoe. "But his head is now inhabited by a greater brain than his own." And he chortled in his mirthless way, as if he had made a joke.

"Why do they call this the Island of the Forgotten?" Bridget asked.

Stitgoe gave her a curious look, which she found difficult to read. For a moment she thought he was going to treat her question with scorn. But his face became serious, and he said with only a slight touch of bitterness: "Is it not clear that we, the misshapen, the malformed, the people shunned by others, that we are the forgotten?"

And he walked quickly away.

They disembarked. There were no buildings here at the landing stage, only a stony grey track which led up through the fields and the broken-down dwellings they had seen from the boat, ever upwards towards the great crack in the mountainside.

Lulby appeared to escort them off the boat. "Welcome to the home of the Lady Vencengea," he said with his leering smile. "Welcome to the Isle of Iprades."

Chapter Thirty-Six
Blam's Kitchen

Soon they were passing into the giant gash in the side of the mountain. Bridget stared up at the massive sides of the cave entrance, worn smooth by countless years of rainfall, and at the great slabs of rock overhanging the cavern's mouth which looked as if any moment, at the merest sound, they might slip loose and come crashing down on anyone who dared pass beneath.

Then they entered a twilight world, halfway between grey daylight and the deep night of the underworld. Their guides lit torches and held them high over their heads, though the strangely crimson glow they afforded only seemed to intensify the darkness around them. Their path wound laboriously round and over great mounds and ridges of rock, on into the depths of the sinister black cave.

After endless twists and turns, the track came to a flimsy wooden bridge across a swift, silently churning stream, black as pitch. On the other side there was nothing but total darkness, the darkness of the unknown. Even their guides, in their monk-like robes, seemed to hesitate for a few moments, before plunging on across the bridge, their reddish light gleaming eerily in the black waters of the icy river.

Their route now followed a ledge along the underground river for a good ten minutes, until the path took a sudden turn to the left, in under an archway which seemed to have been carved by hand in the rock. Over the archway Bridget glimpsed mysterious symbols – triangles, crosses, animals' heads and so on, possibly intended to have some occult significance. But she had no time to study them in any detail, for their guides and captors hurried them on under the sinister arch.

Now they were in passageways, endless passageways cut in the rock, some broad and straight, others narrow, twisting and undulating. On and on they went. Later it all seemed to Bridget like a dream, or rather a nightmare inspired by the malevolent spirit that inhabited the place. They passed underground lakes, with water still and black which seemed to watch them as they walked by, challenging them, demanding to know why they were trespassing on these unseen, unknown places. They walked along narrow ledges, on one side of which were seemingly bottomless pits, where one wrong step might have plunged them into heaven knows what awful dungeons deep in the heart of the rock. At one point they crossed over a natural bridge of stone, curving out over a black, bottomless gulf. The narrow band of stone trembled as they walked on it – indeed the whole cave around them seemed to tremble with deep malevolence at their coming…

Finally, their path began to rise, and soon Bridget was struggling to control her breathing as they climbed steeply up sloping galleries broken here and there by a series of crude steps cut in the stone.

And then, quite suddenly, they emerged into a broad cave, and at last there was daylight streaming in from a series of uneven openings high up on its further wall…

And also wind, a persistent moaning wind whining in through the ragged windows, tugging at their clothes and rushing past their faces.

Someone barked a curt command telling them to stop, and Lulby and Stitgoe detached themselves from the group and disappeared into a passage on the far side of the cave.

Bridget approached one of the roughly hewn windows, the only one which was not above head height.

It opened on to a very different world, a world of wind and driving rain. She winced as the force of the blast hit her. Far below them she could see the wild waters of the lake and serried ranks of wave upon wave being driven relentlessly by the hurricane towards the high cliffs of the island. She could not see the shoreline, but she heard the endless booming of the huge waves as they came crashing, one after the other, on to the rocks below.

She moved closer still to the opening and now she could see a high promontory, shaped like the prow of a battleship, and the angry waves bursting in huge columns of spray round its base. The promontory was at the end of a peninsula connected to the rest of the island by a precipitous ridge which fell away vertically on either side. This peninsula was dominated by a bizarre, jagged mass of rock, culminating in a great stone pinnacle like a giant finger pointing up to the sky.

And on one side of the peninsula, halfway between the pinnacle and the churning waves beneath, she noticed a sort of natural bowl in the rock, a massive amphitheatre evidently hollowed out by the forces of nature. At the bottom of this bowl, as far as Bridget could make out, there was an expanse of water.

Then, as she watched, as if the breath-taking grandeur of this scene was not enough in itself, the thick layer of grey, tumbling clouds above them parted, and for a moment – out beyond the rolling waves – she glimpsed a terrifying sight.

High above them, much closer than she had imagined, loomed the massive, intimidating form of the great volcano itself. The enormous conical shape of Fles towered up above the whole wild scene, overpowering in all its awesome grandeur.

Then the clouds closed again, and the terrible vision was gone.

Bridget had only a few moments to take in this stupendous spectacle. Their guides were already ushering them on into a further warren of small caves, miserable, pokey little spaces for the most part, though now they were at least connected by roughly constructed wooden doors. One of the caves, larger than the others, was clearly a kitchen. There were several people there, not monks like the others, but men and women in dirty white tunics, chopping and hewing at various edibles on a broad table in the middle of the cave.

195

One of them, an enormous, chunky man with huge biceps, turned to them as they came in.

"Ah, Brother Stitgoe, Brother Lulby," he said in a whining, mocking voice, "so you've brought me some new human fodder for the kitchen!" And immediately he burst into a high-pitched, honking laugh.

"Yes, Brother Blam," replied Stitgoe, in his driest tone. "A nice girl and boy to add to your human recipe… and a rather less tender specimen to go with them – though he has plenty of meat on him! They are to be kept under strict supervision, you understand?"

"Indeed I do!" answered Blam, and again launched into his irritating, grating laugh. His mirth came to a sudden halt, however, when Stigrath's giant form emerged fully from the shadows.

"Flabberguts of Fles!" he exclaimed. "This one would feed us all for a month if he were worth…!"

The words froze in Blam's mouth as Stigrath moved towards him. Blam was not exactly small himself, but his pale sweaty features suggested he was not in peak shape. The head cook – for that is what he evidently was – had gross, bulbous features and a lascivious leer on his pinkish-brown face. His eyes protruded from their sockets whenever he spoke, and now, as he looked away from Stigrath towards Bridget and Orin, it was indeed as if he were assessing their suitability for inclusion in that evening's stew. He kept wiping his enormous hands across his mouth and then on a filthy rag which he kept tucked into the broad leather belt that he wore round his midriff.

For the first time in days Bridget reached instinctively towards the pendant which hung round her neck. Then something told her to stay her hand, and in the end she simply adjusted the collar of her shirt to make sure the stone was well hidden. A moment later, and she saw Blam's probing eyes settle on her, and on the arm raised to her neck.

"And the young lady is to be looked after properly," Stitgoe added severely.

"Is she now?" said Blam, his face twisting into a leer.

"… Or you will answer to the Mistress herself!" added Stitgoe.

Blam scowled and turned to one of his female assistants. "Noos! Show the creatures to their quarters!"

Noos was a large blond woman with an enormous bosom. Her gross features wore the same brazenly mischievous look as that of the head cook. She surveyed them with a contemptuous stare, then sniffed and signalled to them brusquely to follow her.

Their quarters turned out to be a small cell-like cave like the ones they had already passed through. Around its walls was a stone ledge covered with rough, sack-like blankets. The cell was connected to others by a twisting, irregular cave-corridor, at the end of which was a space with a crude earthenware bowl full of water.

"That there is where you wash," said Noos, and laughed heartily, her gross body shaking all over. "When you've finished your doings, you just throw them out the window. Don't worry… ain't nobody below!" And she let out another guffaw.

Then the smile disappeared suddenly from her face and she said curtly: "Report back to the kitchen in ten minutes. There's work to be done. The Mistress herself has only just returned. And she'll be hungry after her long sleep!"

Then Noos disappeared.

Chapter Thirty-Seven
The Feast

"Ha, if it weren't for the Mistress Vencengea, you'd all still be in the gutter!"

It was the big-bosomed Noos who said it as she loomed over the kitchen staff toiling away in Blam's kitchen.

"Picked you up off the streets, she did, and gave you a reason to be living!"

Bridget and her friends had been on the Isle of Iprades for over a week now, but in that time they had neither seen nor heard anything of the Dark Mistress. It had been a time of unremitting labour in the foul kitchen complex, a week of chopping tough, misshapen vegetables and fatty, stinking meat – from what animals it came she would not like to have guessed. It had been a week of being constantly bullied by the malodorous Blam and his even more disgusting assistant Noos. She felt constantly that she wanted to rebel, no matter what the consequences, and just tell their new master and mistress she was no slave, that she refused to do any more. But she knew that would be unwise. While Stigrath was in sight the bullying never became too gross. Noos, however, was constantly sending the giant sailor off on pointless errands – like carrying gigantic barrels of water up from a dark well deep inside the mountain. It was almost as if Noos had been given special instructions to persecute Bridget and Orin at every opportunity she could find. But just when it seemed that Bridget was about to snap and fly at Noos over some needless harassment of the innocent Orin, the faithful Stigrath would suddenly appear and glower at his torturer. And she would back away, scowling. Even she, with her enormous bulk, did not dare try her chances with the giant river man. He would not actually say anything. He would simply raise one huge threatening finger and point it in Noos's direction. That was enough.

Bridget had managed to speak to a number of the other kitchen workers. What Noos said to taunt them was basically true. Many of them had been picked up from the poor quarters of Orotworm or other cities, with the promise of a better life in a 'happier place'. They were from among the very poor, or homeless, or people without family. Some seemed at least partly disabled, while others had misshapen limbs or distorted features – rather like Stitgoe and Lulby and the robed acolytes, Bridget thought. They had looked for sustenance not from the forbidding Vysou-Salem, with its mournful and unsmiling priests, but from the Ellektys, the place of noise and sound and cheap entertainment. And the Ellektys had put them in touch with Vencengea… So much, thought Bridget, for the Dark Mistress's supposed patronage of the Vysou-Salem and the Ravenites! Clearly she had links with both the deviant cults which broke away from the Order of the Balance…

Bridget wondered if some of the kitchen workers would be promoted to the ranks of the dark-robed monk-like retainers with whom Vencengea surrounded herself.

Clearly, something big was happening on this particular evening. Some special celebration in the refectory nearby. The kitchen was all a bustle and both Noos and Blam were there to push, shove and generally hassle the kitchen workers into ever-greater efforts. Bridget had been given an enormous pot of pungent-smelling purple stew to stir. Was it soup or gravy? She wasn't sure. She wasn't even sure it was meant to be eaten! All she knew was that if she had to go on leaning over it much longer with her long wooden spoon she might easily keel over and fall into it.

"Come on, stir it, stir it, girl!" Noos suddenly appeared behind her. "It's no use to anyone unless it's properly stirred!"

Bridget looked across the kitchen to where little Orin was manfully struggling to carry a pot almost as large as himself which contained some sickly green liquid. He caught her glance and winked back cheerfully. *He* was all right, then!

Her look turned towards Stigrath. The sturdy captain had been ordered to hack to pieces various coarse vegetables and rough bits of meat and throw them all together into an even larger pot than Bridget's. This task he was fulfilling with remarkable forbearance. Bridget noticed with alarm, however, that Noos was rapidly approaching him.

"Come on, you great oaf!" she growled, for once abandoning the timidity she had previously shown towards him. "Hack it about properly! We don't want the people who eat this to know what's gone into it, do we now?"

To Bridget's relief she saw a smile flicker across Stigrath's craggy face. *Good, he won't cause any trouble*, she thought, *at least, not for the time being.*

The gross figure of Blam appeared at the cave's entrance. "Right!" he shouted in his remarkably cracked, squeaky voice. "They're ready for it. Start ladling it out. And hop to it!"

A well-rehearsed routine then followed. Great trays of plates were brought *en masse* from the neighbouring caves and food from the bubbling pots was thrown carelessly into them. The tray-carriers then whisked their food-spattered trays off through an entrance at one end of the great kitchen, through which, above the tumult and clatter of the kitchen, they could hear the murmur of an assembly of many voices.

"You too, come on!" Blam's voice came from right behind her. She grabbed one of the trays and followed a sweating, limping little man through a rough passageway into a large cave brightly lit with candles and torches.

It was the cave looking out over the sea from which Bridget had caught her first chilling glimpse of Fles. Only it was dark outside now, and the noise of the wind and the crashing sea which had so dominated the room at the time of their arrival was now obliterated by the clamour of animated conversation and raucous laughter.

The room was full of the robed 'brothers', Vencengea's followers, waiting impatiently at long trestle tables to gorge themselves on the highly spiced and coloured foods that were being brought in from Blam's kitchen.

The 'brethren' all had their hoods drawn back, revealing their features, and Bridget stopped in her tracks in surprise, almost dropping her tray. She had seen one or two of the brethren's faces since their arrival – strange, twisted features which made them look as if they had been in some horrible accident. Her immediate reaction had been one of pity. But now she realised that not just some, but all of the members of this sinister community were misshapen, in body or face. All of them without exception were damaged or scarred in one way or another. Some had enormous ears or lop-sided, knobbly noses. Others had jaws which jutted out or protruding foreheads, or flat tops to their heads. Almost all of them, like Stitgoe and Lulby, had something odd about their features, though none of them, she reflected, were quite as bizarre as those two.

Who, she wondered, were these strange creatures who seemed so devoted to the 'Dark Lady'? In her imagination, Bridget began to think of them as the warped offspring of Vencengea's ill-famed experiments.

The place was so full that she did not immediately catch sight of Vencengea. But finally Bridget spotted her, at the head of the central table, joining fully in the merriment. She appeared to be swapping jokes and stories in a loud voice with those of the brethren closest to her.

A sudden hope flickered through Bridget's mind, and she glanced quickly round the tables. But she soon realised, with an intense pang of disappointment, that her friend Pageya was not there.

Yet she must surely be on the island. Bridget wondered where Vencengea was keeping her.

The feast continued for some time. Bridget could not remember how many trays she carried in and out. She began to feel annoyed. Why, after all, had they been brought here? To serve Vencengea and her loutish followers? No, she was sure Vencengea had some other purpose for them, but was biding her time before revealing it. And in the meantime, it seemed, she was intent on humiliating them as much as she could.

Fine, thought Bridget, *let her try. I shall not rise to her little provocations.*

Gradually even the brethren's evident gluttony began to reach its limits, and the process of removing plates and trays began. Bridget was passing the end of the table next to Vencengea with a tray loaded with empty dishes when the Dark Lady suddenly rose to her feet.

"And now, everyone, pray silence," she called in her deep but piercing voice, "for I have something to tell you."

Her tall figure suddenly seemed to tower high above Bridget. The girl turned towards her and was immediately transfixed, frozen by the icy glare of Vencengea's eyes looking straight down on her. Bridget was forced to look away. Her limbs weakened involuntarily, and she was forced to lay the tray down heavily on the nearby table.

When she looked up again, Vencengea had turned back towards the assembly.

"In a moment," Vencengea continued, "we shall move down to the amphitheatre, to the Pool of Edath, to view this evening's show!"

The brethren, evidently quite well oiled with whatever drink it was they had been sampling, raised a raucous cheer.

"But first I have to say welcome to a special guest. I have to introduce to you the lady Bridget, who has graced us with her presence, and to her companions…" (Vencengea lowered her voice in mock awe) "…full-blooded natives, can I say, of the Green Vale!"

This provoked a loud jeer of derision.

"To our new guests!" roared someone at the back of the drunken assembly.

"Our new guests are to be treated with respect," Vencengea continued, her tone sounding almost serious. "As they have been so far, is it not so, Blam?"

Blam, at the entrance to the kitchen, bowed in mock agreement. The company, obviously thinking this was all part of some huge joke, burst into another noisy round of laughing and shouting.

A scuffle seemed to break out at that moment somewhere down at the end of the hall, but Vencengea's voice rose imperiously above the hilarity and it quickly died down.

"Brethren, are we going to disgrace ourselves in front of the newcomers?" she shouted.

"No, no!" came back the response.

"Then let us move off with some order and dignity!"

"Ooo-oooh, dignity!" some of the diners cried and made round eyes at each other. Then they all to a man (Bridget noticed that the community was made up exclusively of men) rose from their tables with much scraping and banging of stools and benches, and began to jostle each other, pushing their way in a very undignified manner towards an exit at the far end of the cave.

Vencengea too pushed back her throne-like chair from the table and turned towards Bridget. Stigrath, Bridget noticed out of one eye, had appeared from the kitchen and was hovering in the background, ready to intervene. He was evidently taking his duties as her guardian very seriously.

"You, dear Bridget, will of course come too," said Vencengea in her most unctuous voice, "and bring the bear and the elf as well, if you like! We have some fun prepared specially for you this evening."

Vencengea's words sent a shiver of foreboding down Bridget's spine. Whatever it was that Vencengea had prepared as a 'show', she suspected it could not be anything too pleasant. She felt absolutely certain she did not want to accept Vencengea's invitation. Yet clearly she was not being given a choice. Several of Vencengea's robed acolytes had formed a circle around her. In desperation, Bridget signalled across the room to Stigrath and Orin to join her. The acolytes stiffened as Bridget's friends approached, but Vencengea gestured with a swift movement of one long, thin arm to let them pass. Then she turned sharply towards the door at the end of the refectory through which the other Brethren had disappeared, and Bridget and her friends had no option but to follow her.

The door led outside on to the windswept face of the cliff itself. A narrow path led along the precipitous side of the island, with a sheer drop to their left, plunging down to the restless lake beneath. It was now totally dark, and some of Vencengea's followers had lit large, guttering torches which they held aloft to show the way. Some of the torch-bearing brethren had already progressed some way along the path, and their pools of reddish light began twisting and turning along the cliffside, high above the unseen waters beneath.

With growing trepidation, Bridget followed Vencengea's tall, commanding figure along the exposed pathway. The wind was rising again, and although it was not nearly as strong as on the day they had arrived, it pulled and tugged at her clothes. A false step or a moment of indecision, she realised, could send her tumbling down the sheer face of the cliff.

They turned a corner, and Bridget suddenly realised where they were going. Their party was heading in the general direction of the promontory Bridget had seen on their arrival. In another couple of minutes they would reach the thin ridge which connected the island with the rocky promontory she had seen from their quarters. She remembered the high pinnacle she had seen rising from the centre of the promontory. Although the night was terrifyingly dark, apart from the line of torches proceeding along the cliff, Bridget she could just make out the contours of the giant rock tower, blacker, if that were possible, than the rest of that black night.

They reached a point where the track swung out on to the perilously narrow ridge heading out towards the dark pinnacle. Without a moment's hesitation Vencengea plunged out along the ridge.

Although Bridget could not see the water far beneath them, she could hear it thundering against the rocky shore hundreds of feet below. And the water, she now realised, was on both sides, with the ground on either side of the path plunging steeply away into the darkness. As they made their way out on this horribly exposed place, the path seemed to grow narrower and narrower. In places it could not have been more than a couple of metres wide.

Vencengea, her mantle streaming out in the wind, turned back towards them.

"We call this the Ridge of Resolution," she called to them above the blast of the wind. "Those who cross it need strong nerves and belief in themselves!" Then she turned away from them again, laughing her loud, melodious but strangely chilling laugh.

Bridget clutched at Stigrath's sleeve and clung firmly to it as they made their way tentatively out along the ridge. Orin in turn clung to her. The path was not only narrow. It rose and dipped, and was extremely uneven. Several times Bridget stumbled, but felt Stigrath's grip tighten round her hand as he guided her onwards.

The icy blast of the wind took their breath away. It had tremendous force, and it was uneven, coming in sudden squalls which would attack them unexpectedly, tearing wildly at their clothes, and then die away with equal abruptness, so that they almost toppled over the edge on the windward side.

She saw Orin glance nervously downwards.

"Don't look down, Orin," she urged, even though she knew he could probably see nothing. "Don't look down. Just keep on walking across."

At last they came to the other side.

Here, unexpectedly, the path split in two, with one branch turning off to the right and losing itself among the jumbled rocks of the high promontory. Bridget could now see much more clearly the outline of the giant stone finger looming threateningly above them.

The left-hand branch of the path cut off at an angle down the sloping side of the headland. And this was the one they followed. They were now directly above the great natural amphitheatre that Bridget had noticed when she first gazed out towards the peninsula. Their path began to plunge downwards, twisting and turning in a series of switchbacks round the sides of this awesome, vertiginous hollow in the rock. Those who had gone ahead, both monks and servants, were already some way down the path. The torches or lanterns which they carried, guttering and flaring in the wind, made a vivid zigzag of light on the side of the precipice as the column of dark-robed figures snaked down towards the sea.

The path here was steep, so steep indeed that at times they had to cling to the rocks on the inner side. The wind went on tugging and pulling at their clothes. The sea itself was invisible, but as they progressed downwards Bridget began to see what looked like a flat space at the bottom of the giant rock bowl. When they descended further, Bridget could see that it glistened in the reddish light of the torches.

It was water! A small lake or pool on the floor of the amphitheatre.

Vencengea turned to them again.

"Behold!" she said, "the Pool of Edath. For many it is the last place on earth they visit…"

Chapter Thirty-Eight
A Deadly Duel

They were nearly at the bottom of the zigzag path before Bridget noticed something unusual about the tiny lake. Near the centre of the water was a dark shape, possibly some sort of island in the middle of the pool. When the first of the torches arrived at the bottom of the great rocky bowl, she saw it more clearly. It was an island all right, though little more than a flat slab of rock.

The spectators had begun to assemble on a broad ledge which stretched all the way round the pool, about ten feet above the water level. Their torches reflected on the rippling surface of the water, broken as it was by the ceaseless wind. The whole scene created an eerie impression of restlessness and turbulence.

Vencengea took up position on a platform of rock slightly higher than the circular ledge and stood motionless above the water. Bridget and her friends were left to their own devices, and for a fleeting moment Bridget thought of trying to disappear into the shadows. But she realised at once that it would be hopeless. There was little likelihood that there was any other exit from this dark and sinister place other than the path by which they had descended. Her friends evidently felt the same. They approached the poolside not far from where Vencengea was positioned, still not knowing what to expect, yet strangely drawn by an inexplicable curiosity.

They had not long to wait. Some sort of hatch opened on the flat rock in the middle of the pool and several figures emerged, some pushing the others. Then a number of them retreated back down the hatch, leaving just four men, dressed in ragged clothes and grasping long poles.

On their appearance, the crowd of monks and servants immediately started to hiss and boo, and set up a hostile chant of, "Skomiar, Yenomi, Skomiar, Yenomi!"

Stigrath leant over to Bridget and muttered in her ear: "Skomiar people not popular with ordinary Orotworm folk! Also not like… Yenomi!"

"Yes, that's pretty obvious," commented Bridget in return. "So these are both Skomiar and Yenomi, put together. I bet they don't like that much. But what's going to happen to them? What are they going to do with those poles?"

Stigrath shrugged. He seemed as baffled as she was.

At that moment a small stream which had been quietly spattering down the cliff into the pool at one side rapidly began to grow in size. Clearly, someone had released a sluice gate further up the stream or diverted a much larger watercourse into it, for it quickly became a torrent. The assembled company gave a cheer and waved their torches and lanterns in approval.

The level of the pool around the rock began to rise.

Bridget was beginning to have a very bad feeling about what was going to happen. But she could do nothing but stand there and watch, her mouth growing gradually drier. The water's level was now rising rapidly. Bridget glanced at the four figures on the rocky island with their flimsy poles, and she began to have an inkling of what sort of show this was going to be.

Something was moving in the water. It was something large and smooth and pale, and which swam very fast. An awe-struck 'ooh' went up from spectators, and Bridget saw several of the women from the kitchen staff clutch at each other.

"The Engra!" one of the monks declared, with grim satisfaction. "The Engra is hungry!"

The sleek white creature in the water began to swim round and round the island. What was it? A shark? Some sort of fresh-water crocodile? It was impossible at first to see. But its circling round and round the rock had a hypnotic effect, building up within the watching crowd a palpable feeling of tension and anticipation.

Bridget wanted to look away, but couldn't.

Perhaps it's another of Vencengea's illusions? she told herself optimistically.

The level of the water was now only just below the level of the flat rock. The four men seemed, for the first time, to realise how the poles they had been given were meant to be used. One of them, she saw, was examining the end of his and appeared to be grinding it deliberately against the rock. Clearly, the poles were intended to give the four men some means of warding off the creature in the water. The poles, in other words, though clearly inadequate as weapons, were supposed to create some sort of contest for the spectators.

The water was now lapping over the rim of the rock, but the creature still kept its distance, circling slowly round and round the island. Bridget tried to make out what sort of animal it was, and now and again thought she caught a glimpse of tiny, cruel eyes and a broad mouth full of whiteness.

She looked at some of the faces around her. They were clearly gripped by the drama of the coming confrontation, half-excited, half-horrified. Some of them were muttering to themselves or their neighbours. Bridget had the distinct impression they had seen similar 'shows' before and knew what to expect.

She looked at Vencengea. The Dark Mistress, to her surprise, seemed to be the only one who was not particularly enjoying the drama of the situation. At first she thought that the look on Vencengea's face was one of indifference, but then she revised her view. No, Vencengea's expression was one of distaste, even of pain. What! Was it possible that the mistress of the island was actually feeling sorry for the unfortunate men she was using to impress the baser instincts of her followers?

Bridget turned back to the pool just in time to see the creature make its first move. It slunk with deceptive indifference to a corner of the pool just under Vencengea, as if to pay her homage, and then turned with a sharp splash and raced at remarkable speed towards the now submerged island.

The four men were ready for it. They were now up to their waists in water. At a bark of command from one of them, they raised their poles and pointed them in the direction of the oncoming beast.

At the last minute, however, it veered away and took to circling the rock again, slowly and deliberately. *It's just playing with them,* Bridget breathed to herself. *The horrible thing's just playing with them. The water's not deep enough yet.*

A moment or two later, however, the creature made its second pass, this time from quite close to the rock where the men stood. By now the water was well above the level of the flat-topped rock, and the men were up to their chests in it, struggling to keep their feet. But again they were ready. There was a lot of splashing around the rock and for a moment a shiny white body slid up out of the water, but was pushed to one side and plunged back into the deep water. The combined strength of the poles had deflected its attack and the men were safe.

But not for long. The creature kept attacking, at different angles and from different distances. It was only a matter of time before it succeeded.

The monster was deflected by the poles for perhaps the fifteenth time, but this time twisted with remarkable alacrity and plunged back towards the men. One of them gave a scream and disappeared.

To Bridget's disgust and horror many of the spectators round her burst into spontaneous applause, cheering and clapping wildly at the success of the creature. They were clearly supporting the creature, not the men.

For a while there was silence from the pool. The three remaining men were left circling warily, back to back, watching for the reappearance of the creature. Though Bridget could not see their faces, she could feel their fear and tension even from this distance. One of them began to babble something in his native tongue, though it was not clear whether they were prayers or curses and whether they were addressed to the Fates, the audience or the creature.

Several of the audience laughed and threw jeers at the doomed men.

The men shouted back defiantly. There were further taunts.

Then the creature struck again. Its new attack came so unexpectedly that the men missed its direction. The man who had been cursing saw it too late and was borne away into the deep water. As he went under he let out a long, terrible roar of hatred and defiance.

Now there were only two. The crowd waited with anticipation for the creature to finish them off.

It launched itself again. The two men, in what appeared to be a rehearsed move, jumped apart and let the sleek white body slip through between them. For a moment or two it seemed to flounder in the deeper water. It had, for the first time in this unequal contest, miscalculated.

It tried again, and the men fell apart as before, leaving it to slide through. This time it turned quickly, as it had when it captured its first victim. But the men were equal to it. They had their poles ready and managed to repel its sudden twist.

The creature swam backward and forward, apparently perplexed by this new turn of events. The crowd was suddenly silent and tense, sensing that the contest was no longer the old, one-sided show they had come to expect. The creature faced real intelligence and a resourcefulness it was not used to.

Bridget saw the two remaining men talking to each other, evidently discussing their next move.

The creature swam close to the submerged rock and made a feint as if to swim away again, but at the last moment changed direction and launched itself at the men at full speed, an upper row of sharp white teeth showing just above the surface of the water. One of the men shouted a sharp command and their two poles rose simultaneously above the water and formed a prong aimed directly at the creature's open jaws.

There was a violent splashing and both men disappeared under the water, evidently driven out into the deeper part of the pool by the momentum of the attack.

For several moments there was silence. Then something broke the surface of the pool. It was the creature, still swimming. It began to go round and round the pool again, as it had done before, as if in triumph. There was no sign of either man.

The spectators broke into a roar of approval.

Then it slowly began to tail off. There was something protruding from the creature's mouth, like a double-pronged fork. It was the poles that the two men had rammed down its throat. And they had not sharpened the ends of their poles for nothing. The creature was bleeding, bleeding profusely as it swam round the pool, going more and more slowly.

Then it disappeared.

Two heads emerged from the water just under the platform on which Vencengea was standing. The two men who had killed the monster swam easily to the bank and pulled themselves slowly out of the water, obviously weary and bruised. One of them was bleeding from a gash on one arm. Deliberately, almost insolently, they climbed up the rocks towards Vencengea.

One of them, a squat muscular man dressed in a rough leather tunic, pulled himself up straight and addressed the Dark Mistress.

"We have overcome your monster, Lady Vencengea. As you see. I believe that the reward for winning this contest is our freedom, a free passage away from this isle and back to our homelands."

This bold statement was greeted with hissing and a low muttering from some of the nearby spectators. But Vencengea held up her hand to silence them.

"You are correct, Skomiar. Those are the rules of the contest… And they will be honoured."

The second man, taller than the first and dressed in a simple garment of high quality cloth, now stepped forward.

"Then we demand that a boat be put at our disposal at once."

Bridget looked at the men curiously. They were so dissimilar, one a Skomiar and one obviously a Yenomi. Yet they had worked together so well to defeat the creature. And something about the taller one seemed very familiar, as if she had seen him before. But she could not think where.

A slow smile spread over Vencengea's face.

"You demand a boat, proud Yenomi," replied Vencengea, feigning surprise, "but the rules of the contest say nothing about a boat! Go by all means! But you will have to provide your own boat. We have none to spare."

There was a moment's silence. Then the spectators who had followed this exchange burst into laughter and cheering. Their leader had outwitted the stupid Skomiar and Yenomi and punctured their inflated pride!

The Yenomi officer looked thunder-struck, but recovered his poise quickly.

"Then will you, proud lady, grant us lodging in your domain and enough freedom on your island to seek materials to build a boat?"

The spectators looked eagerly towards Vencengea, to see what her reaction would be. She hesitated, but only for a few seconds. Then she nodded and said:

"By all means... though I do not think you will find it easy to collect what you are looking for. And... be aware that my servants are unlikely to aid you!"

There were more approving noises from the onlookers.

The squat Skomiar bowed, in acceptance of this judgement. But his tall Yenomi companion was still not satisfied. "Just one more favour, milady," he said.

Vencengea looked irritated, but nodded reluctantly.

"We would like assurances about the two companions who arrived with us on your island, the boy and the woman. We need to know if they too will be safe."

Vencengea frowned. "Why should they not be?" she asked sharply.

The Yenomi swallowed hard to suppress his anger. "As we have seen today, Lady Vencengea, not all your guests survive the honour of your hospitality... As our comrades Kotz and Erash know to their cost!"

Again the two names he mentioned stirred memories in Bridget's mind, but still she could not think where she might have met this man or his dead comrades before.

The Mistress of Iprades waved her hand impatiently. "You have no need to know what I plan to do with the boy and the woman. Perhaps I shall change my mind and sell you, Yenomi, as a slave to the Skomiars and you, Skomiar, to the Yenomi... So be warned! Do not cause me any trouble..."

"As for our other guests," said Vencengea, turning on Bridget and her friends. "Take them back to the kitchens. And Blam, tonight you will lock them in their quarters, do you understand?"

Chapter Thirty-Nine
Images in the Dark

It was only when they were half-way up the zigzag track to the top of the cliff that Bridget remembered where she had seen the Yenomi knight before. He had been one of the Silver Knights who came to collect the levy of young people at Wesomethe! What had his name been? Something like Piltoc… or Pailtac… The more she thought about it, the more she was convinced that it was he.

And that made her think about what he had said to Vencengea. He had said something about a boy and a woman. Could that possibly mean…?

No, surely not, she said to herself. They had left Tom in Teivos, not in Tekram. And Madge had stayed at Nirei. Why should she think they had now come to this god-forsaken island? She was letting her imagination run away with her.

Yet for the next few days she couldn't get the idea out of her mind that Tom and Madge might be on the island. And it was with a small thrill of excitement that she caught sight one afternoon of the self-same Yenomi, Pailtac, apparently arguing with Blam at the entrance to the kitchen about some goatskins used to hold water and which the head cook was about to jettison.

"If you do not need these old skins any more, then give them to us, fat man!" the already irate Yenomi was saying.

"I would rather give them to the Evil Fates themselves," replied Blam with a leer. "Even an overused goatskin is too precious a material to give to a Yenomi!"

"But you heard the Lady Vencengea herself say we were free to gather material for our voyage off your island," said the exasperated Yenomi lord.

"But of course! You are free to try… and I am free to refuse!" And Blam laughed his grating, corncrake laugh.

Bridget sidled up behind Blam and before he could stop her she spoke to the Yenomi knight.

"Excuse me, sir, but if you are in touch with the boy and woman who arrived on the island with you, could you tell them that there's somebody here who may be a friend of theirs?"

The Yenomi's eyes almost popped out of his head. Blam, meanwhile, let out a roar of anger and tried to hustle Bridget back into the kitchen.

"Tell them my name is Bridget!" she called to the Yenomi knight as Blam dragged her round a corner.

Blam was livid. From a nearby hook on the wall he grabbed a leather belt which Bridget had seen him use to beat others who had offended him. Luckily for Bridget, Noos appeared just at that moment.

"Don't be a fool, Blam," she hissed. "You know the Mistress said the girl was not to be touched."

"Then you punish her!" snarled Blam. "Put her in Cell Three! And no food or water for the rest of the day!"

In fact, Bridget escaped all punishment because at that very moment Lulby appeared and announced that "the girl from beyond" and her companions had been summoned before Vencengea herself.

"Go and fetch your friends," he ordered impatiently. Clearly, he was not in a very good mood. "You are to follow me at once."

Bridget went and called Stigrath and Orin. Hurriedly, they tore off the dirty white overalls they wore for kitchen work and followed Lulby.

He led them to the refectory where they had served at the great celebration meal and continued across it out on to the cliff path. Soon, they were in sight of the soaring headland they had visited several nights before, culminating in the lofty finger of rock at its peak. The wind was not as strong as it had been on the night of the deadly duel in the Pool of Edath. But by the time they had reached the vertiginous neck of rock which stretched out towards the cliff-lined peninsula Bridget had decided that in spite of the calmer weather she definitely preferred nighttime crossings. In daylight they could see in all their horrific splendour the dizzy drops down on to the jagged rocks and seething waters hundreds of feet below.

Nonetheless they crossed the ridge safely. But instead of taking the left-hand path down towards the amphitheatre and the sinister pool, Lulby led them up the right-hand fork, heading off in among the boulders of the rocky pinnacle.

Almost immediately the path cut into the rock and passed under a stone archway. They found themselves in some sort of vestibule. It was still and dark, lit only by a single guttering torch high up on the stone wall. Bridget detected an odd smell, as of incense. To the right she noticed a spiral staircase twisting upwards towards an unseen light. But Lulby ignored this and led them straight to the other side of the vestibule, to a heavy, dark blue curtain.

He yanked it back and, casting a whimsical look in their direction, disappeared beyond it.

They followed and found themselves in a large cave, so large that the feeble torchlight filtering through the curtain from the vestibule very soon lost itself in the darkness. Bridget could make out neither walls nor ceiling. But she sensed the empty space in front of them. And Lulby had vanished completely. They were alone, it seemed, though Bridget suspected they would not be alone for long.

"Do you have the feeling we've been somewhere like this before?" she murmured to her companions.

"I think Vencengea might be somewhere near at hand!" Orin suggested.

"Different place. Same old tricks!" grumbled Stigrath.

It was no surprise, then, when a torch suddenly flared in the middle of the dark space in front of them, some distance away. And then a second... and a third. Five torches in all, set in different places around the cavern. Or maybe five reflections of the same torch.

"You see," Stigrath muttered darkly. "Her Ladyship... doubtless... appear directly."

As if on cue Vencengea did appear, not far away, on what appeared to be a balcony some fifteen feet above them, to their right. She was leaning on a parapet, staring into the darkness beneath her, not looking directly at them. She had a playful, half-amused look on her face.

"So, my dear friends," she began, "how are you managing with deciphering the messages so carefully encoded, it seems, by that old rogue and would-be magician Kalmom? Have you come any closer to finding what he fancifully calls the 'Opening'?"

None of them said anything in reply. So after a pause Vencengea spoke again.

"But of course I was forgetting. You have not spoken to your friend Thomas recently. And he has taken a different itinerary from yours... I assume by design... so that he may have some of the answers, and you the others."

The friends glanced at each other in surprise. A sudden hope flared in Bridget's heart. Did this mean that Tom and Madge really were on the island?

Yet she knew she must still be on her guard. She had seen before the sort of game that Vencengea liked to play with people's hopes and fears.

"Do you know where Tom is?" she called anxiously. "And his Aunt Madge?"

Vencengea did not answer at once. "Ah, I am sure you would like to have some news of them, would you not? Yes, I'm sure you would..."

"Tell us what you know. Please. Are they safe and well?"

Vencengea said nothing. She went on staring down into the darkness beneath the balcony where she was standing. Or was she in fact standing there, or somewhere else, and this was just an image, projected into the cave...?

It's as if this is a recording of her image, prepared in advance, Bridget thought. *It's as if she's not even here at all...*

The answer to her musings came in the form of a low laugh from the balcony.

"Oh, I am indeed here, child... I am indeed here with you."

Bridget felt a chill pass down her spine. How did this sinister person know what she was thinking?

"Please tell us something," she pleaded.

But there was no answer. Bridget was beginning to feel an increasing frustration. Perhaps she should show her anger? Would that work? Would that impress this haughty and heartless person?

Then the 'Dark Mistress' disappeared, and there was nothing but darkness...

When she reappeared she was much closer to them, under one of the nearby torches, and was pacing from side to side beneath it. *Perhaps it's a trick*, Bridget thought. *Perhaps Vencengea doesn't know where Tom and Madge are at all. Perhaps she's trying to trick **us** into revealing their whereabouts!*

"I have had certain reports," Vencengea said in a low voice, "that your friends have been sighted not far from here, in the neighbourhood of this island.

What they are doing here, of course, is a good question. I am not normally very tolerant of people prying into my affairs, and I consider any attempt to land on this island an invasion of my privacy. That usually is punished very severely…"

Something at the far end of the cavern caught Bridget's eye. Focussing on a point in the darkness beyond the last of the torches, she saw a dim picture taking shape. It began to come closer and clearer, and they saw what appeared to be a wild and windy coastline, with high waves tumbling on to jagged rocks along the water's edge. Slowly the scene moved upwards, passing over a jumble of crags and on to an expanse of sloping rock and sparse grass. On the further side of this slope they could make out a blurred shape, dazzlingly white against the background of the dark rock. As the picture became more focused, they saw that it was some sort of wreckage, with metal spars lying twisted together with shreds of a silvery white cloth material. On one portion of this material, which flapped and twisted in the wind, Bridget deciphered the letters, in a familiar sloping script: "GOO…"

"It's the Goodcheer," whispered Bridget in horror.

"Where are our friends? What's happened to them?" she demanded, turning to where Vencengea had been standing. But Vencengea was no longer there.

"You know what's happened to them, don't you?" Bridget shouted accusingly into the darkness. There was no answer.

The picture of the wreckage had in the meantime faded and now, right beside them, another picture appeared. Bridget's legs almost buckled with surprise.

There, almost within touching distance, it seemed, were Tom and Madge. They were sitting, or so it appeared, on crude bedsteads covered with rough blankets in a room with bare stone walls and little or no decoration. Bridget noted with concern that there was no door, only iron bars along one side.

Both Madge and Tom looked totally bored and fed up. Bridget imagined she could hear in the background a constant noise, either of the wind or the sea… Then to her ever-greater astonishment she heard Tom and Madge begin to speak.

"How much longer are they going to keep us here, do you think?" said Tom, suddenly jumping up and pacing around the room. *"It's been at least ten days since we landed and they said they'd take us back to Orotworm as soon as possible."*

"Weather's been bad, as you heard that priest chap say," replied Madge in a weary voice. *"What did he say his name was? Rayil? The boat doesn't sail in bad weather, and he says they haven't had storms like this in years."*

"Tom! Madge!" shouted Bridget towards the images. "Can you hear us? It's Bridget! And Stigrath! And Orin!"

But clearly they didn't hear a word. They continued their conversation.

"I wonder what they've done with Yentsilbor and Pailtac and the others," Tom was saying, as he slumped back down on his bed, looking totally despondent. *"I could have done with their company. It's utterly awful here. The sooner we get out of this place the better. We've got to get back to that Teivos place to look for Bridget and Stigrath and Orin…"*

"We're here. We're here!" Orin and Bridget called together, as loudly as they dared.

"O Tom! O Madge! Please hear us," murmured Bridget. "You can't go back to Teivos without us!"

"Hm, yes…" Madge was saying, *"…but remember we'll also have to come back some time to repair the Goodcheer."*

"I think our first priority is to find the others, and the other key-words…"

"Our first priority is to find Bridget, I agree. But the second is to repair the Goodcheer and get out of this crazy place as quickly as we can! What good has this mad quest for clues done anyone? No, we have to get out, young man! As soon as we've found Bridget."

"But I'm here, I'm here," pleaded Bridget. "You've found me!"

The images of Tom and Madge suddenly sat upright.

"What was that?" asked Tom. *"I'm sure I heard a voice."*

"Mm… Sounded like a girl…"

"Madge, Tom… did you hear me?" Bridget cried with sudden delight.

But this time they didn't react. *"Must have been my imagination,"* said Madge. *"The wind plays all sorts of tricks in this draughty place."*

"No, I heard it too," said Tom. *"How strange…"*

"Tom, please answer me," Bridget called again. She rushed forward into the heart of the dark space in front of her and called again. But it was no good. She collided with some sort of mirror. Suddenly, there were pictures of Tom and Madge all round her. But their voices could no longer be heard. And no matter how loud or long Bridget pleaded, it was clear that neither Tom nor Madge could hear her any longer. And then their images suddenly faded.

Bridget felt the anger welling up inside her. "Vencengea!" she shouted again into the dark. "Why are you playing games with us?"

Vencengea's melodious laughter rang out nearby. "Games? My dear girl, this is all far too serious to be described as a 'game'."

Vencengea's voice was now very quiet, but crystal clear. She still had not reappeared on her balcony, or anywhere else in the cave, but they could hear every word she said.

"Firstly, I can tell you that you can give up your search for this so-called Opening to the Beyond."

There was a moment's silence. Then Vencengea continued.

"All along you thought you were drawing closer to some great secret, the hidden way to some gateway to the Beyond… and you had worked out that this 'Beyond' might lie on the other side of the great Crystal Lake, near the volcano of Fles. Is that not so? And that you might, you just might, locate there the mysterious Kalmom, the author of the messages you had been reading… Am I not right?"

Again neither Bridget nor her friends replied, so Vencengea went on.

"I can now tell you that you will never reach this 'Opening'. If it exists, you will never live to see it."

Bridget's mouth had gone dry. She did not want to think too much about what Vencengea' words might mean.

"Where is our friend Pageya and what do you intend to do with her?" Bridget demanded. "You have no right to abduct her like this. You should allow us to take her back to her family in the Vale…"

Vencengea's image, bright and fiery, loomed suddenly out of the darkness right beside her. The deep, dark eyes flashed bright in the gloom, glaring down at Bridget, boring into her, larger and more threatening than she had ever seen them before. Her whole figure blazed with anger.

Bridget shrank back, genuinely frightened.

"Abduct her! Take her back to her family! What do you mean?" Vencengea literally screamed. "I am her mother! Do you not understand? I am the only family she has!"

Chapter Forty
A Vision Through the Mist

Vencengea vanished as suddenly as she had appeared. All at once, Lulby was beside them again, this time accompanied by Stitgoe ushering them impatiently out of the long cave, back into the vestibule. But instead of taking them back outside, the two misshapen retainers directed them up the spiral staircase they had seen when they entered.

At the top was another heavy curtain, which Stitgoe drew back.

Another surprise. Before them lay a comfortably furnished and restful room, well-appointed with padded sofas and armchairs which had, Bridget noticed, curiously carved wooden handrests. The walls were entirely covered in rich tapestries and draperies of many colours, though a deep claret red seemed to predominate. The mellow light of three or four candles in glass jars, also tinted red, fell on the carpeted floor. In a hearth to one side, there burned a bright log fire.

The room was empty. Occasionally one of the heavy curtains that surrounded the room was stirred by a draught of air, evidently coming from some passageway hidden by the hanging cloth. Bridget could hear the low moaning of the wind through hidden nooks and crevices somewhere beyond the room.

That, she guessed, must be some sort of *inner sanctum*, Vencengea's own very private space. Yet it did not fit well with the image Bridget had formed hitherto of the Mistress of Iprades. She had always thought of the tall, proud woman as forbidding, sinister and, yes, probably evil. Yet this comfortable, homely chamber seemed to suggest there might be another side to her, a more human side, embittered possibly by disappointment and perceived injustices. Nothing in these rich tapestries and ornate furniture, the mellow lighting or the faint musty smell that hung in the air spoke of anything inherently bad. On the contrary, Bridget decided, it was a very human room.

Bridget's eyes were drawn to the wall above the fireplace. Over the hearth where the fire burned so brightly, there hung a picture. It was the picture of a young person, evidently a girl, standing in a forest surrounded by high mountains. The girl had long, blonde hair, just like Pageya's. Strangely, however, her face was turned away from the artist, towards the highlands, and only the outline of her cheeks was visible.

Bridget would have liked to approach and examine the picture more closely. But Stitgoe ushered them brusquely across the room. At the far side of the room, he pulled the curtains roughly aside and herded them through into a bare corridor. Bridget felt an acute feeling of disappointment. She would have liked to spend more time in the warm and cheerful room.

They found themselves in another short passage, lit dimly by guttering candles in glass jars. It ended in a stout door. Lulby braced himself, as if expecting some shock, glanced at them with a capricious glint in his eye, then flung the door open.

Bridget and her friends were almost bowled over by the blast. As she struggled to keep her feet, Bridget heard what she thought was a mischievous chuckle from the over-sized acolyte.

On the other side of the doorway was a sort of covered balcony, open to the elements. It was, she thought, something like a captain's bridge, with a roof above their heads supported by rock pillars but no glass windows between the pillars to protect you from the fury of the wind. It was now blowing a gale once more, and it howled across the exposed gallery from one side to another, tearing maliciously at their clothing.

Battling as she was to stay upright, it was a few moments before Bridget caught sight of Vencengea. She was sitting on a low bench some distance away at the very apex of the triangular gallery, her back towards them, looking out over the fearsome scene that opened up before her in what was left of the fading grey daylight.

As Bridget fought her way forward, she saw that they were at the very extremity of the island, on a point high over the tumbling waves of the lake beneath. With a deep sense of awe, she glanced right and left, surveying the wild panorama of the storm-torn lake. Huge waves came sweeping towards the island, row upon row of them, seemingly intent on crushing anything and everything in their way. Never had Bridget seen, in any of her many holidays on the coast, a sea so totally unrestrained and vicious as this one. The wind was roaring head on into their covered balcony. And although they were high above the surface of the water, probably hundreds of feet, the spray from the waves as they crashed against the rocks below came spinning up on the ferocious wind and every so often, splashed across the more-exposed side of the balcony.

The Mistress was staring steadfastly out into the storm. It was not immediately clear to Bridget what she was looking for, for there seemed to be nothing at all visible from this gale-blown watchpost but a featureless grey blanket of mist framed between the swelling waves beneath and the ragged clouds above, whipping past over their heads.

Then, as Bridget approached the seated figure in some trepidation, her eyes were abruptly diverted to something happening in the maelstrom in front of them. The clouds parted for just a moment and revealed a wide vista out over the tormented surface of the lake.

And then, right ahead of them, looming over everything else around it, there again was the mountain. It seemed so close that it took Bridget's breath away. Its huge conical shape literally towered above their island refuge. In an instant, Vencengea half rose from her seat and held up an arm, as if saluting the very mountain. Then the curtain of cloud fell back into place and obliterated the stunning vision of volcano and lake as suddenly as it had been revealed. Vencengea sank back into her chair.

It's almost as if she's worshipping the mountain, Bridget thought to herself.

Lulby went up to her and respectfully leaned over her shoulder. She jumped up and whipped around to face them. Bridget saw that she was soaked to the skin. She expected Vencengea to be angry at their intrusion on what had obviously been a private moment.

But to her surprise, she saw that Vencengea was smiling.

"Welcome to my private cliff-top retreat," she shouted above the wind, her face wreathed in smiles. Bridget had never seen her like this before. Vencengea was positively glowing with pleasure.

"This is where I come," she shouted again, "to look out across to the fateful mountain, the great volcano of Fles…"

Vencengea laid her hand on Bridget's shoulder in an almost-motherly way and led her back away from the worst of the wind.

"Yes," she continued, "I know you cannot very often see it these days… In former times, however, it was there… almost all the time. And you saw it just now! Was it not imposing, was it not the most incredible sight? What did you feel? Excitement? Inspiration? Fear, perhaps?"

She glanced back towards where the mountain had been.

"Often I have come here and gazed on it… and contemplated the mysteries that it holds deep within it…"

Bridget did not know what to answer, so she said nothing.

Vencengea went over to one side of the balcony and leaned pensively on the rock, staring again out into the clouds, as if hoping to see the giant volcano one more time. The wind ripped at her clothes and her hair. At that moment, the Mistress of Iprades presented a wild, an almost-frenzied, sight.

But no longer, Bridget thought, so threatening. No longer quite so frightening. Almost a real human being.

Vencengea turned back to her. The others, whether by accident or design, stayed at a distance. It was just the two of them now, her and the Dark Mistress.

"Do you not understand?" Vencengea asked her, fixing her suddenly with her bright piercing eyes wide open with mock surprise. "Do you not understand why I am so happy? The daughter I thought was lost forever has been found. That is why I hold feasts and sports and other celebrations, every –"

She cut off and gave Bridget a look which the girl did not understand. It seemed to be full of anguish and pain, and yet there was also some hidden pleasure in it, some deep night. And the other… joy. And a certain steely determination. The old familiar Vencengea, Bridget decided, was slowly returning.

"Come with me," she said, taking Bridget by the arm. "Come and talk with me…"

Chapter Forty-One
Vencengea's Plan

Vencengea led Bridget to one side of the balcony, the more sheltered side.

It turned out that it was more than a balcony. It led on to a covered pathway, man-made, which continued round the side of the great rock citadel which Vencengea had chosen for her home. They were at the end of the jagged promontory jutting out into the sea which Bridget had seen from the main island. Over the low retaining wall which divided the path from the precipice they could still see the angry waves crashing with undiminished vigour on the rocks at the base of the promontory. And now and again, as the path dipped or curved, they glimpsed above them the giant stone finger which topped the mass of jagged rocks that formed the headland.

For several minutes, as they walked, Vencengea was silent, apparently lost in deep thought. She no longer looked out on the tempest. She had drawn in on herself and seemed to be studying the rock floor they were walking on. Bridget also remained silent. She simply did not know what to say.

Then Vencengea began to talk again, and her words were still directed only at Bridget. The others were following at a distance, but remained some way behind. It was as if Stitgoe and Lulby were keeping them away from their mistress and Bridget.

"It is difficult to describe to you what the finding of my daughter Pageya means to me! For years I have sought her. For years that treacherous and self-righteous upholder of the so-called Balance Kalmom has hidden her from me! But she is my only child, the only one surviving of the twins I bore…"

Vencengea paused for a moment to look down at the angry surface of the lake.

"For months I could not accept that her twin, Pathemy, was no longer alive. I returned over and over again to the high place where the rock had tumbled down and covered the path towards the snowy mountains. Hopelessly I searched through the tangled rocks for some sign that they could have survived, the child and the one called Maani, who had also, as I thought, perished. I used all the means I knew to move some of the rocks… I employed local villagers to prize the rocks away so I could look underneath. I even produced explosions with the powers I had developed and sent rocks careering down into the valley below…

"But all my efforts were in vain. I found nothing, and when I managed to disturb the rocks which blocked the path, it only brought new rock falls down from above, so that the place was even more perilous than before…

"Then, in desperation, I resorted to calculations that the rock fall might have

218

been narrow enough to miss them. Perhaps they had escaped and climbed on up into the high range! I took food and clothing and climbed up beyond the valley where the rock fall had occurred, up into the snowfields and gorges above, ever higher and higher… But the winter had come, and I was driven back by the fierce storms, the driving snow and the bitter cold.

"… And so, finally, my thoughts turned to the child that I knew had survived and the person who had taken her, Kalmom."

Vencengea paused again, as if overcome with emotion. A fierce gust of wind ripped along the open walkway, almost knocking Bridget from her feet. When she recovered, she found that Vencengea had continued along the covered path. The others were still about fifty yards behind them. Bridget hurried on to keep up with the Mistress. Vencengea was still speaking, almost as if she were talking to herself.

"I returned to the Mephadore… but they were not there. Nor were they anywhere that I could find! I made enquiries, used subterfuges so that people were obliged to tell me what they knew. But they genuinely, it seemed, knew nothing… I pursued him, Kalmom the kidnapper, to every corner of the Realm. Everywhere, over plain and mountain, up rivers and across lakes, convinced that sooner or later he would betray where he had hidden the girl. I sent my agents to infiltrate the fraternities in whom I thought he confided. Once or twice I almost had him. But he proved more resourceful than I expected…"

They continued to walk in silence around the promontory. Now they were above the tall and narrow neck of rock which led out from the main island, and Vencengea stopped again.

"I had for years devoted myself to studying the science of thought-transmission. I had become adept in reading the thoughts of others, even from some distance off. I tried to track down Kalmom this way. But somehow, though I never thought very highly of his skills in this domain, he managed to block all my attempts to surprise him…

"I realised that the girl would not always be with him. And of course my search for her was even more painstaking than my search for him. But strange to relate, though I often found tracks of *him*, of the hypocrite and traitor Kalmom, I never found any trace of the girl… of my beloved daughter.

"I tried all the ways I knew to find at least some small piece of information about her. But I found not a trace, not a scrap…

"I used to think longingly, with pain in my heart, of my girl, my lost daughter, of how old she would be, of what she would now look like… I fell into moods of deep depression and despair… What had he done with her? I began to fear the worst. Had he killed her, by design or accident? Only this, I began to believe, could explain why she had so totally disappeared from the physical and psychic world…

"After that I hated Kalmom even more fiercely… if that were possible. And I was even more determined to track him down and exact my revenge… And what a terrible revenge that was to be, when I found him!"

With a sudden jerk Vencengea turned and strode further along the pathway.

It only partly sheltered them from the wind and rain, and Bridget found that her face was now wet with spray and drizzle, and glowing from the chill wind.

They were now moving on to the windward side of the promontory, and the gale began to beat on Bridget's ears. Vencengea had to raise her voice to be heard. But she continued her tale, talking to the wind as much as to her companion.

"Gradually, another possibility dawned on me... Even if the Maani himself had not survived the rock fall, could he have passed on to Kalmom the secret of how to find his land across the mountains of the Great Divide? What if Kalmom had found a way of reaching it himself, taking my daughter there with him and leaving her there? Could it be that on those occasions when I had managed to find traces of Kalmom, but not the girl, it was because only he had returned? Had my daughter all along been untraceable for the very reason that she was not in this Realm of ours, but in a totally different one, a world which was unreachable? Was it his intention to keep the girl, my precious daughter, there on the other side of the mountains... where I could not find her or even detect her existence?

"And suddenly my heart began to glow, warmed by a new hope! What if Pathemy too was over there, on the other side? What if the other child, the one I had lost all hope for, he had all along survived the rockfall and been taken by the Maani to his world?

"Then the day came when my agents brought a report which I did not at first believe. They said the Maani had returned. He had come back across the High Mountains and had arranged to meet his associate Kalmom in a small hut high in the snowfields...

"Could it be true? My heart leapt...

"Did I dare trust the report?

"If it were true, I could not believe my luck! Here at last was my chance, not just to catch up finally with Kalmom the betrayer, but also meet once more the strange, dithering creature who had been my friend, the man they called the Maani!

"Would he also have the child with him? Or maybe both children? And the jewel they had worn round their necks? My spies said there was no sign of any children... but that did not matter. If I was able to confront Maaniriv, I would find out soon enough where the necklace was... and the children...

"With all speed I travelled to the Green Vale, with Lulby and Stitgoe... For years, during my long search, I had built up a following of men, and some women, among the outcasts and the ill-favoured. I had trained them here in Iprades in the skills of survival and retaliation in this cruel world where the strong dishonour and persecute those who are not favoured with riches or good looks or artfulness... Lulby and Stitgoe were my favourites, those who had particularly won my trust..."

A new gust brought them to a halt, and for several moments both Vencengea and Bridget had to struggle to keep their feet. Then, when the wind died again, they continued along the path. Vencengea, however, had suddenly become remote and silent. When she finally spoke, her voice was subdued.

"We captured one of Kalmom's followers. But the kidnapper himself, and the Maani, escaped. By sorcery... Yes, yes, I underestimated Kalmom's sorcery. He escaped us, and fled back to the Vale. And the Maani... I do not know... perhaps he went back over the high passes... That is what I assumed, anyway."

Vencengea was silent again, this time for several minutes. She had stopped and was now looking vacantly out over to the stormy waters. When she spoke this time, her voice had changed again. It was hesitant and soft, almost like a whisper.

"It was the moment of my deepest despair. I had lost everything. My friends, my children, my revenge, and last but not least my hope of transforming the life of the people of the Realm. For I believed the stones, the pendants, could give me the power to do that..."

She paused. They had now reached a point which looked down on the Pool of Edath, where they had witnessed the terrible duel between the Engra and the four men. Vencengea turned to Bridget, a strange, mischievous smile on her face.

"... And then, high up on the slopes of those snowy mountains, I had an idea. 'What,' I said to my comrades, 'if we ourselves were to cross the mountains to the world of the Maani? And there look for him, and for my lost children, Pageya and Pathemy...'

"Lulby, of course, did not even understand what I was talking about, but agreed to go with me anyway... And Stitgoe was quite tickled by the plan...

"And so, after long preparations, we departed...

"I will not describe all the things that befell us on that terrible journey. I will only say that after many accidents and adventures, we came to the place called Havenmouth and discovered that this was where the Maani had dwelt. And also that he had returned there, not once, but twice... but was now, we were told, dead – of old age and, they said, of a broken heart... "

Vencengea was gazing down at the pool of Edath, far below.

"The question that now tortured me most," she went on, "was whether Pathemy had indeed survived the fall of rock in the ravine. And whether Kalmom and the Maani, those artful conspirators, had indeed managed to reunite Pageya with her twin?"

She moved off again, and soon they were approaching once more the covered balcony at the apex of the promontory. Bridget had listened all the time in silence, and as she listened to Vencengea's extraordinary tale, a host of conflicting emotions began to grow inside her. Now, as the story evidently neared its end, she felt an enormous lump rising in her throat.

"For weeks, even months," Vencengea continued, "we found no trace of either child."

Then she paused, as if wondering how much more to say. But after a moment broke into her low, throaty laughs.

"All we found was his bookshop... and the notebook."

Vencengea stopped again, and for the first time in all this long monologue Vencengea looked directly at Bridget

"We found it in the little house in the back street which he had turned into a bookshop. We found it among all the other nonsense that he had evidently accumulated over the years… And in the notebook he had put the messages, the messages he had received from his fellow conspirator Kalmom…

"But when it came to reading them, what did we find? He had hidden them behind a screen of codes, so that only the Maani could have understood them. At first I was furious. I could read only the opening passages, which were in the language of Maaniriv's country. But after that the traitor's writings were in some sort of indecipherable code… Clearly, they contained an important message – otherwise he would not have hidden it in this way. My companions and I poured over them for weeks, for months, but could make no progress towards deciphering them. I was frustrated and enraged. I cursed Kalmom, the evil and devious one, and Maaniriv, with his deceptively naïve manner which covered such a cunning mind… I even cursed my own children, for not allowing me to find them!

"…But then I thought again… And slowly a plan crystallised in my mind."

A smile spread slowly over Vencengea's face, but it was a smile tinged with sadness.

"In his notebook Maaniriv made no mention of what happened to the second twin, Pathemy," she said. "Perhaps the child had not survived the rock fall, after all… Or perhaps it had. If such were the case, then when Maaniriv died he must have made provision for the child, had it adopted perhaps by some other parents… All that Maaniriv spoke of in his confused jottings was the need to send somebody clever and resourceful back to the Realm, to help combat the troubles which were increasingly besetting it. I also understood that although he had been in touch with Kalmom, their messages must have taken months, maybe even years, to cross the Great Divide. And that Kalmom probably would not have heard of Maaniriv's death…

And that gave me an idea!"

They had reached the balcony again, and the wind was growing ever stronger. It was now tearing at their clothes and trying to push them back the way they had come, as if it did not want them to reach the sanctuary and safety of Vencengea's apartments. There was now an almost constant booming noise as the waves thundered against the rocks beneath. The spray came lashing across the exposed balcony almost without cease.

"My idea was simple. It would require a lot of patience… I would persevere with my efforts to locate my lost children, Pageya and Pathemy, continuing to search through the Maani's own writings for clues. And I would continue my efforts to decode the messages of his confederate Kalmom… But realising that I might well fail in that quest, I devised a secondary plan…

"I would ensnare that trickster Kalmom! I would find two children of similar age to Pageya and Pathemy, my twins, and take them back to the Realm. I would recruit two children, a boy and a girl, and return to the Realm, and let it be known that I, Vencengea, had visited the land of the Maani… and brought back his children…"

A huge wave hit the side of the cliff and came crashing over them.

"We were bait!" cried Bridget. "You used us as bait!"

Vencengea turned away from her, heading for the doorway into her apartment. But Bridget could still hear her words as she struggled to follow her, slipping and sliding in her distress on the treacherous wet surface of the rock floor.

"There would be a second coming, a Second Coming from the Land of the Maani beyond the white snows! I imagined it clearly. The Child of the Maani… no, make it Children, a boy and a girl, whom I would present as Twins! My twins! And they would speak in riddles, the way he did!"

Finally they had reached the doorway which led to the corridor with the guttering candles.

"Our people are so credulous, you know. They have this touching belief in the mystical qualities of all twins! And even more they love people who speak in riddles and interpret them for others!" Vencengea laughed.

"And Kalmom, I knew, would be forced to reveal himself!"

"Why?" Bridget shouted defiantly as the Mistress turned to enter the doorway. "What did you plan to do with us that would make him break his cover?"

Vencengea stopped for a moment, but did not even turn her head. And she did not answer the question.

Bridget felt numb. She did not know whether to laugh or cry. She felt such a dupe.

Suddenly, she felt Orin's hand on her arm. He had come up quietly behind her. Clearly, he had heard Vencengea's final words and understood just how awful Bridget felt. Stigrath had also come up and was mumbling angrily into his beard.

"You can never imagine how difficult it was!" Vencengea's voice was fast receding down the passage. "All the children in that wretched Havenmouth place seemed incredibly stupid, or suspicious, or cowardly."

Then Vencengea turned back to face them, standing in the doorway of her chamber.

"But finally, finally I found what I thought was the perfect pair!"

Bridget and her friends had now come up to her again. Vencengea looked past them, as if they were not there, with her proudest expression.

"Of course, I did not expect you really to decipher the codes… That, I suppose, was a bonus. But whether you did or not was irrelevant. I would make sure that you came here to the Realm and would search for the trail that Maaniriv had apparently concocted with the aid of Kalmom.

"And I would follow you! And sooner or later, you would attract the attention of the man I had grown to hate the most in this world, Kalmom the kidnapper. And you would deliver him into my hands."

Vencengea's figure suddenly straightened as she gazed past them. Bridget turned to look in the direction the Mistress was looking.

For an instant the clouds lifted again for just a moment. And there once more, looming high above them, stood the sinister conical shape of Fles.

"And now, indeed, I have them both!" Vencengea concluded triumphantly.

Bridget caught her breath. "You mean, you have found Kalmom as well as Pageya?" she whispered, unable to believe what she was hearing.

"Yes, and it was you, my dear, who led me to him!"

Chapter Forty-Two
Pageya's Choice

"Is he here, on Iprades?" asked Bridget hoarsely, standing squarely in front of Vencengea.

The Mistress's face darkened. "Alas, no. One more time he has managed to evade my grasp. But at least I know that he is not far away and what disguise he is using."

They had passed along the corridor and re-entered Vencengea's chamber. Bridget, numb in more senses than one, was more than thankful to be back in the warmth and shelter of the richly furnished room. She went straight to the fire and began to warm her hands before its glowing embers.

Vencengea watched her for a moment, then broke into a sudden peal of wild laughter.

"Of course it has happened the wrong way round!" she chuckled. "Of all the stupid yet wonderful things to happen! The idiot Skomiars who were supposed to go and capture you and bring you to Lusedion, brought me the wrong girl and boy... But one of them, wonder of wonders, was my own daughter, my long-lost daughter Pageya!

"...I knew who she was at once. When they brought her to Lusedion. She had the look of her father about her. Those long blond eyelashes and dreamy eyes. And she had a lot of her mother about her too, of course. Practical, sharp, intelligent – she did not inherit those qualities from her father..."

"So why have you brought *us* here?" murmured Bridget. "You found your daughter, if Pageya *is* your daughter. Why do you need us? Why, after you left us to our fate in Lusedion, did you change your mind and bring us here?"

Vencengea gave her a probing look, as if weighing up whether or not to answer. Finally she said:

"At first I thought I had no more need of you... But then I reconsidered."

"But why?"

Vencengea smiled indulgently.

"Why? Because you have not yet delivered to me the one who calls himself Kalmom..."

Bridget could not stifle a small gasp of surprise. Vencengea laughed.

"But my dear girl, why do you find this so unexpected? As I have explained, this was the main reason for bringing you here in the first place. As you say, you were my bait! As I have explained, since I first located Maaniriv's notebook... and the messages it contained... I have been watching over you and willing you to make contact with my oldest adversary, the author of all my woes, that

225

supposedly upright hypocrite whose birth name was Kalmom – though in recent times he has used other names!"

Stigrath, who had said absolutely nothing since they had arrived on the pinnacle, now broke his silence.

"You, Mistress of Dark… cannot keep us here… against our will!"

"Oh but I can, my dear captain. I can keep you here as long as I like!"

The big man stepped forward, but Bridget signalled urgently to him, and reluctantly he backed off, rumbling something incomprehensible in the depths of his vast chest.

Vencengea's eyes twinkled.

"I see you have your bear well tamed," she said with amusement.

Bridget ignored her. "Just how long do you intend to keep us here?" she asked.

Vencengea smiled at her indulgently.

"Until I have accomplished my objective," she said coyly.

"Your objective?"

"Ah! Once again you ask too much. I am not prepared to reveal anything about my intentions, except to say that it may take me some time to fulfil them."

The wind howled miserably outside, billowing out the curtain at one side of the room.

"Quenrie will know what to do!" piped up Orin, who had also been listening in silence. "He will guide us and lead us off this awful island!"

Vencengea's face underwent one of its many rapid transformations. Suddenly, she was alert, on her guard. She stood over the little Elonym, her eyes flashing.

"So who is he, this Quenrie? And why have you so much confidence in him, my little elf? Why does he hide himself so carefully and not come to rescue you?"

Bridget tried to signal to the little Elonym not to say any more. But Orin, as if himself sensing danger, was already trying to turn attention away from Quenrie.

"My sister Geya will not go with you, not by her own will!" he declared defiantly, tears coming into his eyes. "And she will not do what you want her to do, whatever it is!"

Vencengea' features suddenly lost all their benevolence. She glared fiercely down at Orin and for a moment Bridget feared she would do something terrible to the little boy. But then her face relaxed and she merely smiled.

"You would, I am sure, like to see Pageya and speak to her yourselves."

Before they could reply, Vencengea rose and walked over to the curtain leading back out to the stairs. Holding the curtain open she indicated another spiral staircase, this one leading upwards.

"Shall we go and visit her?" she suggested.

Bridget's heart leapt. So her friend was here! But in what condition and what state of mind? Bridget found her own mind was in turmoil, an inner jumble of conflicting emotions – hope, apprehension, puzzlement… anger.

The steps continued up another two spirals before opening out on to a corridor curving away into the darkness to one side. Opposite the head of the stairs was a low wooden door, which Vencengea unlocked with a key attached to a chain round her waist.

They entered a small room. It was tastefully furnished, like the one downstairs, with coloured tapestries and thick woollen rugs. One small window looked out on the leeward side of the promontory and was covered by a pane of yellow tinted glass through which the dying embers of daylight seeped, giving the whole room an artificially warm glow.

At the far side of the room was a small bed, and on it sat Pageya. She was reading what appeared to be a storybook. It had, Bridget saw as she approached, bright but faded illustrations, where armed men appeared to do battle with various ferocious looking monsters.

With a small cry Pageya jumped up and ran across to embrace Bridget.

"Bridget, you are somehow here! It is wonderful to see you! I have missed your company so much!"

For a moment Bridget could not speak, she was so overcome by emotion.

"It's lovely to see you too, Geya!" she finally managed to say. But her words did not convey even part of what she felt.

Pageya also gave Orin a tight hug and then pressed herself against the massive chest of Stigrath, who had knelt in order to embrace her. Bridget noticed that the large captain quickly wiped a tear or two from the corners of his eyes.

"It is so good to see you all!" Pageya exclaimed. "You must tell me all that you have seen and done since we last met."

Bridget glanced at the door, where Vencengea was standing with an enigmatic smile on her face, playing with the key in her hand. Abruptly, as if on an impulse, the Mistress of Iprades slipped out of the room, closing the door softly behind her.

Orin went up to Pageya and said: "Geya, you are not really going away with… with this lady Vencengea, are you? Tell her that you want to come back with me to the Vale!"

Pageya's face fell. She looked down at the covers of her bed and for some moments did not speak. Then she said quietly:

"Orin, I must do what this lady wishes."

Bridget looked at her friend in horror. "But why, Geya? Vencengea is a person of… well, a person who performs dangerous magical tricks, for some incomprehensible reason! Who knows what she may have planned for you? And look, she has locked you away in a remote prison. If she really were a loving mother, as she claims, would she do that?"

Pageya looked at her sadly.

"Bridget, I am convinced that this is indeed my mother, the only one I have… And she has been very kind and understanding to me. Also my illness is getting better under her care. I must respect her will…"

"But she intends to take you away, goodness knows where, and make you a pawn in some mad plot she has concocted! I am sure of it. And heaven knows what the consequences will be… for all of us, but especially for you!"

Pageya look down at the ground.

"My mother has worked hard all her life for the good of ordinary people… ordinary and unfortunate people, like the people here who are her followers. I see that now, though I did not see it before. I was never told by… by those who brought me up… about her efforts to cure illness and make people happier…"

Bridget couldn't believe what she was hearing.

"But Quenrie is your friend. He is devoted to you!"

Bridget suddenly felt someone looming over her. She turned and found that Vencengea had somehow re-joined them and was staring down at her menacingly.

"This Quenrie," she said in a voice which was barely a whisper, "you say he was the… friend of my daughter? This same Quenrie who has been helping you? And where… where, pray, is this Quenrie now? Do you know?"

Bridget, startled by Vencengea' sudden reappearance, replied truthfully:

"I don't know… I really don't. The last time we saw him was in Teivos, in a cell in the Ghalug."

Vencengea uttered what sounded like a low curse. But she did not look too upset by what Bridget had said. On the contrary, it seemed to give her some grim satisfaction. Pageya looked at Bridget pleadingly.

"My friend Bridget," she whispered, "I believe that Quenrie did not mean badly. It is just that he did not know all the facts… He only knew what Kalmom had told him."

A warning bell sounded deep in Bridget's subconscious. She knew Pageya was trying to tell her something. Desperately she searched her friend's face to find what it was.

"You believe," she asked hesitantly, "that Quenrie has been working for Kalmom all along?"

Behind her, Vencengea gave a low chuckle. Pageya's eyes were fixed on Bridget, pleading ever more urgently.

"Quenrie just repeated what his master Kalmom told him," she said softly. "But you must believe, dear Bridget, that the events of my life are more complicated than I once believed. My mother is not the bad person Quenrie told me she was…"

"Bad?" Vencengea whipped round and confronted them both. Her face contorted into a fierce grimace. "Is it bad to want justice for all the wrongs which Kalmom did to me? Is it bad to ask him to return what he stole from me?"

Bridget stared at her, this fierce woman with hatred in her dark eyes, almost demented with rage, and any feeling of sympathy that Pageya's words might have stirred very quickly evaporated.

"If you mean your daughter Pageya, she has been returned to you… So what else is it, Vencengea, that you want?"

To her surprise, Vencengea made no attempt to hide the truth.

"I need the stone," she said, "the other part of the stone!"

And she drew from her bosom the misshapen pendant on a leather thong, the one which for so long had hung round Bridget's own neck. Vencengea held it up before them so that it caught the flickering red glow of the flames in the nearby hearth. The distorted semi-circle of normally dull stone began to glow with an ominous, pulsating redness.

"This is what Thirdrol stole from the mountain," Vencengea went on in a strangled voice. "Or at least, this is half of it."

She turned the stone first one way, then the other.

"No one knows how it was done, but Thirdrol split the stone in two equal parts, giving one half to each twin, or rather to their false guardians, Kalmom and the Maani. I am convinced that when the twin part of this stone is found… and it will be found…" Bridget felt Vencengea's gaze dart in her direction. "… it will join with the other and become one stone again!"

Bridget gazed at the pear-shaped stone, glinting dully in the firelight, so familiar, it seemed, and yet now, suddenly, so alien.

"And what will happen when they are joined?" she asked hoarsely.

"Ha!" said Vencengea triumphantly. "Then we shall have restored something which should never have been so wantonly divided, something unique and infinitely precious… The Eyestone, the one and only Eye of Truth!"

Bridget blinked, unable to hide her astonishment. Vencengea laughed.

"You have not heard of the Eye? It once resided deep within Fles, behind a great glass wall which Thirdrol named the Mirror. And it was the Eye, this stone, which projected its light on the Mirror, and subjected what was before it to a merciless Truth…"

"But… but how? I don't understand…"

"No, no more do I, a mere mortal! All I know is that Thirdrol found this phenomenon, deep within the mountain, and it transformed him, from a vague, dithering old man, into a confident and powerful leader who commanded the respect of all who met him…"

"So… so why did he divide the Eye? If it gave him such power…"

A bitter glint came into Vencengea's eyes.

"Thirdrol was a coward and a hypocrite," she said grimly. "He divided the stone because he did not dare use its power himself. Yet neither did he want anyone else to hold its power and make use of it…"

Stigrath, who until now had remained silent, now made a curious, strangled noise.

"Thirdrol," he muttered, "no way a fool. He knew some men… and women… dangerous with too much power."

Vencengea turned on the giant captain. Once again her expression had totally changed. Gone was the condescending and amused tolerance. Now there was only black anger. For a moment Bridget thought she would bring down some terrible curse on the unfortunate riverman. But then she turned away from him and strode to the door. With a flick of one hand, she opened it and stood back, indicating clearly that it was time for them to go.

"I have perhaps said too much and been altogether too generous with my time… I shall ask you to leave now…"

Stigrath rumbled ominously but again Bridget signalled to him to do nothing.

She rose to her feet, anxious not to alienate Vencengea too much.

"We shall go if it is what you want. But please can we come again to visit Pageya?"

Vencengea made a dismissive sound, as if to indicate that she was really not in a mood to discuss it. Pageya herself came forward to say goodbye.

"Thank you for your visit, dear Bridget," said Pageya. "I am so pleased you are here. Perhaps we shall see each other again tomorrow, or the next day at least."

They embraced and clung to each other for as long as they dared, conscious that Vencengea was standing behind them at the door, waiting. Then Bridget turned to leave, giving her friend a last, tearful smile.

Then she stopped. A powerful urge suddenly welled up inside her to tell Vencengea everything she knew. She wanted for some reason to taunt the tall and haughty woman, tell her that she would never find the other part of the stone, tell her that Quenrie was more powerful and wiser than she was…

Bridget turned back towards Vencengea. But she found that Pageya was looking straight at her. It was as if her friend had detected her intention and was warning her, urgently, to forget it.

So Bridget said simply: "We shall be thinking of you all the time, Geya. And we shall do all we possibly can to help and support you!"

Vencengea made another scornful sound and started to herd them out of the room, as if she somehow feared their influence over her daughter. Pageya said quickly: "Please do not do anything unwise, my dear Bridget. Try to respect my mother. She tries hard to bring happiness to people's lives."

Bridget thought of the 'happiness' which Vencengea had organised for her people at the Engra's pool, and grimaced.

Lulby appeared, to lead them away. As Vencengea closed the door behind her, Bridget's last glimpse of Pageya was of the slender blond girl sitting on her bed staring into space, a look of anguish and indecision on her face.

They were led down the spiral staircase and out into the stormy night. Then back across the dangerous ridgeway to their quarters. This time the crossing was made more difficult still by a thin rain which had begun to fall, making the rocks even more slippery and treacherous than before.

Bridget felt trapped and helpless. She was stunned by all she had learnt from Vencengea. She desperately wanted to get off this dreadful island. Yet there seemed no way of escape. And there seemed no way to rescue Pageya from the ruthless woman who claimed to be her mother.

What was it that Vencengea was not saying?

And why was she, Bridget, so alarmed that Vencengea apparently had Pageya so completely under her control? She could not help feeling that even if Vencengea was Pageya's mother, her intentions were almost certainly not in Pageya's interests.

Had Vencengea herself not more or less admitted that her intentions had much more to do with acquiring the second part of the pendant than the welfare of her daughter, much as she may have loved her?

Bridget decided there and then that she must rescue her friend from the clutches of her passionate and sinister captor. Mother or not, Vencengea has some well-formulated plan in which Pageya would play a significant role, probably as an innocent pawn. Of that Bridget was more than sure.

Chapter Forty-Three
A Plan of Action

The following afternoon Bridget was gloomily working in the kitchen, chopping some tired-looking vegetables on a table beside one of the windy openings that looked out on to the cliff face. She felt very low. She had spent a restless night tossing and turning on her uncomfortable bed wondering if she would see Pageya again before her friend was taken from the island, and coming to the gloomy conclusion that it was unlikely.

Suddenly, a figure appeared in the opening in front of her, standing on the rocky ledge outside, and she had to stifle a little shriek.

"Just go on working," whispered the man, "and don't look in my direction."

She had dropped her knife into one of the bowls on the table. Carefully she picked it out and went on peeling and chopping, though her hands were trembling. She now recognised him as the man who had survived the deadly encounter with the Engra in the Pool of Edath and whom she had seen arguing with Blam about the goatskins. She was ever more certain now, when she saw him close up, that this was indeed the Yenomi knight who had come to take the young people from Wesomethe, the one called Pailtac.

"There's a rough track in the rock from here, beside the window, to the path that leads to the ridge and then down to the Engra's pool."

"The Engra… You mean…?"

"The many-toothed monster that Vencengea feeds people to… Can you find your way down to the pool after you have finished work? I have news for you, from friends."

A small thrill of excitement made her almost drop the knife again.

"Yes… I mean… Well… I think so. We usually finish quite late, though, after it's dark."

"All the better. But be careful on the path… It is quite tricky in places."

"I know," she replied.

And then he was gone.

Bridget told Stigrath and Orin about the visit during their lunch break.

That evening it was extremely late before they were allowed to leave the kitchen. Nevertheless, when Noos and Blam had finally retired to the latter's quarters with several jars of an unidentified liquid, the three of them crept back to the kitchen and out through the window. Their quarters were not normally guarded. Clearly, Blam did not think there was anywhere on this bleak island his 'volunteer' kitchen staff would want to escape to.

The path along towards the promontory was easy enough to follow, even in the darkness. But when they reached the rock saddle they were forced to stop. It was pitch black, and the wind, though not as fierce as the previous day, was still strong. Hundreds of metres below, they could hear the waves crashing angrily against the foot of the cliffs.

"This is madness," said Bridget. "We can't see a thing, and as the man said, the path isn't an easy one."

"Do not fear, Bridget," said Orin. "I have the eyes of our people. We see well and very clearly, even in the dark. I shall guide you."

"Must guide… also… heavy-foot Stigrath!" said the big captain, who was obviously as nervous as Bridget.

Cautiously, with the nimble Orin leading the way and holding Bridget's hand, and Stigrath following as best he could, often on his hands and knees, they began to make their way along the path. At certain points there seemed to be nothing at all between them and the thundering waves far beneath. Again Bridget felt grateful that it was so dark and she could not see what was beneath them.

As they approached the far side, Bridget half expected some night patrol of Vencengea's monks to step out of the shadows and challenge them. But there was nobody.

They found the track which led to the left towards the amphitheatre and were soon winding their way downwards. This time there was no zigzag line of torches to follow, so again they had to make their way carefully, following Orin's instructions and warnings.

At last they reached the bottom and trod warily on to the circular platform that surrounded the pool. The water was low, as it had been when they first arrived on the night of the 'celebration'.

A noise came from a rocky outcrop near where they had stood with Vencengea. Then there came a soft call. They approached, and Bridget felt a firm hand close over her wrist and pull her gently behind the rock.

It was the man she had identified as Pailtac.

"Did anyone follow you?" he asked anxiously.

"No, I don't think so," she replied.

The other man who had survived the fight with the Engra, the broad-shouldered Skomiar, was also there, and he greeted them with a formal dip of the head.

"My name is Yentsilbor," he said. "I am an officer of Teivos… But have no fear. I do not eat children!" And his pockmarked face creased into a toothy grin.

"Pay no attention to this Skomiar dolt," said Pailtac. "Come with us. It is important that you do not make a noise."

They left the shelter of the rocks, crossed over the broad ledge which skirted the pool and, to Bridget's astonishment and consternation, began clambering down towards the edge of the water.

"Are you sure there aren't any more of the creatures?" she asked in an anxious whisper.

"You mean Engras?" asked Pailtac. "Oh yes, there is a whole family of them."

"I take it that's a joke."

"No, no joke. There are at least six of them…"

Bridget stopped in her tracks.

"Do not worry," Yentsilbor intervened. "Only one of them is released into the pool at a time. More importantly, the water is too shallow at the moment for it to swim into the pool. It lives in a deep cave over there near the waterfall. They can only come out when the water is raised."

Bridget wondered if that were true even for smaller ones. Pailtac had said there was a whole family of them. But when they came to the water's edge he jumped unceremoniously in. The water only came up to his waste, but Bridget felt sure that was quite enough for any Engra to swim in. She hesitated again before entering the water.

"Do not worry, young mistress," said Stigrath behind her. "No Engra monster was ever a match for this river captain."

Only slightly reassured, she dropped into the water. She winced at the cold.

"Have no fear," Pailtac said, taking her by the hand. "There will be no Engras tonight."

She stayed very close to the Yenomi knight as they waded across to the island, reminding herself that he and his comrade had already killed one of the creatures. Stigrath had lifted Orin and was carrying him across the circular pool.

They reached the small island without incident and were soon out of the water. Yentsilbor went straight to the stone slab at its centre and pulled it up with little difficulty. Bridget gazed downwards and saw that it opened on to a flight of stone steps, damp and worn by the flow of water which clearly seeped through when the level of the pool was raised.

At the bottom of the steps they came to a roughly hewn corridor which led off in the general direction of the sea. After a few minutes of tortuous progress, they reached a bare stone gallery, one side of which opened on to a rocky expanse at the foot of the cliff, while on the other were ranged a row of doorways, each of them barred by an iron grill.

"Is that you, Bridget?" came an eager voice.

Bridget gave a little cry. It was Tom. It really was Tom!

"Tom, Tom! Is it really you?" she whispered. "Are the others with you too?"

"I don't know which others you mean," came Madge's voice, "But I'm certainly here, for what it's worth!"

Bridget was now at the first iron grill, clasping her friends' hands through the bars.

"But you are locked up!" exclaimed Orin, coming up behind her.

"Here there is no problem," said Yentsilbor, and he simply lifted the iron grill out of its sockets and set it to one side. "The local masons do not have very high standards," he said.

A match flared and Bridget leapt nimbly past Yentsilbor Pailtac and gave Tom an enormous hug.

"Hey, hey," he said, "we're still only good friends!"

Then Madge appeared out of the gloom and even she dropped some of her normal reserve to give Bridget one of the tightest hugs she had ever experienced. Then she did the same to Orin. When it came to Stigrath's turn, she just took him by the hand.

"No hugs for you, I'm afraid, old Bearskin!"

There came a deep, incomprehensible rumble from the sailor's massive ribcage. Bridget realised that he was laughing.

"Are there no guards?" asked Bridget in surprise.

"The Engra is the only guard they think necessary," said Pailtac. "That and the weather…" He glanced at the high waves beating against the rocks below them…

As briefly as he could, Tom explained how they had got there and how once on the island the black-robed crew of Vencengea's ship, the Maibiton, had overpowered them and led them down to these cells under the Pool of Edath. He explained that the two men who had lost their lives in the battle with the Engra were, alas, the knights Erash and Kotz.

Bridget felt a stab of sorrow. She remembered the two men from Wesomethe and though Kotz had not been very gracious then, she felt sorry he had perished in such a way. As for Erash, he had seemed such a cheerful and pleasant man, behind the knightly swagger. Then she felt a sudden surge of anger. How dare Vencengea, who had organised this outrage, pretend to be a caring and loving mother! Did Pageya know what her supposed mother had done?

It was then Bridget's turn to outline her adventures with Orin and Stigrath. Tom was particularly excited that she had found at least one more key word.

"I found one too – on the island of Thifa!" he exclaimed. "If you've worked out more of the messages, then we can compare notes – the bit I deciphered didn't altogether follow on from what went previously."

"I have it here with me!" exclaimed Bridget in excitement, delving into the inner pocket of her anorak.

"Some other time," said Madge, "We don't have enough candle power in this wretched dungeon to read the writing on a cornflakes packet."

It was true. The light in the cave was very dim.

Bridget noticed that Yentsilbor and Pailtac were busy talking to Stigrath at the back of the cell.

"Can it be," she said, "that Yenomi and Skomiar have buried their old enmities and are actually working together?"

"Aye, young lady," said Pailtac, a note of bitterness in his voice, "and more than that. Skomiar and Yenomi have been fighting and dying together."

Yentsilbor nodded. "My friend is referring to our comrades Erash and Kotz. I fought as strongly as he did to save them."

Out of evil, Bridget reflected, some good may come.

"Why were you not included in the fight, Tom and Madge?" Bridget asked quietly.

"Well for heaven's sake, I'm just a woman," snorted Madge. "It would dishonour the wretched monster if I put in an appearance!"

"And I was considered to be 'a mere boy'," Tom muttered, "no fair game for the punters!"

"And where is Quenrie?" Bridget asked, suddenly realising the little sage was not with them. "Is he not here? You said he escaped from the Nilmerk too…"

Tom shook his head. "Quenrie refused to come here to Iprades, and now that we've come to know the island, we can understand why." He looked nervously round him. "Given Vencengea's extraordinary talent for eavesdropping, it's probably dangerous even to mention where we last saw him…"

The business-like Pailtac was beginning to lose patience with the general chatter.

"It's time we discussed important matters… like when we are going to escape from this island. I take it that our new companions also want to dispense with the hospitality of Lady Vencengea?"

Stigrath agreed volubly, but Bridget hesitated.

"What's the matter, Bridget?" asked Madge. "You haven't fallen in love with this secluded paradise, have you?"

"I shall not leave without Pageya," she said firmly.

"Pageya, she's here too!" exclaimed Tom.

"Yes, and Vencengea is claiming that Pageya is her daughter."

This news was greeted with a baffled silence.

"And I'm convinced Vencengea also has some mad idea of taking her off to meet the Messengers…"

Madge raised her eyebrows.

"You mean the blokes who disappeared to the other side of the Volcano?"

"I don't know exactly where they're supposed to be – beyond the Volcano or at the top of the Volcano or inside the Volcano! And Vencengea doesn't seem to know either. But she seems pretty convinced they are somewhere over there on the other side of the lake. And she clearly intends to go looking for them – with Pageya. She also seems to have some sort of role mapped out for us…"

They explained to Yentsilbor and Pailtac who Pageya was and why they needed to rescue her as well. Pailtac was not impressed.

"So we have to put the whole enterprise in danger for the sake of this one sick girl?" he asked incredulously.

"She's not just 'a sick girl'," Bridget protested angrily. "She's a very special person and… she's my dearest friend."

There was a silence. Then Stigrath's gruff voice said:

"I too… not leave without the Princess Pageya. If need… I carry her."

Bridget went over to him and squeezed his hand.

"But where is she kept?" asked Tom. "If Vencengea says she's her daughter, she must be kept somewhere near where Vencengea is."

"Yes," replied Bridget. "She's locked in a small room above Vencengea's quarters, in the headland up there."

Pailtac muttered a curse. Yentsilbor sighed.

But Madge stood by Bridget. "If that's the case," she said, "we'll just have to put our brains together and include some sort of rescue in our escape plan!"

"You have an escape plan!" exclaimed Bridget. "Just how do you intend to escape from this awful place?"

Madge put her finger to her mouth.

"I don't think it's safe to discuss any plans here," she said.

Bridget nodded. "Yes, Vencengea has, actually, been eavesdropping on you! She even showed us an image of you, here in this cell, discussing what had happened to you…"

"You saw us here?" Tom exclaimed.

"Yes, I don't know how she does it. She seems to be able to hack into other people's thought patterns and then project it to other places… But perhaps we should continue this conversation outside, where the sound of the waves may make it more difficult for her?"

The others agreed, and they left the cells and walked down a narrow path to a level patch of ground just above what looked like a tiny natural harbour. The waves crashing against the cliffs all round made it difficult even for them to hear each other, and they felt confident that even if Vencengea were listening, she would not be able to understand too much.

Pailtac was still deeply unhappy at the proposed delay in their escape. Tom began to explain what their plan had been.

"We've known about this harbour since we came here. And since Pailtac and Yentsilbor now have the freedom of the island, they've been collecting a certain amount of material in order to make a raft…"

"A raft?" exclaimed Stigrath contemptuously.

"Alas," said Yentsilbor, "that is about the only sort of vessel that we can possibly assemble with so little time or material. Nor do we have the sort of knowledge that you may have, captain, about ship-building…"

Stigrath acknowledged the point, but was still unhappy. A raft! Stigrath sailing on a raft! Would his dignity ever recover?

Pailtac took up the explanation.

"The lake, although very tempestuous, is not as large as it seems. It can only be fifty or sixty arrow shots to the nearest coastline, the one underneath Fles. It will be easier, however, to go in the other direction. The winds almost always blow away from Fles, towards the coastline of the Great Plain of Tworm… which is where we want to go, in any case. That is a bit further away, maybe a hundred or a hundred and fifty arrow shots."

"I suppose that means ten or fifteen miles," said Bridget with some misgiving. "And how far have you got with building this raft?"

"Building the raft will take only a few hours," answered Yentsilbor, "once we have assembled enough materials."

"Which we have done already!" said the impatient Pailtac.

"So there is nothing really to prevent us going at once," explained Yentsilbor, "except that…"

"Except that Tom asked us to take you too," said Pailtac, "And now you want us to wait further, for the sorceress's daughter!"

"But rescue her we shall," said Madge forcefully. "We must! She cannot stay here and be either brainwashed or tortured by this foul woman! Even if she is her mother!"

Chapter Forty-Four
Burning Mirrors

"Where did the fire start?" Vencengea snapped.

"In the stores, mistress," replied Lulby shamefacedly, "the food stores and…"

"Yes?"

Lulby hesitated, but Stitgoe, bowing deeply as if in contrition, completed what his colleague had been about to say. "The piles of goods that Blam has stored away over the years, things he has confiscated from the people brought from Orotworm."

Vencengea muttered something angrily under her breath. They were standing outside the archway leading to Vencengea's quarters on the headland, looking across at the cliffside caves which housed the dining hall, Blam's kitchen and the living quarters of the main community. It would soon be dusk, but the gathering gloom was lit up by a lurid red glow from the entrance and windows of the community.

"It is getting worse," the dark mistress muttered. "It is growing."

Flames were now beginning to lick at the upper edges of the community's windows.

"There was a lot of cooking oil spread over the stores, Blam says," said Lulby.

"So it WAS sabotage!" Vencengea snapped. "Where are the two who fought the Engra? This must be their doing…"

"We cannot find them anywhere, Mistress."

"And the other prisoners?"

Stitgoe looked embarrassed. "They too have vanished… the ones in the cell that is."

"And the girl Bridget and her friends? Please tell me that they are safe in their quarters…"

"We… we think so."

Vencengea uttered a poisonous sounding blasphemy. Her eyes narrowed.

"You two had better go over there and sort this out. Otherwise that corrupt fool Blam and his useless floozy Noos will allow the whole place to be destroyed! And the community servants to escape… I mean, try to leave."

Stitgoe cleared his throat. "Ahem, if you do not mind my suggesting it, mistress, I think it would be best if you yourself went over to put things straight. I think this is a major crisis!"

Vencengea again uttered a low curse, but waited no longer. She summoned the three guards who were standing nearby and, gathering the ends of her long dark robe, threw them over one shoulder and set off down the path towards the saddle.

Tom, Madge, Pailtac and Yentsilbor had heard all this, crouching in the darkness among the rocks nearby. They were all out of breath, having just hurried up the zigzag path from the Pool of Edath.

"So far, so good," murmured Madge.

But to their dismay Vencengea turned to Lulby and Stitgoe after a few metres and snapped:

"What are you following me for? Go and guard the girl! And watch her well, or you will pay for it!"

Lulby and Stitgoe bowed slightly and returned up the passageway between the rocks which led to Vencengea's quarters.

"It looks as if we'll have to deploy Plan B as well," whispered Tom.

Madge nodded grimly.

This was the first hitch in their carefully elaborated plan. They had hoped that Vencengea would take her assistants with her, along with most of the guards from her promontory retreat. For that was where they had to venture to rescue Pageya. Into the Queen Wasp's nest itself!

Tom and his friends followed Stitgoe and Lulby, at a distance, along the alley in the rock and watched them enter the stone archway into the darkened vestibule beyond. They waited outside for several tense moments. Then there was a faint sound, like the patter of small feet on the stony ground.

"Orin, is that you?" Tom whispered anxiously.

"Yes, it is I." Orin's waif-like figure appeared through the archway. "You can go on and begin. The two chief scarecrows" (this was his name for Lulby and Stitgoe) "have ascended the stairs. Are the kitchens already on fire?"

"Yes, you can see the glow clearly… You had no problem getting across the ridge?"

"No, I hid in the place in the rock you showed me, just outside the community door… then I came across when I knew the scarecrows would be having their dinner."

"And Bridget and Stigrath should be on their way now as well…"

Tom shivered. What if the hiding place on the far side of the saddle was not good enough and Vencengea detected his friends?

They would just have to hope. Their whole plan was extremely risky. So many things could go wrong. They had to depend not only on the element of surprise, and Pailtac's supposed skill in picking locks. They also had to hope that Vencengea had temporarily switched off whatever psychic powers it was she possessed.

They now crept cautiously into the rock vestibule. Orin had already scouted out the lie of the land and located a niche near the entrance to the Hall of Mirrors which suited their purposes. This is where they now took up their position.

"Orin, you go and keep watch outside…"

Orin darted out through the archway.

They waited five more minutes.

Pailtac was becoming impatient. "They are late," he muttered. They will be caught on the crossing of the ridge…"

"Patience, Pailtac my friend…" murmured Madge. "Have patience."

"Our friends will be caught," Pailtac said again. "I knew it was foolishness to try this mad plan… We should have gone without the girl. Vencengea has ways of tracking people down…"

"But Pailtac, it is working," whispered Madge. "Vencengea has already left the promontory, as we had hoped."

"But where are Bridget and Stigrath?" he hissed. "They were supposed to come across before anyone noticed the fire in the kitchens…"

"Give them more time," Tom urged. "They may have seen Vencengea and the guards crossing and had to wait…"

Pailtac's fears were unfounded. A moment or two later Orin came scurrying back.

"They have crossed, they will be here in a moment!" he whispered. "You can begin."

Without waiting any further Pailtac lit the three torches in his hand and passed two of them to Tom and Yentsilbor. Now the time of action had come, his irritation had vanished. He smiled at them both.

"Good luck!" he said, and clasped each of them by the hand.

They entered the hall of mirrors. Tom immediately headed down to the bottom of the cave, threading his way among the angled plates of glass. At last he found the spot. They had assembled a small pile of rubbish, wood and old curtains and cloths and doused them with cooking oil from the kitchen. Tom set his torch to it and immediately a bright flame sprang up.

Almost at the same moment a similar flame burst into life in another corner of the cavern.

The effect was dramatic. The cave immediately became an inferno. Reflected in the mirrors, the flames looked as if they had taken hold of the whole place.

A little of Vencengea's magic turned back against her, thought Tom with grim satisfaction.

Tom hurried back to the entrance and took up his position with Yentsilbor and Pailtac in the niche near the foot of the spiral staircase. Orin dashed outside again to take up his position as lookout. Pailtac had now assembled a second pile of rubbish, by the foot of the staircase, and set light to it so that the smoke and smell would be bound to rise up to the rooms above.

A moment or two later they were joined in their hiding place by Bridget and Stigrath.

"She was on to the saddle before we were," Bridget explained breathlessly. "We had to dodge back into the hiding place until she got across…"

Then Tom and Yentsilbor disappeared into the burning hall. Not a moment too soon, for now they heard the clatter of heavy steps coming down the staircase. Bridget held her breath.

It was Lulby. He stared, eyes bulging, at the fire at the bottom of the stairs, then caught sight of the conflagration in the hall of mirrors and at once ran back up the stairs.

The smoke in the cave was becoming thicker and thicker. Bridget and the others were supposed to have equipped themselves with wet cloths to help them breath, but Tom wondered if that would be enough. There was little time to worry, however. Again there were footsteps on the spiral staircase and Lulby appeared again, this time with Stitgoe and several black-robed acolytes. Tom noticed that they were all armed with long daggers in scabbards stuffed in their rope belts.

Stitgoe saw the flames and his thin face turned into a mask of anger. He gave a sharp word of command and several of the assistant-guards disappeared outside, evidently in search of water to douse the flames.

"Who has done this?" he shrieked. "Who is there?"

The only answer was a dismal moan from the far end of the hall, as of some lost soul in torment.

"Who is that? What are you doing here?" screamed Stitgoe, advancing into the hall with Lulby and the remaining armed guards in his wake.

There came a high-pitched cackle of laughter, which was joined a moment later by a deep, rolling guffaw. It sounded, Tom thought, remarkably like the recording of the Laughing Sailor which children could play for fifty pence in one of the arcades at Havenmouth.

A voice came from the flames. "You who serve the Mistress of Iprades, your time has come! You have dabbled too long in mysteries you do not understand!"

The voice of doom had a strong Skomiar accent.

The friends waited no longer. As Stitgoe and his retinue advanced further into the mirrored hall in search of their tormentors, Bridget and her remaining friends slipped out of the niche and onto the lower steps of the twisting staircase. Had Stitgoe or Lulby seen them? They did not wait to find out. Pailtac sprang up the steps, three at a time, with Bridget and Madge following close behind, and Stigrath lumbering up the steps as best he could.

They came to the level on which Vencengea had her rooms and passed on upwards, until they reached the door on the third level.

While Stigrath held his torch high, Pailtac pulled a ring of rough metal hooks from a pocket in his tunic.

"Hope one of these will do it!" he murmured.

He poked first one hook into the lock in the door, then another, and another, each time twisting and turning it to try and get a hold on the bolt which would release it. He tried five, six times, and still there was no success.

"A damnably complex lock," he muttered. "Just what one would expect from Vencengea!"

"Hurry! Quick! No time!" growled Stigrath.

"I am doing my best, you Naisur river-rat!" snapped Pailtac.

A voice came from the other side of the door: "Please, who is that? And what is happening? Please tell me…"

"Geya, it is Bridget! Don't worry, we have come to rescue you…"

242

"O please, I do not need to be rescued! I am with my mother. She will be so upset if I leave now…"

"It's all right, Geya. We mean your mother no harm…"

At that moment there was a click and the lock gave. Pailtac turned the ring that served as a door handle and pushed the door open.

Pageya was standing there in a nightgown, her long blond hair dishevelled and her face pale as a sheet. Tears were streaming down her cheeks.

Bridget stepped forward to reassure her, but Pageya turned away and went to the far side of the room.

Madge then stepped into the room and went over to the anguished girl.

"Look, my dear," she said, "you may not want to be rescued from this here island paradise, but we intend to rescue you anyway! We're just a little bit worried about what this woman intends to do to you, even if she is your mother!"

Bridget could see that Pageya was in a very troubled state. Her illness, clearly, was only in remission, despite what she had said about Vencengea being able to cure her.

"Please, I do not want to cause my mother anguish…"

Bridget went over to plead with her, but at that very moment Pageya's body went limp and she literally swooned into Bridget's arms.

"Perhaps it's just as well," muttered Madge. "This way we'll be able to take her without argument."

They wrapped Pageya quickly in the covers from her bed and Stigrath gently took her up in his arms. Bridget gathered some clothes from a chest near the bed.

"She is so light," said Stigrath, marvelling. "So let us go. As fast as we can!"

They hurried back down the curved staircase. The smoke was now billowing up in their faces, making it hard to see or breath. They passed Vencengea's quarters and on down to the lower level. At the bottom, to their immense relief, Tom, Yentsilbor and Orin were all waiting for them.

There was no sign of Lulby or Stitgoe. "They've gone off towards the mainland," Tom whispered breathlessly. "Probably to bring back the guards… and their Mistress."

At that moment they heard someone approaching from outside. Quickly they dodged into the hidden alcove which had served them so well earlier.

It was Vencengea herself, and alone. Her face was set in a grimace of anger and determination. With a sweep of her robes, she turned the corner and began to climb up the stairs.

"Quickly! We must go quickly!" Pailtac urged them.

They moved swiftly out of the shadows and hurried towards the exit.

Bridget ran with the others out through the arched entrance, half expecting at any moment to meet Lulby and Stitgoe and half of the armed guard. But they safely reached the path that led down to the Pool of Edath and turned into it. Fortunately, it was a relatively clear and calm night, and there was enough moonlight filtering through the clouds for them to make their way down the rutted path.

They had gone only a few metres when from above, high up in the pinnacle under the great stone finger, there came a most dreadful, heart-rending wail.

"They have taken her!" Vencengea shrieked, her powerful voice piercing the night air.

"They have taken my treasure! Stitgoe! Lulby! Find them! They must not escape!"

Chapter Forty-Five
The Pool of Edath Again

They hurried on down the twisting, turning path, not even daring to look upwards.

Orin ran on ahead, with Stigrath, carrying Pageya, following as quickly as he could. Madge, the least athletic of the party, was finding the path difficult going in the dark. Bridget and Tom lagged behind to help her over the trickier sections. Pailtac and Yentsilbor brought up the rear. They had equipped themselves for the possibility of hostilities with makeshift shields of wood and leather and short stabbing spears they had cobbled together from kitchen implements.

"Please! You must move more quickly!" Pailtac called down to them. "It can only be a matter of time before they search this path."

Indeed, now that they had reached the far side of the great natural bowl, they could see back up to the entrance into the pinnacle. A group of people had gathered there, holding torches which shone red and menacing in the gathering darkness. And even as they watched, several of the torches moved away to the left, towards the path they were following.

They moved on as quickly as they could. After another five minutes of laborious descent, they paused, at Madge's request, to catch their breath. Bridget glanced anxiously upwards. She saw that a group of dark-robed acolytes were indeed coming down their path. The menacing red glow of their torches was moving swiftly across the cliff face.

It had already reached the spot, several zigzags above them, from which they had first observed the pursuit.

"Can we go on now, Madge?" Bridget asked.

Madge nodded.

But as she spoke there came a sort of whirring noise and a sharp crack, as something hit the cliff face above their heads. A number of loose stones tumbled downwards just ahead of where they were.

"Quick! Let's push on," Tom cried. "I don't know what it is, but they're throwing something at us!"

There was another whirr and they saw a rolling ball of blue flame fly through the air and burst against the rock above them. This time there was a loud roar and a sizeable chunk of rock detached itself from the precipice, crashed on to their path and then, most of it, bounced or rolled on into the void beyond.

"Vencengea must be among them, and they've obviously seen us!" shouted Tom. "She's trying to cut off our line of retreat. We have to go on quickly!"

They stumbled on over the rubble which the rock fall had left on the pathway. A third time the whirring noise came, the ball of bluish fire and the sharp explosion, this time somewhere below their path.

It was Tom who saw first what was happening. "Madge, look out!" he shouted. "The path's giving way, just in front of you!"

But it was too late. Madge, concentrating on avoiding the debris in her way, did not see the cracks appearing in the path just a few feet in front of her. With a terrible groaning noise, the ledge carrying the path began to subside.

Tom and Bridget had already passed the spot weakened by the explosion. They looked back in horror as Madge tried to pull up, but overbalanced and was carried over the edge as the ground collapsed beneath her feet. Desperately, she flailed out with her hands and, by good fortune, caught hold of a protruding rock as she slid off the path. Wildly, she scrabbled with her feet to gain some hold and save herself from plunging down into the Pool of Edath itself.

There was now a gap of ten or fifteen metres between Tom and Bridget and the struggling form of Madge.

"Hold on, Madge, Pailtac will help you!" Bridget encouraged her. But would he get there in time, she thought. Madge was groping in vain for a firmer grip on the crumbling rock.

Then she stopped struggling. She seemed to have gained some sort of foothold and at least seemed in no immediate danger of falling. Yentsilbor and Pailtac had now reached her.

Pailtac called across the yawning gap.

"You must go on! We shall save your friend Ont-Maj. Go to the raft and escape this foul island!"

Yentsilbor concurred.

"We shall hold them back – and try to stop them crossing this gap! And then we shall make our peace with Vencengea… someway or other!"

And they heard his low chuckle.

"They're right!" This time it was Madge's breathless voice. "You two go on! And quickly. Go! Do what you're told!"

Bridget and Tom knew they had no alternative. If they stayed behind, then all of them would be caught. And at any moment Vencengea might send another of her blue bolts down and cut off the path further down. They could now see their pursuers' torches, turning the bend only a hundred or so yards away. Bridget and Tom turned and ran for all they were worth down the path, in pursuit of the retreating figure of Stigrath.

They came to a point where the track dipped behind some rocks and stopped to take stock of the situation. By this time the pursuit had reached the point where Madge had been desperately clinging on to her rock. Pailtac and Yentsilbor had hauled Madge to safety. Now they laid down their arms before the advancing acolytes.

Tom and Bridget did not stop to see any more. They ran on downwards.

At last they reached the sinister Pool of Edath and jumped down on to the platform of rock that surrounded it. The small figure of Orin appeared.

"Come across, quickly! Stigrath is already on the rock, with Geya."

They started to clamber down towards the water. Suddenly, Tom exclaimed: "The water, it's much higher than it was the last time we crossed!"

"Look!" cried Orin. "Someone has opened the waterfall!"

It was true. The gentle splash of the water as it dropped into the pool from its hidden source above was rapidly changing into a torrent.

"Quick!" Stigrath shouted across to them, from the flat-topped rock in the centre of the pool. "Cross quickly or it will be too late!"

Bridget helped Orin down into the icy cold water, then plunged in herself.

The water came up above her waist. And there seemed to be a swirling current, which made it difficult to keep one's footing on the slippery stones beneath.

"Orin, where's Orin?" cried Tom.

"I am here," piped up poor Orin, who was desperately trying to keep his mouth above the water. "I am here, but the bottom of the pool is hard to find!"

Tom clutched at him and helped him lift his head clear of the water.

They ploughed onwards. They were now half-way across. The water was nearly up to Bridget's neck. How could Orin possibly go further?

"It is all right, Tom," she heard Orin splutter. "I shall swim. I was born beside a lake, remember?"

It was at that point that Bridget felt a rush of water behind her and something white and sleek slid past her.

"An Engra!" Tom cried. "I think it's one of the Engras."

She heard a heavy splash in front of her, and Stigrath's voice came through the night.

"Where do you think it has gone, friend Tom?"

"I don't know, Stigrath! But I wouldn't meddle with it if I were you!"

Bridget caught the dull gleam of a metal blade several metres in front of her.

"This is me!" she said clearly. "And I don't bite!"

Stigrath laughed grimly.

"Do not worry, my young friend Bridget. Tonight my knife is trained to hunt only Engras!"

His giant frame moved past them through the water.

Tom and Orin were already pulling themselves out on to the rocky island. Bridget was doing her best to follow and had just taken hold of a rock above her to heave herself up when the water behind her suddenly burst into a terrible maelstrom of foam and darkness.

She hauled herself on to the flat surface of the rock and turned to look. There was now silence again. But then she saw a whitish blur swimming round the pool, near the far bank.

What had happened to Stigrath? Had the monster killed him already?

Then, just beneath the overhang where Vencengea had watched the contest, there was another frantic thrashing in the water. The white blur swam rapidly one way, then another, as if feinting for an attack. Another burst of foam and spray. And then all lay still.

Something appeared just beneath their rock.

"Why have you not lifted the stone?" came Stigrath's voice. "We have no time to lose."

"Stigrath!" cried Bridget. "I thought it had got you!"

"Not me, nor anyone else, ever again. But we must hurry. The chase is almost on us!"

Sure enough, there was a shout from above and they saw torches descending rapidly towards the pool.

They found the stone slab and pulled it open.

"At least pool will delay them," grunted Stigrath. Bridget noticed that at this time of emergency he seemed to be speaking with more freedom. "Probably takes long time to drain."

Down the steps they went and past the cells where Tom and Madge had been kept prisoner.

The path now descended steeply towards the sea. It had begun to rain now, and to Bridget's consternation the wind was also rising.

"Do we still have to assemble the raft?" she asked anxiously.

"No," answered Tom. "Yentsilbor and Pailtac did it all earlier today."

They were now near the shoreline itself, on the level stretch of rock that ran along one side of the small natural harbour. And there Bridget saw what looked like a pile of assorted junk nestling on the rock near the harbour entrance.

She realised with a jolt that this was the raft!

It looked so extraordinarily flimsy. When they reached it, she saw that the main frame of the structure was made of long wooden planks. Where Pailtac and Yentsilbor had found them she could not imagine. These were strapped together by what appeared to be leather thongs, possibly taken from the goatskins that she had seen Yentsilbor begging from Blam. More of the goatskins had been inflated and had been strapped beneath the wooden frame, to give it buoyancy.

Above the wooden frame there was a sort of rough shelter, also made of skins and of the same curtain material they had used to lay the fires in the hall of mirrors.

Bridget looked nervously at the heaving, pitching water of the small inlet. If this was what it was like in sheltered waters, what was it going to be like out on the stormy lake?

But Stigrath had no such qualms, it seemed. With some sporadic help from Tom and Bridget, he set about pushing the rickety structure towards the edge of the water.

It was only at this juncture that Stigrath suddenly realised that Madge, Pailtac and Yentsilbor were not with them.

"Captain Ont-Maj?" he grunted.

"She will not be coming with us, Stigrath. The rock path was destroyed in front of her and she stayed behind with Pailtac and Yentsilbor. But they urged us to go on."

She was suddenly afraid that the big river-man would refuse to go without them.

But he only grunted.

"More room on the raft!" he muttered.

"But the raft's going to be bobbing about like mad!" cried Tom. "How on earth are we going to get on to it?"

"It will be like a game we played when I was small," said Orin. "We called it: 'Riding branches in the wind'. It was great fun on windy days in the big trees!"

Bridget gulped.

The raft tumbled heavily into the water and sank into it alarmingly. Then it bobbed up again and crunched noisily against the rocks.

"Quick, jump on board," called Stigrath, "before it is dashed to pieces!"

He grabbed two loose hide ropes attached to the raft's side and tried to keep it steady as Tom and Bridget leapt simultaneously on to the swaying, pitching vessel. They slid and tumbled across the rolling, uneven deck and, more by good luck than design, ended up under the awning in the middle of the raft, which was attached to a short mast. Here they attempted to make themselves as secure as possible, wrapping themselves in goatskins which they in turn attached to the mast. Orin, who had followed close behind him, huddled in beside them, clinging to Tom for safety.

The question now was, would Stigrath also make it on to the pitching, rolling craft, with Pageya in his arms?

The giant captain waited for the raft to rise again to the level of the rock, then released his grip on the two hawsers, grabbed Pageya up from the rock, and leapt on board, clambering with remarkable alacrity for such a big man up towards the rude shelter in the centre of the heaving, plunging deck. Bridget undid the goatskin belt around her middle and ventured out to help him. Immediately she lost her grip on the slippery wooden surface and began to slide towards the edge. At the last minute a hand grabbed her arm and pulled her towards the awning.

"Our voyage has only just started," said Tom. "Why leave it so soon?"

Stigrath had made it to the shelter. They all clung on, staring into the darkness round them. The ramshackle collection of planks and goatskins was suddenly torn away from the side of the rock into the middle of the frothing inlet. It heaved alarmingly beneath them as a particularly large wave swept in from the open waters. Then the raft was swept up into the cove, and then out again, flying past the crude rock jetty from which they had boarded.

Bridget was sure the next wave would take them back into the cove, or maybe crush them on the cruel rocks which towered all round it. But instead, it pushed them only as far as the entrance of the tiny harbour, and from there they began to slip away steadily from the shoreline.

They were afloat and out on the wild waters of the lake.

From under the awning Bridget anxiously scanned the cliffs around the inlet. She thought of their friends, now at the mercy of Vencengea and her followers. What would happen to them?

For the moment there was no sign of the pursuers.

It was Orin, who was nervously clutching Bridget's arm to steady himself on the pitching deck, who suddenly tensed and pointed upwards.

High, high above them on a jutting spur of rock that looked down over the little harbour they saw Vencengea. She was holding above her head a torch that guttered madly in the wind, illuminating her tall frame and flapping garments. She was looking directly down at them, and as they lurched and swayed laboriously out of the tiny natural harbour, snatches of her voice came down to them in the intervals between the gusts of wind.

She was calling to them, and though Bridget could not make out the individual words, she understood that Vencengea was promising pursuit. And revenge.

Finally the sorceress's voice broke into a piercing high-pitched wail, though whether Vencengea was laughing or weeping it was impossible to say.

Chapter Forty-Six
The Raft

But at least they were away! They were off the dread island of Iprades.

Stigrath unfurled the small sail and he and Tom hauled it up their vessel's flimsy mast. Bridget realised that the wind, which had seemed to be blowing directly on-shore, was in fact racing from right to left, along the length of the island, towards the plains of Orotworm. And that was the direction they wanted to go!

The sail flapped madly and then filled, with a sound like a whipcrack. It billowed out and bore them away from the shore, though slowly, ever so slowly, and out into the high waves.

The unwieldy craft lifted on the swell of a wave, then dropped with a heavy splash into the trough between that wave and the next. There was suddenly water everywhere, at their feet, in among their bodies, all over them. And as the next wave came and lifted them, the raft tilted at a crazy angle, so that Bridget was sure that she and the others were all going to be tossed off into the swirling waters round them. She tightened her grip on the goatskin strap that held her to the mast and helped Orin to do the same. The raft, their only shelter and their only hope of salvation, suddenly seemed very fragile and vulnerable indeed.

Again they rose and fell. And once more. Already they were soaked through and freezing. They did all they could to make the still sleeping Pageya as secure and comfortable as she could be, wrapping her in skins and tying them to the mast.

"Together! Huddle together!" roared Stigrath over the noise of the tossing waves. "We have to keep each other warm."

Another five minutes and Bridget had overcome the initial shock and was becoming more accustomed to the constant lifting and falling, pitching and rolling. As they drew slowly away from the shore of the island, the waves became significantly larger. That meant that the rising and falling was not so jerky and sudden, but it also meant that they rose higher, and sank further, and the water often poured all the way over the raft, so that they had to cling tightly to each other, and the rough animal hide fixings around the mast.

Bridget looked back towards the dark mass of the island… and for a moment her blood ran cold. There, high up on the pinnacle which housed Vencengea's sanctum, the very place from which they had descended that night, was a light, a single bright red light. It seemed to be searching for them, with a steady, menacing glow from near the top of the rocky projection. It was motionless, but so bright that Bridget felt it could not have been just a beacon. She tapped

Stigrath on the shoulder and pointed.

Stigrath looked and nodded. "Eye of the Night," he said grimly, spitting out some lake water from the latest wave that had broken over the raft. "Can see it from Isle of Thifa… from other end of lake even."

"The famous 'Eye of the Night'," cried Orin. "I have heard stories about it. Is it not said that it hypnotises sailors and lures them to destruction on the Isle of Iprades?"

Stigrath grunted something that was probably an affirmative, then spat again.

The wind and waves were taking them along the coast of the island, heading – as they had hoped – away from the side of the lake dominated by the giant volcano. But the wind was getting fiercer by the minute, and their frail craft was being lifted up on to the rolling crests of the gathering waves, then flung down the other side at a sometimes-alarming angle.

To make matters worse, the bindings with which they had tied their raft together were beginning to unravel. One particularly large wave rose above them, a great black shape in the general gloom, and came crashing down on top of them, soaking everything under the goatskin shelter that was not already soaked. And then one of the inflated goatskins at Bridget's side of the raft worked itself loose and before anyone could do anything, disappeared into the darkness. The ramshackle assembly of inflated hides, ropes and planks was now developing a distinct list to one side.

O why, o why did we embark on this crazy venture? Bridget thought to herself. No matter how bad things had been back in the kitchen-cave, and whatever ignoble or evil intentions Vencengea may have held towards them, could it possibly have been as bad as the danger they now faced, the danger of extinction itself?

Their makeshift craft was soon threatening to break up altogether. They lost another of the inflated goatskins, and now there were only seven or eight of them left. That was all that was keeping them afloat. Bridget and her friends clung to the hide ropes that held the whole ramshackle assembly together, knowing that if they once slipped off into the icy waters of the lake, their companions could not possibly save them.

The waves continued to crash against their frail vessel, drenching them time and again with spray. The wind continued to tear at their clothes and the few remaining possessions they had – the rucksack, the bundle of food, the gourds with the water. These last Stigrath guarded carefully with his body. Clearly, if they were to survive, drinking water would be essential in the long term.

Bridget tried to distract her thoughts from their plight by thinking of people she held dear. At least she was facing this terrible danger with the comforting strength of Stigrath here by her side and the cheerfulness of Tom… what a good friend he had been. And with little Orin, with his quaint, amusing ways…

And of course there was Pageya too, here by her side, who in so short a time had become such a firm and loyal friend…

She thought also of the people they had left on Iprades. Madge… good, resourceful, no-nonsense Madge. She had even grown fond of the proud and dismissive Pailtac and the crudely jocular Yentsilbor.

For a moment she thought also of her parents. And her disabled brother Tim. Poor, brave Tim, who confronted life with such cheerfulness... Tim, her adopted brother... But who was he really? No, she would not allow herself to speculate about that.

An overpowering nostalgia flooded over her, mingled with guilt...

After what seemed like an age, it slowly began to grow light. But the grey light of dawn brought little comfort or consolation. The scene around them was bleak and, if anything, more intimidating than in the darkness. Now they could see row upon row of wild, breaking waves, stretching as far as the eye could see. The wind tore at the crest of each wave, flinging spray over everything, including their frail craft. Bridget no longer thought about being wet. She had grown used to the feeling of being soaked to the skin. She pulled Pageya nearer to herself and huddled closer to the others to keep warm.

"At least we're out of sight of the island," shouted Tom above the roar of the wind and waves. "If they do set out to find us, it won't be easy to see where we are!"

It was true. The horizon on all sides was grey and empty. The waters were covered by a sort of grey mist, formed partly perhaps from the spray whipped up by the wind.

But Stigrath shook his head doubtfully.

"Vencengea is not such a fool. She knows a raft like ours is borne along by wind... and in same direction as the wind."

That thought depressed them all. But when she looked around Bridget was suddenly seized by new hope. The waves, she was sure, were not so high, the wind not so wild as it had been even five minutes previously. The raft was still rising and falling, rising and falling, but the water was no longer spilling over its sides.

Bridget looked at Stigrath. "Is the wind falling, or are we... are we perhaps nearing land?" She couldn't keep the optimism out of her voice.

But Stigrath was looking worried. "We could, I suppose, be coming close to land, little lady. But something worries me..." His speech seemed to be becoming clearer and clearer. He looked up at the clouds scudding across the sky above them.

"What is it?" she asked anxiously.

"The wind. The wind seems to be changing direction."

There were a few moments silence.

"But that means..." Tom began his sentence, but didn't end it.

The wind died down further, until it was almost still. The raft rose and fell as before, in an eerie silence.

Then the first puffs of wind blew again across their chapped faces. It was coming from quite a different direction.

"Stigrath!" said Tom tensely. "Is my sense of direction wrong, or...?"

Stigrath shook his head.

"No, my friend. I think sense of direction is right. Wind is beginning to turn, blow different way, from the opposite direction. If continue like this… it blow us back… maybe towards Iprades."

Chapter Forty-Seven
A Twist of Fortune

It was now fully daylight, but they could see no further than a few hundred metres on any side, initially because of the mist, and then increasingly – as the wind began to whip up the waters once more – by a driving spray whipped up by the ever-strengthening gusts. Very soon it was howling round them as fiercely as before – only from the opposite direction!

They clung together, not just for warmth but in Bridget's case at least for the comfort of human contact. Could it be that all their endeavours, all the risks and heartache of their perilous descent to the rocky harbour, of their battle with the wind and waters, would be brought to nothing by a freak change of wind direction?

For a moment she wondered whether it was just by chance. Was it conceivable that the wind itself could have been manipulated? By Vencengea? Or some other evil force even more powerful?

She forced herself to dismiss the thought. It just was not possible. Vencengea might pretend to have supernatural powers, but this was ridiculous.

Yet the idea kept forcing itself back into her mind. Were they, after all, in Vencengea's clutches? Was it ever going to be possible to escape here? Bridget closed her eyes and tried to forget about it all, about the wet and the cold and the sea tumbling around her, about the horrible nightmare she was going through and could not escape.

Then she opened her eyes again and looked towards the horizon with an ever-increasing sense of foreboding, expecting at any moment to see, ahead of them, the dim outline of the dread island.

But for a while there was nothing, only the blank grey ceiling of the sky and the driven spray that whipped your cheeks if you looked up, and the looming, threatening waves which rose with boundless malevolence above the frail piece of flotsam to which they clung.

And then it was there! A dim, very dim suggestion of a darker grey rising out of the whiteness of the foam. It was ahead, almost dead ahead, and they were being driven relentlessly towards it.

The dim contours of the island took firmer shape, and now there could be no doubt that it was indeed Vencengea's island, the sinister bastion of broken rock from which they had escaped so recently. For a moment an irrational hope suddenly surged in Bridget's heart. The great block of rock was a little to the right of the course on which they were being driven. Might it just be possible that they would miss the island itself and be swept past?

Then her hopes fell as suddenly as they had risen. The island was only just off their course. Even if they were not swept on to its rocks, they would pass so close to them that Vencengea or her watchmen up on the pinnacle would have no difficulty in spotting and intercepting them.

But maybe that would be for the best, she decided disconsolately. It was a miracle that their ill-assembled raft had not already broken up altogether. The towering waves continued to pour relentlessly over its stern. They would constantly be lifted up on to a crest, but just as they thought they would ride up and over it, the crest would break and the water tumble over them, drenching everything and everyone.

The great jagged cliffs were now clearly in sight, with all their clefts and gullies plainly visible, and the spray of the waves, rising and falling, crashing mercilessly against the rocks all along the shoreline. They were drifting ever closer. They passed the high promontory which marked the northern end of the island, a great wedge of sheer cliffs ploughing into the wild waves like the prow of some enormous ship. They slid down the eastern coast, and now they were within sight of the strange rock formation that marked the entrance to the tunnel opening on to the inner lake, the tunnel through which they had themselves passed so recently in Vencengea's black-sailed ship, the Maibiton.

And again Bridget had the sensation that she was hallucinating…

Something was moving steadily and stealthily along behind the ragged line of rocks that guarded the entrance to the inner lake. At first she thought it was some sinister, slithering animal, but gradually she made out the dark cloth and rigid struts of masts and upper rigging.

It was the Maibiton herself, clearly on its way to intercept them!

So their return had been detected! There was to be no escape.

Stiffly Bridget raised an almost frozen arm and pointed. But either the others were too numb to react or they had already sighted the black sails behind the rocks. They all stared dumbly as the darkly arrayed ship, like some loathsome giant spider, crept steadily on behind the protective line of rocks that lay between their two vessels, towards the exit point.

It arrived there just as their raft was also just approaching the gap in the rocks that marked the channel entrance. Now they could see the whole of the black ship in all its sinister splendour. It was no more than half a mile from them and was now beginning to turn slowly, deliberately, so that its prow was pointing outwards towards them, and with all its oars deployed it was ready to make the plunge towards the open water and its intended prey.

And that, without any question, would be the end of their little escapade.

Bridget watched, transfixed, as the dark vessel gathered pace in the narrow lagoon beyond the high rock by the entrance.

As it approached the exit point, it met the wash from the waves that were sweeping past the mouth of the channel. It rose gracefully to the crest of the swell, but at the same moment was thrust powerfully to one side, so that it ended up perilously close to the high bastion of rock that marked the left-hand side of the narrow entrance. It gathered itself in the trough before the second wave and came onwards. This time the second wash lifted the huge vessel even higher and bore it down, its masts leaning at a crazy angle, towards the jagged shore below the high rock.

Bridget suddenly realised that the black-rigged ship was in trouble! Despite its crew's undoubted skill and knowledge of the perilous harbour entrance, they clearly had not reckoned with the conditions that day. Perhaps they had been ordered out to intercept the raft by Vencengea, against their better judgement. Perhaps on another day they would have waited for the weather to change.

The small company on the raft watched in awe as the great vessel struggled for its very survival. Bridget suddenly found that she did not know whether to rejoice at the plight of the sinister ship or feel pity for the desperate people on board. They heard shouts of anger and dismay above the roar and splashing of the waves, and the oarsmen desperately tried to back-paddle and bring the vessel back in out of the storm to the safety of the inner channel. Clearly, if the ship came any further, it would be crushed mercilessly against the rocks.

The ship touched the sides of the cliff, and they heard a great crunching sound and more cries of distress from the men on board. But by now the storm had carried their own frail vessel on out of sight and past the channel entrance. Vencengea's ship was now hidden from them, though they still heard cries of alarm and the sound of wood grating against rock. Then even that was drowned under the noise of the maelstrom around them.

What had happened to the black-rigged vessel? They were left to guess its fate. Was it possible that their luck was changing? Could it be that they might escape Vencengea's grasp after all?

The waves and wind were now bearing them swiftly along the side of the island, and it seemed only a few minutes before they caught sight of the lofty pinnacle at the southern headland where Vencengea had her living quarters. Bridget could not throw off the feeling, irrational as it was, that Vencengea was still up there, watching them with her all-seeing, malevolent eyes.

Now they were passing the tiny cove where they had embarked on their foolhardy venture. They were being carried along at an incredible pace, though it was hard to tell whether it was the strengthening wind or some rapid current sweeping along the side of the island that was responsible. Bridget's worst fear had all along been that, rudderless as they were, they would be swept helplessly on to some jagged promontory that jutted out of the island's shore. But that danger was now receding. The way ahead of them seemed clear. The giant cliffs soared above them, menacing, glowering, but they seemed, if anything, to be further away than before. The companions' flimsy vessel was now being carried past the rocky shore, as if by some hidden will, unharmed, unthreatened and still afloat.

Then they were at the end of the island. Just like the other tip of the island, it rose up to one enormous sheer cliff that plunged straight down hundreds of feet into the churning waters. Huge waves broke on to it, throwing spray out far and wide. There was a great booming as hundreds of tons of water collided with the unyielding rock, to be flung back in a churning mass. If they had been blown anywhere near this cataclysmic scene, their raft would surely have been shattered into splinters in a few seconds. But fate now seemed to be with them. The winds and current bore them past this turmoil of water and out into the open waters of the furious lake.

Again Bridget did not know whether to be thankful or horrified. The scene on the open water was even wilder than before, with great dark waves soaring high above, then breaking right on top of them, so they had to cling on with ever-greater desperation. How much more could they take? How far did this seemingly endless lake stretch in front of them?

For the first time Bridget's heart began to falter. They could not now, surely, have any hope of salvation.

Stigrath moved round inside their bedraggled and largely ruined shelter, throwing a goatskin rope round their bodies and lashing them all tightly to the stump that was all that was left of their central mast. Bridget had not noticed it, but somewhere along the line their flimsy sail had been completely torn off and had disappeared.

But Stigrath, at least, had not given up hope. "Just think, princess," he shouted over the roaring wind, "every other journey by water will be so tame after this!" And he grinned at her through his dripping beard.

What's happened? she thought. *Stigrath has become almost eloquent in the middle of this chaos!*

How long they went on, rising up slowly and then falling each time with a sudden calamitous thump, on and on, over and over again, she had no idea. She knew she was near the end of her strength. Her stubborn determination to stay positive had all but disappeared. Yet she clung on grimly to her goatskin strap, determined not to betray any signs of her failing hope, aware that any sign of weakness on her part might affect the spirits of the others, particularly Orin. But her body was now losing all feeling. She knew that if Stigrath's rope had not been round her, she would several times have lost her grip and just slipped gently off the raft into the seething waters.

She was falling asleep.

Someone was slapping her face. "No, princess, stay awake! Don't give up now!" It was Stigrath roaring into her face.

But how could she hold on? She was at the end of her strength. She forced herself to think again of friends from her past, of her mother and father, of Tim, and for a few moments she felt a glow of warmth towards them all. They had not been such a bad family when she thought of them now. Plenty of family rows, maybe, plenty of indifference and incomprehension by the parents, needless rebellion by the children. But also happy times together, at Christmas, on holiday, playing board games or digging ditches in the sand. Happy times. Lost times which would never come back…

She heard Tom's voice as if it were in a dream. Unconnected words, as if his mind was numb, rather like Stigrath's normal speech. "Is it imagination, or waves not so high? Believe storm is passing."

She forced her eyes open and looked around. At first she thought it was some cruel quirk of Tom's humour. The high waves were still welling up darkly and spilling angrily over their raft. But when she had looked around for several moments she thought that perhaps Tom was right. The wind was not whipping the tops off the waves so violently, the waves themselves didn't seem quite so high, their flimsy craft was not being hurled along and buffeted quite so venomously as it had been only a few minutes ago.

And the sky seemed to be clearing. The air above the frail raft was no longer so full of wild, driving spray. They could see further into the distance.

"Land! Look, land!" shouted Orin.

They looked ahead, and there, sure enough, right across the horizon from one side to another, from the level of the lake itself up to the ceiling of cloud that lay above it, there rose a solid, dark mass which could be nothing else but land – real, solid land!

Bridget looked at Stigrath, and he smiled back at her. Then, frozen and numb as they were, they both burst out into joyful laughter. "We're saved, we're saved!" she couldn't help shouting, over and over again.

Then she caught sight of Pageya, who finally, after all the buffeting and tossing, was beginning to regain consciousness. She was lying there, propped against the mast, a strange look on her face, fascinated, even mesmerised, but at the same time deeply troubled.

"What's the matter, Geya?" she asked. "Are you still upset that we left your mother? Or do you see something we don't see? Aren't we safe? Haven't we escaped from Iprades after all?"

Pageya turned a pale and slightly frightened face towards her and smiled. "Perhaps we have escaped," she said. "But this land, this land ahead of us…"

"What's wrong with it?"

"Maybe nothing," said Pageya dreamily, "maybe nothing. But I have fear in my heart… We are about to land beneath the volcano, on the shores of Fles itself."

Chapter Forty-Eight
The Paradise Shore

Bridget awoke.

What was the matter? Everything was so still. The place she was lying on wasn't heaving and swaying, it wasn't surging dizzily upwards... and dropping sickeningly back down again...

Then she remembered, vaguely, dimly, as if she had dreamed it all. The huge breakers swelling up beneath them as they neared the shore. The thunder of the waves breaking on the featureless beach somewhere up ahead of them. The sickening lurch as their raft landed on the hard shingle. How Stigrath had shouted to them to jump off before they were swept back out to sea... and how she had been so exhausted she just fell off the disintegrating jumble of goatskins and planks.

And continued falling. Through the water. Deeper and deeper...

She could remember no more after that. Only that for one heart-stopping moment as she sank into the swirling water she thought that this must be the end. After all their efforts, after all the struggle to stay alive on the raft, this was the end. When they were so near...

So where was she now?

She opened her eyes.

On either side there was nothing. Only bare, endless shingle stretching off into the mist.

She became aware of something or someone behind her. Slowly, painfully she pushed herself up on to one elbow and turned her head.

She almost bumped her forehead against the trunk of a long dead tree, lying flat on the smooth stones of the shingle. And just beyond it was the skeleton of a second tree, this one still standing, its gaunt frame high above her head, its bare arms stretched out on either side as if it were appealing for pity to the wind, or perhaps simply mourning the passing of its fallen comrade at its feet.

Her head slumped back. She felt so tired she had difficulty keeping her eyes open. And when she tried to get up, she found she had no strength in her limbs. She lay back and allowed her eyes to fall shut.

Gradually she became aware of voices, muffled voices which seemed to be echoing down a long tunnel. Then suddenly they became clearer, and she thought she recognised them. But then they stopped.

Her eyes opened and once again she managed to lift herself just enough to look around. But there was no one there. She was quite alone.

Instantly, she felt a rush of panic, and raising herself a little further she managed to peer over the top of the stricken tree trunk. Tom and Stigrath were sitting there, munching some cold meat from the rations they had brought.

"Welcome back, little princess," boomed Stigrath. "Thought to let you sleep a while, recover strength."

"Where are…?"

"Pageya and Perorin? Over there, exploring." Stigrath pointed to a spot a couple of hundred yards away where some mounds in the shingle seemed to indicate some form of previous inhabitation.

Bridget looked at the big sailor. His speech definitely *was* improving.

Then she saw Orin and Geya coming back across the shingle towards them. Geya approached almost shyly. Clearly, she had recovered from whatever fit or seizure she had suffered during their escape. She and Bridget stood and looked at each other for several moments. Geya looked alive and well and happy in a way that Bridget had not seen for some time.

There was relief in her look but also, it seemed, a little sadness. Bridget knew that it was nothing less than a miracle that they were both still there, alive and unharmed. And she suddenly felt hugely grateful to be living, even in this barren waste, lost as they were and with little food and no means of escape.

She and Geya fell into each other's arms and for several minutes stood there, not moving or speaking.

Then the whole group took up their meagre belongings, a few rough bags of food, and the faithful rucksack, with its precious documents still wrapped in cellophone, and wandered in the direction of the ruined farmstead. Orin reported they had found nothing there, nothing but stones. But it would give just a little bit of shelter.

"How did I… get out of the water?" Bridget asked.

Orin grinned back at her. "Why, it was me of course! Who of our number is so strong as to carry not just three sacks but two girls, even in the most splashing water?"

Bridget gaped at him, but then caught the twinkle in his eye. She turned to Stigrath.

"It was you, Stigrath, wasn't it? It was you again who rescued us, me and Pageya!"

The big man looked away, as if her show of thanks almost irritated him.

"When you are given the strength to do something," he mumbled, "it is a big sin if you do not do it."

The shingle beach seemed to be endless on either side. And the barren ground extended far back from the lakeshore. Indeed, the whole landscape around them was one of pure desolation. Not a green stem or shoot was anywhere to be seen, either on the shore or the nearby hills or the long grey slopes above them. Nor indeed was there any soil. There was nothing but stones.

Bridget looked in the direction she thought the great volcano should be, but again saw nothing. A solid grey layer of cloud hid everything above a couple of hundred feet. The conical summit must have been far, far above the thick mass of the clouds. Yet as she looked up the barren slopes towards the cloud line,

Bridget sensed its unseen presence and found she was filled with an irrational sense of gloom and foreboding. It was as if the enormous, hidden mountain knew they were there and disapproved.

She shivered and tried to shake off these fanciful notions. But her eyes, and thoughts, were constantly drawn back towards the brooding presence above them.

They built a fire in the shelter of the ruined farmstead, using the scattered and bone-hard branches which were all that remained of a copse that had evidently once sheltered the cottage. Stigrath lit it, with some difficulty, by rubbing two stones together over some dried leaves they had found sheltered by fallen stonework in the farm's dead orchard. They dried themselves as best they could in its glow. Then they began to eat some of the meagre provisions they had brought with them from the island.

"We shall have to find more food soon," murmured Tom.

They all stopped eating and looked at each other. "Perhaps we'd better save this," said Tom, looking at the hunk of bread and cheese he held in his hand. But Stigrath shook his head.

"Eat some now. We are all hungry and need to recover strength. We shall find some more food some way – I don't know where, but must be some living thing here in this wilderness."

"Perhaps we could fish in the lake?" suggested Orin brightly.

But Stigrath shook his head mournfully. "You look at the water? Nothing live in that."

It was true. The water was little more than a foul grey slime. And here, where the Pestilence seemed to dominate everything, there was also a smell. Not so much a smell of rotting, more a biting chemical smell, like that of a laboratory.

There was something Bridget had been dying to ask Tom, but in all the excitement of the last twenty-four hours had not had the opportunity.

"Tom, you mentioned that in the last section of the 'message', the one you deciphered at this Thifa place, it says there's a final key – the name of a place, wasn't it? – and that together with all the other 'keys' we had discovered it would unlock the mystery of the Opening…"

"Yes… So?"

"Well, we've deciphered all the riddles between us, haven't we? So if we could work out what this mysterious place is we should be in a position to find this last clue, shouldn't we?"

Tom nodded doubtfully. "Yes, I suppose you're right. What was it Kalmom said in that final section? It WAS the name of a place, a place of destiny… whatever that means… where many people had struggled… and come to a gloomy end."

"That could be almost anywhere," Orin chirped in, and he grinned at them brightly, in spite of the mournful gist of the conversation. Bridget was suddenly very glad the little Elonym was with them. He had recovered all his normal cheerfulness, and that in turn was helping her regain some courage.

Tom nodded. "Yes, it could mean anywhere. So where do we go from here?"

Stigrath grunted. "Anywhere!" he said. "But must go from here."

Bridget suddenly glanced at Pageya. She too seemed to have recovered most of her spirits. And yet she looked preoccupied. She was frowning deeply, and now she began muttering to herself and waving her fingers in the air in an agitated way, as if something was on the tip of her tongue but she couldn't quite find what it was.

"I know... I should know," she said. "A place of destiny... Recently... Seen. Been there! Cannot think... Oh there is an idea at the back of my mind. But it will not come out!"

"Don't fret, Geya," Bridget tried to calm her. "It's bound to come back to you at some point. Do you think it was somewhere YOU have been recently? Or somewhere where we all have been recently?"

"A place where people have struggled and met a gloomy end?" Tom mused, scratching his head. "I wonder if... if he means that great temple in Orotworm, what did they call it...? The Vysou-Salem?"

"Yes, it certainly was gloomy enough. And lots of people were waiting there... for something. But a place of destiny? And struggle? It doesn't quite fit..."

"The Nilmerk?" suggested Tom.

"Struggle? Yes, maybe... but destiny?"

"I think maybe...," Stigrath began.

"You think what?" asked Tom.

"Maybe I know..."

Orin suddenly jumped to his feet. "I Orin am SURE I know!" he cried in excitement.

Tom and Bridget looked baffled.

"For once," said Orin proudly, "it is not you, Bridget and Tom, who have read the riddle! It is us poor no-brains from the Vale!"

"Come on then," said Bridget, smiling at the little boy's excitement. "Tell us where this mysterious place is."

"Why, it is the place in which many have struggled and many have died, the awful and frightening Pool of Edath!"

Stigrath grunted.

Pageya made a strange sound. "I am not sure," she said. "Maybe you are right, little Orin. Or maybe it is something else, similar to that..."

"Maybe the Isle of Iprades itself?" Tom suggested.

"Yes, well maybe..." said Bridget, "though I've absolutely no desire to go back *there* in the foreseeable future!" She found she was slightly put out, unwilling to accept that one of the others might possibly be right, while she, frustratingly, had no idea at all what this mysterious place of struggle might be.

"Kalmom doesn't say we have to actually go there! Just that we use the name of the place, and the other key words... That's what he seems to be suggesting, anyway... But what do we do with them?"

"Let us," said Orin, who was clearly on top form, "let us throw all the letters of these words up in the air and see what saying they make when they fall to the ground!"

"I think you mean," said Tom, laughing at his small friend's enthusiasm, "let's jumble all the letters up and see if we can make a sentence out of them! Is that it!"

"Very much and yes so!" said the little Elonym proudly.

They sat down and compared notes. First they wrote down the six keywords they had used to decipher Kalmom's diary.

MERCY HEART BOLDNESS HARMONY LIGHT TRUTH

Then they added the name of the place they thought the last message referred to:

POOL OF EDATH

And for fifteen minutes or so they mixed up all the letters and tried to make sense of them.

But their labours were interrupted by Stigrath. He had not taken part in the 'game with letters', as he called it, and had been pacing up and down the shingle outside the ruined farmhouse, looking anxious and taking no part in their endeavours. From time to time he glanced towards the lake.

"It is time to move," he said, surveying the misty horizon. "Weather calmer now and Vencengea surely starts searching for us as soon as she can. We must leave the shoreline."

"But we saw Vencengea's ship being wrecked on the rocks!" Tom protested. "And I didn't see any other boats like her while we were on Iprades."

Stigrath shook his head. "We not know for sure if Maibiton wrecked. Could escape rocks and go back. We not know... Not sure. And I think maybe more than one such boat. Need to go from this beach."

Bridget anxiously at Pageya. What would she say? Geya too had been looking in a strange way out over the lake, towards Iprades. Was she still under whatever spell it was that Vencengea had put over here? Would she agree to go with them? Had she forgiven them for kidnapping her against her will?

When Bridget asked her, however, if she felt strong enough to walk, Pageya simply nodded and began to struggle to her feet. *Perhaps her mother's influence over her is weakening*, Bridget thought. She looked at her friend's face. Pageya's lips were pursed together, and her expression showed a quiet determination which Bridget had not seen before.

Tom suggested reconstructing the raft and sailing along the coast, but when they went over to it they saw at once that it was hopeless. What remained of it was in the last stages of disintegration, and several of the remaining goatskins had punctured on the sharp stones of the shore.

"So we must go on foot, but which way shall we go?" asked Bridget in despair. She looked along the desolate shoreline, then up the barren and rocky slopes of the volcano, its summit still hidden by the grey pall of mist that covered the sky.

"If we climb that hill over there, we shall be better able to scout out the land," suggested Tom, pointing to a low ridge of land running out into the lake about a mile away.

So they set off and soon were climbing up towards the top of the promontory Tom had pointed out. It did not take long to reach one of the knolls in the ridge. They turned for a moment to look out over the grey waters of the lake.

Orin, who had the keenest eyes, suddenly made a strange noise and pointed.

"Look!" he cried, grabbing Tom's sleeve.

They looked out across the broken surface of the lake and Bridget too caught her breath. There, only a few miles from the shore, a dark shape was floating smoothly over the furrowed waves.

There was no mistaking what it was. It was Vencengea's vessel, the Maibiton, or one exactly like it.

"So it didn't sink when they tried to intercept us!" Bridget breathed, a cold fear seizing her heart.

"She is coming, she is coming to hunt us!" whispered Stigrath, for once allowing a flicker of concern to cross his calm features. "We must hurry on. We must not tarry. Need to get off skyline. Must not show our presence here."

*****

None of them, not even Pageya, needed any prompting. They moved hastily off the ridge and down the other side towards a small pile of rubble a hundred or so metres away.

"Was this once also a house, do you think?" asked Tom, looking round at the surprisingly symmetrical pattern of what at first had seemed a jumbled heap of stones.

Stigrath nodded grimly. "Either that, or one of many monasteries which once welcome pilgrims to these shores. Slopes between volcano and lake once thickly populated," he noted sadly. "Well known for their greenness. Even called this the Paradise Coast. And now look what is left!"

"Where are we going to hide in this moonscape?" Bridget asked despairingly.

There was simply nowhere to hide. The monastery ruins were too obvious a place to hide, and the rest of the mountainside was open and bare. Had there been trees and woods or hedges or fences it might have been possible. But the Pestilence had killed all vegetation. The trees were mere skeletons or stumps, there was no sign at all of hedges, and the borders of what had been fields were only marked by the occasional barely visible ridge in the ground.

They paused in the ruins for a while to plot their strategy. Tom suggested they should follow the coast round the lake until they came to the plains and then make for the nearest inhabited point.

"It can't be that far distant," he said. "Twenty miles along the lake and then maybe another five or ten round to the nearest village. When we were over the other shoreline of the lake, in the Goodcheer, there were still things growing on that side. The trees and bushes were badly affected by pestilence, but there was enough growing to sustain life of some sort."

Orin looked doubtful. "But which is the shortest way? The way we are going now, or back the way we have come? It is important for me, because I have very small legs."

"If we continue the way we are going, we shall have to pass right under the volcano," said Pageya, looking up apprehensively to where the great mountain should have been visible.

"But from what I remember from the map we found back in Havenmouth," Tom interjected, "it is shorter this way… I'm pretty sure of that."

Bridget was not convinced. She looked at Stigrath.

The sturdy captain was gazing gloomily at his feet. Without looking up he said:

"Dear friends, I am afraid we have only one choice. We must climb up the volcano."

The others stared at him in disbelief.

"Go up the volcano!" exclaimed Tom. "But who knows what there is up there! And that's where the pestilence comes from. It'll kill us all before we get anywhere!"

But Stigrath's face was set hard. "All the same," he said, "we have no choice. If we go any other way, they will catch us. We must hide in the cloud…"

"Where would it lead to, Stigrath?" asked Bridget, trying to understand. "What is there up there?"

"I know not."

"You don't know!" Bridget almost shouted. "Yet you want to take us up there! Stigrath, have you taken leave of your senses?"

"No," said the big man quietly. "But if we do not go above clouds we shall be hunted down by the Daughter of Darkness before this day is over."

They all looked at him in despair. But they were beginning to realise that he was right.

"If we follow coast at the shore level, we shall be always within sight of Vencengea. There is nowhere, as you can see (he made a wide sweeping gesture with his arms) where we can hide. All she has to do is track us along the shore. And her ship travels faster than we do. She can out-distance us, and drop her men off on coastline wherever she likes, ahead of us, behind us, all round us if she wants. We would be trapped easily."

But his reasoning was interrupted by Pageya, who was obviously in some distress. Her breathing had become agitated again and her eyes betrayed genuine fear.

"I cannot go up this volcano," she said. "It smells of evil! Never! I just cannot do it!"

There was a moment's pause, and the friends looked at each other uneasily. Everyone felt much the same about the volcano. But Bridget said finally:

"I'm afraid I think Stigrath is right. We don't have any choice, Geya. On the other hand we don't have to go all the way up the volcano. Let's go just above the cloud line. Then we can turn to one side, away from the summit itself, and come down again in another place."

They gazed gloomily up towards the hazy line where the mountainside disappeared into the cloud, with the growing realisation that this was the direction they were going to take. Whatever lay up there, it was their only chance of escaping Vencengea.

Chapter Forty-Nine
Edge of the Unknown

They decided to follow the ridge they had just crossed, up towards the cloud line, keeping to the side hidden from Vencengea's ship.

The ubiquitous stone of the shoreline had given way here to slightly softer ground, a mixture of a moss-like growth and open earth. But their progress seemed painfully slow. Perhaps it was because they were tired and cold and hungry, but each time they looked behind them, the shoreline seemed no further away than it had been before. And the shoreline was the threshold of danger. Once the pursuers had landed there they would be within striking distance.

But gradually the ceiling of cloud above them came closer. Bridget looked at a rocky outcrop just to their right, on the crest of the ridge, and saw it quite suddenly disappear behind a blanket of mist. Soon she was watching wisps of cloud as they floated past just above her head.

A sudden cry of warning came from Stigrath. "Move behind the rocks!" he said urgently, pointing to a pile of boulders just to their left. "But no running. Not want any sudden movement."

The reason for his anxiety was soon apparent. When they had taken shelter behind the rock, they peered out over its rim. Stigrath nodded grimly. The black-sailed ship had just rounded the promontory at the bottom end of their ridge. It was close to the shore, as if searching for somewhere to land.

Then the mist came down over them and obscured their line of vision.

They hurried on upwards, hoping upon hope that they had not been seen from the vessel. Now they were hidden by the cloud, but this knowledge brought little comfort. Vencengea, they knew, had quite special powers of divination and detection.

Stigrath called another halt and went off to reconnoitre ahead. Bridget did not want him to go. She felt uneasy as she scanned the flank of the mountain, colourless under the dark grey cloud. For the moment all seemed quite ordinary and safe. There was no wind, no thunder, no dramatic flashes of lightning – only a thin rain falling from the dreary clouds. The upper slopes of the volcano were still shrouded in impenetrable mist. But Bridget felt the tension rising within her all the time, growing stronger the higher they climbed.

Then she became aware of a sound which did not seem to fit in with the surrounding landscape. At first she thought she might be imagining it, but then it came again, more distinctly. It seemed to come from a long way away across the barren slopes of the great volcano – a thin crackling noise, like someone unwrapping the paper from round a chocolate bar.

It came a third time, this time much closer. Now it was more like the crackle of fireworks at a display – not the loud, banging sort, but the spitting, popping kind. It came from some way up the mountain, to the left.

There was silence for a minute or two, then the noise began again… but this time in a quite different place, she was sure, closer to them, and to the right.

"Listen," she said to Tom, as he caught up with her. "What is that noise?"

He listened intently for a moment, and the sound came again, a sharp crack this time, followed by a series of low buzzing noises.

Tom shook his head. "Sounds like something electrical," he said, puzzled.

Then from over a ridge to one side they saw a series of blue flashes, and the crackling noises repeated themselves. A few moments later, there came the first puff of wind. It turned into a breeze, and within a minute it was almost blowing a gale.

There was a violent flash over the nearby ridge, and the mountainside was rocked by a loud crack of thunder. The clouds all round them had darkened as they watched, and there was an indescribable, unbearable tension in the air.

Stigrath came stumbling down the slope towards them.

"Follow me!" he shouted. "We cannot stay out in this."

At the same moment the clouds seemed to open directly above them and they were engulfed in a deluge.

But it was not just rain. The heavy raindrops were mixed with a swirling mass of greyness.

"It's the pestilence," shouted Orin. "The pestilence is upon us!"

Bridget slipped and slithered in the quagmire created by the grey deluge and had to keep wiping her face to keep the mixture of rain and sludge from pouring into her eyes. But somehow she managed to keep behind Pageya, who in turn was following Stigrath. The others were somewhere behind.

Stigrath led them to an outcrop of rocks with an overhang. Here they found a small cave which gave them shelter from the worst of the grey fury that had engulfed the mountainside.

It was almost as dark as night now, and eddies of wind kept blowing flurries of the greyness in on top of them. Stigrath organised them into building a barrier of loose rocks and stones around the cave entrance, as much to keep them warm and occupied as to protect them.

At least, Bridget thought, *it will make life difficult for Vencengea and her search party.*

But how long was it going to last?

The storm, if anything, seemed to be getting worse. It was now almost pitch black and the wind was increasing…

And then the storm stopped, as suddenly as it had started. The sky overhead suddenly cleared, and for the first time that Bridget could remember since they came anywhere near the lake, they even caught a glimpse of sunshine.

It only lasted a few seconds, though, and when they emerged from the cave, flicking off the flakes of grey matter from their clothes, the sky was once again covered by a thick blanket of cloud. The wind had dropped again to almost

269

nothing.

They looked round in disbelief. The mountainside was, if anything, even bleaker than before the unexpected storm. The ground was totally covered in the grey sludge, which glistened dully with the water which had soaked into it. A torrent of muddy water poured down through a nearby gully.

Orin wanted to stay there in the shelter of their rock, fearful that another tempest might catch them on the mountainside. But Stigrath was reluctant to stay still while there was any chance of being caught by Vencengea and her followers.

"We must try and climb just little higher, then turn to left and try follow side of the mountain," he said.

"What would happen if we just went on climbing?" asked Tom innocently. "The summit of the volcano is over to the left, surely. Is there no pass or plateau here above us?"

"There is a ridge," said Stigrath simply. "There are several summits on it, small mountains, not so big as Fles… Holy places for the seekers who came to this shore. One was called Izon, I think. And another Masli… Mountains, but not as big as Fles. People used to go there for pilgrimage. Some sought the Opening near these places…"

"And what is there beyond the ridge?" asked Bridget sceptically.

Stigrath hesitated. Then, finally, he spoke.

"According to the mariners who once plied this lake, there lie the Wastes of Serped. It is also called the Great Unknown. About them there are many fables, but no certain knowledge. No one has ever returned from there, though there was a time when many set out in that direction."

"And what do these fables say?" asked Bridget.

It was Pageya who answered, her voice thin and melodious as usual, but with a tremulous note which made Bridget glance up quickly at her. "Mostly," she said, "they speak of an empty world of sandy desert. Some versions talk also of fertile oases beyond the sands and maybe also rich cities. Nowadays, I think, few believe these are more than fairy-tales."

There were a few moments of silence.

"Well, I suppose a sandy desert couldn't be much worse than this place," grumbled Tom. "And if there are oases there must be some food! That would make it an absolute paradise. I'm getting mighty hungry."

But Stigrath was convinced they needed to turn along the side of the mountain and head back for Orotworm rather than risk the uncertainties of the 'Great Unknown'. He agreed, however, to their sharing out a little more of their meagre rations. Then they set off again up the mountain, through the sludge.

Bridget was slowly becoming aware of an increasing listlessness taking over her body. She felt so tired that after a while she had the impression that she was sleepwalking. Several times she found her eyes falling shut, and she had to shake her head to keep them open…

And she was also beginning to see things that didn't quite make sense. At one point she thought she saw through the mist something that looked like a telegraph pole, with several lines passing through it. But then the cloud closed in

Chapter Fifty
Guardians of the Gateway

They moved cautiously up towards the giant stone archway. As they approached, it became increasingly obvious that this was no natural phenomenon. The arch was definitely man-made. It was built on level ground overlooking the slope they had been climbing. Beyond was a plateau, bleak and bare and covered, like everything else just at that moment, by the grey sludge.

They stared up in awe at the giant structure. Here and there stones had fallen out of the otherwise perfect masonry. Elsewhere the sides were smooth and undamaged. The mist swirled round it, billowing past on the rising breeze.

All at once Tom, who was leading the way, froze. He pointed ahead of them, through the arch of the gate. Bridget looked in the direction he was pointing and saw a number of figures standing there in the mist, motionless.

They were tall and thin and wraithlike, and stood there defiantly, blocking the way, without any trace of movement.

"Ho!" called Stigrath. "Who are you, guardians of the gateway? Have we your leave to pass through?"

There was only silence, except for the gentle sighing of the wind through the cracks in the enormous structure above. The figures did not move, nor did they answer.

Stigrath moved forward again, walking under the giant archway itself. "Say, is this the fabled Gateway to the Opening, that which leads to Paradise?" he asked. "What must we do to gain your permission to pass?"

Bridget touched Stigrath's arm. "I think... I think..."

But the captain continued to go forward. "We come in peace. We are refugees from a land afflicted by evil. We seek to know how to enter the land of peace which, it is said, you guard."

The 'guardians' remained motionless. One of them had his arm raised in some ungainly gesture, though whether it was a sign of welcome or of warning was not clear.

The companions could now see that several of the guardians seemed to be holding high poles or spears in their hands. Bridget, however, was becoming more and more convinced that these were not spears. Nor were the figures guardians.

"Stigrath," she called. "I don't think you should go any closer."

It was clear that Stigrath had not noticed the wires, wires that spread out across the end of the archway passage where they stood. Bridget had seen them from the start, and she could see they were definitely wires, strung horizontally between the poles which she had at first taken to be spears. And she also saw that it was the wires which were supporting the figures Stigrath insisted on addressing as 'guardians'.

Bridget grabbed at Stigrath's leather belt and tried to pull him back. He pulled up in surprise and turned to look at her. He had stopped no more than a few paces from the figures.

"What is, Princess... Why?"

And then he too saw the wires.

The motionless figures – there were five of them – all had their backs turned towards Bridget and her companions. And Bridget now understood why they had appeared so tall and gaunt.

They were dressed in rags, and here and there through the rags there protruded the whiteness of a femur or a humerus.

The guardians were nothing more than bare bones.

"Don't touch the wire!" said Bridget urgently.

She need not have said it. Her friends were all so frozen with horror that none had made any move towards the fence.

"Stand back a bit," she said.

Bridget delved in the bundle she was carrying on her back and pulled out an empty metal can which they had been using as a cup for drinking water. Gingerly she lobbed it towards the wire fence.

As the can touched the wire, there was a sharp crack, and with a loud spitting noise it jumped back and landed with a clatter only inches from Bridget's feet.

Stigrath walked up and down the fence, looking for gaps. But the wires, thin and barely visible though they were, seemed to be in remarkably good condition, as were the iron poles that supported them.

The friends walked round to either side of the great archway, but found to their dismay that the flimsy but deadly fence stretched away endlessly on both sides. They followed it for a couple of hundred yards on one side, but there were definitely no gaps. And the dully-gleaming wires were too close to each other to allow anyone, however slim, to work their way through to the other side.

"What are we going to do now?" asked Orin despondently.

"One thing for sure," said Stigrath. "We do not stay anywhere near this arch. Vencengea's huntsmen cannot be so far behind, and that" – he nodded at the great archway looming out of the mist – "is most visible thing for miles around. They will head for it as soon as they see it."

"All we can do then," suggested Tom, "is follow our previous plan and make our way across the mountainside, round the flank of the volcano. That way we may still escape them."

No one disagreed. They were now trapped between this remarkably well maintained electric fence and the party or parties of Vencengea's followers they presumed were advancing upwards from the lakeshore.

"Do not forget," said Stigrath quietly, "that Vencengea has special powers of vision. She can also read thoughts, even from far away."

"Well let's hope then," said Tom cheerfully, "that this mist bungs up her radar!" And he patted Stigrath reassuringly on the back. The big man gave him a mournful smile.

"I like your good cheer, young Tom," he said.

They set off across the mountainside, leaving the fence away to their right. It seemed, in any case, to be veering up the mountain towards the volcano's summit. And that was not the way they wanted to go. Gradually they steered a course further and further away from it, hurrying from one rocky outcrop to another, peering anxiously down the slope towards the lake for any signs of Vencengea's black-robed followers.

After a while, they stopped behind yet another large cluster of boulders, rested and consumed what little of their rations they dared. They kept silence, listening for any telltale sound. But there was none. No voices, no birdcalls, no tinkling of water. Only the cold unfriendly sound of the wind moaning in the rocks.

All of them, except perhaps for the indomitable Stigrath, were nearing exhaustion. Their feet and lower legs were covered in the heavy grey slime formed when the pestilence became damp. And somehow it had also got on to their hands, their arms, even their faces. Bridget wondered if it were the grey dust that was making her feel so tired and downhearted.

It was beginning to get dark, and they had begun to look for a suitable place to spend the night when Bridget saw the figure again, the one she had seen earlier, as she thought, waving to her.

Was this just another unfortunate traveller caught on the electric fence? No, this figure was facing towards them, and as she watched, it raised its arm again and signalled.

This time there could be no mistake. The person was standing on a flat-topped mound several hundred yards away, a single grey-robed figure carrying what appeared to be a staff or spear in one hand. This time Bridget stopped the others.

"Look! I'm not hallucinating, am I? There's a person over there with a staff, signalling to us…"

She waited for one of them to say something, fearing that they might for some reason not be seeing what she saw. Then Pageya said in a soft voice.

"Most definitely a person," she said.

"You have sharp eyes, Pageya, and you too, Orin. Can you see who or what this person is? All I can see is that he's carrying some sort of pole or staff, probably of wood."

Pageya shook her head. "I cannot see his face because his hood covers it."

"How do you know it's not a woman?" asked Tom.

"I feel it is not a woman," was Pageya's simple reply.

"Look, it signals us," grunted Stigrath. "It waves us to follow…"

"And it's disappeared!" said Tom in annoyance, as the figure dropped out of sight behind the mound.

"What do we do?" asked Tom. "Follow it? Or run a mile in the other direction?"

"I think we follow it," said Bridget, "but keep our eyes open. It didn't look at all like one of Vencengea's beings, and if it were hostile, it presumably wouldn't beckon to us to follow."

"Perhaps it is leading us towards a trap," said Orin nervously.

"Let us take that risk," said Stigrath, a pensive look stealing over his face. "Something about this grey person seems familiar to me. We go, but we go carefully!"

They set off towards the mound where they had seen the figure, glancing here and there over the mist-covered mountainside. The appearance of the stranger had somehow given them new energy and motivation. The mound where he had been standing was only a little way off the path they had been following, so did not seem a wasted journey. But when they had clambered up to the top of the mound, the mysterious grey figure was nowhere to be seen.

"Look!" cried Orin suddenly. "There it is again."

For several moments Bridget could not see anything, but finally she caught sight of the figure, this time standing at the entrance to a broad gully running down the mountainside.

"If he starts going downwards, back towards danger," asked Tom, "do we want to follow him?"

No one was sure, but they started making for the gully anyway.

The gully had obviously once carried a stream of some considerable proportions flowing down from the upper reaches of the mountain. This torrent, however, seemed to have dried up in spite of the recent rain. The bottom of the small valley was nevertheless a quagmire, a dull morass of treacherous grey mud.

Bridget, who was in the lead, stopped. "How do we get across this lot?" she asked despondently.

"We must cross somehow," said Stigrath. "We dare not go down too far towards the lake, for fear of being seen."

"But we shall have to descend a little way, to find a suitable way across the gully," said Tom.

Stigrath nodded grimly and took the lead. At first the gully was broad and by keeping to its sides they found it easy enough to follow. But then it entered a narrow, rocky ravine and on their side began to fall away steeply. The further side seemed to offer a wider and more manageable path. They decided to try and cross the gully as best they could. That meant they would have to clamber over rocks grey with the slime.

Stigrath again led the way, doing his best to guide them by pointing out suitable footholds.

By the time they had reached the other side of the gully it was rapidly growing dark. And there was neither sight nor sound of their mysterious grey guide.

"Useless to go on," said Stigrath. "Only put ourselves in danger. Look, there little further down valley is another overhang in the rock. Looks free of grey dust and slime. Seems good place to rest until morning."

The others agreed only too readily. They were all tired, dirty and dispirited.

Bridget felt that she just wanted to forget about things for a while, sink into a deep sleep and find a few hours respite from the awareness of their hopeless position.

"I don't think we'll be easily spotted here," Tom commented. "If Vencengea's people are still searching for us, they'll have a job to find us."

Bridget hoped he was not tempting fate, but was too tired to say so.

They scrambled over the remaining rocks and boulders and reached the overhang. It was indeed dry and relatively clean, and went some way into the darkness under the rock, to form a narrow cave, so they could be fairly confident of not being spotted from a distance.

They settled down in the welcome darkness, wrapping themselves in the dirty blankets they had retrieved from the raft. Bridget had barely laid her head on the hardness of the rock when she noticed that Tom, somehow, had lit a candle and set it on a rock ledge at the back of their narrow cave.

"Don't worry," he said softly, "the light won't be seen anywhere except inside the cave."

She wondered if he were right, but hadn't the energy or will to protest.

"Do you still have the pendant, Bridget?" Tom whispered anxiously.

"Yes, of course," she murmured sleepily, and reached inside her collar to clasp the ornament.

Tom, meanwhile, had taken out his pencil stub again and was working away, scribbling letters, staring at them, and then rapidly crossing them out. She was much too exhausted to help him and was soon dozing off.

The last thing she was aware of before falling asleep was Tom, muttering to himself:

"It must be that! But what a strange sentence… What on earth does it mean?"

Then there was a pause, in which she must have fallen asleep. Because Tom's next words seemed to come from a long way off, and she was so drowsy that she could not rouse herself to respond. "I think I've got it, folks!" he was saying. "I think I've worked out the last clue!"

Through her drowsiness Bridget felt just a small tingle of excitement, and for a moment she thought of fighting her physical exhaustion and forcing herself to wake up. But she had just found a really comfortable position on the rough bedding beneath her.

For once her will power failed her and she drifted into a deep, calm sleep.

Chapter Fifty-One
The Opening

She woke to find an unusual light all round her.

The sound of the wind was also there, the same steady soughing sound which had lulled her to sleep the night before. So she was not dreaming. She rubbed her eyes and looked out from beneath the underhang.

Only then did she realise to her astonishment that what she was seeing, for the first time in weeks, was sunlight, real steady sunlight. It was, admittedly, a very pale sunlight, but sunlight it was nonetheless.

She turned towards the others, only to find that they had all gone!

Their bedding, and the crude rucksacks they had made for themselves from the raft's awning, had also vanished. Her own precious rucksack, the one with Kalmom's manuscript, had disappeared too...

In near panic she jumped up, grabbed her blanket and ran out into the gully. First she glanced upwards, but there was nothing there. So she turned to the right and scanned the course of the former torrent down the gully.

And there, to her enormous relief, she caught sight of them. They were standing in a little group on a rocky platform, on the rim of what looked like a precipice. The channel of the dried up stream ran to one side of their rock and then came to an abrupt end. Beyond it was an enormous gulf.

Bridget hurried down to join them, breathless, and was about to chastise them for deserting her when Tom turned and said:

"Orin saw the man again. The one in the grey cloak. He was standing here, pointing downwards."

Bridget now caught sight of what lay on the other side of the platform and pulled up abruptly. It was a huge natural amphitheatre gouged out of the mountainside, maybe a hundred feet deep, surrounded on all sides but one by cliffs. The floor of the bowl, far below, was a jumbled mass of rocks and debris. In among the boulders there flowed a river.

"Where does the river come from?" Tom asked, frowning. "It doesn't come from up here. This gully is dry, except for the mud and sludge."

"It must come out of the rock somewhere beneath us," said Orin.

Tom was already moving off round the uneven rim of the great bowl. The others followed. It was heavy going. They kept having to clamber up rocky outcrops and then lower themselves down on the other side. But nobody complained. They all seemed eager to find out where the river came from.

Tom was going so fast that he was soon well ahead of the others. Bridget was the only one able to keep him in sight. She overtook him at a point where the ground leading down to the bottom of the circular cwm was not nearly so precipitous. They glanced at each other and then, without a word, set off together to scramble down the remaining slope.

They reached the point where the stream flowed out of the rocky bowl into a deep ravine. Looking back up into the circular bowl, they had a clear view of the precipice on which they had been standing only a few minutes before.

Tom pointed. "There's your answer," he said triumphantly. "The river comes out of the rock up there, half way up the cliff."

She saw it. The upper half of the cliff was bare and dry, but a little more than half way down, where the cliff was no longer perpendicular and was more like a jumble of fallen rocks, water suddenly appeared, gushing out of the rock and tumbling down in a series of cascades, dividing and then rejoining until finally they collected in a pool which then spilled out across the floor of the amphitheatre to form the torrent by which they were now standing.

"How very interesting!" said Tom.

"What?" Bridget asked.

"Don't you see? There must be a cave entrance there, half way up the cliff. Or maybe several. Yes, I think I can definitely see a slit in the rock, where the main flow of water appears... But it's a cave that would have previously been hidden!"

"How do you mean, hidden? I don't understand..."

Tom laughed. "You're extraordinarily slow sometimes, Bridget," he said condescendingly. "This opening would have been totally hidden behind the waterfall which once must have come hurrying down through the gully and poured over the precipice!"

Bridget was peeved by the way he had said it, but had to admit he was right. "Yes," she agreed, "it would have probably concealed the opening, wouldn't it!"

Tom was now off again, climbing over the rocks on the floor of the depression, following the stream upwards.

Bridget still felt annoyed.

"Shouldn't we wait for the others?" she called after him.

But he didn't answer, so she set off as fast as she could in pursuit, allowing her annoyance to give way to a mounting excitement.

She caught up with him at the bottom of the series of cascades which came tumbling down over the rocks. He had stopped, and as she approached, he pointed to something.

"Look!" he said. "These stones aren't any old common boulders. Lots of them have been chiselled and sculpted."

It was true. And there were also steps in among the jumbled rocks, leading upwards.

"This could have been one of those old temples Quenrie told us about," she suggested.

"Or a monastery," Tom replied. "You know, like the one where old what's-his-name... Thirdrol... had his community."

Bridget felt a sudden glow of excitement. She could feel it – they were on

279

the verge of finding something new and unexpected, and very important.

They looked at each other again.

"Shall we start climbing, then?" she whispered. All thoughts of waiting for the others had vanished.

Tom rolled his eyes. "A ruined temple!" he said. "Who knows what you might find in a ruined temple!"

So they began to climb up over the jumble of rocks, without so much as a glance backwards.

It was quite easy to climb the cascade because the rocks were so uneven and gave plenty of handholds. In among the debris were more of the carved stones, some of them shaped into beautiful patterns and carved figures, human and animal. Bridget also caught sight of broken stone tablets and she realised with a little thrill that they were inscribed in the now familiar letters of the ancient Elonyms. She wanted to stop and examine them, but Tom kept up a relentless pace and she didn't want to lose him. After a couple of minutes, however, he stopped in his tracks.

"Look," he said, "someone has been here before us!"

He pointed to what looked like a piece of soiled and blotched paper that had become wedged between two rocks.

Bridget examined and then extricated it, taking care not to tear it. It was the corner of a page.

There was writing on it, again in the Elonym alphabet, though the page had obviously been drenched in water and the characters were smudged. Bridget could just make out a few of the symbols she had learned to read in the last few weeks.

"H… R… U," she read. "It's all jumbled up, like Kalmom's messages."

But then something else struck her.

"Tom," she said softly. "This is exactly the same sort of paper that Kalmom's message was written on."

Tom took the torn page. He thought for a moment and then said:

"Do you know what? It's something we hadn't noticed before, but I think it's also exactly the same sort of paper that we've been using to transcribe and work out Kalmom's riddles…"

"Which we were given…"

"…Back in Quenrie's tower…"

"…By Quenrie."

They stood in silence for a few moments, trying to take in the implications of what they had just said.

"Hm," said Tom finally, and looked up towards the point where the stream emerged from the rocks.

"Let's go on."

They went on in silence. Bridget was finding it more and more difficult to keep up with him. The rocky slope was now growing steeper and dustier, and she was soon covered in the grey, clinging ash which had dried in the sun but still covered many of the rocks.

After five minutes or so, she stopped to regain her breath and brush as much of the powder off her clothes as she could. She looked ahead and found she had lost sight of Tom.

Suddenly, a hand grabbed her shoulder.

She shrieked and pulled away, turning to face an extraordinary figure. It was clothed entirely in grey, and its face was a hideous mask of the same, ashen colour.

"Sorry, did I frighten you?" Tom asked.

"I just didn't recognise you!" she cried in relief, "with all that…"

"I knocked against a dead bush and this lot fell all over me! By the way, you're not very recognisable yourself!"

She looked down at her clothes and her hands and laughed.

"Yes, we both of us look like something out of a bad pantomime!" she agreed.

"The Opening is just over here, behind this boulder," said Tom nonchalantly.

"The Opening?" asked Bridget eagerly.

"The Opening," replied Tom, "or at least that's what I think it is."

"Do you mean…?"

"I mean the Opening."

He led the way, squeezing past an enormous boulder and dropping on to a small space of even rock.

And there it was, an irregular gash in the rock wall with water gushing out from the black recess beyond. To one side was a shelf of rock which led off into the darkness of the mountain.

Chapter Fifty-Two
A Dead End

"We can't go in there without any light," said Tom. "We'll need candles and Stigrath's flint to light them. He's got them in the bundle he carries."

Bridget nodded. Yet she felt really impatient at the need to wait. This, after all, might well be what they had been looking for, without really knowing it, for weeks and weeks.

They looked back down towards the centre of the great bowl of a depression and saw their friends labouring up through the broken rocks and boulders. Bridget slithered down to where Stigrath was struggling to pull his considerable bulk up the first stretch of the cascade, with Pageya doing what she could to aid him.

"Where's Orin?" Bridget asked anxiously.

"He went back to scout out the deep ravine," Pageya replied. "He and I thought we heard something in that direction. Perhaps only an animal moving…"

What animal could there be amid this desolation? Bridget thought. But her mind was preoccupied with other matters.

"There's a hole up here, a hole in rock. We need the candles from your pack."

Stigrath frowned. "Yes, we saw hole. But why enter? We only get caught in this place. Once we go in cave, Vencengea's men easily trap us. Very bad idea."

A small figure came slithering up the rocks from below. It was Orin, a very breathless Orin.

"There are men," he said breathlessly, "many men and approaching fast. They are coming up a path through the lower gorge. The men in black…"

Stigrath looked round the bare hollow where they were standing.

"So," he said grimly, "I change my mind quickly. Perhaps best choice is to go in cave!"

Bridget nodded.

Soon they were all together in front of the slanting gash in the rock. The water was gushing out of one corner only. On the other side there was plenty of room for them to stoop down, one by one, and enter.

They had only three candles, improvised affairs made from animal fat that they had stolen from Blam's stores. Stigrath lit them with the flint that he carried in his pocket. He kept one and gave the other two to Tom and Bridget. The flames guttered slightly in the breeze which blew into the cave, but by shielding them with the hand it was possible, they found, to keep them alight. Cautiously they moved on into the dark.

Tom pushed his way to the front, past Bridget and Stigrath. "I found the hole first," he said. "I want to go into it first."

Stigrath glanced inquiringly at Bridget, but she only smiled and nodded. "Let him go," she said.

Tom lowered his head and plunged ahead into the darkness. Bridget followed close behind, eager to find out what lay ahead.

At first the tunnel was no more than a wide crack in the rock, obviously formed by natural processes. Several times she found herself stepping in the water and on another occasion she had to turn sideways on in order to pass through a particularly narrow passage. She wondered vaguely whether Stigrath would be able to negotiate these stretches, but was so eager to press on that she didn't stop to check.

Soon the passage broadened out a little, so that she could clamber forward without too much difficulty, always following the guttering light of Tom's candle a few feet ahead of her. They rounded a bend and the passage suddenly opened out into a cave. It was a cave so large that they could barely see its roof or walls.

Directly in front of them, however, and clearly visible, was a pool of water. It lay perfectly still, with the candlelight shining eerily on its mirror-flat surface and then penetrating deeper, right down to the pool's stony bottom. Tom and Bridget approached and began to walk slowly along the edge of the water. At first Bridget had the impression there was some sort of glow emanating from the water itself. After a while, however, she came to the conclusion that this must be a trick of her imagination. The pool must simply be reflecting the light of their candles.

Tom stopped suddenly just ahead of her. They could now make out very dimly the rock wall on the far side of the pool, and he was staring at it intently. Bridget joined him and turned her eyes in the same direction.

For a moment or two she imagined that the rocks on the far side were looking at her. She closed her eyes for a moment and then reopened them. The impression had gone. There was absolutely nothing there but rock, she was sure.

"Did you see something over there?" Tom asked.

Bridget shook her head. "Well, just for a moment… But no, there's nothing there, is there?"

They walked on along the side of the pool. But Pageya, who had now entered the cave, stopped at the very same spot that they had and pointed.

"Look, there is a horrible face! There on the rock!"

Bridget came back and looked again. This time, by peering steadily for a few moments, she saw that she had not, after all, been imagining things. On the rock overhanging the pool of water there was a face, a severe, frowning face. And above it there was some rough lettering, which Bridget, try as she might, could not decipher.

"What does it say, Geya? Can you read it?" she asked.

Pageya peered at the letters above the pool.

"It is a very old script," she said, "but as far as I can make out it says: 'BEWARE…'"

Bridget shivered. "Is that all?" she asked.

"'BEWARE... ALL YE WHO APPROACH!"

"Not very welcoming!" commented Tom.

"No, it is not," said Pageya quietly. Bridget thought there was a slight tremor in her friend's voice.

"There must be more than that, Geya," Bridget said. "There's far too much script there for it just to say that..."

"Yes. Then it also says... NONE WHO ENTERS HERE... WILL EVER LEAVE..."

Chapter Fifty-Three
The Final Answer

Bridget shivered again.

"It's creepy," she said, surveying the hostile stone walls of the cave. "Let's get out of here... Somehow."

"It's certainly got a sinister feel about it, hasn't it," said Tom.

"Sorry, there's another word," Pageya interrupted them.'...WILL LEAVE... UNCHANGED!'

"'None who enters here will leave unchanged'... Now that sounds a bit more encouraging," said Bridget.

"But what are we supposed to enter?" asked Pageya innocently.

They all laughed. "Why, this cave, of course," said Tom.

"But we've already entered the cave," Pageya answered logically. "Is there not another place to enter?"

Bridget reflected for a moment. "Geya's right, you know. Our unfriendly face here certainly seems to be suggesting that we still haven't entered whatever it is that's going to change us!"

To Bridget's immense relief, Stigrath had made it through the narrow passage, and he and Orin now joined them.

"We heard sounds back in the tunnel," said Orin in a scared voice, "as if the men are already entered into it."

"Robed men will have a few sore heads if they try to capture us," growled Stigrath, choosing a few loose stones from the ground nearby. Quite how he intended to use them was not entirely clear to Bridget.

Meanwhile Tom was deep in thought.

"I wonder," he said, "I wonder if *that* is what it means..."

"What are you talking about, Tom?" Bridget chided him. "You're talking to yourself again."

"Well, you know that we've been trying to make some sense of what Kalmom said in the last section of his Message..."

"Of course. You mean about the six keywords and the place name, which Orin guessed was 'Pool of Edath...'"

"Yes, have you come up with any explanation or solution yet?"

"No, you know I haven't." Bridget knew she was sounding just a little bit irritable. "Get to the point. Vencengea and her crew could be here any minute, remember?"

"Well the letters we have at our disposal... I've memorised them, every one. They are:

And last night, up under the overhang, I couldn't sleep so I began going over it again in my mind... For some reason I thought of the word 'MIRROR'... the jumbled letters of our keywords had all its letters. Then I looked at the keyword 'Truth' and at first it looked as if it might provide the letters for 'thought' – if you have an extra O and a G from somewhere else..."

"Tom, we haven't time! Tell us what you found!"

"I decided a more likely and useful word would be 'THROUGH'... I then tried to fit words which might go with 'THROUGH THE MIRROR'... and I decided a good one was PASS..."

"Pass through the Mirror, Tom? But what mirror?" asked the ever practical Orin.

"Well that's what I couldn't figure out until now..."

Bridget looked round her in exasperation. "And where do you see a mirror here?"

"There!" said Tom, pointing to the glassy surface of the water.

Bridget was not at all convinced the water could be called a mirror. "What was the full sentence you worked out?"

"**Pass through the mirror coldly, then to the flame beyond!**' It uses all the letters of our keywords, every one of them – no more, no less."

"Now he's seeing flames as well as mirrors!" Bridget grumbled.

But then she looked again.

The pool did not, as she had at first thought, plunge straight downwards at its edge, but sloped gently away from where they were standing. Bridget could see clearly the cracks and the tiny pebbles in its bottom...

She looked up and across at the rock wall on the far side. Once again a strange sensation came over her as she caught sight of the outlines of the face staring over at her. She shivered. As Orin had commented, it was not a very pleasant face. It looked rather like the grimacing mask of tragedy, scowling across at her with blank, hostile eyes and down turned mouth...

No, definitely not a friendly face...

In fact, it seemed to be giving a very clear message: "Go away! You are not welcome here..."

But then... then suddenly she caught a pale reflection of the face on the still surface of the water and had to repress an impulse to laugh. The reflection of the face on the rock wall was inverted, and... now instead of the grim mask she had been looking at hitherto she saw another face... a face which was totally different. A calm gentle, smiling, welcoming face...

Bridget looked at the reflection again, and suddenly things began to fall into place. *Pass through the mirror coldly, then to the flame beyond*, she repeated to herself.

Bridget took off her sandals and picked them up. Then she gave her candle to Pageya and put one foot into the water, on to the gravel bottom. She shuddered as the icy water wrapped itself round her foot.

She took a second step, and a third.

"Hey, where are you going?" exclaimed Tom.

"Just stand there and hold the candles," she replied.

Soon she was up to her middle in the water. She found it was not nearly as cold as it had first seemed. She went on stepping further and deeper into the pool.

She turned her head and saw that the others were watching her with a mixture of disbelief and fascination.

She smiled, waved to them, then turned away from them and walked on steadily, down into the water. She took a deep gulp and plunged her head below the surface. She felt the icy water come up over her face, her eyes and, finally, the top of her head...

END of 'The Search for the Opening'
Part Two of 'The Mountain on the Other Side of Light'